298

Love in anoth...

"An extraordinary reading adventure you cannot pass up."

—*Rendezvous*

A LOVE DENIED

"We are returning to Bimordus Two," Teir acknowledged quietly. "Our trip was just a short delay. You knew that."

"But I asked you to take me someplace else," Sarina said. "I don't want to marry Rolf."

"You might still fall in love with him. If there is any truth to the legend, you have to give the councilor a chance. It is your duty as Great Healer to form an alliance. I cannot countermand my orders." He stood stiffly, his eyes forward. If he looked at her, his resolve might weaken.

"How can you send me into another man's arms, after all we've shared?" she cried, fear striking her heart at his cold demeanor.

It made Teir sick to think of her in the councilor's bed. Outwardly, he merely shrugged. "I'll still be around when Cam'brii bores you."

"Bastard!" she shrieked. "You don't even mind that I'll be killed? They'll condemn me because I'm not the Great Healer!"

He hardened his heart against her fury, knowing that he had to return her to Lord Cam'brii. "Your disposition is for the High Council to decide," he told her curtly.

Sarina picked up a metal astrocompass and threw it at him.

CIRCLE OF LIGHT

NANCY CANE

Book Margins, Inc.

A BMI Edition

Published by special arrangement with Dorchester
Publishing Co., Inc.

To Richard, my real-life hero.

With special thanks to the following:

Marilyn Campbell, colleague, friend, and mentor, for her generous guidance, support, and encouragement.

Barbara DeWitt, friend and neighbor, for believing that I would achieve my dream; for listening to my plot lines during our morning walks; and for many hours of reading.

Theresa Di Benedetto, Deborah Shelgren, Ona Bustos, and Nancy Grant, for getting me started.

Chapter One

Smoke billowed into the air, swirling and blending into a murky gray fog whose tendrils reached into every hidden corner of the city. Mantra remembered the pungent smell even though it had been ten months since he'd fled his home. A lot of good it did him to hide in the countryside. The deadly plague called the Farg had spread its tentacles until it reached him even there. The pestilence touched everyone, regardless of location or station in life. It was a great equalizer, as Mantra had come to learn.

Huddling in the shadows of a doorway, he clutched his cloak tighter around his trembling body. It wasn't the cold that concerned him. Mantra dared not risk being seen. The telltale ugly swellings on his thick tan hide would condemn him on sight. If he were caught, he'd be sent to the pest-house. He wanted to die in his own bed, not in a chamber of horrors.

A paroxysm of coughing struck him, and he stooped, hacking and trying to clear the phlegm from his lungs. When at last he straightened, his face was red, his breath coming in short, painful bursts. In the dim light of the streetlamps, he could see the winding cobblestone street disappearing into the mist ahead. Only a few more blocks to go, then he'd be home. With a stab of fear, he wondered if anyone was left to greet him. His mother and father . . . his sisters . . . had they all succumbed to the plague? It was selfish of him to return like this, to put them all in danger, but he craved one last glance of his loved ones before he died.

It was difficult to breathe the dry air after the relatively moist freshness of the country, and he had to stop every few paces to catch his breath. He was grateful that the streets were deserted. Public gatherings were forbidden, and all transportation had come to a halt. It was as though the very lifeblood of the city had stopped. Sewage flowed freely in the streets, and even the wooden structures surrounding him seemed to lean inward with despair. Mantra cringed from the shrieks and lamentations he heard as he passed the homes still inhabited. Nearly everyone was affected by the horrifying visitation, if not themselves, then their dearest relations. The city had become a harbor of death.

Mantra's shoe slipped on a water-slicked stone. He flailed, catching his balance and cursing, but voices ahead made his words choke in his throat. Quickly, he sagged against a wall, his heart thumping. *Go away!* he cried silently. It was a searcher and a chirurgeon, hurrying together on their gruesome mission to examine the dead. One of them held aloft a red rod, warning off anyone approaching not to come near. Mantra held his breath as they passed, for all the good it would do him. He was already infected, and he shivered, knowing they would soon be coming for him.

When the voices faded, Mantra stepped out and moved forward at a faster pace. His head began to hurt, and dizziness threatened to overwhelm him.

He pushed on, determination giving him strength. He nearly sobbed with relief when he rounded the corner of his street.

What he saw made him stop short.

Oh no! Was that a watchman with a halberd in hand guarding his front door? Mantra slowly approached. A large red circle was painted on the door with the piteous words scrawled across it, *HAVE MERCY UPON US!*

Terror struck his heart. "What is this?" Mantra cried.

"You approach a closed house. Be gone," the watchman said. He was a stout fellow whose facial hair was thick and coarse. From the set of his shoulders, he appeared muscular beneath his robe.

"I must enter," Mantra replied, frantic with concern. "It is my home!"

The watchman took a closer look. "By the sun, citizen, are you ill?"

"Aye." Mantra grinned heinously as he thrust up his sleeve to reveal a rash of purplish blotches discoloring his thick hide.

The watchman's eyes widened and he stepped back. "You have the Farg!"

"Unlock the door. I wish to join my family."

The watchman hurried to obey. Withdrawing a large key from the folds of his garment, he fumbled with the lock, swung the door open, and stood aside for Mantra to pass. "The faith be with you, citizen," he said, making the sign of the circle as Mantra went by.

"Mantra!" his mother screamed as he entered. She flew down the stairs, and Mantra barely heard the door bang shut behind him, or the key turning in the lock a second later. He was racing to greet her, flinging his arms around her and sobbing her name.

"Alas, I forget myself," he said, suddenly pulling back. "I am infected by the Farg."

"Mercy!" his mother cried.

Now he saw how haggard she looked as he stood back to examine her. Her hair, once her crowning glory, hung in stringy reddish-brown strands down her back. Her luminous eyes were dull and sad. Even her garment, a softly woven fabric in green to match her eyes, was creased and stained. A wave of guilt swept over him as he thought about how he'd left.

"Who else is ill?" Mantra asked, afraid to hear the answer.

Malika's shoulders slumped. "Your sister Zunis. She has the fever."

"And Father?" His supply station should have kept them all well fed, at least until they were shut in.

Malika looked away. "He took sick all of a sudden. Two days didn't pass before the dead cart came to take him away."

"*No!*" Mantra howled, rage and grief overwhelming him. He sank to the floor, squeezing his eyes shut to hold back the tears.

"Mantra, promise me you will not die, too!" Malika cried, kneeling beside him.

"I'm so sorry, Mother." He gazed at her with sorrowful eyes. "I should not have left as I did. I ran at the first sign of the plague. I was a fool and a coward."

"Hush, my son." Her voice was gentle as she put out a hand to soothe him. "You were not the only one trying to flee. The streets were thronged with carts and beasts of burden, with wagons and goods, with people and baggage. You were lucky to get out before the barriers went up."

"The barriers are useless. The distemper is everywhere." Mantra ran his fingers through his rusty brown hair. "Curse this *maug* planet. If we lived closer to the sun, we might not be so horribly affected."

Malika straightened. "It is harmful to listen to rumors from offworlders."

"We have to ask the Coalition for help. It is the only way."

"The only way is for the Coalition to leave our planet alone. We joined for the trade only. Any other contact is forbidden." Malika's voice was firm. "This is an old discussion. Come to bed."

Mantra rose slowly, his limbs stiff and sore. He ached in a hundred places. "Joining the Coalition isn't enough. We need to become active members. We need to progress—"

"Progress brings corruption. We will talk no more of this." Malika peered at him closely, and her eyes darkened with anxiety. "You are trembling, and your face is a ghastly hue. How long have you had the distemper?"

"It's been five days since I got sick. The fever was the worst. It was not thought I would survive, but a kindly caretaker gave me a posset-drink, and I recovered." A rattling wheeze choked off his words, and he struggled for breath. His chest constricted as though a painful vise were around him, and he coughed, clearing the obstruction. "But as you can see," Mantra said, gasping, "the infection has spread to my lungs."

His mother's countenance paled. "Upstairs with you," she ordered, lifting her skirt and preceding him.

"Mantra, you have returned at last," his eldest sister Sita greeted him from the second landing. Her voice was cool, her expression disapproving. At least she hadn't suffered from their quarantine, Mantra thought. Sita's eyes were heavily made up in a rich lavender shade to match the silky cloth that draped her slender form. She looked as though she were ready to go out on a social visit. Mantra bet she hadn't lifted one finger to help Malika in the whole time he'd been gone. But then Sita had always considered herself first.

As had I, Mantra thought, feeling the familiar wave of guilt.

He regarded his sister calmly. "Where is Kairi?"

"Here!" His next elder sister came flying out of the room she shared with Sita, book in hand. She was about to throw her arms around him when he stepped back, a look of warning on his face.

"Stay away. I have the Farg."

"Oh, no!" Kairi's expression turned to horror as she observed him more closely. "You look terrible. Let me help you."

"Keep your distance," Malika cried. "You girls must remain in your room. I will attend him as I do Zunis. Go now, quickly. I'll bring you both a sulfur balm as soon as I'm free."

Sita wrinkled her nose. "Not that awful stuff again!"

"It's been an effective preventive, hasn't it?" their mother said. "Now off with you!"

Kairi cast Mantra a regretful glance and followed her haughty sister back into their room. Mantra made haste for his own bed. It was as he had left it ten months ago, his possessions untouched, his bed made up as though he had just gone out for an afternoon. A sob of grief tore at his throat. If only he had seen his father one last time.

He made no protest as Malika turned back the coverlet and motioned for him to get into bed.

"Show me how bad it is," she demanded, leaning over him, her eyes soft with concern.

His modesty had long since gone. Mantra stripped, averting his eyes from the expression of horror on his mother's face when she saw the extent of his blisters.

"I'll check on Zunis, and then I will get you some poultices. The poison must be drawn from your body." She listened for a moment to his wheezing. "I will also brew a tea of *lalith* leaves for the congestion."

Malika bent down, and a tear escaped from the corner of her eye. "Rest, my son. I am glad you have returned." She squeezed his hand, and a brief expression of hopelessness flickered across her face before she turned away.

It was much later when Mantra was awakened by cries from downstairs. Throwing his cloak over his shoulders, he hobbled out of his room. "What is it? What's the matter?" he called.

Sita and Kairi emerged from their room, their frightened faces pale against the vivid blue hues of their nightclothes. "It is Zunis," Sita whispered. "When the fever spikes, she gets delirious."

"How long has she been like this?"

"Three days. The fever shows no sign of breaking."

Mantra frowned. That was a bad omen. "Is Mother tending to her?"

"Aye," Kairi replied in a low tone. "She won't allow us to help."

"I must go to her." Despite their protests, he went down the stairs, stopping every few steps to catch his breath. The mucus in his chest seemed looser, so he coughed some of it up. A burning pain stabbed his lungs and Mantra winced, holding on to the rail and waiting for the discomfort to pass. Finally the pain subsided into a dull ache and he was able to continue his descent.

"Mantra, please go to bed!" his sister Kairi pleaded from above.

"Don't waste your words," Sita said to her. "Mantra never listens. He didn't listen when Father asked him to help out in the food station. Father might still be here now had Mantra been around to share the burden."

Feeling the blood rush to his face, Mantra whirled to face her. "Shut up, Sita!"

"Go back where you came from," Sita hissed. "You're just more work for Mother. You're sick. You should never have come here."

Mantra took one glance at the shocked look on Kairi's face and suppressed his retort. Turning on his heel, he shuffled to the library which had been converted into a sickroom. He found his mother huddled over the writhing form of his youngest sister.

Mantra drew in a sharp breath when he saw the livid color of Zunis's face. Her eyes were glassy and wild as she thrashed about, muttering incoherently. Her reddish-brown hair, the same color as their mother's, lay tangled about her face. She looked like a different person from the last time he had seen her, a sweet young maiden about to breach her sixteenth year.

Malika straightened, and he saw she had been applying a wet cloth to Zunis's forehead. Instead of remonstrating with him for coming downstairs, his mother seemed glad of the company. She drew a weary hand across her brow. "I know not what else to do," Malika said. "Either the fever must break, or it will take her. This goes on too long."

Mantra stared at her helplessly. He didn't know the ingredients of the posset-drink that had helped him, so he couldn't offer any advice. "The room is cold, Mother. Would a fire not help?" He drew his cloak tighter around his body.

"I think not. Zunis must be kept cool."

"But see how her limbs tremble."

"It is the distemper. Did you not find it so?"

"I suppose," he said, shrugging. "In truth, I was not aware of much when I passed through this stage."

Malika sighed. "I pray it will end soon. I grieve to see her suffering so."

Mantra stared at his sister, wishing he could will her to get well. She looked so frail as she lay there. He remembered her laughter, her happy innocence, and he thought how everyone's innocence had been destroyed by this onslaught of pestilence.

Returning to the hall, Mantra trudged up the stairs, knowing he would be more useful if he could recover his own strength. Kairi awaited him in front of his bedroom door.

"How is she?" Kairi whispered. He noticed she

carried a book. Kairi was always reading, and he'd found he could talk to her about the things that interested him far more easily than with anyone else in the family. He supposed it was because Kairi drank up new ideas the way some people drank water.

"Alas, Zunis is not doing well. I fear for her survival." They commiserated a moment in silence. "Mother is worn-out and needs a rest herself."

"I know. She nursed Father, and now poor Zunis. I wish she would let me help."

"Can you talk?" Mantra asked, suddenly eager for a sympathetic ear. "I promise to keep my distance." At Kairi's nod of assent, he placed a chair for her in his doorway, and sat on his bed. Regarding his sister, he decided he liked the way she had braided her hair. It hung down her back nearly to her waist, while wispy bangs shaded her brow. Her face was a petite version of his mother's.

"I can't talk to Mother about these things," he began. "She doesn't understand. I heard a lot of talk when I was away . . . talk about the Coalition, and about the legend. It is said the time is right."

Kairi leaned forward. "How so?"

"The blazing star appeared in the sky as it was foretold, a full moon cycle before the onslaught of the pestilence. You saw it, do you remember? Its dull, languid color and heavy, solemn motion were supposed to predict a horrible judgment. So it has come to pass. The plague is slow but severe, terrible and frightful. And it's not happening just here on Tendraa. It is all over the galaxy, on planets not only similar to ours but different as well. Don't you see?" His eyes burned with zeal. *"Death and confusion will reign throughout the heavens. And then the Great Healer will appear."*

Kairi gasped. "But it's just a legend."

"More than that," Mantra contradicted. "All that was predicted has come to pass: the Farg, the arguing factions within the Coalition, even the Morgots."

"The Morgots!" Her eyes widened with fear. "They are not in this sector, are they?" Mantra had told her about the warrior race from a distant solar system who had been attacking planets neutralized by the plague.

"The last I heard from Ravi, they were in the Quk system," Mantra said grimly.

"How long ago was that?"

"Six months past."

Their cousin Ravi was a renegade. He'd stowed away on a freighter to escape from Tendraa, then joined the Coalition Defense League. His prowess at flight school had earned him the prestigious position of first mate to Captain Teir Reylock. Mantra had secretly kept in touch with him, eager to hear the forbidden news from other worlds. But the spread of the pestilence had disrupted their communications.

"The Morgots could be anywhere by now," Kairi whispered.

"That is true. Ravi said the Coalition had their hands full just trying to deal with the plague. Their resources are limited. Even the ruling High Council is looking to the Great Healer for salvation."

"I wish I had such faith." Kairi's eyes were filled with despair.

"Open your heart, Kairi. The prophecy will be fulfilled."

"But who is this savior? When will the Great Healer be revealed?"

"I don't know, sister." A paroxysm of coughing struck him, and as Mantra struggled for a painful breath, he gasped, "I only pray it will be soon."

"You want me to do *what*?" Captain Teir Reylock said, scowling. He stood facing his superior officer across the man's desk. Leaning forward, Teir clenched his fists. No way was he going on this worthless mission, he thought.

Admiral-in-Chief Daras Gog glared back at him,

aware of Teir's doubts. If it weren't for Captain Reylock's excellent reputation, Gog would rake him over the hot fires of Alpha Gomaran Two for his insolence. But Reylock was the chief troubleshooter for the Coalition Defense League, and this mission demanded Gog recruit the best. He could overlook military protocol if Reylock listened and obeyed.

"You heard me," Admiral Gog said quietly, fixing a steely gaze on the captain. "You are to deliver the Earthwoman to the High Council for her marriage to Lord Cam'brii."

"Just like that?" Teir snorted. "The woman hasn't any notion of the legend. How am I supposed to get her to come? Should I tell her she's been identified as the wondrous Great Healer who will save the universe from destruction and despair?" He laughed, a harsh sound in the stillness of the office. "To her it will mean nothing."

"You'll manage." The admiral stood behind his desk and began pacing, his hands clasped behind his back. He was shorter than Teir, but with his military bearing and decorated uniform, he was nonetheless impressive.

"By the Suns, Earth isn't even a member of the Coalition!" Teir said, his blue eyes stormy. He tucked his hands into his flight jacket pockets. "Considering it's their solar year 2007, that doesn't say a whole lot for the planet."

Admiral Gog stopped and raised his eyebrows. "It is to your advantage that Earth is still in the primitive stages of development. Your small reconnaissance vessel can enter its orbit undetected."

"Reconnaissance vessel?" Teir said, his voice ominously low. "What about my own ship?"

"Your spacecraft is too large. The vessel you will be assigned is small and swift. It is better for eluding radar."

"The hell it is! I take my own ship or I don't go." Teir thrust his jaw out stubbornly.

"Captain Reylock!" the Admiral thundered, losing patience. "Do you have any idea of the significance of this mission?"

Teir's gaze was defiant. "I don't believe in the legend of the Great Healer. You want me to do the job, I'll do it, but in my own way."

"By the moons of Agus Six, you'll obey orders! Do you want the plague that is devastating our galaxy to reach your home planet? Do you want the Morgots to enslave the few people who will survive?" He narrowed his eyes. "Worlds are falling one after the other, first to the plague, then to those accursed aggressors. The Great Healer is our only hope of stopping them both!"

"An ignorant Earthwoman? Come on!"

"All the signs point to her as being The One."

Teir saw the fervor burning in the admiral's eyes and wondered how this obviously intelligent man could believe in such mythological garbage.

"If anyone's going to save the galaxy, it's ourselves," Teir growled. "The diplomats in the High Council argue like a pack of *borks*. We're facing two major threats, and the ROF still calls for a vote to dissolve the Coalition. No wonder the Morgots are moving in. Dissension makes us ripe for takeover."

"That's why Sarina Bretton—the Earthwoman—is the key," the admiral told him. "With the recent problems facing the Coalition, membership in the Return to Origins Faction has swelled, and the High Council is hard pressed to focus its attention on external matters. If the Revelation occurs as predicted, the ROF's push for all species to return to their respective home worlds will be nullified. Coalition unity will be strengthened. That's why it's so important for us to retrieve the Earthwoman."

His eyes took on a heightened glow. "So far, the prophecy appears to be coming true. As it was foreseen, the harmony of the galaxy is disrupted by internal strife. Pestilence has struck us down.

Hostile invaders are conquering our worlds. It's really happening, do you not see?"

"No, I don't." The only thing Teir saw was a religious fervor spreading throughout the galaxy, a sort of spiritual defense against odds stacked too high against them all. "But I realize the High Council won't try to solve its own problems until the legend is proved false," he concluded. "So I'll bring the woman."

"Good." It didn't really matter to Gog what Reylock believed as long as he did the job. "And you'll take the reconnaissance vessel."

Teir opened his mouth to protest, but at a quelling look from the admiral, he thought better of it. "Aye, sir." Snapping a crisp salute, Teir turned and left.

K'darr, chief of the Morgots, paced the bridge of the battlecruiser, *Krog*. The flagship of the Morgot fleet, the *Krog* had been named by K'darr himself. The word stood for demon in the language of his people. With his horned ears, ridged brow, and fiercely black coat of fine fur, K'darr appeared as the very Evil One himself, an image he liked. He wanted his enemies to quake at the sight of him.

"The Assimilation is going well, Your Eminence," said Grand Marshal Zen-Bos. He wasn't as tall as his leader, but since K'darr was over six foot seven inches in height, that wasn't unusual. Still, it made him feel awkward having to look up at K'darr, and Grand Marshal Zen-Bos didn't like feeling awkward about anything.

"Continue," K'darr barked. He stood with his hands inside the folds of his voluminous black robe, his one vanity being its trim of solid gold. He knew the robe made him look even more forbidding with his stiff posture and perpetual dark scowl.

Zen-Bos wished he could look into his leader's obsidian eyes without feeling a tremor of fear. But he'd heard too many stories about what happened to those who displeased his master not to feel a quivering in his gut. Still, he forced himself to meet K'darr's harsh gaze with a strong, determined one of his own.

"Two-thirds of the sentient planets are converted, Your Eminence. The satellite monitors are in place for the rest."

K'darr glared at him. "Then what are we waiting for? Set course for the Tendraan system."

What are *we* waiting for? The marshal swallowed. He'd thought K'darr was here for an inspection tour. His transport ship had arrived barely an hour ago. "Sir?" he queried apprehensively. A trickle of sweat itched beneath his light coat of golden fur, and he resisted the impulse to scratch it.

K'darr's mouth tightened. "I'll be coming along. Planet Tendraa is rich in flavium. If we secure the mineral's source, our new superweapon can go into production."

Zen-Bos nodded. He'd heard about the tectonic missile under development at the heavily fortified research center on Morgot. If the weapon could be implemented, their superiority over the Coalition alliance would be assured.

"A brilliant conception, Your Eminence. You may use my quarters for the duration of your stay."

K'darr's opaque eyes brightened. "I've already had my things moved in. You must come and view my plants."

The marshal shuddered. "I'll look forward to seeing them," was his careful reply. He'd heard about K'darr's plants. The leader's collection traveled with him wherever he went. It consisted of the most exotic specimens from the planets they'd conquered— souvenirs, in their own way.

K'darr's favorites were said to be the vicious man-eating *thrum* from Antiguas Two, and the thorny swinging fodus vine from Souk. Zen-Bos remembered the report of the last warrior who had viewed the

leader's collection. He'd annoyed K'darr by disobey-
ing a direct order, and when he didn't show up
for duty the next morning, a lieutenant had gone
to check on him. K'darr had grinned and pointed
to the pieces of fur and skin scattered about the
thrum plant.

Zen-Bos gave the order for the change in course
toward the Tendraan system. "Will there be anything
else you require, Your Eminence?" he asked in a
deferential tone.

K'darr nodded. "There is one more thing."

Zen-Bos held his breath. "Sir?"

K'darr drew Zen-Bos into a corner and lowered his
voice. "The Legend of the Great Healer—" Zen-Bos's
face paled "—I understand the time has come for the
Revelation."

Zen-Bos swallowed hard. "I have heard rumors to
that effect, Your Eminence."

"They are more than rumors," K'darr roared.
Everyone on the bridge turned to look at him
but just as quickly averted their eyes. "Intelligence
reports that the Coalition has identified the one they
call the Great Healer," he continued evenly. "It is an
Earthling female known as Sarina Bretton. If there
is any truth in the legend, she could pose a threat to
the fleet. Teir Reylock has been assigned the duty of
retrieving her."

"Reylock!" Zen-Bos had heard of the man's reputation. He itched for the opportunity to confront the
meddlesome troublemaker. Eagerly, he watched his
superior's face.

"I want you to contact Cerrus Bdan," K'darr
ordered. "The smuggler has an old score to settle
with Captain Reylock. He should enjoy this challenge.
Tell Bdan we'll pay him well if he delivers the Earthwoman to us. He can take care of Reylock himself."

A slow grin spread over Zen-Bos's face. It made
sense to let someone else do the dirty work for them.
This way, no one would suspect the Morgots were

involved. "I will send the message at once, Your Eminence."

"Good." K'darr swung around, his robe swishing at his feet. "No one must interfere with our Supreme Plan," he muttered on his way to the turbolift. "No one." His eyes blackened into two chunks of coal, and anyone in his path moved swiftly out of the way.

Chapter Two

Sarina Bretton stared out of her office window at the dazzling cityscape below. The Miami skyline dipped and blended into the pristine blue of Biscayne Bay. Numerous white sailboats plied the glistening sun-drenched waters, and far in the distance, a barge chugged out to sea.

Her eyes glazed over, and in her mind she saw another scene from the space adventure film she'd viewed over the weekend. In her imagination, she became the pilot of the starship. With supreme skill, she evaded enemy laser blasts, dodged asteroids, fired photon torpedoes, and soared over new planetary horizons. . . .

Sarina sighed and drew her attention back to the client list on her desk. She was an attorney, and she dealt in facts, not fantasy. To imagine herself in any other role was a waste of time. *Toughen up, girl.* Those were Mother's words, but she was right. Sarina always needed reminding to curb her soft side.

A few stray wisps of hair tickled her face, and

Sarina pushed them back. Determinedly, she focused on the work in front of her. Before she could accomplish anything, the viewphone rang and broke her concentration.

"Sarina?" Her boss, Hiram Simmons, looked harried as he stared at her from the monitor screen. "I've assigned you a new client by the name of Pierce Mitchells. He should be on his way there now. Can you come up and see me when he arrives?"

"Certainly, sir." She straightened her shoulders, feeling uncomfortable under the scrutiny of the gray-haired managing partner of the firm.

"I'll fill you in on the case when you're in my office."

"That's fine, sir." Sarina was about to hang up when another call came through. She pushed the flash button. "Hello?"

"Hi, babe." Her fiance's face came into view, his solemn brown gaze warmingly familiar. Robert, one of the partners in the firm, had an office upstairs along with the rest of the upper echelon. Law clerks like herself were relegated to the lower floors. She'd been working here for just over a year now and didn't even have her own secretary, but hopefully that would change soon enough.

"I got wind of the Goroka case," Robert said. "How the hell did you get involved in something like that?"

Uh oh. She'd known he wouldn't approve. "I couldn't help it. The woman was so pitiful. She had nowhere else to go."

"She can't pay, for God's sake!"

"I'm only giving her legal advice, and I'll work on it in my spare time. Don't worry, it won't cost the firm anything."

"That's not the issue. If you're going to be accepted as a full-fledged Associate, you have to stop being a sucker for these hard luck cases. This isn't the first time you've used your time unwisely. Simmons won't like it."

Sarina's lips thinned. "Not everyone can afford the high fees he charges, you know."

"So let them go elsewhere. What do you want, a welfare job or a position that's going to pay your bills for a long time to come?"

"Some things are more important than money, Robert."

"Yeah, like what?" When she didn't answer, he went on. "You're up for the big promotion, sweetheart. Simmons is considering your application to become an Associate. Don't screw up now."

"Why? Are you going to delay our wedding again if I miss out?" Sarina asked bitterly. He'd already changed the date twice.

"I'm only interested in your career," Robert said, his tone sincere. "This week is crucial. Simmons is going to put you to the test."

"What do you mean?"

"He'll tell you he's sending you a client, but it'll be some wacko. Your reactions are what count. We all have to pass this nutty psych test to move ahead."

Her heart thumped with excitement. "Robert, Mr. Simmons called right before you did! He said he's sending in a new client, and we're to go up to his office together."

Robert sucked in his breath. "This might be it, then. You can do it, babe. Just stay cool."

"What should I expect?" Sarina's nervousness was growing and she could feel her palms getting damp.

"If your test is anything like mine, the 'client' will tell you a totally wild story. Simmons will be observing your responses, so act professionally. Go along with it and pretend you believe every word. He wants to see how you'd handle a difficult situation."

"But I'm supposed to take the client up to Mr. Simmons's office. Won't he refute or validate the man's case?"

"Only after he's satisfied you've passed the test." Robert chuckled. "You might not exactly end up in his office either. I was led to a special suite of rooms he uses for this purpose. It was decorated like a boudoir. The client told me that if I handled his case satisfactorily, I could have my choice of any of the lovely ladies present. Of course, it was all a ruse, but the women sure acted their parts convincingly!"

"You never told me about that!"

He grinned. "I thought you might be jealous."

"Not on your life. So you're telling me I can expect a really crazy scenario?" Sarina couldn't imagine what was planned for her, nor could she picture her staid boss getting his kicks out of games like these, but apparently there was a side to him she hadn't known existed.

"Good luck," Robert said, his eyes dancing with amusement. "Call me later and let me know what happened."

"Wait!" She wanted to ask him how he'd solved his own test situation, but he hung up without giving her the chance. Damn the man! Now she'd have to struggle through on her own.

Annoyed, Sarina tapped her fingers on the desk. They'd been engaged ever since she graduated from law school and took the clerkship at the firm. Robert's recommendation had helped her land the position, and she knew his influence was important in getting her promotion approved. She knew she should be grateful to him, but gratitude wasn't what she felt. He kept postponing their wedding, saying she should concentrate on getting ahead, and Sarina was beginning to wonder which was more important to him—her job status or herself?

Their wedding was set for December, five months from now, and if Robert put them off one more time, she'd need to reevaluate their relationship. During the past few weeks, she'd felt increasingly dissatisfied. It was difficult to pinpoint the cause. Yes, Robert irritated her, but that could be because she felt pressured. She'd applied for the Associate position because that was what he kept urging her to do, yet this job didn't fulfill her expectations. She couldn't admit that to him without starting a big argument. But she knew these problems were not the root of her current distress. Something else bothered her, but she hadn't a clue as to what it was.

Realizing that the new client might walk in at any moment, Sarina patted her French braid at the back of her head. It was still smooth and sleek, so she reached into her handbag to freshen her makeup before he arrived.

Just as she was putting her mirror away, a loud rapping sounded at the door. "Come in," Sarina called.

The door opened and in strolled the most gorgeous man she had ever seen in all of her twenty-six years. He was tall and powerfully built, but the dominant feature that held her was the strange color of his eyes. Never had she seen a hue so deep, so celestial. It was as though the sky was mirrored in his gaze. His eyes locked on hers as he approached.

"You are Sarina Bretton?" His voice was deeply resonant. The masculine tone reverberated throughout the room and seemed to touch a chord within her very soul.

"Yes," Sarina said breathlessly, moistening her lips as the man strode forward. He stopped directly in front of her and bent his head to examine the identification badge pinned to her crimson and white shirtwaist dress. Her I.D. picture showed her in a relaxed pose, her wavy blond hair hanging down her back, gray eyes wide in an oval face, and her pink lips parted in a silly grin.

Sarina noticed his thick black hair grew long in the back, curling at his nape. His features were angular, firm and strong. Then her gaze wandered down to the strange silvery jumpsuit that he wore. It was molded to his powerful body like an animal skin.

"Excuse me—I had to make certain," the man said.

Sarina looked up, startled. He was watching her, his face expressionless. Sarina searched his startlingly blue eyes for contact lenses, but saw no telltale outlines. The intense color fascinated her.

"Certain of what?" she asked, flustered.

"Of your identity." He grasped her right hand and turned it palm up. "You are the one I seek," he said, indicating the round area of pigmentation on her soft flesh.

A shiver of delight ran through her as she felt the warmth of his touch. "That's just a birthmark."

A small smile played on the man's mouth. Sarina grew uneasy and withdrew her hand from his grasp.

"Look, Mister, uh—"

"You may call me Teir."

Teir? She looked down at her desk where she'd scrawled the name Pierce Mitchells on her message pad. When she gazed back at him, her eyes mirrored her confusion.

"You are needed. I am to escort you," Teir stated, a hint of irritation in his tone.

"Escort me?" Sarina asked. "Where?" But then she answered her own question. "Oh, you mean to Mr. Simmons's office." Obviously this man, with his weird outfit and strange manner, was the test case Robert had mentioned. Remembering that her fiance had advised her to act professionally, she stuffed a notebook into her handbag.

"You won't need that where we're going," Teir said.

"I may have to take notes." Smoothing out her skirt, she rose and asked briskly, "Shall we go?"

A look of astonishment dawned on the man's face, as though he hadn't expected her to be so cooperative. Sarina wondered at that but decided to play along. Simmons's test might even be fun.

Smiling at the idea, Sarina stalked past the man and out into the carpeted corridor. Teir followed silently, his footsteps thudding behind her.

She waited until he caught up. "Has the initial data on your case been filed?" she asked as they began walking down the hallway. The main bank of elevators was situated at the opposite end.

Teir did not respond. He marched beside her, his expression stony. Halfway down the corridor, he came to an abrupt halt. "This way," he said, pointing to a closed door.

Sarina shot him a sharp glance. "That's a storage closet!"

Wordlessly, Teir opened the door, and Sarina gasped. Facing them was an elevator car.

"A private lift!" she exclaimed. "I never knew this was here." She narrowed her eyes. "Where does it go?"

"Up," Teir said, without a trace of a smile.

It must go to Mr. Simmons' penthouse suite, Sarina decided. She'd better be on the alert—her boss might be watching them via hidden cameras.

At Teir's urging, Sarina stepped inside the padded interior. Teir entered the elevator after her, his tall muscular form seeming to take up most of the small space. Sarina's breath quickened at his nearness. She edged away until she bumped into a wall. Her apprehension rose when she noticed there was no control panel.

"How do you operate this thing?" she asked.

As the door slid silently shut and they began a slow ascent, Teir showed her a small remote control device he held in his hand. It resembled a miniature pocket calculator.

"You'd better hold on," he said, securing the object in a previously hidden pocket of his jumpsuit. He slipped his hands into two loops protruding from the padded walls of the lift. "This thing starts slow, but it accelerates fast."

How peculiar, Sarina thought. There was little time to speculate because just then a big thump rocked the elevator. Sarina grabbed for the two remaining loops on the wall and clung tightly as the lift shot upward at an incredible speed. She felt as if she'd left her stomach somewhere far below. A whoosh of air sounded in her ears, and a smell like that of a pressurized airline cabin filled her nostrils.

Just as suddenly as it had started, the acceleration stopped. An eerie sense of motionlessness gripped her.

"What—what happened?" she asked, alarmed. Her head was reeling, and she felt completely disoriented.

"The antigravity device activated," Teir said. "We're out of the atmosphere now. That's the worst part of the ride, but it doesn't last long." He did a quick calculation on his remote control instrument. "Another one of your Earth minutes and sixteen seconds and we'll be there."

Earth minutes? Boy, when Robert had said she'd be sent a wacko client, he really meant it!

"You can let go now," Teir said in a curt tone.

But the elevator swayed, and Sarina's throat constricted. She maintained her grip with frozen fingers. A gentle bump rocked the lift; then the motion stopped. Tentatively, Sarina withdrew her hands from the loops. As she massaged the ridges they left on her skin, a buzzer sounded somewhere outside. The steel door slid open to reveal a short corridor with a blank white wall at the far end.

Sarina peered out into unfamiliar territory. This was definitely not the penthouse suite where Mr. Simmons had his offices, nor was it anywhere else in the building that she recognized.

"After you," Teir said, thumbing toward the exit.

"Right," Sarina mumbled, swallowing. She wondered where he was taking her. Would Mr. Simmons be waiting to join them? If so, she'd better not show any hesitation.

Boldly, Sarina stepped forward. As Teir followed her out into the corridor, the lift door closed behind them.

"Now what—" she began, but Teir prodded her along until they reached the white wall. He pressed his hand against a raised panel, and a hidden door slid open with a hiss. Sarina gasped as a new view unfolded in front of her. Never in all her daydreams had she conceived of such an amazing sight!

It reminded her of an airplane cockpit, with rows of buttons and computer panels blinking in various colored lights. The symbols were in an unrecognizable code. But her attention did not linger on the instrumentation, as Sarina's eyes swung to the huge viewscreen. In front of her was a blackness so profound she could only wonder at it. Far in the distance, tiny lights that resembled stars shone brightly.

"What is this place?" she whispered in awe.

"My ship," Teir responded matter-of-factly. He pointed to the two modular seats facing the viewscreen. "Sit there," he commanded, indicating the one on the right. When Sarina didn't move, he made a sound of impatience and tugged her forward. Feeling suddenly weak in the knees, she didn't resist when he pushed her down and buckled her into a safety harness.

"What's going on?" Sarina was thoroughly confused by now. "Is this some kind of a flight simulator?"

Surely Mr. Simmons wouldn't go to such extremes just to tap into her favorite fantasy. No one in his right mind would incur such exorbitant expense merely to test an employee. And for what purpose? This scenario had nothing to do with legal expertise. Come to think of it, Robert's hadn't either. He must have been tested to see if he would take a bribe, albeit in the form of seductive women. But Robert had at least known where he was while Sarina wasn't certain of anything.

"I think there must be some mistake," she said, but Teir ignored her comment. He was already dropping into the pilot's chair beside her.

He strapped himself in. Then, releasing a lever, he manipulated the steering column and a different view was revealed on the screen.

"Say farewell," Teir said quietly.

Sarina's mouth dropped open. That greenish-blue globe spinning against the dark backdrop looked very much like the planet Earth!

Numbly, she turned to stare at Teir.

"Firing thrusters," was all he said. He punched a button and a roaring noise sounded. She felt a huge surge from somewhere underneath and then suddenly they seemed to be moving at the speed of light.

"Will you please tell me what's happening?" Sarina demanded, her heart thudding.

Teir entered a code into the computer and then leaned back, his hands behind his head. For a long moment he didn't look at her. He was amazed at how willingly she'd come with him. He'd been prepared to render her unconscious if necessary, but the woman had cooperated readily. Teir ran his hand through his unruly hair. What did it matter? She was here, and accomplishing this mission was his prime concern.

He glanced at her. The woman was waiting for an answer, her face lit with curiosity. His orders were to brief her, but he wasn't sure how to start.

He decided he might as well spill it out. "You have been identified as the legendary Great Healer," Teir began. "A terrible disease called the Farg is sweeping through the galaxy, killing billions. Those who survive are being enslaved by a warrior race known as the Morgots. You are destined to stop these horrors and save everyone."

His tone was sarcastic, but he couldn't help it. The woman certainly didn't look like a Savior. "I'm taking you to the High Council where you will wed our esteemed prince, Lord Cam'brii of the ruling House of Raimorrda. Supposedly, the prophecy will be fulfilled through this marriage."

Sarina stared at him, unable to believe her ears.

This man had never claimed to be Pierce Mitchells. But if he wasn't the client Mr. Simmons had sent to her, then who the hell *was* he? Surely his story couldn't be true? No, it was too preposterous! This had to be a simulation, or some kind of theatrical set.

But even as Sarina tried to find a rational explanation, her imaginative mind discarded it. That view of Earth had been much too realistic. She didn't know of any technology that could produce such an effect. And if this setup was real, she had just been abducted in a spaceship by an alien!

Panic swept over her and she fumbled with her safety strap, feeling an intense need to find an exit.

"Stay in your seat!" Teir thundered. "We're about to enter space warp."

Sarina's anxiety escalated into sheer terror. She tugged at the buckle, but her hands were trembling so much she couldn't unlatch it.

"Nine seconds to go. Eight, seven . . ."

Her neck whipped back as the ship lurched forward. The stars became a kaleidoscope of color, a blur of passing images as they passed at lightning speed. She felt herself being pressed back into her seat. Then just as suddenly, the ship slowed, and they were gliding smoothly. Some of the stars seemed larger, closer than they'd been before.

Sarina couldn't comprehend what was happening but she was desperate to return to a familiar environment. Wrestling with the catch on her safety harness, she finally unhooked it and jumped up.

"I want to go home. Where's the exit?" she cried, peering frantically around. Even if she did find one, she had no idea where it would lead. If this really was a spaceship. . . .

"Get back in your seat," Teir snarled.

Despite his ominous tone, Sarina charged for the opposite wall. Behind her, she heard a growl of rage as Teir leaped up and grabbed her by the wrist.

"You're hurting me!" she cried as the pressure of his fingers forced her to turn around. His use of brute force confirmed her suspicion that he wasn't an actor hired by her boss to play the part of a client. She wasn't even sure he was a man. Maybe he was an alien life form who'd taken on the shape of a human male so as not to frighten her. If that was so, it wasn't working. She was terrified!

"Either you do as you're told, or I'll have to lock you up," Teir said in a dangerously quiet voice. "The ship's on autopilot right now, but there's some tricky navigation ahead. I have to pay attention to the helm. You must not interfere."

"Let me go!" Sarina struggled to free herself but it was like fighting against solid rock. Teir maintained his tight grip on her arm, and even as she kicked and squirmed, he drew her against his body.

"You'll obey me, woman!" He looked into her wide, defiant eyes. The silvery flecks in them reminded him of the mists of Quava Plain on his homeworld of Vilaran. He hadn't been home in ages, and suddenly he felt an overwhelming desire to return. His grasp on her loosened, and his gaze drifted down to her slightly parted lips. She tempted him, this woman, with her spirited behavior. With a sound of disgust, Teir thrust her away.

Immediately, Sarina raced to the door at the rear of the cockpit. She couldn't be trapped here! The walls felt as if they were closing in on her. Frantically, she searched for some way of opening the door, hoping it would reveal the elevator or a familiar corridor.

"Storms of the sun, woman, get away from that wall!" Teir ordered. "You can't go anywhere."

Slowly, Sarina turned to face him. He had to be speaking the truth. This man, or whatever he was, had lured her here and used her misinterpretation of the situation to his advantage. Now she was his prisoner. Her head whirled as she remembered what he'd said. She was needed. She had to marry someone. It didn't make any sense, but then again, none of this did.

Glancing at him, she noted the way his muscles bulged, stretching the fabric of his silvery jumpsuit. He was strong, and from the demonstration he'd already given her, she had no doubt he could easily enforce his demands. She'd better do as he said until she learned more about what he had in mind.

Teir saw the play of emotions on her face, fear mixed with doubt and confusion. She might find this easier to accept if he gave her a fuller explanation. "Sit down while I check our heading," he commanded. "Afterward, I'll answer any questions you might have."

Sarina reluctantly obeyed, taking her seat while Teir dropped into the pilot's chair to peruse the instrument readouts and punch commands into the computer. "Where are we going?" she asked, not sure she really wanted to know.

Teir regarded her with relief. At last, she was acting rational. His jumpsuit itched, and he scratched at a spot below his knee. He hated wearing it, but it was the standard uniform issue for sensitive missions and the sensory-laden material was invisible to radar, enabling him to enter Sarina's office building undetected.

"We are on our way to the High Council," Teir said tersely. "According to the legend, your healing power will be activated when you fall in love with a member of the ruling family. Hence your marriage to Lord Cam'brii."

"The ruling family of what?" Sarina asked, hoping to gain all the knowledge she could. She suppressed her panic, determined to find some way out of this situation.

"Earth is not yet a member of the Coalition of Sentient Planets, an alliance of star systems in this quadrant of the galaxy. The House of Raimorrda has ruled the High Council for eons past. Lord Cam'brii is their most valiant noble. He was chosen to fulfill the prophecy."

Teir spoke with derision, Sarina noticed, as though he didn't believe any of it. Maybe she could convince him to take her home. "Where do you fit in?" she asked.

Teir glowered at her. "I'm an officer in the Coalition Defense League. I was assigned the enviable job of transporting you to the High Council."

"You don't seem too happy about it."

"This assignment is a waste of my ability," he snapped.

"I see. What is your normal job function, Captain?"

He gave her a wicked grin. "I hire out my services."

"What kind of services do you mean?" she asked, deliberately ignoring the sexual innuendo in his tone.

Teir focused his attention ahead. They were entering a new star system, and heading for a large copper-colored planet. He punched a code into the computer and took over the steering column, guiding the ship around the planet's edge.

"I'm a troubleshooter," Teir replied when the maneuver was completed. "When the Defense League doesn't need me, others pay me to solve their problems."

"I see," Sarina said. "What if I paid you more to take me back home?" she asked eagerly. "I'll double your usual fee, no matter what it is!"

Teir shot her a disdainful glance. "No way, *princess*," he said, using the title she would assume after her marriage. "The High Council has summoned you, and it's my job to deliver you."

"You don't have to tell them you found me. Make up some excuse," Sarina begged.

His voice hardened. "Forget it!"

Too bad, Sarina thought. Noticing the outline of

a doorway on the opposite side from the escape hatch, she decided to explore on her own, whether her captain liked it or not. Meanwhile, maybe she could figure out some other way to make him take her home. She wasn't going to give in so easily.

"Sarina," Teir growled, "come back here!"

Anger at the inconvenience she was causing roiled his blood. Jumping out of his seat, he saw she'd already ducked through to the next passageway. He hurried after her.

Sarina found herself in a series of rooms that opened into each other, storerooms and gunnery decks from the looks of them. At the sound of footsteps behind her, she glanced wildly around and grabbed a hefty rod-shaped object from what looked like a pile of tools on a shelf just as Teir came racing through the portal.

"Don't come any closer or I'll brain you," she warned, waving the object threateningly in the air. It was so heavy she could barely lift it, but she put on a brave front and faced him.

Teir paused, then took a step in her direction. "We're approaching the Yxon asteroid belt. I have to guide the ship. Stop this foolishness immediately!" His tone was icy, his eyes furious.

"No! I want to go home!"

He shrugged. "You've sealed your fate. I'm going to lock you up for the duration of the voyage."

"Over my dead body!"

"Over your *unconscious* body, maybe."

Sarina swallowed a large lump in her throat. Her arm was starting to ache, and she couldn't hold up the heavy rod much longer. She doubted she could swing it effectively to hit him anyway, but it was the only weapon she had.

"Will you stop waving that blasted electrifier around? It's dangerous," Teir growled, still advancing.

"I don't like the way you're giving me orders.

Turn this—this vessel around and take me back to Earth!"

"You leave me no choice," Teir sighed. Setting his jaw, he pounced.

Sarina swung the rod, but Teir easily sidestepped the blow and chopped her forearm with the side of his hand. A sharp pain stung her below the elbow. The weapon fell from her numbed fingers and clattered to the floor.

He caught her by the wrists and forced her backward toward one of the cabins. "Stop!" she cried. As he shoved her around a corner, her braid loosened and her long hair came tumbling down.

"Inside," Teir commanded, his eyes glittering.

Sarina clung to the wall. Teir pressed his body against her, trying to force her in the direction he wanted her to go. Her breathing was labored as she struggled, wrestling with him in the doorway. His thighs were muscular and strong, and he used them to push her sideways. She felt herself helplessly sliding. Then suddenly she stumbled to the floor, and he was pulled atop her. His body pinned her down. With her skirt raised halfway above her hips, and her limbs tangled with his, she became acutely aware of his growing bulge between her legs.

Fury surged through her as she glared up at him. "You bastard, *get off me!*"

"Look, princess," Teir said, trying to ignore the effect she was having on him, "I never asked for this assignment. It's time you and I—"

Boom! Something crashed into the ship. The hull shuddered, and another deafening *boom* followed.

Cursing, he quickly rolled off her.

"What was that?" Sarina gasped, sitting up.

Teir regarded her with icy cobalt eyes. "We're under attack." He yanked her to her feet. "You'd better obey me, woman, because both our lives are in danger. Stay here."

He turned toward the cockpit, but just as he cleared

the archway, a blast hit the ship and the area in front of him exploded. Sarina screamed, throwing her hands up to protect herself as a cascade of fiery debris crashed down.

Sarina staggered forward. She found Teir on the floor, leaning against a wall. Blood oozed from a large jagged wound on his arm. His face was ashen, pinched with pain.

"Oh, my God!" Sarina gasped.

There was no doubt about it—this was real, all right.

The planet Earth was far behind. Everything she'd ever known was gone. Sarina was alone in a spaceship with a strange man and they were being attacked by hostile alien forces!

Chapter Three

"There are medical supplies on that shelf," Teir muttered, pointing. His hand shook, and Sarina wondered what she would do if he passed out. But he remained alert.

"Help me out of this blasted jumpsuit," he said. "Hurry! I have to get to the controls." Another thump racked the ship, and Teir tried to rip off his sleeve in his impatience. The effort was too painful, and he stopped with a groan.

"Lie still," Sarina said.

She knelt beside him and tugged at the tight-fitting material until his upper torso was bared. Her gaze swept over his massive shoulders, then down to the dark tangle of hair on his broad chest. The hair tapered and disappeared at his waistline. A warm flush crept up her face as she stared.

"Don't get shy on me now, princess." Teir's dark eyes bored into her, and fortifying herself with a deep breath, Sarina yanked the jumpsuit down below his hips—and gasped. Dear God, he was naked!

"Stop gawking," he snapped. "My regular clothes are in the master cabin. You can get them after you dress the wound." Annoyed, he kicked the jumpsuit the rest of the way off by himself.

"Aye, aye, sir," Sarina retorted, saluting. Rising, she went to retrieve the medical supplies. As Teir barked out instructions, she cleansed and dressed his wound. Part of her responded to what he was saying, and part of her tried to assimilate all that was happening. She still couldn't believe the spacecraft was real, until another shuddering *whump* reminded her they were under attack. A pungent odor remained in the air from the previous explosion. Yes, this was truly happening, she told herself, feeling a sudden rush of exhilaration.

When she'd finished bandaging him, Teir complimented her efficiency as a nurse. If he weren't so worried about what was going on up front, he might have taken more pleasure from her touch on his skin. His flesh tingled where she made contact. But there was no time for such indulgent thoughts and Teir got up.

He stumbled naked into the cockpit while Sarina went to get his clothes. The sight on the viewscreen stopped him cold. Poised in space was a huge cigar-shaped vessel, its deadly weapons turrets aimed at his ship.

"By the corona, it's Cerrus Bdan!" Teir muttered. A sinking feeling hit him as he realized he was facing his old foe. What rotten luck! Even if he didn't believe in the legend of the Great Healer, his mission was to deliver Sarina to the High Council, and Bdan's untimely appearance could put quite a crimp in those plans.

His jaw clenched, Teir dropped into the pilot's seat and punched in the code to activate the ship's defenses. He should have done it before, but he'd been too distracted by Sarina. Now it was too late. The console refused to respond, and his shields remained off line.

"Blast!" Deftly his fingers moved over the controls, but before he could activate a backup system, a flash erupted from Bdan's vessel and another resounding *boom* rocked his ship. One thought consoled Teir. If Bdan wanted to blow them out of space, he would have done it already. The smuggler obviously wanted them alive.

"What's happening?" Sarina asked, rushing in with his clothes in her arms. She dropped them on his lap, averting her gaze from his nakedness to look at the viewscreen. Her eyes widened in astonishment when she saw the armed vessel poised in front of them.

"Our main tangent beams are out," Teir explained as he stood to put on his pants and vest. "The laser cannons won't fire, and we've lost maneuvering ability." He glanced at her, his face expressionless. "We're defenseless. We have to wait for their terms."

"Terms?" Sarina's voice cracked. She stared at Teir as he fastened his trousers. The hip-hugging black pants and leathery vest were all that he wore. With a fresh white bandage around his muscular arm, a dark shadow around his jaw, and his unruly midnight hair, he made a rakishly handsome picture.

Teir seem unaware of her appraisal as he took his seat. "Cerrus Bdan owns that ship. He's waiting for our surrender. We're lucky, princess—we could have been dead by now." While there was still time, he keyed a message and transmitted it on subspace radio using a prearranged code.

"The stinking buzzard isn't even allowing us to negotiate!" he grumbled. A shuttle had just cleared the enemy vessel and was turning in their direction. "I should have known Bdan wouldn't give us any options, especially not where I'm concerned. They're coming for us."

"Who is he?" Sarina asked.

"Cerrus Bdan is a notorious smuggler who deals in the slave trade. We haven't exactly been on friendly terms," Teir explained. He'd disrupted a number of

Bdan's illicit runs, and the smuggler had a grudge against him. "It's unfortunate that he caught up with me just now."

"Will he kill you?" Her brow furrowed with concern. Not that she cared about the man, Sarina told herself, but he was her only protection.

Teir shrugged casually in response. He was more worried about what Bdan might do to her. Sarina's silky blond hair floated about her shoulders like spun gold. With her porcelain complexion, large smoky eyes, and full trembling mouth, she was more than pleasing. Add to that her curvaceous assets he'd felt earlier, and she'd bring a high price in the slave market.

Of course, Cerrus Bdan might decide to keep her for himself. Teir was fully aware of the smuggler's cruelty to his female slaves, and Bdan might take particular delight in tormenting Sarina if he thought she belonged to his old enemy.

Thrusting that unpleasant thought aside, he said, "There's no point in resisting. We'll plot our escape once we're on their vessel." He only hoped that the plan he'd already set in motion would work without a hitch.

"What? You're just going to sit there and let them board us?" Sarina asked incredulously. If he didn't care about himself, the least he could do would be to fight for her freedom. "What kind of defense is this of your future . . . your future—" She couldn't remember what her title would be once she'd married Lord Whoever.

"Princess," Teir supplied. "Now listen carefully. Say nothing about yourself, or about why I brought you here. Let me do the talking, understand?"

Sarina nodded, and the anxiety in his expression made her fear increase. Before she could reply, a bump jostled their ship as the enemy shuttle docked. Teir rose and nudged her to do the same. They turned to face the exit portal.

The door slid open and in marched a formation of heavily armed troops. Sarina sucked in her breath. It wasn't the uniforms or even the shooters pointed in their direction that alarmed her. It was the strange blue hue of the soldiers' skin, the doglike appearance of their faces, and the floppy ears.

A husky officer stepped forward, barking out an order. His dark eyes looked small and menacing behind the wide brim of his helmet.

"What did he say?" Sarina asked, frustrated and not really expecting an answer. The alien's voice was a harsh growl, and to her the sounds were meaningless and jumbled.

"He said we are to come with him to Bdan's ship."

"You speak their language?" Sarina glanced at him with awe.

"No, I wear a linguist patch. It translates any of the known sentient languages." He pointed to his temple where she could see a slight scar. "You'll have to get one implanted. I didn't think of it before. Your disability could be an inconvenience to us."

She started to respond, but the officer—whose face resembled a vicious bulldog, she thought—snapped a few sounds that made Teir stiffen beside her. Touching her elbow, he urged her forward.

"Now what?" Sarina asked in a trembling voice.

"He says he'll be more than happy to roast us for dinner if we don't do as we're told."

She gasped. "Would they really *eat* us?"

"Probably not, although cannabalistic tribes still exist on their planet in the more remote areas. Bdan is a harsh taskmaster, however, and he wouldn't appreciate their doing away with us. He has something far more interesting in mind, I'm sure."

The alien soldiers flanking them, Sarina and Teir were marched through the airlock into the waiting shuttle. Standing beside Teir, Sarina tried to control her fear as the uniformed figures spoke in harsh, guttural tones.

A short time later, they entered Bdan's spacecraft. Sarina was trembling violently, but Teir seemed unconcerned, his stride long, his shoulders squared. Dear God, Sarina thought, how does he remain so cool?

In reality, Teir was worried as hell. As they headed down a long, steel corridor, he wondered what Bdan had in store for them. He needed time to give his escape plan a chance to hatch.

They approached a set of double doors that hissed silently open at their approach. The officer of the guard barked a few commands, and Teir indicated to Sarina that they were to enter. Making a quick decision, he gestured to her that they should each go in alone. Better they should be apart, he thought, so Bdan wouldn't think she was his woman. Unable to explain his reasoning aloud, he strode past her, ignoring the look of surprise and dismay on her face.

"Well, if it isn't my old friend," Teir drawled, approaching the large figure seated on a small dais. His peripheral vision assessed the number of attendants inside the chamber. The room was ringed with them.

The corpulent smuggler looked up from the naked slave girl he was fondling on his lap. She was humanoid and could have been obtained from any one of the pirate's illegal raids on Coalition vessels. Teir tightened his mouth in anger.

"Captain Reylock. A gr-r-reat pleasure it is to gr-r-reet you again." Bdan's beady eyes shifted to Sarina who'd followed close behind. "And you br-r-ring with you such a lovely companion."

Sarina stiffened, not understanding his words but getting the gist of his meaning. Never had she seen a being so gross. With his bluish skin, hanging jowls, and large bulbous nose, Cerrus Bdan reminded her of an ugly bloodhound. Even the sounds coming out of his mouth were a mixture of grunts and snorts.

"She doesn't understand you, Bdan," Teir said. "The Earthwoman lacks the linguist patch."

"Easily can we r-r-remedy that." Bdan rumbled his r's with a guttural tone that made him even more unattractive to Sarina. She tried to keep her expression neutral as he pushed away the slave girl and beckoned with his finger for her to approach.

At an almost imperceptible nod from Teir, Sarina moved slowly forward until she was close enough to the fat smuggler to smell his foul breath. She cringed as he ran a stubby finger along her cheek. Turning his head, Bdan snapped out an order. A short-legged attendant whom Sarina thought resembled a dachshund waddled out of the room.

She glanced fearfully about, surprised by the luxuriously decorated chamber. The silken drapes and plush furnishings were in bright rainbow colors, but they didn't cheer Sarina. She could very well end up like that girl who was trying to slink off, unnoticed.

But Bdan noticed the slave's movements and he let out a series of high-pitched barks that froze her in her tracks. An angry purplish blotch suffused Bdan's face as he screamed invectives at her. The girl looked clearly terrified.

Sarina didn't dare move, but she felt Teir come up behind her. "What's the matter?" she whispered out of the corner of her mouth.

"He didn't give her permission to leave."

One of the attendants withdrew an ominous-looking rod from his belted tunic. The girl shrieked and as she turned to run, the guard pointed the object at her. A crackling beam shot out, striking her in the back. She slammed against a wall and slithered to the floor. The attendant strode forward, lowering his weapon, and another beam struck the girl, then another, until she writhed in agony. When she finally went limp, Bdan ordered her removal.

"Is she dead?" Sarina rasped, her throat so dry

she could hardly breathe. She'd recognized the rod-shaped object. It was similar to the one she'd picked up to use against Teir, the thing he'd called an electrifier.

"Probably," he responded, but shut up when he felt Bdan's glowering attention return to them. The dachshund-like attendant reentered the chamber, and after a rapid verbal exchange with his master, he started toward Sarina.

"What's he doing?" she asked Teir, her voice rising in fear.

"Don't worry," Teir muttered, knowing what was coming but powerless to prevent it. This method was crude, at best, but it would work.

As the dachshund approached, Sarina saw he held a tiny rectangular object in his hand. As he grasped her arm and yanked her close, she cried out. The attendant grabbed a handful of her hair, jerking her neck back and silencing her. He pressed the object against her temple. There was a loud snapping noise, and a blinding pain shot through her head. Sarina swayed and felt herself being propped up by the dachshund. After a few seconds, the discomfort passed and she was able to stand by herself.

"What—what happened?" She blinked her eyes to clear her vision.

Bdan replied, "You have r-r-received the linguist patch. Now can we communicate. Aware am I of the reason for Captain Reylock's escort, your r-r-royalness. But the truth he may not have told you." The smuggler's dark eyes gleamed as he glanced at Teir. "The captain usually pursues his own agenda. Fortunate are you that I intercepted his ship."

A small smile curved Bdan's mouth as he regarded Sarina. "Together shall we dine; then can we discuss your disposition."

Teir smothered a curse. So Cerrus knew her identity. There could be only one way the smuggler had found out. Someone from Defense League headquarters had leaked the information. No wonder Bdan had intercepted him so easily. Teir only hoped the rest of his plan hadn't been screwed up, or they'd really be in trouble. What did Bdan intend? To ransom Sarina to the High Council? Other than settling the score between the two of them, Teir couldn't see how else he would stand to gain.

"Bring him forward," Bdan barked, pointing at Teir.

Two husky attendants grasped Teir's arms, ignoring his stifled groan of pain when one of them clamped a hand around his bandaged wound.

"I can walk, you animals," Teir gritted, twisting to free himself. But the movement only aggravated his wound, so he swallowed his pride and stopped struggling.

Sarina watched helplessly as Teir was dragged directly in front of the fat gloating face of Cerrus Bdan. She didn't envy him his position.

"Wounded in my attack, eh?" the smuggler growled with delight. "Don't worry, fix you properly we will . . . after you answer a few questions. Then have I other plans for you." His jowls quivered, and drool formed at the corner of his lip. "Looking forward to this have I been for a long time, Captain. I hope you decide to resist so we can prolong your interrogation. Take him below," he ordered the two goons.

"Hey, wait a minute," Teir protested, seeing the look of terror come over Sarina's face. But he was hauled through the doors before he had a chance to reassure her. He wasn't certain he could have, anyway. The cards being dealt so far were stacked in Bdan's favor. He only hoped Sarina could come up with a trump.

As Sarina watched Teir being dragged away, she felt utterly lost. How could she possibly defend herself against this repulsive creature? Slowly, she turned to stare at the smuggler who was observing her intently.

"What do you want from me?" She tried to make her tone sound bold and confident.

Bdan grinned and gave a slight bow, making his pumpkin-colored caftan swish at his feet. "Your r-r-royalness, we wish only to please. Prepared have I the appropriate quarters for you to refresh yourself and change. Then shall we dine together and talk." He clapped his hands, and an elderly female appeared. She was of another species, her bent humanoid form covered with a thin coating of filmy substance. As she moved, her face shimmered. She wore a coarse sack-like garment.

"Come," the woman said in a flat, toneless voice and Sarina obeyed, following her through an adjacent room, then to a lift. On a lower deck, Sarina was shown into a sumptuous dressing room. "A bath has been prepared for you, my lady," intoned the old woman. She indicated a partitioned area off to one side. The expression in her pale yellow eyes was vacant, and Sarina wondered if she were drugged.

"What are Bdan's plans regarding Teir and myself?" Sarina asked. She felt a strong sense of dread. The smuggler was giving her the royal treatment, but she didn't trust him. Surely there was more to his purpose in holding her than he let on.

The woman gave her a blank look. "The master honors you, my lady." She selected a gown from a large wardrobe. "This suits your coloring." She held the fabric up against Sarina's skin.

"It's beautiful." Admiringly, Sarina fingered the silken material. The diaphanous gown was a vibrant tangerine interwoven with silver threads. It had a tight laced bodice, long sleeves, and a long flowing skirt. Recalling the slave girl, Sarina could just imagine Bdan undoing those laces and putting his paws on her breasts. The thought made her shudder.

"I'm comfortable in my own clothes, thank you," she said quickly, thrusting the dress back into the older woman's hands.

The woman's face hardened. "You will put this on after you are cleansed. Your water cools. Need you assistance?"

"Where is Teir?"

Receiving no response and realizing the woman was not going to budge until she bathed, Sarina stepped behind the partition and quickly undressed. She had to admit that the warm water in the sunken bath felt good once she'd immersed herself. She hadn't realized how grimy she'd become since leaving her office.

Her office. God, that seemed ages ago! Was Robert worried about her? Was he trying to find out where she'd gone? Tears suddenly sprang to Sarina's eyes. Why did this have to happen to her? All that was familiar was gone. She was in a strange place among hostile alien creatures. How was she ever going to get back home?

Sarina sank deeper into the soothing water until it reached her chin and closed her eyes, letting her imagination bring Robert's comforting face into view. But it wasn't her fiance's visage that appeared. It was Teir's. And she knew she had to help him.

"It is getting late, my lady." The slave woman stepped around the partition and lifted Sarina's clothes from the floor.

"How do I dry myself?" Sarina asked. "I don't see any towels."

"You have merely to get out." The woman's shimmering features shifted, as though a hint of a smile had appeared, before she went into the dressing room beyond.

Sarina stepped out of the bath and waited. Instantly, the walls and floor began to glow. A pulsating vibration started, and her body warmed as waves of radiant energy washed over her. Seconds later, the vibrations stopped, and the stones went cold. As she looked down, Sarina saw that she was completely dry. Since she was also completely naked, she called out, "Excuse me, I need my clothes back."

"In here," the woman's voice commanded.

Sarina walked around the barrier, to find the slave holding up the tangerine gown.

"I guess I have no choice," Sarina muttered. Her own clothes were nowhere in sight, and neither were her undergarments. As she allowed the woman to dress her, she couldn't help feeling vulnerably exposed. The silken material covered her down to her ankles, but it was so transparent she was sure Bdan would be able to see right through it. Of course, that's probably what he had in mind.

The slave stepped back and examined her. "Suits you, this does. Now will I fix your hair." She indicated a dressing table with a seat. Sarina watched in a mirror as her hair was combed off her face and fastened with jeweled clips, the rest cascading down her back. "Good," the woman said when she stepped back to examine her handiwork. "The master will be pleased. But you need color to your lips." She rummaged in a drawer and handed Sarina some cosmetics.

Sarina applied the makeup unwillingly. The last thing she wanted to do was attract the lascivious attention of that old dog. As it was, she felt like a lamb being offered up for slaughter. She closed her eyes while the woman sprayed her with perfume. Her only hope was that Bdan would truly treat her as royalty. To that end, she'd have to play up the legend for all it was worth.

As she tried on the soft shoes the woman gave her, Sarina had a fleeting vision of Teir locked in a cell, his body sweaty and unwashed, his arms chained to a wall. Maybe they were torturing him even now. The idea filled her with horror. She shook her head to clear the vision, but it remained. She wanted so much to help him, but dear God, what could she do?

Cerrus Bdan was waiting for her in a room that appeared to be a dining hall. A long oblong table of a white marble-like material was set for four. Crystals mounted on the walls provided a soft, muted light, and billowing purple and gold ceiling drapes added color. Gold was everywhere, in the serving pieces, ornaments, and tableware. Bdan sat smugly on a cushion at the opposite end of the room. Sarina thought the effect was like a desert sheik's tent.

Standing in the doorway, she swallowed apprehensively.

"Enter," Bdan commanded. He too had changed his outfit and was resplendent in an olive military uniform, complete with many glittering decorations.

Sarina tilted her chin and strode forward, then halted several feet from the smuggler.

"Come closer," Bdan growled, his beady eyes gleaming. Drool ran down his chin as he leered at her. "The dress becomes you, it does," he said, licking his lips and staring at her breasts.

Sarina cleared her throat. "You are expecting others?"

Bdan leaned back against his cushioned chair, never once removing his eyes from her. "Arrf," he acknowledged.

A side door opened, and an incongruous pair entered. Bdan said to Sarina, "Allow me to introduce my *gima*. This is Ava Bet." A tall, stately female dressed in a shimmering jade gown nodded at Sarina, a look of displeasure on her face. She was heavily made up, her green eyes rimmed in black. Her wild auburn hair writhed about her head as though it was alive. Her other, much more unusual attributes were the four arms she sprouted, two from each side. Her twenty long, clawlike fingernails were polished in black. Sarina could guess Ava Bet's function, which accounted for the *gima*'s irritation at Sarina's presence.

"And this is Lieutenant Otis, my executive officer," Bdan said, indicating the uniformed creature beside Ava Bet. He, too, was humanoid in shape but there the resemblance ended. His face was lizard-like and cold. Harsh onyx eyes glared at Sarina without even a nod of acknowledgment.

"Be seated," Bdan said, and as though by hidden signal, attendants appeared to wait on them.

Sarina sat opposite Ava Bet who stared at her, a low growling noise coming from her throat. Sarina folded her hands in her lap and waited.

"Tell me," Bdan roared at her, "how came you to be aboard R-R-Reylock's vessel."

Sarina jumped at the loudness of his tone. "Teir— Captain Reylock—came to my office and I went with him, thinking we were going to see my boss," she explained.

"Once on board his ship, did you not try to escape? Or were you already aware of the prophecy?"

Three pairs of eyes centered on her. Sarina decided to be honest. "I was not aware of it until Captain Reylock told me," she said quietly.

"Had no notion, did you, that you were the Great Healer?"

"No." She lowered her eyes to her plate and the weird concoction which looked like worms squiggling on a bed of blue rice. She tightened her mouth as her stomach heaved and bile rose in her throat.

"And now?"

She wondered at Bdan's probing questions. His beady eyes glared at her eagerly as though he hoped she would make a mistake. No doubt he lusted to add her to his collection of slaves, she thought in despair. How could she get out of here to help Teir if she was trapped herself?

"The High Council wishes to wed me to Lord—uh, Lord—"

"Cam'brii." An unpleasant smile played across Bdan's mouth. "According to the legend, fall in love with this nobleman you must in order for your power to become activated." He leaned forward and lowered his voice. "Tell me about this power, your r-r-royalness. How does it work?"

Sarina looked him straight in the eye. "I have no idea. I don't understand how I was identified as this healer in the first place."

"The Auricle in the Great Hall glowed with the fire as it was predicted. An answering light came from Earth. From you, Sarina Bretton. So was I informed."

"Ah." Sarina nodded as though she understood. In truth, she didn't understand anything except that she wanted desperately to go home. She wanted to be with Robert, to return to familiar surroundings with normal people. Inside, she cried out for this to be a horrible dream. But it wasn't, and she was here, facing these repugnant aliens all by herself.

"Where is Teir?" she asked.

"Captain Reylock is being interrogated," stated Lieutenant Otis.

Throughout the conversation, he'd been staring at her, his expression unreadable. Ava Bet, on the other hand, was trying to pretend uninterest by noisily slurping her food.

"We are trying to determine Reylock's purpose in abducting you," the executive officer continued. He'd barely touched his food, Sarina noticed.

"Teir said he was ordered to—" Sarina stopped, biting her lip. Perhaps some of the information he'd given her was confidential.

"Take you to the High Council? Of course. But what would he stand to gain?"

"For that matter, what do you?" she asked point-blank.

Bdan spoke, ignoring her question. "Serves his own ambitions, Captain Reylock does. R-R-Raided my ship numerous times with his scurvy crew. Stole my cargo and sold it for profit. A thief, he is!"

Sarina frowned. She wouldn't put it past Teir to do as Bdan said, but what other plans could he possibly have for her? He seemed sincere about taking her to wed Lord Cam'brii.

"I just want to go home." She addressed Bdan, who was stuffing his mouth with some sort of green leafy substance. "Maybe you can help me."

"An excellent idea," purred Ava Bet, taking an interest in her for the first time. She flashed Sarina a feline smile. "Why don't we just take her back where she came from?" she suggested, turning to Bdan and raising a hopeful eyebrow.

Bdan growled, "Not possible."

"Why not? Because your plans are every bit as traitorous as Reylock's?"

Bdan's blue face purpled and he rose in anger, knocking his chair over in the process. Cushions scattered to the floor. "Be silent! Overstep your boundaries, do you. I'll have your *mzips*—" he pointed at her writhing hair "—yanked out and served in my soup if you don't guard your tongue," he roared.

Ava Bet's expression turned sullen. "Then excuse me, my lord master. My appetite has suddenly vanished." With a swish of her skirts, she left the room.

"Ar-r-r-r," Bdan snarled, turning his narrowed gaze on Sarina.

She felt a rush of fear. But before she could find out what he intended, Sarina was aware of a sudden silence. There was no engine noise, no whirring of machinery. She noticed that the sensation of movement had stopped as well.

Lieutenant Otis leaped out of his chair and was racing for the entryway when an armed soldier entered the dining hall.

Halting in front of his leader, he saluted.

"Report," Bdan snapped.

"Defense League forces have surrounded our ship, master leader. We are caught in a tractor beam wheel. Demanding our surrender, they are."

A string of expletives was the response. "Find us, did they? How?" Bdan barked.

Lieutenant Otis, who had stopped by the doorway, snorted. "You might ask your prisoner that question."

The corpulent smuggler glared at him. "Go to Security Level Six and ask him yourself! Make arrangements, I will." He glanced at Sarina. "Confined to your quarters are you."

At a hidden signal, the old slave woman appeared to escort her out.

Like hell I'm going to my quarters! Sarina thought. This was her chance to free Teir. Security Level Six, huh?

She was on her way.

Chapter Four

Sarina docilely followed the old woman into the lift. She kept a calm expression on her face, but inside her thoughts were racing. Somehow, she had to elude her guard. Then she had to find out where Security Level Six was located.

She smiled meekly at the woman as the turbolift descended, noting that their destination had been spoken aloud. It shouldn't be hard to get to the Security Level this way, she thought, hoping access wouldn't be denied once she was free to try. Unlike Teir's, this ship's computer seemed to respond to voice-activated commands. As long as identification wasn't required, she shouldn't have any trouble getting where she needed to go.

Sarina glanced down at the tangerine gown. It certainly would be easier to move around if she had her own clothes on. Those soft shoes weren't made for running, either. As her eyes lifted back to the face of the old woman, the glimmer of an idea dawned.

By the time they reached the residential deck, she'd formulated her plan.

"Enter," the woman ordered, thumbing her into the same sumptuous chamber as before. Stepping inside, Sarina noticed an inside door was open, revealing a bedroom suite adjacent to the dressing room. Was there an exit from there as well? she wondered. Pretending to be fatigued, she sat on the bed, trying the overly fluffy mattress. No, this suite had only one entrance and one exit which was through the dressing area. An odd arrangement, but given Bdan's predisposition for fondling nude females, she wasn't surprised he placed more emphasis on dressing or the lack of it.

"I'm terribly thirsty," she said to the old woman, who had taken a rigid stance in the archway between the two rooms. Wasn't she even to be allowed to rest by herself?

A glimpse of a smile showed in a shift of skin on the woman's face. "Fatigued you must be. I'll get you a *sedit* beverage."

"What's that?" Sarina asked suspiciously.

"A drink to help you relax." The woman moved across the bedroom to a small recess in the wall. Punching a code on the raised panel beside it, she explained, "This is a fabricator unit. Every stateroom on the ship has one. It can synthesize over three thousand types of food." Smirking at Sarina's obvious ignorance, she stood waiting for the beverage to materialize.

"Why don't you order a drink for yourself?" Sarina suggested. "The air is so cool in here. Your throat must be dry."

As she talked, Sarina's eyes darted around the room, then lit on a piece of artwork, a marble pyramid set in an alcove on a tall pedestal. This was her chance, while the woman was occupied. Slowly, she slid off the bed and sauntered toward that side of the room. With a sudden movement, she grabbed the pyramid by its point and rushed toward the slave with the flat side held outward.

Crack! The sound of the impact on the woman's head made Sarina cringe. She dropped her make-shift weapon as the woman crumpled silently to the ground. Sarina knelt beside her. She hadn't hit her too hard, had she? She hadn't meant to kill the poor thing, just knock her out for a while. Risking a precious moment to feel the slave's pulse, Sarina was glad to feel a strong beat.

Then she set about pulling off the woman's drab, sack-like garment. Dressing as a slave would be a good disguise. With a grimace of distaste, Sarina slid the itchy fabric over her head, only to see that the tangerine gown peeked out from underneath. It was too long, Sarina realized with dismay. And her dainty slippers would be a dead giveaway, too. Kicking them off, she decided to go barefoot; then she remedied the other problem by tucking the silken gown up high under the slave robe where it wouldn't show.

Fortunately, no one was in the corridor when she tiptoed outside. In a flash, she was at the end waiting for the turbolift.

"Security Level Six," she ordered the computer once she was inside. She was relieved when the turbolift responded, whisking her first vertically and then horizontally. She'd been afraid the computer might not respond to her, or that it would sound an alarm at her unfamiliar voice. Also, a special clearance might have been required for entry to the security level, but so far her luck was holding out. She wondered if the computer would provide any other information. It couldn't hurt to ask.

"Is there a schematic available for this destination?" she asked.

A wall lit up with an illuminated diagram of the security sector. She peered at it closely, memorizing the details. There were six clusters of detention cells, each centered around a command quadrangle which featured guard stations, surveillance, a lounge/ready room, and an armory. The turbolifts stopped right in front of each quadrangle. Great news, Sarina thought. How was she going to get past the guards?

"Ah, computer, is there a rear entrance into the security level, by any chance?"

"That information is not available," came the toneless reply.

So, she was left with a dilemma. Sarina was still puzzling how to solve it when the turbolift came to an abrupt halt and the door slid open. Facing her was the command center for Detention Block Six, and it was bustling with armed guards. When she emerged, one of them detached himself from the group and strode over to her. His uniform was different from the others, and she assumed he must be the warden in charge.

"What are you doing here, *sumi*?" he growled, giving her a look of suspicion mixed with disapproval. His dog face wasn't hidden by a helmet, and his fierce features reminded Sarina of a bullterrier. She wondered nervously what he was thinking about her appearance. Her bare feet might not be unusual for a slave, but her made-up face probably was. At least she'd had the foresight to remove the jeweled clips from her hair. It hung loose, and she bowed her head so that long strands of hair shielded her face.

"I've been sent to run a test on the fabricator unit," she answered, slumping her shoulders in a subservient posture. "There has been a malfunction in other sectors."

"Why was I not notified? Let me see your identification."

Sarina swallowed hard and fumbled inside a pocket. Something cold and hard met her touch. It was a rectangular object, like the one Teir had held in the elevator at her office building when they'd soared off into space. She handed it over.

The warden scanned the device for her ID. Then he

looked at her again and frowned. "Check your orders with my superiors will I. R-r-remain here. You may retain your data link." He gave her back the device, and Sarina resolved to learn how to use it as soon as possible.

Relieved that the warden had turned his back on her, she surveyed the area. None of the guards were paying her any attention. Her gaze swept to the other end of the command center. The beginning of the detention block stretched out from there. How would she be able to tell which cell was Teir's? Would he be inside, or was he being interrogated elsewhere?

She didn't have time to consider her next move because suddenly a loud claxon hooted throughout the ship. "All stations, prepare for boarding," announced the computer's disembodied voice.

The guards moved in a flurry of activity, and Sarina realized that this was her opportunity. Keeping her head lowered, she shuffled around the command center to the other side. No one stopped her when she entered the detention block. Row after row of identical steel doors met her gaze. A wave of helplessness washed over her as she regarded them. Now what?

She had reached an intersection and was trying to decide which way to go when someone emerged from a cell off to her right. With a shock, Sarina recognized Lieutenant Otis, Bdan's executive officer. Quickly, she veered left, rounding a corner and hugging the wall. Heavy booted footsteps stomped her way, changing direction at the last moment. She waited until the sounds receded before letting out a sigh of relief.

Her knees shaking, Sarina scampered down the corridor toward the cell Otis had just vacated. She remembered he'd been sent to question Teir, so hopefully the captain would be inside. But as she faced the massive door, she felt despair. How was she to open it? There was no lock, no handle, at least none that was evident to her inexperienced eye. She ran her fingers around the edges of the door but found nothing.

"Teir, are you in there?" she hissed. No response. The door was probably too thick for him to hear.

Shouts came from the guard station, and Sarina froze. But after a breathless moment, she realized they weren't getting louder. The commotion must be due to the imminent boarding by Coalition forces. Turning her attention back to the door, she was startled by a sudden loud click.

The door moved slightly ajar, as though a magnetic lock had just been released. Or maybe it had never been adequately shut to start with. In any event, Sarina didn't stop to count her blessings. She shoved the door wide open.

Teir was inside, stretched out on a cot, his eyes closed. He didn't seem any the worse for wear, but when she softly called his name, he twisted sideways with a groan.

"Are you hurt?" She rushed over to him. "I've come to rescue you."

Recognizing her voice, Teir's eyes snapped open. He sat up, swaying slightly, and gave her a sardonic grin. "Well, aren't you a welcome sight." He looked her over and his eyes narrowed. "Then again, you don't seem to have fared so well yourself."

"This is just a disguise. Get up, will you? The guards are occupied, but they might head this way at any moment."

"What's happening outside?" He got to his feet, wincing as he leaned to one side. Sarina wondered what they had done to him. His face was pale, with a darkening bruise over his cheekbone. His hair hung untidily over his forehead, and she noticed a fresh bloodstain on his bandage, too. But it seemed to be his leg that was bothering him the most.

"Coalition forces have surrounded the ship. We're about to be boarded," she told him. "Can you walk?"

He raised an eyebrow. "I could probably use some help." He held out his good arm, and she hurried to support him. She tried to ignore the quickening she felt inside when he leaned his weight against hers. His body was as taut and strong as she remembered from the cabin aboard his ship. The memory brought a rush of warmth to her cheeks.

"My people will be looking for me," Teir explained as they hobbled toward the door. "I arranged for a backup unit to follow our route. When Bdan's ship intercepted us, I sent out a distress signal."

"So that's how the Coalition found us so fast."

"Right. I thought it best not to take chances when I had such an important dignitary aboard." His tone was sarcastic, but his gaze held something more, making Sarina's breath catch in her throat.

"I'm sure Lord Cam'brii will be most grateful," she murmured.

Teir's grip on her tightened. Just as they reached the doorway, two guards rounded the corner in the corridor. They spotted Teir and Sarina at once. One cried out a warning shout as both reached for their weapons. Cursing, Teir shoved Sarina aside and threw himself into the air in a leaping kick that connected with one guard's nose, and then he punched the other. The next minute, he was dragging both bodies in her direction.

"Give me a hand, will you?" he grumbled. "I've got just one good arm."

"You bastard!" Sarina replied. She put her hands on her hips. "What happened to your injured leg for which you so desperately needed my support?"

"I had a miraculous recovery." Teir shoved the bodies inside the cell and disarmed them. "Here, take this shooter." He tossed her a heavy weapon.

She caught it, then nearly dropped it. "I don't know what to do with this!"

Teir almost laughed at the absurd picture she made with her blond hair loose, her face made-up, the coarse slave dress, and her bare feet. The sight of her would stop any guard in his tracks whether or not she pointed the shooter.

"Just hold the grip, and point the energy emitter end forward," he said tersely. "Your finger goes on the trigger. The setting should be on number three." He watched to make sure she understood. "Now let's go find my men." Gesturing for her to follow, he headed back into the corridor.

"Maybe Bdan was right," Sarina snapped.

"What's that supposed to mean?" Teir whirled around, facing her. She stood unmoving in the doorway.

"He said you followed your own agenda. You let me think you needed my help when you were faking it. Why?"

"I *did* need your help."

"Sure. And were you going to keep pretending if those two goons hadn't shown up when they did?"

A wicked grin lit his face, and he started toward her. "Would you like to find out what else I had in mind?"

She lifted her chin. "No, Captain. Keep your distance, please."

He regarded her a moment before he responded. "All right, I will. And now unless you want to be stranded here, we'd better go. Agreed, *princess*?" He used her title to remind himself that she belonged to Cam'brii. By the corona, that nobleman was going to get more than he bargained for!

Panicked cries came from the command center and Teir realized his men must have arrived. He hurried on, hoping Sarina had the good sense to follow.

A thin figure charged around the corner in front of them and came to an abrupt halt. "Captain! I was just coming to free you!"

Sarina gaped, as Teir and the tall stranger slapped each other on the back in welcoming friendship. The other male was humanoid but of a different species.

Instead of skin, his body was covered by a thick tan hide, what she could see of it beneath his flowing white shirt and dark pants. His hair, a rusty brown color, was cut short.

"Alas, you have been hurt," the stranger observed, noting Teir's bandaged arm.

"Sarina took care of it. Let's move out."

The stranger glanced at her. His jade eyes had a luminous quality she'd never seen before. She looked back at him with interest.

Teir noticed. "Pardon me, I am remiss in my introductions," he drawled. "Ravi, this is our wondrous Great Healer, Sarina Bretton."

Ravi strode forward, flashing her a grin that was quite attractive. "*Mira*, it is an honor to greet you," he said, bowing. His voice was low and pleasant and she smiled in response.

"It's nice to meet you, too. You must be one of Teir's crew, I gather?"

Ravi glanced at Teir. "I serve as Captain Reylock's first mate on the *Valiant*."

"Are there many of you?"

"Mistress?" He frowned, puzzled.

"Are there many crew members on board your ship?" Sarina asked. She hadn't given up hope of going home. Maybe she could find a friend among his crew to help convince the captain to return her to Earth.

"You'll meet everyone soon enough," Teir said, suspicious of the cunning look on her face. "Where's Wren?"

"He is supervising the cargo transfer," Ravi answered, refocusing attention on his commander. "I am afraid I have bad news. Cerrus Bdan jettisoned away in a distress pod."

"Blast!" Teir knew what that meant. Bdan wouldn't let him rest until he evened the score. Later, he would think about how to meet the smuggler's threat, but right now he had other priorities.

He turned to Sarina. "Come on, it's time to get you aboard the *Valiant*." His eyes lit up. "Wait until you see her. She's nothing like that reconn vessel we were on before."

"Could she give me a ride home?" Sarina suggested hopefully. Maybe he'd reconsider after this episode.

Teir glared at her as an odd sense of disappointment swept through him. "Your duty lies elsewhere," he said tersely. Then he left her and strode on ahead.

"My cousin Mantra will be thrilled at your arrival," Ravi said, falling into step beside her. He had a slow, even gait and it was easy for Sarina to keep up with him. "Mantra has long been a believer in the legend. Seeing you, I can say my own doubts are relieved."

Sarina gave him an astonished glance. "How so?"

"I can see it in your eyes, *Mira*. The radiance of the true light is present."

"If you say so," she vaguely agreed, wondering how many people she was going to disappoint when her so-called power didn't materialize.

They entered the command quadrangle. Bdan's guards were lined up against a wall, disarmed, with their hands folded on their heads. A squad of uniformed Coalition troops held them at bay. One of them, an older officer who appeared to be in charge, snapped Teir a salute.

"Captain, the ship is secure. Our men are on the bridge."

"I understand Bdan has escaped," Teir said, striding over to the control console. "Bridge," he said into the comm unit. "Lieutenant Rodan, how's the cargo transfer coming?"

"Nearly finished, Captain," came the immediate response. "The *Omnus* was carrying about forty thousand credits worth of calgonite ore. It's being transferred to the *Valiant* as instructed."

"Good. I'm going to take our guest to the *Valiant*. As soon as the transfer is completed, we're leaving."

"And Bdan's crew?"

"Place them under arrest according to regulation number forty-two under the Treaty of Kidaren. You'll be responsible for securing the *Omnus* and towing it to the nearest starbase. I'll check in with you later."

"Do you wish to have an escort, sir?"

"No, we'll manage ourselves. Reylock out." Teir turned to Ravi. "Let's go," he ordered his first mate, gesturing for Sarina to precede him into the turbolift.

She bit her lip and walked in, trying to keep her questions, of which she had many, for later.

The shuttle bay was bustling with Coalition troops. Teir found a craft that was loaded with cargo and ready to go. "We'll hitch a ride," he said, indicating the boarding ramp, then glanced at the men hauling ore into the other shuttles.

"That's not the only cargo he's carrying, I'll bet," Teir said. He turned to Ravi, halting halfway up the ramp. "Give me your data link."

At the other's questioning look, Teir explained, "Bdan's guards took mine. And that reminds me— the reconn vessel needs to be returned to starbase also." He gave that order to Lieutenant Rodan, then patched into his crewmate Wren who was busy directing operations in the cargo hold.

"Wren, I'll bet if you search further, you'll find another type of cargo on board."

"Such as?" Sarina heard the melodious tone, and it primed her curiosity to meet this other crew member.

"Same thing we've caught him at before."

"I'll check it out."

"Timing?"

"Shouldn't be more than one haura."

"Okay. We're heading over now. Reylock out."

Compared to the luxury of Bdan's vessel, Teir's ship the *Valiant* seemed positively austere. Unadorned metal corridors and bulkheads met Sarina's eye as she followed the captain aboard. He and Ravi went immediately to the bridge where they immediately took their places in the command chairs. Sarina stood behind them, watching while they flipped switches and punched in computer codes. The huge viewscreen in front showed Bdan's fat cigar-shaped vessel the *Omnus* poised against a backdrop of velvety space. Surrounding it were combat spacecraft with a round insignia she couldn't quite make out, but assumed was the symbol of the Coalition.

Teir's ship was unlike any of those sleek, birdlike vessels—Sarina had gotten a glimpse of it through the shuttle porthole. The *Valiant* was larger, with an A-frame design in the back tapering off to a snub nose in the front. Gun ports jutted out from various angles. It looked peculiar, menacing, totally functional.

"What kind of ship is this?" she asked. "It's different from the others."

Teir swiveled in his seat to answer her. "This used to be a freighter, princess, until I—uh—acquired her. I've made a number of modifications."

"I see." She didn't, but she was glad to have found a subject to which Teir would respond. "How many crew members are there altogether?" Sarina asked. She, Teir and Ravi were alone on the bridge, but she was sure other men were working elsewhere. Someone must have been responsible for maintaining the ship's position while Ravi and Wren transferred over.

"There are six of us. Lieutenant Wren is our navigator. Currently, he's supervising the cargo transfer from Bdan's ship. Wren is a Polluxite," Teir added, grinning. He could imagine Sarina's reaction when she met him. "Then there's Datron, who's in charge of engineering and maintenance. Korox is our weapons officer, and Moff'tt handles science and systems control. They're down below. You'll meet them later."

"Perchance the lady would like a tour now, Captain," Ravi suggested in a gentle tone. "You have assigned her a cabin? If not, she is welcome to use mine." His friendly green eyes met Sarina's.

"No, she'll have my stateroom. I'll move in with you," Teir said. Turning to Sarina, he added, "I suppose you'll want to freshen up." His gaze dropped to her bare feet. "And you could use a pair of shoes."

Sarina decided to learn her way around this ship as soon as possible since it was, in effect, her newest prison. Despite being treated like an important guest, her wishes were completely disregarded. She had to do what they said or Teir would throw her into the brig, or whatever they called it on board his ship. He'd made it clear that he wouldn't accept any challenge to his authority, nor would he take her home. Sarina's only hope was to ingratiate herself with his crew and sway them to her cause.

So she smiled and politely accepted his offer.

Sarina had never turned the full force of her dazzling smile on Teir before, and the effect nearly took his breath away. "Take the helm," he said to Ravi, rising.

At the rear of the circular bridge section was a turbolift on one side and a hatchway on the other. "There are three decks," Teir said, pointing to a schematic on the wall. "Level One contains the bridge, crew quarters, and conference lounge. Level Two holds the warp drive and sublight engines and deflector shield generators. Level Three is where we came up from the shuttle bay. It's also where the cargo hold is located." His face radiated pride. "She's tight, but well outfitted."

"I'm impressed," Sarina said. His ship wasn't as luxurious or as large as Cerrus Bdan's, but it suited Teir. Even in the brief time she'd been with him, she could tell he wasn't the type to go for frills or embellishments. His first devotion was to duty and it showed in the organization of his vessel.

It also showed in his attitude toward Sarina. "Please," she said, turning her wide gaze on him.

"Won't you reconsider and take me home? You've brought me here against my will. I don't know or care about any legend! Your Coalition is wrong—I'm not the person they're looking for."

His mouth tightened. "I don't want to hear this again."

"But what about my friends and family? They'll be worried about me, and I miss them terribly. You can't just take me away!"

"But I have, haven't I?" Steeling himself against her pleas, Teir gestured for her to enter the hatchway. On the other side was a short corridor. "Go left," he said.

Afraid of making him angry, Sarina obeyed, peeking inside the first room to the left. It held a long table and six chairs.

"This is the lounge," Teir said in a flat tone. "It doubles as a mess hall and conference room." Sarina was glad to see a row of portholes lining the outside hull. The room would have been totally bleak otherwise with its plain gray walls. If he allowed her to come in here, she could at least watch the stars while figuring out a way to get back home.

"Crew quarters," he said, pointing down the corridor. With Sarina at his heels, he threw open the nearest door and stood aside for her to enter. "This is my cabin. You can use it for the duration of the voyage. I'll just get my things."

"Will it be a long trip?"

Sarina was wondering how much time she'd have to work on the sympathies of his crew. Getting friendly with them seemed the best course of action, as did learning all she could about this ship and her captain. She wasn't going to give up hope, not by a long shot.

"Bimordus Two is 29.4 parsecs from this location. We should be there in approximately eighteen days if we hold maximum speed—and if nothing more interrupts us."

"You don't anticipate any more trouble, do you?" she asked, noting the dark look in his eye.

"No." Teir ended the conversation abruptly and went inside. The cabin was sparsely furnished but comfortable, with a low bunk, a single armchair, and a console with drawers. A compact computer sat on a separate small desk.

"Is that a fabricator unit?" Sarina strode over to a recess in the wall and touched the raised panel beside it. "I thought you said the lounge also was used as a mess hall."

"We usually like to eat together, but this device can supply all your needs: food, clothes, toilet articles. You merely have to program in your orders."

Despite the desperation of her plight, Sarina was intrigued by the idea, and interested in learning more about it. "How do I do that?" she asked.

"The computer can fill you in on the necessary details," Teir replied.

"First I want to get rid of this ugly outfit!" Sarina began to yank the slave robe over her head.

He stared in astonishment as the coarse robe dropped at her feet, revealing the most transparent gown he'd ever seen. The filmy tangerine fabric clung to her body, exposing every curve. His gaze lingered on her breasts, then traveled to her tiny waist. From there, the skirt flared out, seeming to float about her ankles. Her dainty bare feet peeked out from underneath.

"By the corona, is that what Bdan gave you to wear?" he snarled.

Sarina stepped back at the fierce expression on his face. "Yes. A female attendant took me to a room to change, and she took my clothes." She smirked. "Later, I took hers!"

A consuming rage shook through him. The urge to capture Bdan and make the Souk pirate pay for his crimes was overwhelming. It took him a moment to regain control of his temper. "I'll get you something decent." He stalked over to the fabricator unit and rapidly punched in numbers on the control panel.

Sarina watched as a shimmering haze descended upon the recess in the wall. The next moment, a pile of clothing, complete with shoes, met her astounded gaze.

"Get dressed. I'll see you later."

Teir didn't even wait to retrieve his own personal belongings. He rushed out as though he didn't trust himself to be alone with her. Of course she was probably imagining his reaction, Sarina told herself. He wasn't the slightest bit interested in what she wore, other than to have her suitably attired for her presentation to Lord Cam'brii. Sarina picked up the items from the fabricator. How odd, then, that he had made the selection he did.

Chapter Five

Pajamas. That was what the clothes resembled. The loose-fitting black pants and long-sleeved top conjured up images of ancient Chinese peasants toiling in a rice paddy. Why on earth would Teir want her to wear these ugly things?

Frowning, Sarina spread the clothes on the bunk. It seemed to her as though Teir had deliberately chosen this shapeless outfit to make her look unattractive. But why? An intriguing notion came to her. Perhaps this was a clever ploy on Teir's part to make Lord Cam'brii reject her. If that happened, Sarina could return to Earth and Teir would have fulfilled his duty of delivering her to the High Council. But he'd be helping her at the same time.

Upon further consideration, she decided Teir wouldn't be so considerate. He was too bound up in concepts of duty and honor to take any path other than the one assigned him. In any event, if Cam'brii didn't like her, there was no reason why she wouldn't be paired with another member of the ruling family.

Apparently the legend didn't specify Lord Cam'brii. It just said her healing power would be activated when she fell in love with a member of the House of Raimorrda. Doubtless there were other eligible males descended from the bloodline who could be mated with her.

But if Captain Reylock hadn't chosen these clothes to make her appear unattractive, why had he picked them? Sarina wondered. Was this what females normally wore in the Coalition? The only other members of her sex she had observed were the ones aboard Bdan's ship, and she couldn't count them. None of the Coalition troops had been female. What about Teir's crew? She had yet to meet the other three members. For all Sarina knew, she could be the only woman aboard.

That's it! she decided. Teir didn't select the outfit because females in the Coalition normally dressed this way, nor because of Lord Cam'brii. Captain Reylock simply didn't want his crew to be distracted by her feminine charms.

Damn the man! All he thought about was accomplishing his mission. Well, Sarina would decide how she'd dress, whether he liked it or not!

Turning to the fabricator, Sarina frowned. How was she to work the thing?

A loud knock sounded at the door. "Come in," she called.

"Mistress," Ravi greeted her with a friendly smile, "is there anything you require? I was passing on the way to my quarters and thought I would attend to your needs."

Sarina gave him a sweet smile. "I wish to learn how to use the fabricator unit."

"Ah. May I enter?" He cocked his head, awaiting her permission. Once again, she found his warm gaze comforting. Ravi didn't seem in the least surprised to see her in the silky tangerine gown. It was as though he'd accept anything from her because of who she was—or who he thought she was.

"Please come in." Sarina stood aside for him to pass.

For the next few minutes, Ravi went over the basic instructions for using the fabricator unit. Each category had its own code. For example, food was preceded by a zero-zero-one prefix. Clothing was zero-zero-two, and so on. Then the requested item was typed in.

"How does it work?" Sarina asked in awe when she'd selected a pair of jeans and a burgundy sweater. She picked them up and placed them on the bed next to the black pajamas. After Ravi left, she'd order some underwear. She was too embarrassed to do that in front of him.

"The method utilizes molecular alteration. If you wish a more complete explanation, you can access the files on the computer. It responds to voice activation." Ravi ensured that her voice could initiate commands, then turned to her with a stiff bow. "I will leave you now, Mistress. If you require anything further, pray ask the computer to locate myself or the captain."

"Wait!" Sarina said. "Ravi, you know about this legend and the prophecy. Do you really think it's right to force me into becoming the Great Healer if it's not what I want?"

His luminous eyes cooled. "It is your destiny, Mistress."

"I don't agree with that. My destiny is on Earth, with my friends and family. There are people who need me! How can you think it's right to take me away from everything I've ever known?"

"You will adjust," Ravi replied calmly. "There are others who need you more. I will assist you in any way I can."

"Then tell your captain to take me home!"

"That is not possible, *Mira*," he said quietly. And with those words, he was gone.

Disappointed, Sarina sank onto the bunk and

covered her face with her hands. True, she hadn't met the other crew members yet, but Sarina felt she'd get the same reaction from them. They were all loyal to their captain and the blasted Coalition. Was no one willing to help her? Was she doomed to be separated from her loved ones forever? As she contemplated never hearing their voices or joining them in laughter again, tears rolled down her cheeks and despair overwhelmed her.

After a while, Sarina's tears gave way to anger. Rage surged within her, giving her new strength. What right did the Coalition High Council have to change her life? On whose authority had she been kidnapped? How dare these faceless individuals interfere with her future!

Standing, she clenched her fists and vowed to find a way out. She'd scan the computer files to see what kind of information was available. If no one aboard this ship was going to help her, she'd have to rely upon herself to come up with a viable plan, and learning all she could about her new environment was the first step.

Sarina ordered her underwear and dressed, perversely hoping she'd annoy the captain with her choice of clothing. She'd have to obey his orders until she figured out what to do, so this was the only way she could rebel. Meanwhile, as long as he allowed her access to the ship's data files, there was hope.

Sarina became so engrossed in the information the computer offered that she didn't even feel the vibration that indicated the ship was under way. Nor did she hear the knock on her door until it had swung open. She whirled to see Teir facing her on the threshold.

"The crew is eating in the mess hall if you wish to join us," he said, without waiting for her to acknowledge his presence.

Sarina regarded him wordlessly. Despite her enmity toward him, she had to acknowledge his masculine appeal. His dark hair swept low over his forehead. He'd shaved, and his jaw was taut and angular. Her gaze descended to the clean white shirt he'd put on under his black leather vest, open at the collar. His eyes boldly raked her body. She couldn't tell what he thought of the low V-neck of her sweater or the tight fit of her jeans, because his expression gave nothing away, as though he were purposely hiding his thoughts.

"You've been busy," he drawled, sauntering inside her cabin. *His* cabin, she reminded herself, flushing.

"This computer is a gold mine of information," she countered, rising.

His gaze focused on her cleavage. "Is it?"

Sarina felt another rush of heat to her face. "I learned a lot."

"I'll bet. You accessed the crew profiles. Did you learn everything about me that you wanted to?" His eyes slowly moved up to meet hers.

Sarina took a step backward, her heart thumping. "No, I . . . uh . . . still have some questions."

"Such as?"

He was barely a foot away now, his eyes glittering. Craning her neck to look up at him, Sarina moistened her lips.

"You're from the planet Vilaran," she said. "You are human, but there's something special about your people—"

"Yes?" His face hovered inches above hers.

Sarina couldn't say it. It was about their mating instincts. Vilarans were highly sensitized to pheromones, chemicals produced by the body to stimulate sexual response. Once a Vilaran met a member of the opposite sex with a compatible scent, their body chemistries melded and they were joined for life. Staring into Teir's heavenly blue eyes, she wondered how he had evaded that fate thus far.

"I d-didn't get all the information," she stuttered.

He smiled, reading the truth in her expression.

By the corona, she was alluring in those strange form-fitting clothes. He should be angry that she'd discarded what he'd chosen for her. He'd purposely selected garments that would make him less aware of her feminine attributes. But her independence attracted him even more, dissipating his anger. In fact he was teetering on the brink of kissing her. Her soft, parted lips tempted him, as did the vulnerable expression in her eyes. Teir didn't remember ever feeling such an irresistible urge for a female before, and it confused him. Sarina was from Earth. Such a magnetic attraction should only be for one of his own kind.

Frowning, he stepped back. Regardless of how he felt about her, he'd never made it a habit to toy with another man's possession. Sarina belonged to Lord Cam'brii—in a manner of speaking. Keeping his distance from her was crucial.

Sarina let out a sigh of relief when he moved away. For a moment, she'd thought he was about to kiss her. What was worse, she'd wanted him to! Disgusted with herself, she tossed her head and strode out the door. She heard loud voices coming from the lounge, male voices laughing and talking.

The crewmen looked up from their seats around the table when Sarina and Teir arrived. An awkward silence fell over the group.

"You already know Ravi," Teir said, gesturing. "This is Lieutenant Wren."

Sarina's mouth dropped open. The Polluxite was large, even bigger than Teir. Liquid hazel eyes were set wide over a straight nose, a smiling mouth, and a firm jaw. His eyebrows were unusual in that they had three lines of color, a white streak between two chestnut layers. A thick thatch of brown hair covered his head. But what really astonished her was the huge pair of wings sprouting from his back.

"Wings!" she gasped. "You can fly?"

"No," Wren chirped. "I'm sorry if they startled you."

He pinched his face, and the wings folded, collapsing into his body.

"Where did they go?" Sarina asked, oblivious to the amusement of the others in the room. She walked behind the Polluxite to inspect his back but saw only his shirt with two narrow vertical slits. "Forgive me, I'm being rude," she said, blushing, but Wren just tittered.

Teir was chuckling too, and their entertainment at her expense riled her. "You might have warned me," she snapped at the captain.

"And deprive my men of a good laugh? Your reaction was priceless."

She folded her arms across her chest. "Aren't you going to introduce me to the others?"

"Of course. Datron, Korox, and Moff'tt, this is Sarina Bretton."

She nodded to each one in turn. Datron and Korox appeared humanoid, whereas Moff'tt was small and elfin in shape, with large ears and a wide forehead. He was dressed in a peculiar short tunic. White tufts of hair in irregular patches decorated his head. He looked so funny that Sarina couldn't help smiling at him. He grinned back, his small white teeth flashing.

"You can choose your own food from the fabricator," Teir said curtly. "A menu from your home planet has been entered into the basic programming. I hope you'll find something you like."

Sarina's stomach growled at the suggestion, and she realized she was starved. She hadn't been able to touch anything on her plate at dinner on Bdan's ship. Hungrily, she approached the fabricator and requested a large steak medium-rare, french fries, and a soft drink. Her mouth began to salivate as the food materialized.

"Meat!" Wren commented sniffing the aroma. "How barbaric!"

Sarina saw he was nibbling at a plateful of berries

and nuts. "You don't eat meat at all?" she asked as she took a seat. From the corner of her eye, she watched Teir order his own meal and wondered what he ate.

"Plant food is nature's gift," Wren replied in his melodious voice.

"You may be right, but after the day I've had, I need something more substantial."

Sarina cut into her steak, thinking that Wren didn't appear to be undernourished. Maybe he consumed huge quantities over the course of a day. That would account for his large size.

Teir sat beside her. His plate was loaded. "What do you have?" she asked him curiously.

He named some items she'd never heard of, then tried to explain what they were. Sarina gave up attempting to understand. "Never mind. When I'm in the mood, maybe I'll taste them," she sighed.

Bending her head over her plate, she tried to hide the sudden tears in her eyes. Everything was so *alien*, even the food! It only intensified her determination to return home, where all was familiar.

Her thoughts drifted to the people she'd left behind. Robert must be frantic, wondering what had happened to her. Mother would call her apartment and when no one answered, she'd be worried to death. And her friends—Good God, she'd almost forgotten about Abby! Every Sunday, Sarina visited her friend in the convalescent home, and Abby depended upon seeing her. She'd been injured a year ago in an automobile accident. Her legs had been paralyzed and she was still undergoing rehabilitation. But she wasn't expected to regain complete mobility, and she looked forward to Sarina's visits to boost her morale.

Lifting her fork with a piece of juicy beef on the tip, Sarina pretended an interest in her food. She'd lost her appetite but knew she had to eat. No matter what she had to do, Sarina resolved, she *would* get home. She didn't only have herself to think about.

Others were relying upon her.

Of course, that was what Ravi had said about the people in the Coalition. Glancing at him, she wondered idly what would happen if the legend were true. Would she actually become this Great Healer they all waited for? Sarina had wanted to be a doctor, but she hadn't pursued a medical career because of her mother's objections. But what if now she had the chance to be a healer?

Choking down the meat, she decided she didn't want to find out. It meant marrying a total stranger and no matter how noble he was, she didn't care for the prospect one bit. All she wanted was to go home.

The days passed without further incident. As she got to know the crew better, Sarina recognized the deep respect they had for their commander. Teir remained an enigma to her, his behavior courteous but aloof. Never again did he allow himself to be alone with her, but Sarina didn't let it bother her. She focused on acquiring knowledge, knowledge that would help her accomplish her goal of returning home. To that end, she spent hours at the computer terminal in her room, absorbing history lessons and technical data easily processed by her analytical mind.

She questioned each crew member in turn, learning all she could about their roles in daily ship operations. For their part, they seemed to like her. Wary at first, they soon accepted her at face value and included her in their discussions. Moff'tt was funny, with an impish sense of humor that Sarina appreciated. He was always trying to make her laugh. Datron and Korox were the fall guys for a lot of his jokes, but they didn't mind because it relieved the boredom of the mission. Sarina was aware they all thought it was a waste of time—all except Ravi who couldn't seem to do enough for her. His devotion warmed her heart and made her wish she truly was a healer, especially when she learned of the devastating effects of the plague which he called the Farg, on his planet, Tendraa. He told her what little he knew, horrible tales of death and despair, but he'd lost contact with his cousin Mantra, the source of his news. Ravi feared Mantra had become ill, and he was beside himself with worry.

"If the Liege Lord would ask the Coalition for help, it would improve matters greatly," he explained, seated beside her at the table one day. They were alone, and she was sipping a fruit drink while he spoke. "Contact with the Coalition is forbidden on Tendraa except for trade. I can do nothing."

Sarina frowned. "Why is contact forbidden? Isn't Tendraa a full member of the Coalition?"

"Not really. My people are xenophobes—afraid of outsiders. You see, Mistress, eons ago Tendraa was much more technologically advanced than it is now. Trade with other worlds was widespread. We learned of many wonders from other cultures and made great progress, but our people were not prepared for so much so fast.

"A devastating civil war nearly destroyed the planet. The weapons used had been built with the knowledge we'd gained from other worlds. A new government arose from the ashes and decided it was progress that had led to our destruction. As a result, all trade was banned, and all contact with offworlders was forbidden in order to avoid further contamination."

Ravi shook his head. "In my opinion, the life that ensued has been one of ignorance and suffering. Even now, we live in complete isolation except for the treaty, and that came about because our leaders got tired of smugglers raiding our mineral-rich planet. By making an agreement with the Coalition, trade is restricted and visitors are controlled."

He leaned forward, his expression brightening.

"You are our hope, Mistress, our symbol that progress must occur. Destiny moves on the winds of change, and you are the force behind it. Do it, *Mira*, show your power to my people and save my world from the Farg and its own oppression."

"How, Ravi? I don't think I'm this Savior you need." Sarina trembled at the expectations Ravi and his fellow believers had of her.

"Follow the prophecy. It will come true."

He spoke with such fervor that she wanted to believe him. "I'll do my best." But all she could think was how in God's name could she aid his people when she couldn't even help herself?

Hoping to relieve the heaviness in her heart, Sarina sought out Teir the next day. Ravi was on the bridge, and she knew Teir was alone in the cabin they shared. She knocked lightly on the door.

"You!" he said, jumping up from the bunk on which he'd been resting when he caught sight of her.

Sarina's face grew warm. He was bare-chested, and she'd obviously disturbed his rest, but he needn't be so rude.

"May I talk to you a moment?" she asked, her tone hesitant.

Teir cleared his throat. As soon as he'd seen her outlined in the doorway, his heart had begun palpitating wildly. She looked lovely, her fair hair floating about her shoulders, a wistful expression on her face. She wore a simple royal blue chemise dress that vividly detailed the contours of her body. He didn't need her to come any nearer—his reaction to her was potent even at a distance.

"Come in," he said gruffly.

She stood before him, her eyes wide. He stared down into the silvery depths, mesmerized.

"I wanted to ask you about Ravi," she said, acutely aware of his proximity. The man seemed to be radiating heat. Sarina felt incredibly warm. She glanced at his muscled arm. His wound had nearly healed, she noticed. His biceps bulged under the new pink skin. Lowering her gaze, she stared at the dark swirls of chest hair. "I wish I could do something to help him and his people. Is there any way you can contact the government on his planet, find out about his cousin Mantra? Ravi is very worried about him."

Teir ruffled his unkempt hair. "I've tried, but all communications are out. Our contacts are either dead or they've fled."

"Has anyone from the Coalition gone to assess the situation?"

"It's forbidden unless Tendraa asks for help."

"Couldn't you fly a clandestine mission?"

He stared at her, aghast. "Disobey orders and risk my crew catching the Farg? No way!"

"You're no help at all!" she snapped in frustration.

He grasped her arm. "Don't criticize. You're out of your element here, and you know it."

Sarina twisted in his grip, frightened by his fierce expression. "Watch how you handle me. I'll be a princess when I marry Lord Cam'brii, remember?" It was an idle threat, considering how she planned to get away before that.

"Poor man!"

"Aargh!" She struggled to free herself.

"Curse you!" Teir cried, releasing her. "Why do you torment me?"

"Oh, come on! You've been avoiding me this whole trip. Are you afraid I'll still convince you to take me home?"

"You can't convince me to do anything. You're nothing but a mere—" his eyes raked her over "—female."

"Well, this is one female who's going to make a difference! And I'm going to start right here with your ship." Sarina felt like annoying him, and she knew saying anything disparaging about his spacecraft would do the trick.

"What do you mean?" he asked, frowning.

"This is the dullest vessel I've ever been on," she

said, as though she'd flown in spaceships her whole life. "Nothing but gray everywhere. It needs color."

"Don't you go messing with the *Valiant*."

"You can't give me orders. I'm not one of your crew."

"While you're on board my ship, you'll do as I say."

"Like hell I will!" She saw his eyes darken and his mouth tighten with rage and decided she'd better depart before he retaliated. Spinning around, she left.

The next day, Sarina conjured up some paints on the fabricator and begun work on one of the bulkheads. The cartoon mural took her several days to complete, but she thought the final effect was worth it—amateurish maybe, but cute. At least Sarina thought so. She grinned when she imagined Teir's reaction. He'd probably give her hell. Maybe he'd become so furious that he'd give in and return her to Earth just to get rid of her!

Sarina found she was actually looking forward to his angry response. But to her surprise, Teir took one glance and silently passed by. Disgusting man! she thought, deprived of satisfaction. At least he could have said *something*.

Hoping to provoke some reaction from him, she decided to tackle the lounge next. The crew didn't object. Moff'tt even helped her select the colors. While she was painting, Sarina felt a sense of freedom she'd rarely experienced before. Her mother had never approved of frivolity. "You've got too much to learn. Study hard, and don't let your feelings get in the way," was the refrain Sarina had heard ever since she could remember. Feelings were anathema to her mother. She had always urged Sarina to suppress her emotions if she wanted to succeed. Her mother hinted at the family curse that would descend upon her should she let her feelings control her. So she'd gone into law where facts were life and life followed rules—rules her mother approved of, just as she'd approved of Robert.

Now Sarina had no one telling her what to do, except for the captain, and he seemed to have given up. She kept hoping he would show his disapproval. At least then he'd be speaking to her again. It had been days since he'd uttered a civil word to her. The crew teased her, saying it was because the captain was smitten, but Sarina figured they had it all wrong. The man acted as though she didn't exist. He was probably counting the hours until she'd be out of his hair for good.

"Approaching the Bimordus system," came Teir's terse announcement over the comm speaker one afternoon.

Sarina's heart sank. Nearly three weeks had passed since she'd left Earth, and not once in all that time had she been able to talk anyone into helping her. No matter how often she'd wailed that she didn't want to spend the rest of her life on some strange planet after being married to a man she didn't know, not one of them cared. She was not ready for her so-called destiny, would never be!

Apprehension filled her as she gazed out the main viewscreen from the bridge. Teir and Ravi were in the command seats, maneuvering the ship toward a giant brownish globe while Lieutenant Wren was working the navigational computer off to the side.

"That's Bimordus Two?" she asked in dismay. "It looks totally desolate!"

Teir swiveled in his seat to regard her impassively. "The planet is barren of life. The site was chosen for the centrality of its location."

"What's that huge bubble in the distance?"

"A biosphere. The surface temperature of the planet is too cold for many of our member species, so an artificial atmosphere had to be created."

"Seems to me they could have chosen a friendlier planet somewhere else."

"This serves the purpose of neutrality," Teir commented. He eyed her attire. "You might want to change. You'll be presented to the High Council immediately upon our arrival."

"The ship will be landing?" Sarina asked. She'd thought they'd take a shuttle down.

"Of course, at the spaceport. Bimordus Two is the location for our central government. There's a lot of traffic," he added in a patronizing tone.

"Is this where Defense League Command is located, too?"

"No." Teir compressed his lips, refusing to say more. Despite her status, Sarina did not have security clearance.

"Will you be staying on Bimordus Two for long?" she persisted.

Teir shrugged. "Who knows? Depends on our orders." He turned his attention forward. "You'd better get a move on if you want to look presentable. We don't have much time."

Sarina glared at his back. She was damned if she'd change her clothes to please him or anyone else! Her ivory silk blouse and beige slacks were good enough. What did he expect her to wear, an evening gown and tiara?

Angrily, she combed her fingers through her wispy bangs. She'd French-braided her hair, tired of wearing it loose. She knew Teir liked it down, so she'd done it on purpose to displease him. Now she felt an irresistible urge to annoy him further. She moved closer to his chair, standing behind him and slightly to one side so he could see her out of the corner of his eye.

Teir was acutely aware of her presence. Irritated that she hadn't obeyed him and changed her outfit, he deliberately ignored her. It was a strategy that seemed to have worked for most of the trip.

"Activators coming online," he said to Ravi, monitoring the automatic landing sequence. Sarina sidled forward for a closer look, her arm brushing his shoulder. Teir felt a jolt of electricity charge through him at her touch.

"Get away," he growled. "You're in a dangerous position. If anything should go wrong, you need to be where the automatic restraints can hold you."

"You didn't say that before," she snapped. "You told me to go to my cabin to change."

His face reddened. "The chairs and bunk in your cabin are outfitted with safety restraints should you need them. I suggest you go there immediately."

"I'll stay here, thank you. If anything happens, I'll hold onto you."

Teir gritted his teeth. This female was infuriating! He should give her a lesson she wouldn't forget.

He jumped up and grabbed her wrist. "By the stars, do I need to lock you in your cabin?"

Sarina pressed herself up against him, thrilling at the hard feel of his body. "Why not? You seemed to enjoy it the last time you tried."

Teir jerked back, releasing her as though he had touched fire. "What are you playing at, woman?" He heard Ravi chuckle, and turned to him. "And what's so funny?"

Sarina gave him a sweet smile and turned her back on him. "Let me know when we arrive, Captain. I'll check out the view from the lounge."

Teir stared after her, his fists clenched at his side. "By the corona, I'll be glad when she's gone!"

"Will you?" Ravi asked, raising an eyebrow.

Teir didn't answer. Even though the mission had been successful, he didn't feel his usual exuberance.

Ravi came to get her from the lounge. "We have received clearance to disembark," he said as Sarina rose from her seat and approached him. Noting the look of apprehension on her face, he took her hand

and held it gently. "If there is anything I can do for you while we are in port, pray call on me, Mistress."

Sarina gazed into his warm green eyes. "Thank you. And if I hear anything about your cousin, I'll let you know."

"May the faith be with you." Ravi made the sign of a circle, as though he were a priest blessing her. "Captain Reylock will see you off the ship. I regret that I cannot, but I must file our log entry before the rest of the crew can leave."

Letting go of her hand, he bowed deeply. "It has been an honor, *Mira*." Then he left.

Sarina felt forlorn and alone. Teir's heavy footsteps proceeded down the corridor in her direction. She knew the sound of his steps by now, but instead of brightening her mood, his arrival saddened her more than ever.

"Ready?" he snapped.

She swallowed a lump in her throat at his narrowed eyes and his stern expression. Why couldn't he be friendly at a time like this? "Yes," she replied, tilting her chin. She was determined to carry this off with poise and grace.

"Then let's go."

Sarina strode to the turbolift, her back straight and her head held high. She'd never felt so scared in her life. Doubts swirled in her mind like a mist, all but blinding her. What if the High Council rejected her? Even if they did heed her pleas for compassion, would they send her back to Earth, or would they condemn her to some remote outpost where she couldn't reveal the existence of the Coalition to the people on Earth?

Knowing that her fate hung in the balance, Sarina stepped inside the lift.

Daimon, leader of the Return to Origins Faction and member of the High Council, adjusted his bulky maroon robe in front of the mirror. In just a few minutes, the woman from Earth would be presented in the Assembly Chamber. Everyone would see for themselves that the legend was a farce when they got a look at her. He should be glad. His movement would gain needed supporters.

Yet instead, Daimon felt doubtful. He stroked his peppery beard, narrowing his eyes. The Believers were strong. Their faith had spread throughout the galaxy, and it might take more than a powerless female to dissuade them. Their unifying force was in direct opposition to the ROF. Daimon would have to figure out a plan to counteract their rhetoric if the Earthwoman added any fuel to their fire.

"Daimon, come on!" Ruzbee hissed from the archway.

The councilman whirled and stared at him solemnly. "How soon?"

"Her speedcraft approaches the main entrance."

It was time. Daimon put on his pair of specially shaded glasses. They had been necessary ever since the ancient Auricle had begun to glow. The sacred stone was kept in a transparent receptacle in the rotunda of the Great Hall. It had been nothing more than a cold oblong chunk until several months ago. Then it had suddenly begun to glow, increasing in brightness until special glasses became necessary for anyone in its vicinity. An answering glow had come from Earth—from Sarina Bretton. Thus she had been identified as the Great Healer. Daimon couldn't wait to hear the rationale for this phenomenon from the subject herself.

He strode from the robing room behind the Council Chamber. Leaving the council wing, he crossed the rotunda, veering around the encased Auricle in the center, then entered the assembly wing on the opposite side of the building.

The Assembly Chamber was filled to capacity. Rarely was there a joint session of the General Assembly and the High Council, but today was an exception. Over five hundred seats were occupied. Daimon claimed his place among the other Council members in a semicircular row of twelve seats facing the Assembly. Behind them on a raised dais sat the Supreme Regent. The buzz of conversation was loud, drowning out the drone of the air filtering system.

Emu glanced at him from two seats down. The thin Sirisian was his most powerful opponent. "Our Savior comes," Emu said with a smirk, leaning over so Daimon could see him. His elastic body elongated as he stretched. "The Coalition will be strengthened, Daimon. It is inevitable. Your teachings will be disregarded as worthless ramblings."

"You worship a false god," Daimon countered, craning his neck to glare at his fellow councilman. Emu's bald head was covered by a small ruby turban. The deep red color made his pink skin appear dark, but it complemented Emu's maroon robe. "The Earthling has no power. She is nothing. The plague and the Morgots will destroy us unless we embrace our own kind. A return to our homeworlds is the solution. We can only succeed against them if we fight for ourselves!"

"Traitor! You cloak your words in rhetoric but in reality you seek dissolution of the central government. You promote secession!"

"The Defense League is too overburdened to do any of us much good. We're killing ourselves," Daimon persisted. "When are you going to admit that the Coalition has grown too large for its own needs? You think this woman from Earth is going to save us? Bah! If you rely on her false powers, you'll doom us all."

"Gentleman," a stern voice interrupted from behind, "please be silent." It was Glotaj, the Supreme Regent.

Another voice broke in, quiet but with the force of authority. "You speak blasphemy of my bride, Daimon. I will not tolerate it. Her power will not be activated until she marries into the House of Raimorrda."

Daimon whipped his head around to view the tall blond man who had spoken. "Pardon, my lord," he said, bowing from the waist as he sat. "You are correct, of course. I am only anxious for the ills that befall us to be eliminated."

Inwardly, he cursed. He should have know Cam'-brii's ears would pick up talk of the woman. He'd have to be careful. Daimon sagged back in his seat, glancing at Ruzbee a couple of rows across in the Assembly. The Arcturian gave a slight nod. He'd noticed the exchange. Daimon was certain that Ruzbee would keep an eye on Emu and Cam'brii. And if the Earthwoman proved to be a problem, she'd have to be dealt with as well.

Sarina's heart thumped wildly as she regarded the huge double doors at the top of the wide staircase. It had only been a few minutes since she'd left Teir's ship. She'd been met by an uniformed officer, who had whisked her away on some type of flying motorcycle that landed in front of the Great Hall. Her escort told her that the structure, a rectangular white building with immense columns and a raised portico in front, housed the central Coalition government. There were three entrances, one in the center and two on the sides. According to the officer, she was to enter the assembly wing on the left.

From her studies aboard Teir's ship, Sarina had learned that the High Council consisted of twelve members, and a Supreme Regent ruled over all.

Now she swallowed apprehensively, dismayed that she was not to be presented just to the twelve Council members as expected. Her escort had informed her that a joint session of the Assembly and the High Council had been called. Inside the Assembly Chamber, Sarina would face representatives from over five hundred worlds.

She glanced back at the officer. The bearded trooper was no youth, but his body was still fit and strong, and in his eyes she saw a kindly glimmer.

"Glotaj awaits your entrance," he said, naming the Supreme Regent. He gestured for her to move forward.

Maybe she shouldn't have worn pants after all, Sarina thought, her knees trembling as she mounted the broad flight of stone steps. A business suit might have made her feel more in control.

She stopped before the double doors, which were flung open from inside. Sarina caught a glimpse of a sea of faces and felt dizzy with nervousness, but she overcame it by taking several deep breaths. Stepping inside, she crossed a short marble expanse before entering the Chamber proper. Everyone stood at her arrival.

Sarina gathered she was to proceed forward to the impressively robed figure at the podium. She walked in a daze, awestruck at the variety of species represented. Teir's crew was nothing compared to this! Bird-creatures, humanoids, snake faces, beings who reminded her of erasers with their elongated heads and rubbery limbs—all lined the aisles. Sarina's head whirled.

"Miss Bretton." The robed figure spoke, his voice rich and accented. "I am Glotaj, Supreme Regent of the Coalition of Sentient Planets. We welcome you to Bimordus Two."

Sarina liked the kindly twinkle in his eyes. He was human, she thought in relief, or at least he appeared so. She gave him a tentative smile in return. All the seats faced him, she noticed, except for a row of twelve that were turned toward the audience. Ah, the High Council! Which one was Cam'brii?

She furtively scanned the row of councilors. Only four were male humanoids. Lord Cam'brii had to be one of them. Was he the tall, handsome blond, the glowering one with the beard, the older fellow with white hair, or the redhead with the puckish face?

She looked questioningly at Glotaj. He had observed her assessment, she guessed, noting the amusement in his brilliant blue eyes—eyes that suddenly reminded her of Teir's. A jolt went through her. The similarity was astounding.

Sarina felt another pair of eyes burning into her, and glancing around, she found the source. The tall blond councilman was staring at her. His eyes, too, were a celestial hue. The color must be commonplace here, she thought.

"We wish to ask you some questions," the Supreme Leader said. "Come up here where everyone can see you."

Sarina obeyed, trembling. His black robe reminded her of a judge. She felt as if she were on trial. How foolish—she should feel comfortable in such a setting! The law was her profession, after all. But this was no ordinary court. Her life could be at stake. Sarina had no idea what they would do if she didn't fulfill the prophecy.

After the assemblage was seated, Glotaj addressed her. "How is it that you came in answer to the light from the ancient Auricle?"

Sarina remembered Cerrus Bdan mentioning this to her. It was the reason she had been identified as the Great Healer.

"I have no idea," she responded honestly. "I knew nothing of the legend or the prophecy until Captain Reylock briefed me."

"Yet the glow came from Earth, from your location. Our orbiting observatory was quite definite."

"I have no explanation for that."

"Have you sensed no special power within yourself?"

"None."

"No desire for healing?"

Sarina hesitated. As an attorney, she'd instructed clients to answer only the questions put before them and say nothing else, certainly not to offer any personal information. But in her case, if she gave Glotaj some insight into her character, perhaps he would decide to send her back home.

"I did think of becoming a doctor once," Sarina responded, "but my mother was against it. She said I'd make more money as a lawyer. I wasn't even allowed to consider a medical profession."

"And now?" Glotaj's keen gaze held hers.

"Now I'm—I *was* an attorney. I was about to be offered a promotion when Teir—Captain Reylock—kidnapped me." Her voice ended on a sharp note.

Glotaj inclined his head slightly. "We regret the need for subterfuge, Mistress. It was felt you might not be cooperative."

"And why should I be? What right did you have to bring me here against my will?" Sarina glared at the entire assemblage, as though it was their fault and not just the High Council's. "You took me away from everything that had meaning in my life. Why should I agree to anything you want me to do? I demand to go home!"

"You will establish a new home here," Glotaj said, his tone firm.

She met his gaze. "Can you possibly know what it is like to be torn away from your loved ones, banished to a place where everyone and everything is alien? Can you?"

"Your profile declares you to be intelligent and resourceful. We're certain you'll be able to adapt. And once you become the Great Healer—"

"I have no magic powers, Your Honor."

"Time will tell. According to the legend, you must first marry into the House of Raimorrda. You have heard of the dire situation our worlds are in?" At her nod, he continued. "Our planets are dying, one by one. The plague is taking its toll. Our scientists are working around the clock, but they are unable to find a cure."

His eyes burned with intensity, and his voice rose. "You are our only hope, Sarina Bretton. Let your power come forth. Heal the sick, and inspire our people to fight the aggressors who conquer us. By your marriage, you shall save us!"

He turned to the audience. "Let the rites of betrothal begin according to the customs of the bridegroom. Lord Cam'brii, take your place by your bride."

Before Sarina's stunned gaze, the tall blond man rose from his seat among the High Councilors. In several quick strides, he was beside her.

"I accept my responsibility," he told Glotaj.

"Well, I don't!" Sarina replied.

Lord Cam'brii's clear gaze pierced her flashing rebellious one. "Please, Mistress, be calm. This will all work out for the best."

"Not for me!" Sarina studied him from under her long lashes. At least he was good-looking with his solemn, chiseled face and his full head of curly blond hair, but he lacked the rugged appeal of the *Valiant's* captain. And even though Lord Cam'brii's maroon robe stretched across his broad back and wide shoulders, she didn't get the same feeling of electricity as when she was near Teir. How could she possibly marry this man?

Before she could utter another protest, Lord Cam'brii took her hand, turning her so they both faced the Supreme Leader. Glotaj raised his arms above them.

"By your marriage, I declare the prophecy is fulfilled. You are as one." He muttered an incantation in another language, then lowered his arms and smiled. "Go now and do your duty. And congratulations!"

Congratulations? Good God, were they married? Sarina snapped her head around to stare at Lord Cam'brii in shock.

Chapter Six

Lord Cam'brii strolled alongside Sarina toward the council wing on the other side of the building. The assemblage had been abruptly dismissed, and she still wasn't sure what had happened. Was she wed to this tall, taciturn man beside her, or just engaged?

Glancing at his profile, she thought his noble lineage was aptly delineated in his refined handsome features and his regal carriage. And it was his very heritage that had brought them together.

As they walked, various members of the government stopped to congratulate them and offer greetings to the Great Healer. The alien faces blurred in her mind, a mixture of colors and different exotic styles of dress.

"Are we going to your—uh—office?" Sarina asked, feeling totally lost. The filtered air felt cool, and there was a faint medicinal odor that made her feel even more out of place, bewildered by so many new things happening so fast. These people might be used to meeting new life forms, viewing alien landscapes, and smelling strange scents in different environments, but to Sarina, everything was like a dream.

Her escort gave her a warm smile as though sensing her discomfort. "I wish for you to see the Auricle," he said. "It's just up ahead."

Sarina halted, stopping him with her hand on his arm. She ignored the robed officials scurrying around them.

"Tell me, my lord, are we married?"

He glanced at her in surprise. "Nay, Mistress. What gave you that idea?"

"Glotaj said we were as one, and everybody has been giving us congratulations." Sarina felt stupid. How was she supposed to know what the Regent meant?

Lord Cam'brii regarded her with amusement. "He pronounced the words of betrothal according to the custom of my people. We are considered as one even though we are not yet wed. For the next sixty days, we are to be together. Then comes the marriage ceremony. The rituals are quite complicated, incidentally. You shall need instruction."

"Where are you from?" she asked. "I mean, from what planet?"

"I'm from the planet Nadira in the Regulus system, but my bloodline is descended from the House of Raimorrda."

"And that crosses planetary boundaries?" Sarina deduced.

"Correct. We are a human species, with some minor modifications. But we live on many worlds."

"So these marriage rituals are those of Raimorrda."

"Correct again. I'm glad to see you have an interest in the subject."

Sarina just smiled. She wasn't merely being curious—she needed to learn all she could in order to find a way home. Maybe Lord Cam'brii would take her back to Earth after they'd gotten to know each other. He was bound to notice she wasn't happy here.

But would her feelings mean anything to him? He probably considered it an honor to wed her and to serve the Coalition. Cam'brii might not understand how she felt. Worse, he might not care.

Feeling increasingly like a pawn in a game she didn't understand, Sarina was grateful that at least he was polite and well-mannered. But even though the councilor was attractive, being with him didn't give her the same thrill she got from Teir's presence. She felt a sad sense of loss. Despite their disagreements, she missed him and wished he were here instead of Cam'brii.

They walked on, and as they neared a wide circular area in the center of the Great Hall, Cam'brii donned a pair of dark glasses. "Forgive me, I have forgotten to get you a pair. Everyone who passes the rotunda must wear them. Give me just a moment." He turned away.

Sarina saw that he'd spoken the truth. Everyone in the area wore similar glasses, though no one had had them on in the Assembly Chamber. "Don't bother," she called after Cam'brii, moving toward the strange brightness.

She entered the rotunda. Directly overhead was a domed skylight through which bright rays streamed down. But that light was nothing compared to the brightness of the object standing in a cylindrical transparent case in the center of the marble floor.

"Sarina, step back! It will blind you!" Cam'brii shouted.

She slowly circled the guardrail as he ran up behind her. "Don't worry," she said. "It doesn't bother me."

He stared at her. "How can it not? Others who view the Auricle with the naked eye lose their sight forever!"

She shrugged. "It glows, that's all. In fact, I think the effect is rather beautiful." The stone was smooth, about eight feet in height, oblong shaped with a pointed top. It reminded her of something, but she couldn't think what it was. The fragment of memory nagged at her, but she pushed it away, awed by the phenomenon in front of her. The rock glowed with a pulsating fiery light that was oddly soothing.

Lord Cam'brii seemed stunned, as did others around them. Sarina was indeed the only person without special dark glasses.

"The Earthwoman truly is the Great Healer!"

The cries spread throughout the Great Hall.

"I don't understand," she said, turning to Cam'brii.

"This ancient glowstone is all that remains of a once great civilization on a planet called Shimera," he began. "The legend says that some of the Shimerans who escaped the planet before its destruction possessed special powers. It was prophesied that one of their descendants would arise in a time of great disaster, renew the power, and restore harmony to the galaxy. The Auricle would let us know when the time of Revelation was near.

"And so it has come to pass. After the Farg began to decimate the inhabitants of our star systems and the Morgots started their rampage, the Auricle lit with a fiery glow. It grew so bright that no one could look at it without going blind. One day our orbiting observatory picked up a signal, an answering glow, from Earth—from *you*, Sarina Bretton."

She shook her head. "But that's absurd. I sent no signal. And that business about Shimeran ancestry doesn't apply to me at all." Sarina glanced around at the watching faces. This discussion really shouldn't take place in public, but she wanted to hear more about the legend. Every bit of knowledge could prove useful.

"Could we go somewhere private to talk?" she asked Cam'brii.

"Of course, let's go to our quarters," he replied eagerly.

"*Our* quarters?" Sarina repeated.

He smiled. "We are considered as one. That means we are to share everything."

Good God! Did that mean she was to share his bed also? Speechless, Sarina followed him outside. The Great Hall was on the crest of a hill, and the view was impressive. In spite of her anxiety, she looked around.

The late afternoon light, filtering through the crystal bubble that enclosed the biosphere, formed a bright hazy aura and cast a surreal light on the shimmering city spread out below them. Sarina had been too nervous before to enjoy the dazzling sight, but now she could appreciate its astonishing beauty.

"There are four other biomes besides this one," Cam'brii said, pointing toward the horizon. "This city is the lifestyle habitat. We call it Bimordus Central. I'll show you the other sectors over the next few days as you take breaks from your studies."

"My studies?" Sarina knew she sounded like a parrot, echoing everything he said, but she couldn't help it.

"You need to prepare for your new role. You have much to learn. Tomorrow I will take you to the study center and you can begin."

"Sounds like fun." She grimaced, thinking it sounded like law school all over again—learn the rules and abide by them.

"Today we shall endeavor to get to know one another," Cam'brii said.

It sounded suspiciously like an order. Sarina glanced at the councilor, but his face was impassive. She couldn't tell if the idea pleased him or not. Swallowing apprehensively, she wished she didn't have to be alone with this man, but apparently there was no choice. She'd been delivered into his care, and until she learned her way around, she was stuck.

A squad of armed guards had been waiting for them and now escorted them down a curved footpath heading away from the Great Hall.

"I live in Spiral Town," Cam'brii told her. "It's not far from here. I hope you don't mind walking."

People turned to stare at them as they passed. Feeling self-conscious, Sarina moistened her lips. "Are you always guarded wherever you go?" She felt discomfited by the attention.

"Not until recently. Unfortunately, the guards have become a necessity in the past few weeks."

"Are you in some kind of danger?"

"Let's wait until we're alone for any discussions, shall we?" he said, smiling. His eyes crinkled, and Sarina liked the way the smile transformed his face, but she wasn't interested in Cam'brii as a man. She was only interested in how she could use him to accomplish her goal of returning to Earth.

Her surroundings caught her attention and she became fascinated when Cam'brii pointed out and explained the methods of transportation. The wide paved avenues bustled with flying speeders, slowly cruising airbuses, and crowded people-movers. Sarina had never seen anything like it, and part of her longed to explore. But she reminded herself that she wouldn't be here very long if she could convince someone to take her home.

"Spiral Town houses the members of the High Council," Cam'brii informed her as she quickened her pace to keep up with his long stride. "We each have our own apartment. Space is at a premium on Bimordus Two, so individual dwellings are not permitted."

"The buildings are lovely," Sarina commented. Tall spiraling white towers thrust toward the crystal sky. When she asked what the white stone was, Cam'brii told her it was marbelite. Exteriors of marbelite mixed with glittering pink stone was very attractive, she thought.

"Here we are." Cam'brii stopped in front of a tall building where residential units fanned out from a central spiral. Mirrored casements set into marbelite made the complex appear larger than it actually was. Each multilevel apartment was different from the next, giving the building an individuality all its own. Yet the design integrated the various parts into one fluid whole.

Sarina followed Lord Cam'brii to an entrance framed by large pink stone slabs. "Open," he demanded, and the door slid into the portal. "The guards will remain behind," he told her, gesturing for her to enter. She stepped inside. A spiral staircase rose from the central hallway, at the far end of which was a glass-enclosed lift.

"The lift or the stairs?" her companion asked.

"The stairs," Sarina replied. "The exercise will do me good after being confined to Teir's ship for so long."

Cam'brii shot her a questioning glance, and she realized that she sounded overly familiar with the captain of the *Valiant*. That wasn't proper in her present position, she gathered.

Holding her head high, Sarina started up the stairs. On the third landing, Cam'brii pointed to a door on the right. "Daimon lives there," he said. "The less you see of him, the better."

Leaving her to wonder what he meant, he peered into a lens fixed in the opposite wall. "This is a retinal scanning device," he explained as the door to his residence slid open. He showed her how to deactivate the protective energy field, and then strode inside. Sarina trailed behind him. She felt like a mouse being led through a maze and not knowing how to get out. Danger was in the maze as well but she couldn't sense its direction. The only way to go was forward.

"Why, this is lovely, my lord!" she cried, glancing about at the plush ivory carpeting, the curved furniture gleaming like iridescent mother-of-pearl, and the colorful splashes of paintings on the walls.

Cam'brii evidently had good taste.

"I'm glad it pleases you, Sarina, and please call me Rolf. Would you care for a beverage, or would you rather rest? I can show you to your room if you wish." Rolf towered above her, awaiting her reply.

"*My* room?" Sarina asked, pouncing on the words. "You mean we aren't—I mean, we don't have to—you said we are to share everything!"

Rolf's lips curved upward. "I am afraid you misunderstood. We are to use this period to get to know one another. The only hindrance I anticipate is the presence of your bodyguard."

"What bodyguard?"

"You're a valuable asset to the Coalition, and as such, you must be protected. Regretfully, I cannot be in constant attendance since business occupies me during the daytime hauras. Your personal bodyguard will accompany you at all times, even when we are together."

"What about the troops outside?"

"Their responsibility is to me. Your man can assemble his own team if he wishes."

Sarina put her hands on her hips. "Why is it necessary for us both to be constantly under guard?"

His eyes darkened. "There are those who do not want to see the prophecy fulfilled. They regard our joining as a threat. Once your power is established, I'm hoping the guards will no longer be required." A shadow crossed his face, as though he was contemplating telling her something more, but he remained silent.

"What if it doesn't?"

Rolf frowned. "Pardon?"

"What if my so-called power doesn't materialize?" she asked.

"It will. Have faith," he admonished in his deeply resonant voice.

"Yes, of course," she said sarcastically. How could she forget that she was supposed to fall in love with this man for the prophecy to come true?

"Sarina," he began hesitantly.

"Yes?"

"I know this situation is difficult for you."

"Do you? Do you really?" All her anger and resentment flared and she glared at him.

"Please, don't judge us too harshly. Sometimes over the course of events, new insights are gained. It would be unwise for you to act impulsively at this early stage."

She gazed at him in surprise. His eyes held a look of intense pain, as though he spoke from bitter experience.

"Your High Council didn't give me any consideration. They abducted me and delivered me to you against my will!"

"I know, but your being here is important, Sarina. I'll try to make it easier for you."

She turned away, annoyed by his response. His words were meaningless. The man sympathized with her plight but wouldn't do anything to change it.

"I'd like to get settled now," she said, wearily walking in what she hoped was the direction of her sleeping quarters. Each step on the carpet was accompanied by the musical tinkle of chimes. "What—?"

"That's the *aramus*," Rolf told her. His serious mood had evaporated and he was grinning. "It loves to be trampled. Each step is like a caress to the creature. We keep it warm; it entertains us."

"Really?" Sarina studied him, thinking that it would be in her best interest to learn all she could about him. "When is my bodyguard supposed to arrive?" She wondered how much time they'd have to get acquainted before their privacy was disrupted.

"There must be a delay." Rolf ran a hand through his thick blond hair. "I'd have expected him to be here by now."

"Anyone I know?" she asked jokingly.

His expression sobered. "We are fortunate to be

assigned the best officer in the Defense League—you've already met him. Captain Teir Reylock is to act as your bodyguard."

Sarina's mouth dropped open. Teir! *He* was coming to stay with them?

Her pulse raced with excitement.

Teir whistled low under his breath. "Loopa's here," he hissed to Korox. His weapons officer, a huge, hairy, taciturn man, had joined him for a drink in the bar at the Pleasure Palace, and they were seated at a table in a far corner of the room. Teir watched government workers, mostly lower echelon, chat and joke as they mingled with visitors.

Teir took a sip of his Arcturian brandy. "What do you think he's up to?" He was interested in Korox's opinion. The man's mind was as sharp as a bzoran cat's claws.

Korox raised a bushy eyebrow. "He usually shows up when he's after something. Watch it—he's headed this way."

Teir's hand dropped to his belt, fingering his shooter. His body tensed as the Souk trader sauntered over. Loopa pulled up a chair, turned it around and straddled it.

"Captain R-R-Reylock, a pleasure it is to see you again!"

"What do you want?" Teir asked bluntly. He wasn't happy to see the sly whippet face. Loopa always meant trouble.

"A job for you have I, if you are free."

Teir caught Korox's warning glance. "Oh, yeah? What is it?"

"Cannot yet tell you. If interested, I give first payment. Agree you must to the terms."

Teir leaned forward, narrowing his eyes. "I don't agree to anything I don't know about, Loopa."

Whippet-face squinted. "Can tell you this much. A courier mission it is."

"Transporting what—slaves, illegal data cards, banned pnimx tusks?"

Loopa looked shocked. "Captain, concern myself only in legal cargo I do! Good payment is offered. Give you cash now if you accept."

"How much?" The clever look that had come into Loopa's eyes had piqued Teir's interest, even though he had no intention of accepting.

"Ten thousand credits; twenty thousand more upon completion."

"Why can't you do the job, Loopa? You're a trader."

"Already have contract. Saw the *Valiant* on the manifest and your name gave to client."

"Who's your client? What's the delivery point?"

"Agree to terms first, then r-r-receive information."

"I'm not available, Loopa."

"Your ship in drydock is. Between assignments are you. Good chance to earn extra credits."

"The *Valiant* is being serviced. We'll be out of here in a few hauras."

The Souk trader grinned. "Not what I understand. Major r-r-repair needed. Stuck here are you for some time."

"Captain, may I have a private word with you?" Korox asked.

Loopa got up and walked away, stopping a discreet distance from their table.

"I don't trust him," Korox whispered. "Datron hasn't checked in yet. Loopa could have done something to sabotage—"

Teir cut him off. "Nonsense! Datron's supervising the maintenance. He'd have let us know if anything was wrong."

"You're not thinking of accepting the offer?" His weapons officer looked at him askance.

"Of course not. But I want to know who's behind it." The Souks were known for their fierce loyalty to the commercial cartels that controlled the colonies.

Loopa belonged to the one led by Ruel. *Pasha* of the largest cartel on Souk, Ruel was Cerrus Bdan's elder brother. Loopa could be working for one or the other Souk leader, or for someone else entirely.

Teir signaled for the Souk to come over. "I'll have to think about it," he said. "Where can I contact you?"

"Staying in the Visitor Tower am I." He checked his data link. "Give you one haura to decide."

Teir watched the trader leave. "I've got a bad feeling about this."

Korox grunted his agreement. Picking up his goblet, he swallowed the rest of his drink, a Flaming Starburst that burned its way down the throat.

Teir preferred the smoother glide of his brandy. He was about to raise his hand for refills when the data link in his pocket vibrated. He pulled it out and activated the receiver. "Orders are coming in from Defense League Command," he said with surprise, waiting for the complete transmission.

Korox's expression brightened. "You won't have to worry about Loopa now. We'll be shipping out. Let's hope we see some action for a change!"

Teir's response was a sudden pallor. "Son of a belleek," he cursed.

"What is it?"

"This can't be! I'm going to contact Datron." The engineer didn't respond to his alert signal. "Something's wrong. According to this, our ship is grounded for repairs to the power transfer conduits. We're temporarily reassigned to duty on Bimordus Two."

"What in Zor is wrong with the power transfer conduits?" Korox roared, drawing surprised glances in their direction.

"Moff'tt didn't alert us to any system malfunctions," Teir mused. "You'd mentioned sabotage. You could be right. Let's find Datron and get to the bottom of this."

"If Loopa's responsible, he's out of luck. You

couldn't accept his offer now. What's our reassignment?" Korox's tone was morose. He hated being stuck planetside as much as Teir.

"You're all to report to defense perimeter four."

"And you?"

Teir scowled. "I've been given guard duty of a different nature." He had to force the next words out of his mouth. "I've been assigned as the Earth-woman's personal bodyguard. I'm under orders to stick with her for the duration of her betrothal to Lord Cam'brii!"

Korox studied the look of dismay on the captain's face. Then his mouth opened, and loud bellows of laughter thundered out.

Cerrus Bdan was none too pleased when he heard Teir had been reassigned. "I thought the captain would be free," he snarled to Ava Bet while lying naked on his stomach on a lounger. They were hiding in a safehouse on Starbase Alpha Ten, and the tiny cubicle that served as a sleeping chamber was far from comfortable. He'd managed to take Ava Bet and Lieutenant Otis off the *Omnus* with him while escaping from Reylock's troops. That he'd lost the rest of his crew rankled deeply and made him even more furious with the Defense League captain.

His *gima* murmured sympathetically, rubbing his back with her four hands. Her painted claws scraped up and down his skin in long, sensuous movements that made him squirm with pleasure.

"Loopa was supposed to interest R-R-Reylock in earning extra credits, but the imbecile failed to reach him early enough. Assigned another duty was the captain. He did not have the chance to accept Loopa's offer. Grrrr!" Bdan growled. "Now shall I have to think of another way to get him."

"First things first. You have to get the *Omnus* out of impoundment," Ava Bet reminded the smuggler.

"I hired a squad of geckos. Good they are with

informatics manipulation. They should be able to secure the *Omnus* for us."

Bdan sat up, and Ava Bet noticed that his beady eyes had taken on a malicious gleam. "Work on a new plan to capture the captain shall I. My agents are in place. Keep me informed will they. When the time is ripe, we'll take action. R-R-Reylock must pay for this inconvenience."

Ava Bet ran a claw along his jowl. "Don't forget the Earthwoman. K'darr will be angry with you because of her."

Bdan felt a pang of alarm. The Morgot leader was known to send assassins when an underling failed a mission, and Bdan didn't like to think that could happen to him. It wasn't his fault the Earthwoman got away. Captain Reylock was to blame.

"We'll figure out a way to get her, too," he said. "She's with Lord Cam'brii, but that is not a deterrent. Has plans for the r-r-respected councilor does my brother, Ruel." He saw the flash of surprise in her eyes. "Think you we would let Cam'brii get approval for his First Amendment? A major threat to the Souks is he. R-R-Ruel will take care of him. They've met before, though Cam'brii knows it not."

"How is that?" Ava Bet was more than interested. Perhaps she could use this intelligence to her own advantage.

"An incident in the past that does not concern us. Captain R-R-Reylock and the Earthwoman are our problems." With slow deliberation, Bdan pushed the thin straps of her sleeper gown off her shoulders. As his hand moved to her exposed breast, he said, "Vengeance is sweet, my love. Soon shall we have them. I look forward to inflicting pain upon them both." He squeezed hard, bringing tears to Ava Bet's eyes. It was nothing compared to what he planned to do to Sarina Bretton.

*   *   *

"Someone is at the door," Rolf called to Sarina from the living area.

Sarina was in the sanitary putting her new wardrobe through an ultrasonic cycle. She'd decided to send for the clothes she'd acquired on Teir's ship rather than outfit herself again from scratch. When the carrier containing her personal items had arrived, she began to acquaint herself with the facilities in Rolf's residence. After eating a quick meal delivered by his fabricator, she had begun unpacking.

"Who is it?" she asked.

"It's your bodyguard," Rolf informed her through the closed portal.

Sarina's heart skipped a beat. She'd half expected Teir to connive his way out of the assignment. Quickly, she dropped the blouse she was holding into the cleansing compartment, smoothed her metallic blue jumpsuit, and pulled her hair out of its tight braid. Grabbing a hairbrush, she smoothed her waves until they floated about her shoulders in the fashion that most pleased the dashing captain. Giving one last glance in the reflector, Sarina commanded the portal to open.

When she entered the living area, breathless and flushed, Teir was standing in the doorway. His eyes briefly flickered over her, then rested on Rolf. His expression was grim.

"Captain Reylock reporting," he said, keeping his tone neutral. One look at Sarina was all he needed to feel his blood turn to fire. It was the main reason why he'd objected to this assignment. It would take all his willpower to keep his desire for her under control. With an intense effort, he concentrated on what Cam'brii was saying.

Sarina looked at the two men while they exchanged greetings. Their contrast in dress was remarkable. Rolf had removed his robe of office and was wearing a belted topaz tunic over a pair of bronze-colored leggings. The top was gaudy with gold decorative braid appropriate to his princely status, and a jeweled dagger hung at his belt. If he was a stickler for protocol, he'd probably make her wear formal dress after they were wed, she thought with dismay. She'd have to increase her efforts to get back to Earth! But Teir didn't look too happy. Maybe he would help her now.

He wore a loose black shirt that was open at the chest, revealing a patch of curly dark hair. Her gaze lowered to his waist where the shirt was tucked into snug dark pants. They, in turn, disappeared into a pair of shiny boots. A belt strapped around Teir's hips held a shooter. With his shock of midnight hair falling across his forehead and his electrifying blue eyes, he was magnificent.

His gaze fell upon her, narrowing as he caught her staring at him. "Nice to see you again," he muttered, marching inside.

"We are grateful you have been assigned to us, Captain," Cam'brii said. Teir noticed the use of the word *we* and winced. "Your reputation precedes you. Of course, I heard about the amazing feat you performed on Chanice's World. How ever could you have found the submerged ecolab with the ionic interference in the atmosphere?"

Teir relaxed. He liked talking about his exploits. "Lieutenant Wren, one of my crew, has exceptional navigational abilities. He pinpointed the site of the tsunami and figured out the possible range of drift. After he located the lab, we improvised a levitator."

"And just as you raised the tip of the observatory, another violent storm struck. I hear you went in alone and got the whole team out just before the lab was crushed by another tsunami. I trust you are fully recovered from the injury you sustained?"

Teir heard Sarina gasp. She'd been listening with fascination, not daring to interrupt. He knew she had no idea that he went on rescue missions.

"Injury?" she said, moving forward to confront him. "You were hurt?"

He shrugged. "It was nothing compared to my wounded leg on Bdan's ship."

"What wounded leg?" she asked, confused. "It was your arm that—Oh!" She suddenly remembered and flushed.

Rolf looked at the two of them thoughtfully. "Would you like to discuss the security arrangements, Captain, or can I offer you some refreshment?"

Teir noticed that his voice had lost some of its friendliness.

"Let's go over the security arrangements," Teir said, turning his attention to the councilor. He had a duty to perform, he reminded himself, and ogling Sarina was not part of it.

"Sarina, if you are fatigued, you may retire," Rolf suggested, giving her a meaningful glance.

"No, thanks. I'll just sit here and listen." She settled on a lounger, reluctant to leave when she could feast her eyes on the captain. To satisfy her sudden restlessness, she nibbled from a plate of nuts on the table in front of her while the men spoke.

"I'll leave Sarina at the study center at ten hauras each morning," Rolf was saying. "I should return approximately six hauras later. You'll be solely responsible for Sarina's safety during that time."

"Wait a minute!" Sarina said, sitting upright. "I'm not going to study for six whole hours every day!"

Rolf's expression was somber. "You must acquaint yourself with the important issues facing us. There is no time for frivolous activities."

Teir held up a hand. "Throwing too much information at her all at once could get confusing. What harm would there be in showing her around the city? Besides," he added, "to be informed is to be alert. She should become familiar with her surroundings."

"Indeed," Cam'brii conceded. "Very well, you may

escort her—providing, of course, you take all precautions for her safety."

"I've handpicked my own team, Councilor. They'll
be unobtrusive, and they're tops regarding security
and surveillance." Unfortunately, Teir's own crew
hadn't been available, but they were too well-known
anyway. He needed faces that could blend into the
crowd.

"We can go anywhere in the city without fear,"
he added. "Sarina won't even notice my people are
there."

"Fine. Just be careful where you go. You never can
be too cautious, in my opinion."

"I'd like to see the medical center, if you have one,"
Sarina interrupted. "If I'm supposed to be a healer,
I should familiarize myself with your advances in
health care. And I need to learn about this plague
everyone is talking about." Even though she didn't
intend to stick around for very long, she was curious.
What if the Farg ever made its way to Earth?

"An excellent idea," Cam'brii agreed, nodding.
"Take her on a visit to the Wellness Center." A
melodious chime sounded from above. "Pardon me—
I must receive this message in my work station. Help
yourself to a beverage if you wish, Captain."

With a purposeful stride, he disappeared around
a corner. Soon his booted footsteps were heard
ascending a flight of stairs.

Left alone, Sarina and Teir stared at one another.
At last, Sarina's lips curved upward.

"Tell me the truth, Teir. How did you get stuck
with this assignment? I'd have thought you'd be off
on another mission by now."

He hooked his thumbs into his belt and leaned
against the wall. "The *Valiant* is in drydock for repairs.
There aren't any other ships available."

She lifted her eyebrows. "Repairs? What for?"

"The power transfer conduits are damaged. The
circuits apparently overloaded and burned out. Parts

have to be obtained. It could take weeks for them to get here."

"But there was nothing wrong during our trip."

"Exactly."

She gasped, noting the dark gleam in his eye. "You mean—"

He nodded grimly. "Datron was overseeing the maintenance. He didn't check in as scheduled. When Korox and I went to investigate, we found him at the maintenance hangar, behaving oddly. He couldn't account for an haura of his time. I rounded up Moff'tt who said all systems were clear on the trip here. There'd been no warning indicators of any kind."

"But why?" Teir's problems shouldn't concern her, but for some reason they did.

He shrugged, hiding his anxiety under veiled lids. He'd thought it was Bdan, trying to lure him out with Loopa's lucrative offer while he was between assignments. But someone else was responsible for his orders to remain on Bimordus Two and guard Sarina. Was that person also responsible for disabling his ship?

"Whatever caused the malfunction, I'm stuck here," he said.

Sarina slid off the lounger and stood. "I'm glad you're staying. I need a friend."

Teir's pulse beat erratically as she approached. "You have your betrothed."

She shook her head. "I don't feel comfortable with him. I know the situation is awkward for us both, but . . ." Her voice trailed off. She couldn't complete her thought aloud. *But he doesn't excite me like you do,* she finished silently.

"You're going to wed him. You need to know each other." His eyes fell upon the tendrils of blond hair feathering her face, then upon her soft, full lips. He looked away quickly, before his need for her overwhelmed his self-control.

"You're right, of course." He was reminding her of

her duty, she thought dispiritedly. Those weren't the words of comfort she wanted to hear. She lingered, hoping he'd say more, but Teir was silent. "Well—I guess I'll go to bed. It's been a long day," she said hesitantly. When he still didn't respond, her shoulders slumped and she turned aside. "Say good night to Lord Cam'brii for me."

As she left, Teir's heated gaze followed her all the way from the room.

Chapter Seven

Early the next morning, while Sarina and Lord Cam'brii were breakfasting together, Teir excused himself to head for the Defense League Station on the other side of town. He had unfinished business to complete.

Entering the pink stone and marbelite building, which served as headquarters for the troops stationed on Bimordus Two, Teir went straight to the comm center and requested Admiral Daras Gog at Command Central. As the connection went through, he attached his data link to scramble the conversation.

"Congratulations, Captain," boomed Daras Gog's voice. "You did a fine job of retrieving the Earth-woman."

"Thank you, sir. May I ask the reason for my reassignment?"

"By virtue of her position, the Great Healer has certain enemies, Captain. You're the best man available for the job."

"I thought you might have something else for me to do, something—"

"More active?" The admiral chuckled.

"I was hoping to go after Cerrus Bdan."

"He's headed back to Souk from what I'm told. We can deal with him later. This assignment is more important. Understand, Captain, that we're at a crucial point in Coalition history. The Great Healer plays a pivotal part in what happens next, and you're the one who is solely responsible for her protection."

"Surely any of the other officers stationed here could have taken charge."

"Not as well as you. You're the top officer in the Defense League. Your reputation alone is enough to scare off half the troublemakers in the galaxy. Besides, the woman already knows you. It is thought she might feel more comfortable with someone familiar to her."

Teir jumped on the admiral's words. "Then assigning me was not your idea?"

"Let us say a person in authority strongly suggested you would be the right person for the job."

"What about my ship, the *Valiant*? Was she part of the deal?"

"I don't know anything about that. You would have received this assignment whether or not your ship was grounded. I can put a priority call on the repairs."

"Do it!" Teir didn't care that he was speaking to his commanding officer. "I don't suppose you'll tell me who recommended me?" He wanted the name of the slythian worm who'd set him up.

"Look around, Captain. You might learn a thing or two while you're on Bimordus Two. And don't question your orders!" Sounding annoyed, Daras Gog signed off.

Back at Cam'brii's residence, Teir raised the subject with the councilor. Cam'brii was preparing to leave, dressed for work in a royal blue tunic, navy leggings, and shiny black boots.

"Perhaps you could check into it?" Teir asked him. "I'd like to know who pulled strings to keep me here." *And why,* he added silently.

Lord Cam'brii nodded, his mood mellow as he stuffed a pack of data cards into his pocket. "I'll see what I can find out."

"You're not in any danger, are you?" Sarina asked Teir, thinking that Bdan or his agents might be involved.

"You and the councilor are the ones under guard," Teir answered tersely, "not me."

But Sarina was worried about him. Cerrus Bdan wouldn't forget his defeat so easily. Perhaps he had agents here, scheming to capture Teir. Keeping him planetside would ensure his presence when they were ready to attack him. She didn't fear for her own safety. With Teir protecting her, she felt secure.

They left a short while later, exiting Spiral Town and heading down a wide paved street. Teir suggested taking a speeder, but Sarina preferred to walk and so did Rolf. The councilor gave orders to his guard to remain unobtrusive so Sarina could enjoy the outing. The troops fanned out, dispersing in the crowd. Sarina wondered where Teir's men were— she didn't notice any additional escorts. His team must be experts at undercover surveillance.

As they strolled along, the glittering pink towers, flying vehicles, and alien inhabitants continued to amaze Sarina. Though part of her feared she'd be stuck here forever, another part of her wanted to gape and soak in all the ambiance she could. It was as if her favorite science fiction movies had turned into reality.

Teir walked behind Sarina and Cam'brii. His posture remained one of alertness: his eyes wary, his body tense. The streets were crowded, and opportunities for a sniper were readily available at any one of the mirrored casements facing the main avenue. He had to rely on the scanners his men used to provide adequate warning should anyone aim a weapon. Luckily, Sarina and Cam'brii didn't appear to be attracting too much attention. Most of the inhabitants were intent on scurrying off to business.

"I don't have to be in the council chambers right away," Rolf told Sarina. "I can take you on a quick tour of the city; then we can catch a speeder to the other sectors."

"That sounds fine," Sarina said. She listened while he described the various sights they passed.

"This is the physiolab," he said at one point, gesturing toward a low, rectangular building. "It has a full range of exercise equipment, an indoor pool, and a selection of fitness classes. I try to come here every day after work, and twice a week in the evenings I have fencing practice. You might want to work some sessions into your schedule."

Sarina simply nodded. She hoped to find a way home soon and establishing an exercise routine was not one of her top priorities.

Behind her, Teir tried to focus on his job, but it was difficult not to notice how Sarina was hanging on Cam'brii's every word. By the corona, he didn't know how he could cope with being in such close quarters with her! On his ship, he could occupy his mind with tactical operations. But now, he had to suffer while Sarina enjoyed the councilor's company. His gaze wandered over her body, from her silky blond hair hanging over her shoulders to her sensible low-heeled shoes. He wondered if Cam'brii had noticed how her tight skirt caressed her shapely legs like a lover's kiss.

"We'll just have time for a quick view of the other biomes. I'll show you more another day," Cam'brii was saying. He squinted in the sunlight filtering through the crystal dome. The ceiling was so high that it appeared part of the sky.

"What's a biome?" she asked, acutely aware of Teir's booted tread behind them.

"It's a large-scale ecosystem. Sealed, each system recycles its own air, water, and nutrients. There are four biomes besides this one. The first one we'll stop at is the Nutrition Pod. We use hydroponic and inter-cropping farming techniques for growing fruits and vegetables, and a large aquaculture center raises fish."

She looked at him, puzzled. "Why grow food when you've got fabricators?"

He smiled, his golden blond hair gleaming in the light. It was still early morning, and the temperature was cold enough to chill Sarina's skin. She was glad Rolf had suggested she wear a drape. The climate was temperature controlled, he'd told her, but it was kept cool in the city during early hauras to reduce energy needs.

"Not all of our delegates consume nourishment created through molecular alteration," Rolf explained. "The less developed cultures are used to preparing their own meals. Many of our ambassadors from non-aligned worlds, or new applicants to the Coalition, use this method. We find that when a culture's technology accelerates, the faster pace makes a fabricator more acceptable." He studied her. "The surplus from our Nutrition Pod is offered in various natural eateries around Bimordus Central. Perhaps we should dine in one tonight."

"I'd like that," Sarina said.

They entered a vehicle exchange station to pick up a speeder. Rolf explained the specifications to her. Resembling a bullet-shaped, glass-bubbled car, it held up to four people and had the capacity to glide on wheels or fly through the air. A miniaturized bimanthium krystal reactor provided power.

Sarina gazed in wonder at the other types of trans-portation she'd seen earlier: Smaller-capacity speed-ers; flying motorized cycles; airbuses that cruised slowly just above the ground; and a people-mover that provided easy transport along the city streets. One didn't need to own a private vehicle on Bimordus Two. Everyone had free access to all means of transportation.

The station was bustling with morning activity, but Cam'brii had no trouble requisitioning a speeder. Consulting briefly with his guards, he gave them his proposed itinerary so they could follow in a vehicle of their own. Teir used the communications mechanism on his data link device to notify his team of their plans.

Using this method of transportation, they proceeded to view the Nutrition Pod, Rain Forest, Marine Habitat, and Biogenesis Research Center. After finishing the tour, they returned the vehicle. Teir glanced around the station, unable to spot his men. He'd ordered them to wait there while he accompanied Cam'brii and Sarina to the different biomes. As the councilor led them back into the city, he hoped they were in position. The councilor's troops were good men but they were too conspicuous.

"This whole setup is so complex," Sarina said to Rolf. Teir walked behind them as they strode down a side street. He hadn't said a word during the whole tour, and she wondered what he was thinking. Rolf, on the other hand, had seemed eager to answer her questions. "Are there other biospheres elsewhere?" she asked him.

He nodded. "Colonies have been built on previously uninhabitable worlds utilizing this technology. It allows for expansion of our population base, or for research that cannot be done elsewhere."

"Look at this," Teir exclaimed, striding in front of them. He pointed to a tall obelisk in the center of a courtyard. The monument was covered with strange symbols.

"This is a memorial to the *S.S. Musek*," he said, his voice ringing loud and clear to draw their attention.

"The ship was a commercial passenger liner destroyed by the Korions one hundred and six annums ago."

Sarina had received her own personal data link as a gift from Rolf earlier that morning. Now she pulled it from her pocket and did a quick calculation. Bimordus Two rotated its sun every five hundred days. The disaster must have occurred circa 1929 according to Earth's calendar.

"Who were the Korions?" She'd thought the Morgots were the only threat to the Coalition.

Rolf took her arm and steered her toward a huge circular building made of translucent panels and pink stone. A large set of double doors loomed in front. "You'll learn all about it when you review our history. This is the study center."

Sarina glanced back at Teir, who was staring at them, a pained expression on his face. But he didn't remain still for long. Pushing ahead with his quick stride, he reached the entrance before they did.

"I have reserved a seclusion space for you," Lord Cam'brii told them. "Captain, I assume your men will position themselves at strategic locations?"

Teir nodded. "I've given them their assignments. Some are already inside. Others will watch the exterior."

"Remain alert, just in case. You can instruct Sarina how to utilize the learning facilities." He paused. "May I have a word with you in private, please?"

A wary expression on his face, Teir stepped aside with the councilor. They were out of earshot of Sarina, but she observed them intently.

"I've seen the way you look at my betrothed, Captain," Cam'brii said, narrowing his eyes. "Need I remind you of your duty? The woman is vulnerable. She is in a strange place surrounded by alien beings. Your job is to protect her. Mine is to woo her. Understand?"

Teir nodded, his mouth tightening.

"Good." Cam'brii turned away and approached Sarina. "I'll see you later," he told her with a smile. Bowing, he took her hand and kissed it. Then he was gone.

"What was that all about?" She'd seen the look on Teir's face, and he hadn't appeared pleased by whatever Rolf had said.

"Never mind," Teir muttered. "Let's go inside."

They entered the study center and Sarina was immediately struck by the cavernous interior filled by rows of empty cubicles.

"Where are all the books?" she asked, astounded. Not one tome was in sight.

"Books? We don't use them anymore." He sounded amused. "Come, we'll find the seclusion space Lord Cam'brii reserved for us and I'll show you."

A white robed caretaker who looked to be about two hundred years old took them to a private room at the rear.

"There's nothing here except a couple of chairs!" she exclaimed when they were inside surrounded by four blank walls.

"You simply have to make a request. *Computer*, show us the subliminal learning device," Teir said.

An alcove in the wall opened and a head mask slid out on a slab. Teir picked it up and showed it to Sarina. "You choose your subject, then put this over your head. Pictures will form in your mind's eye—ocean waves, waterfalls, and the like. Relaxing music plays in the background. While you're in a tranquil mood, images and sounds instructing you in the subject you've chosen flash by at a speed too quick for your conscious mind to register. Those images become fixed in your subconscious. It's quite an efficient way to learn."

Sarina examined the device. It reminded her of the virtual reality headgear worn on Earth to play three-dimensional multimedia games. "Does anyone go to school?" she asked.

"Of course." He laughed. "This just teaches facts, not problem solving or analytical thinking. You can only learn that through experience."

"So I have to wear this thing?" It didn't look too appealing.

"It's the quickest way to learn. Your other choice is the living picture method. A holographic display plays out the subject you have chosen."

Sarina nodded eagerly. "I like that much better."

"Okay. Tell the computer what you want to do. It'll provide the rest. I'm going to check in with my men. Then I'll take the other corner to catch up on some reading." He saw her incredulous expression. "Yes, you can actually read. A computer screen will pop out if you so desire. That archaic method is too slow for you, but it suits me fine. I need to catch up on the latest revisions regarding flight procedures, ship maintenance schedules, and news updates." He showed her how to get started and then left her alone.

Sarina set about her studies with alacrity. First she concentrated on the history of the Coalition, instructing the computer to calculate all dates in Earth-time so it would be easier for her to understand. Holographic images sprang to life, giving her the feeling she was living through the history as it played out.

Around 1860, first contact was made between Arcturians and Vilarans. By 1909, relations were established with four other worlds. A conference was held on Sirius IV regarding the formation of a coalition, but it ended in discord. It wasn't until 1919 that the Articles of Coalition were adopted at a consortium held on Bimordus Two. The Souk Colonies offered to join if they were paid a bonus of twenty billion credits. Their request was denied.

Five years later, a cargo ship operating near the frontier of Coalition space was attacked and destroyed by unknown aliens. The following year, another freighter was attacked by the same aliens who did not respond to any attempts at communication. Probes launched with peaceful messages did not return. The need for a Defense League became evident. A hasty force was assembled, and a squadron of twelve patrol craft was sent to obtain information. None was ever heard from again.

Then in 1929 came the incident with the *S.S. Musek*. The passengers and crew were all killed. Fear of pirates seriously curtailed cultural exchange activities. In 1933, a sneak attack by the aliens led to their identification as the Korions.

Time blurred for Sarina as events sped past. A devastating war with the Korions resulted. Later, a peace treaty was signed followed by years of prosperity and expansion. A trade agreement was signed with the Souks. First contact with the Morgots was an armed conflict. . . .

"It's getting late."

Teir's voice broke her concentration. Sarina's eyes burned from the holographic images dancing before her. At her command, the computer shut down.

Glancing at her data link, she saw it was almost time for her betrothed to arrive. "Rolf will be coming soon!" she exclaimed, rubbing her aching head.

"I know," Teir said quietly. Sarina had been so absorbed in her history lesson that until now she hadn't paid him any attention, but his eyes had often wandered in her direction. If she responded to his initiative, he'd be starting something he couldn't finish. Cam'brii's warning stuck in his mind, and he respected the councilor's work enough not to obstruct him.

"He's taking me out to dinner," Sarina said. She regretted not having taken a break with Teir. As it was, they'd gotten a late start. The hauras had seemed to fly by. Now it was too late. She wished he were going to be her dinner partner instead of Rolf.

"Does that please you?" Teir asked, his tone neutral.

"Yes," she said, purposely trying to provoke a reaction. "I believe the man is attempting to be pleasant.

And I think he's quite attractive."

Teir's mouth tightened, and Sarina felt a thrill run through her. She must mean something to him if he cared how she felt about Rolf.

Before he could reply, the councilor arrived.

"Are you ready to go?" Rolf asked. He gave the captain a questioning glance. Teir said nothing.

"Yes, we are," Sarina said, standing. She linked her arm through his with a show of enthusiasm.

"How did you fare today?" Rolf asked as they walked outside, flashing her a white, even smile. She found herself warming to him, but not to the extent that she wanted to marry the man and remain here for the rest of her life. Their purpose in getting to know each other returned to haunt her mind and depress her spirit.

"I've just gotten to the part where the Morgots enter the scene," Sarina said.

It was cool in the twilight, and she drew her drape around her shoulders, glancing about nervously as Teir went ahead to check their path. Danger could come from anywhere, she realized. Rolf, too, was on the alert, although the streets were quiet as most people had left work earlier. There was no sign of any of their guards, but Sarina was sure they were around somewhere, keeping out of sight.

"Carry on tomorrow," Rolf said. "Then you can explore the difficulties facing us."

"The history is fascinating, but I still have no understanding of my role."

He patted her hand. "It will be made clear as you proceed in your instruction."

Teir fell into step on Sarina's other side. She tried to ignore his proximity, but his arm was so close to hers that if she reached out, she could almost grasp his hand.

"What happens if the prophecy is not fulfilled?" she asked Rolf.

"Have faith, Sarina. It will come to pass."

"You keep saying that, but what if it doesn't?" She hoped he would say she'd be sent back to Earth, married or not. He could always get an annulment if such a thing existed in this advanced civilization.

"As you view our history, all will be explained," Cam'brii replied patiently.

Footlights suddenly switched on, casting a muted rosy glow at their feet.

"What if my power doesn't exist?" Sarina persisted.

Rolf seemed reluctant to answer, so she stopped, hands on hips, waiting until the issue was cleared up once and for all.

Her escort cleared his throat, and Sarina could hear Teir's heavy breathing as he stood guard behind them.

"It is understood that it may take some time for you to develop feelings for me," Rolf began, flushing uncomfortably. "The legend states that you must fall in love with a member of the ruling House of Raimorrda for your power to become activated. Therefore, you will be allowed a grace period of one annum after our betrothal date to develop your true inheritance."

"One annum?" Sarina echoed. "You mean a *year*? But what if I don't fall in love with you during that time? Will I be passed along to another Raimorrdan to try again?" The thought that she might be joined to one after the other of the nobility until her so-called power showed up appalled her. What if she never fell in love with any of them? And how could she, when she was already engaged to Robert?

"I have a fiance on Earth," she told him. "My heart belongs to him. It's useless for you to insist on this forced marriage when nothing will come of it. Please send me home, Rolf!"

"I am sorry you were torn from all you hold dear," he said gently, as though some deep, painful experience had affected him. "But according to the signs, it is time for the legend to unfold. All that was predicted must now come to pass. You will understand someday that sacrifices are necessary."

"Why do I need to marry you if I'm just supposed to fall in love?" Sarina asked petulantly. "The two don't necessarily go together."

"The exact wording of the legend is this: *The prophecy will be fulfilled when the Great Healer marries a Raimorrdan who is highly placed and was born under the sign of the circle. The healing aura can only be activated by the power of love.*" Rolf spoke precisely so the meaning would be clear. "I am the only Raimorrdan of eligible age who meets these criteria. Thus am I the one destined for you to wed."

"All right, I understand that much." She was relieved that he was the only nobleman who met the legend's qualifications. At least she wouldn't get passed on to anyone else. But he still hadn't answered her initial question. "What if I don't fall in love with you? What happens if my healing power doesn't materialize after the given time?"

Rolf looked away. "Unfortunately, there is an obscure edict that covers that eventuality."

"And that is?"

He sighed, then turned back to Sarina. "The law was originally passed to discourage pretenders. It has never been repealed." He paused, and his next words chilled her blood. "Should you fail to become the Great Healer within the allotted time, you will be executed."

Chapter Eight

Rolf's words ringing in her head, Sarina was incapable of enjoying their dinner. The very thought of food made her want to choke. She decided she'd better study harder at the library the next day to learn all she could about their society and prepare, if possible, her own legal defense. Execution! How could they possibly accuse her of being a pretender? She hadn't deliberately chosen this path!

Lost in gloomy thoughts, Sarina's eyes roamed the restaurant. Sleek lines of polished iridescent furniture were complemented by etched crystal dividers and indirect lighting. It was a small place, and the patrons represented a variety of species. Their laughter and chatter pervaded the room, but the happy sounds only deepened her despair. These creatures were free to pursue their dreams and goals, whereas she was trapped. How could this have happened to her?

Feeling she'd better make an effort to get to know Rolf, she turned to him. He too had been silent, apparently attuned to her need to assimilate what she'd just learned. Sarina appreciated that and tried to force some enthusiasm into her voice.

"This place has a pleasant atmosphere. Thank you for bringing me here, Rolf."

They were seated in a private alcove. Teir had taken an adjacent booth facing the room so he could watch the entrance. The rest of their guards were positioned outside.

He signaled for a server. "Would you like a beverage?"

"Yes, I'll take whatever you recommend."

Rolf ordered, then cocked an eyebrow as he regarded her. "I want to please you, Sarina," he said. "It's important that we get along."

"For whose sake is it important? Not for mine! No one cares how I feel," she burst out.

Rolf shook his head. "You're wrong. I understand how difficult this is for you and how frightened you must be. But your presence here is essential. The Revelation will strengthen the Coalition's unity and help get the First Amendment passed. The vote must go through."

"What's the First Amendment?"

"Let's just say that it's an issue that vitally concerns me." Leaning across the table, he covered her hand with his. "Stop worrying so much. Everything will work out for the best. Now let's drop the subject of politics for this evening. I want to find out more about you, Sarina. Tell me about your job on Earth. You were an attorney? I read your dossier but I'm not clear as to what that means."

Disconcerted by the warmth of his hand, she slid hers out of his grasp as she proceeded to tell him about her career.

"Nadira has a similar system of advocacy," he said when she had finished. "But you don't sound as though you were satisfied with your job."

"No, I really wasn't very happy there," Sarina admitted.

"Why did you not leave?"

"I wasn't ready to change." She was unwilling to reveal her fear of disappointing her fiance. "How did you become a councilor? Has it always been an ambition of yours?"

"No. I was—persuaded to enter the diplomatic corps. Now it's my life's work."

"Do you enjoy it?"

Rolf shrugged. "I do what I must."

"What does that mean?"

He looked her in the eye. "I made a vow to someone that I must keep. It pertains to my work."

"What vow?"

"We'll discuss that another time," he said smoothly. "This night is for pleasure. Ah, here are our drinks." He leaned back as the server placed two crystal goblets on the table. "These are Moranian Flashers," Rolf told her. "Take a sip like this—" he half-sipped, half-inhaled "—and feel the effect. It's quite delightful."

Sarina peered at the bubbly golden liquid frothing inside the crystal glass and nervously followed suit. She gasped as the effervescence tickled her nose. "Oh my!"

Rolf smiled. "It pleases you?"

"Yes, it's quite good." She took another sip and the cool liquid flowed down her throat, faintly reminiscent of raspberries and champagne.

"I would be remiss if I didn't tell you how lovely you look tonight, Sarina. I like the way you fix your hair," Rolf murmured. The sensual tone of his voice and the warm, appreciative look in his eyes discomfited her.

"I shall be proud to have you as my bride," he told her, "and I look forward to getting to know you more—intimately."

Teir coughed loudly in the booth next to them, and Sarina flushed. Dear God, he must be listening to every word, and Rolf had all but said he couldn't wait to get her into his bed!

"Isn't there anyone else, a girl from your home

planet perhaps, whom you would prefer as your wife?" she asked hopefully.

A shadow crossed his face. "No, there is no one."

"Were you at least *asked* if you would marry me?"

"Yes, Glotaj did me that courtesy, but the dictates of the legend were such that I couldn't refuse. On the day of my birth, a supernova occurred in a nearby star system. The cataclysmic explosion created shock waves that traveled outward at an incredible rate—concentric waves, circles of radiation. A huge gas cloud erupted into space, again in a circular configuration.

"At the time, no one thought twice about these events. Interest in the legend arose when the predictions started to come true, and that only happened in the past few annums. A suitable Raimorrdan was sought. Given my status and availability, those natural events were interpreted as the Sign of the Circle foretold by the prophecy."

He smiled. "I am pleased by our proposed union, Sarina. When we wed, I shall assume the title of Prince on my home planet. It is only fitting that I marry you, a princess of the stars."

"Do you really believe in the legend, Rolf?" she asked earnestly.

His eyes darkened to indigo. "I do. Your destiny is joined with mine."

Sarina wondered if all this might be true. She thought of Robert, of her mother and her friend Abby, of all the other people she'd left behind. Even if the legend was valid, could she sacrifice all she held dear for the sake of total strangers?

Hell, no! She didn't want to live the rest of her life in this strange place, light-years from home, regardless of how many wondrous things occurred. However, no one had asked for her opinion! If she became the Great Healer, would they listen to her then?

Who cares? Sarina thought. I don't want to be here long enough to find out. If I don't fall in love with this man, I'm going to be executed within a year's time!

She had to escape back to Earth before her marriage to Lord Rolf Cam'brii took place.

The next day in the study center, Sarina focused on the problems currently faced by the Coalition so she could better understand what she was up against. Foremost in her mind was the need to mount a legal defense against the execution decree in case she couldn't get home. She began where she'd left off the day before.

By 1998, Earth chronology, the Coalition included over five hundred members. It was becoming so large that only major grievances could be dealt with, a source of concern to many. The Defense League was hard pressed to provide security for all. Then the High Council voted to impose harsh sanctions against Souk companies, ports and shipping interests that participated in the slave trade.

This angered the Souks, who were dependent upon slaves as a labor force. Bitterness against Coalition policy led members of the Souk Alliance, a syndicate of commercial cartels in the mineral-rich Capellan system, to conduct acts of piracy and aggression against Coalition citizens. As a result, Lord Cam'brii proposed a First Amendment to the Articles of Coalition that would permanently ban slavery within Coalition boundaries and establish criminal penalties for transgressors.

Boycotting Souk ports was a controversial move that bankrupted a number of companies that relied on Souk trade. The Return to Origins Faction began on Arcturus II as a protest against Coalition policy. The Arcturians supported trade with the Souks because of the scarcity of minerals on their worlds, and they contended that the Coalition was violating its constitution by interfering in matters of planetary concern. By returning to self-rule, the ROF said, member planets could make their own alliances.

The separatist movement became widespread within the Coalition as the crises mounted. The decimation caused by the Farg and the Morgot attacks further strained the resources of the Defense League, and the ROF, now led by Councilor Daimon, contended that the central government had lost its effectiveness and should be dissolved.

"Why would Daimon oppose the Coalition if he's on the High Council?" Sarina asked Teir. He had been sitting with his back to her all afternoon, concentrating on his reading.

He swiveled in his chair and as his eyes met hers, Sarina couldn't help the swell of warmth that rushed through her. Gazing into his gorgeous cobalt eyes would never cease to thrill her.

"It's the old expansionism story," he said. "At what point does an organization call a halt to growth and put a limit on membership? The Coalition has grown too big and can't meet the needs of all its members. Daimon believes each world could better function on its own. He may be right, but those who believe in the legend refute him. They say the Great Healer will eradicate the threats from the plague and the Morgots. Then the Coalition can focus on internal needs and galactic harmony will result."

"So Daimon doesn't believe in the legend?"

Teir shook his head. "Nor does anyone else in the ROF. Their solution is isolationism."

"Are they a threat to Lord Cam'brii?"

"I don't think so. He's got more to fear from the Souks. They don't want his First Amendment to pass the vote scheduled for next annum. An assassination attempt is likely, backed by the Souks or their allies."

Sarina gasped. "Is that why he needs to be so closely guarded?"

Teir nodded. "The situation is made worse by the plague. Let me explain." He moved his chair closer, and Sarina felt her pulse quicken.

"The Farg first surfaced on Tryst VI, annihilating most of the planet's population," he said. "When the Morgots moved in, they sold the survivors as slaves to the Souks. The plague spread, and so did the Morgot conquests. Pirate runs with slave ships have become a real nuisance for the force.

"Cerrus Bdan is a notorious Souk trader who specializes in slave transports. His brother Ruel is *pasha* of the biggest industrial cartel on Souk, which means he controls most of the homeplanet. Bdan keeps him well supplied with slave laborers and other contraband. I would guess they've made considerable profits from the Morgot conquests. Bdan and I have clashed several times, but always after we haul him in, he finds a legal loophole and is released." Teir scowled. "He's a thorn in my side, one I'd dearly love to pluck!"

"No wonder he wants you out of the way," Sarina said. "He's probably tired of running into you, too. And after this last encounter, he'll really be angry."

Teir appeared thoughtful. "I wonder if he was really after me. Maybe he meant to capture you."

Sarina shook her head. "Rolf is important to the Souks, not me."

"But you're a crucial factor in this whole issue. If the legend is true, it will validate the Coalition's unity. The First Amendment will be passed, and the ROF will be out of business. If you succeed in eradicating the Farg, the Coalition can concentrate on repelling the invaders. You'll help to rid us of the Morgots as well."

"So you're saying the Souks, the ROF, and the Morgots all have a reason to get rid of me?"

He nodded glumly.

"Well, they won't have to worry for long," Sarina said bitterly. "My wedding date is only a few weeks away. After that, I'll have ten more months and then I'll be executed. The High Council will do the others' dirty work for them." She reached out her hand and touched his arm. "Teir, please help me escape! I want to go home!"

Steeling himself, he shook his head. "I can't."

"But I'm not a Great Healer," she cried. "I have no special power. Are you going to stand by and watch me die?"

"Gods, no." Teir's gut twisted as he saw her wide silver eyes fill with fear.

"At least help me delay my marriage to Lord Cam'brii!"

"Did someone mention my name?"

Rolf strode into the room, to find Sarina leaning forward, her hand on Teir's arm, a pleading look on her face. "What's going on?" he snapped.

Teir stood. "We've been discussing the issues affecting the Coalition. Sarina is concerned about you."

Rolf looked at her questioningly.

"That's right," she said, regaining her composure. "It seems you have many enemies, and so do I."

"Indeed. May I remind you, Captain Reylock, that your purpose is to provide protection?" *And nothing else*, Rolf's stern expression implied.

"Of course," Teir said, clenching his jaw. "Just let me scout the area outside before you leave." He turned on his heel and exited.

Outside, he cursed himself for letting down his guard, and he didn't mean in his official capacity as Sarina's protector, either. He'd allowed her vulnerability to pierce his shield. Cam'brii had to remind him of his duty, and that must never happen again. Teir had to harden himself against her.

Teir buried himself in his reading while Sarina studied during the days that followed. Disgusted that he wouldn't help her, Sarina switched to the subliminal learning method so she could acquire knowledge faster. She focused on technical operations, linguistics, and law. Of the latter, she found nothing that would provide a valid defense against the execution decree.

According to the terms of the Ascension Statute, a pretender was defined as anyone claiming to be or *being presented as* the Great Healer, and who did not show evidence of any healing power within one annum of the Auricle's herald.

Teir explained it further. "The time limit was based on the legend, which states that the Revelation will occur within one annum from when the Auricle begins to glow. You've actually been given more time. You have one annum from the date you were betrothed to Lord Cam'brii."

"But who would pretend to be the Great Healer?"

"Many persons might do so, using trickery if necessary, but the severe punishment is an effective deterrent. The law was made to discourage unscrupulous people from seizing power either for themselves or in the name of another person purported to be the Great Healer."

Sarina's panic as well as her homesickness increased as the weeks flew by. Despair filled her soul as she anguished over never seeing her loved ones again. She even missed small things like her hologram collection and the certificate she'd won for an art contest. Everything and everyone she'd ever cared about were just memories.

Rolf introduced her to his colleagues, taking her out in the evening or entertaining callers at home. She interrogated each of them, hoping to find an ally, but to no avail. They were all believers in the legend and supported the preordained marriage that she dreaded more with each passing day.

Sarina couldn't even get sympathy from Teir. He kept his distance except when once or twice, he took her along to meet his friends. Then he laughed and caroused, showing a side of himself she longed to share. She especially enjoyed the visits with his crew.

Ravi's lavish attention more than made up for Teir's lack of it.

In comparison, Rolf's friends were formally polite to her, treating her like the princess she was soon to become. Emu visited often, but all he could talk about was the legend. Most of the discussions Rolf held with his friends were political.

Sarina was desperate, but there was no one to help her.

"At last we are alone," Rolf told her one evening. Teir had gone out to check on the status of his ship, and for once they had no visitors. Rolf seated her on a wide double lounger in the living area and brought her a drink. He was casually dressed in a claret colored shirt and dark pants, his golden hair shining in the muted light from reflectors on the walls. At his command to the computer, the intensity of the light dimmed, and soft, melodious music began to play. It was the oldest setup in the universe, Sarina thought with dismay.

She smoothed her skirt and smiled nervously as Rolf sat beside her. He'd been most pleasant whenever they were together, but they'd had few moments alone. She took a large gulp of her drink and then placed it on the low crystalline table in front of the lounger.

Rolf's thigh touched hers, and she jumped, startled. His steady gaze caught hers as he laid his hand on her arm. "Sarina, I have been neglectful of my duty. It's time you and I got to know each other better." His hand wandered up her arm and touched her face. As he stroked her cheek, Sarina's stomach churned in anticipation of what he would do next.

He traced her facial contours with his fingers. His hand played along her jawline, caressed her cheek, brushed lightly over her lips. He had a very tender touch, and Sarina sat very still, waiting to see if the physical closeness between them produced any effect. It did not; she felt nothing.

He caught her chin in his hand and tilted her face upward. "You are lovely, Sarina. I think we shall both enjoy our union."

"Rolf," she began, intending to discourage him, but his mouth descended upon hers, and the crushing pressure of his lips silenced whatever she'd been about to say. His arms encircled her, pulling her closer. And then she felt his hand roving to the front fastenings of her dress. Pushing against him, she managed a strangled cry.

"I'm sorry. Am I going too fast for you?" Rolf pulled back. His breath was ragged, his face flushed.

Sarina's heart was beating furiously in anger. "Don't touch me! I don't belong to you yet."

"But we are to be wed. It is expected that we are to join before marriage."

"I don't care what's expected. Keep your hands off me!" she snapped.

"You're just frightened. I'll go more slowly. I promise it will be pleasurable for you."

His curly head began to descend again and Sarina jumped up. "You can't make me enjoy something I don't want! And I don't think it's something you really want either. You have no feelings for me, Lord Cam'brii. You view me as a symbol for the Coalition. Well, romancing a symbol won't work!"

"Forgive me." He rose, regarding her with a solemn expression. "This marriage is vitally important to me. I should have realized I could not force the issue."

Rolf began pacing, his hands clasped behind his back. "This is not an easy situation for me either, Sarina. I'm trying to do my best, to fulfill the terms of the legend, but it's difficult for me to woo you when—" He didn't finish his sentence.

"When what?"

He gazed at her with tormented eyes. "We'll spend more time together," he promised, ignoring her question. "I haven't been devoting sufficient attention to you. I see that now."

"Why don't you tell me what's wrong?" She'd seen that pained expression before and wondered what caused him such anguish.

"It's something I need to work out for myself."

"Let me help you!"

"You can only help me by becoming the Great Healer."

So they were back to that again! It seemed to be the only thing he was willing to discuss with her.

"Come," Rolf said, leading her to the fabricator. "We'll find an activity that's less complicated. I'll teach you how to play kather sticks."

"Kather sticks? What's that?"

The fabricator produced a set of colorful twisted sticks with pointed ends and a pair of dice. "It's a game I used to play. I haven't had time for it in a while—I think I've forgotten how to have fun." Rolf glanced at her wryly. "Please, Sarina, bear with me. I still think we'll do well together."

He seemed so earnest in his appeal that she nodded, albeit reluctantly. She didn't want to spend the rest of her life with Rolf, no matter how personable he was. Of course, Teir was another matter. If he had been here tonight, Rolf would never have made that pass at her. But if the captain had tried to kiss her like that. . . .

Seeing the wistful expression on her face, Rolf interpreted it as being meant for him. Perhaps she was finally coming to accept her situation, he thought. She must be hoping as he was that things would turn out for the best.

Feeling a surge of affection for this woman who was about to become his wife, he took her hand and brushed his lips across the back of it.

Teir walked in just then and saw Lord Cam'brii bowing over Sarina's hand. Her hair was mussed and her mouth looked as if it had been kissed. The top fasteners of her dress were undone. Son of a belleek, what had he missed?

His face whitened but he said nothing as he went straight to his room and shut the door. Had Cam'brii seduced her? Was that why Sarina had such a dreamy look on her face? With a groan, he sank onto his bed. It was torture being so near to her and yet so far. The only thing that would get him through this *maug* assignment was to keep his mind on his job.

A couple of days later, Teir accompanied Sarina and Cam'brii to the Rain Forest biome. The other guards were to follow in their own speeders.

"There's a special place I want to share with you," Rolf told Sarina as they strolled down a winding dirt path in the jungle-like setting. "I think you'll appreciate it." His azure eyes were alight with enthusiasm as he took her arm, guiding her forward.

She glanced at him, marveling at how handsome he was. Everywhere they went, feminine eyes were riveted on him. Sarina knew those females envied her and would be thrilled to be in her place. The councilor was both the best-looking and most eligible member of government in the whole city.

But Sarina didn't care how attractive he was or how much attention he lavished on her. She was not willing to die for him, and each day that passed brought her nearer the execution date.

Pushing aside her fearful thoughts, Sarina listened to the sounds of exotic bird cries, rustling leaves, and scurrying wildlife from the thick foliage that bordered the path. A heavy mist permeated the air, gleaming in the rays of light that penetrated the thick canopy of branches overhead. A rich earthy scent filled her nostrils, reminding Sarina of home. A new wave of homesickness hit her and she wished she were there, jogging along the trail at Matheson Hammock.

Behind her, she could hear the heavy tread of Teir's booted feet. She felt his eyes boring into her back and her blood stirred. Why did he have the power to affect her so strongly when Rolf, for all his appeal, left her cold?

Teir didn't like the idea that they'd come here unprepared. Cam'brii had told him where they were going after they were on the way. With the councilor's permission, Teir had given orders for their guards to follow. But now they were alone, and he didn't know exactly when their backup would arrive. He cursed himself for not placing a watch on the place since it was apparently one of Cam'brii's favorite haunts. The councilor was bound to bring Sarina here sooner or later. It surprised him that Cam'brii himself wasn't more wary. He appeared distracted this morning, intent only on impressing Sarina.

Whipping out his scanner, Teir surveyed the area. It would pick up weapons, but not all species were evident to its lifeform sensors. Feeling an uneasy premonition, he shoved himself between the two in front of him.

"Be on the alert," Teir warned. "I've got a bad feeling about this place."

"Perhaps you should go on ahead to check out the terrain," Rolf suggested, wishing to keep Sarina out of harm's way until he knew the path was clear.

Teir immediately charged off to survey the secluded location Cam'brii was headed for. When all seemed secure, he retraced his steps. "I'll stay back here," he said, "and wait for the backup troops." His glance fell upon Sarina but he quickly looked away. Scowling, he drew his shooter and stood guard.

Sarina wanted to remain in his company but Rolf was urging her forward with a hand on her elbow. Unable to think of an excuse to linger, she followed him along the twisting trail. The foliage was so dense she couldn't see around the next turn. Finally, they rounded a curve and came to a halt.

Sarina gasped. A crystal clear lake with a sparkling waterfall spread in a magnificient panorama before them. The lake was surrounded by banks of flowers in all colors and descriptions, and the air was scented with their perfume. Moisture gleamed on the leaves of trees like tiny diamonds. But what made the scene even more exotic was the musical sound of chimes tinkling in the background.

"This is wonderful!" she exclaimed, forgetting all her fears and resentments in the beauty of the moment.

Rolf smiled, the corners of his eyes crinkling with pleasure. "It's called the Rainbow Glen, a replica of the one on my homeplanet, Nadira. Those sounds you hear come from the tupella blooms over there." He pointed to a bed of flowers whose petals alternated colors, orange and firecracker red. "I love this place. It reminds me of home." He sat on a large boulder and stared out over the water, becoming lost in thought.

Sarina lowered herself onto a rock by the water's edge and dipped her fingers into the cool water. It felt marvelously refreshing. Her rust-colored suede jumpsuit, appropriate for the regulated temperature of the study center, was much too confining for this heat. She rubbed some water on her forehead, then picked a large flat leaf from a nearby plant to fan her face. "What's your planet like?"

"Nadira is a lush, tropical world with many areas of unspoiled wilderness," Rolf replied. "It's a popular vacation spot. We have many rare foods and wines not found elsewhere in the galaxy."

Sarina smiled. "It sounds delightful. Why did you leave?"

"My work took me elsewhere. When I entered the diplomatic corps, I had to move to Bimordus Central."

"Don't you miss your home?" she asked. "I miss mine terribly!"

He shook his head. "I left nothing behind."

"What about your family?"

"I am the second son of the Imperator of Nadira."

Her eyes widened. "But that must be a very important position! Of course, you said you'd assume the title of Prince when you wed. Didn't your father want you to remain behind?"

He hesitated, then spoke candidly. "I was disgraced. You should know this before you wed me."

Sarina couldn't imagine Lord Rolf Cam'brii ever doing anything disgraceful. "What happened?"

Before he could reply, Teir shouted, "Sarina, look out!"

A beam of red light shot past her ear, and she heard a crackling noise. Rolf sprang up and his blade was slashing through the air. The trees had come alive, Sarina realized in terror. Dark, hollow eyes glared from their trunks, and their limbs reached out to clutch at her.

Sarina screamed as one grabbed hold of her and began crushing the breath from her body.

Teir's shooter fired again, and the red energy beam hit the bark, charring a gash in the tree. With an unearthly howl, the tree bent, dropping her. The smell of burnt wood permeated the air.

She gasped as Rolf battled two of the creatures with his blade. Teir was trying to take them out with his shooter, but he was being surrounded. "Help!" she shrieked as a scraggly limb reached out for her. She ducked, grabbed a loose vine and ran around the trunk, wrapping the groping branch tight against it.

"Watch your back!" Rolf called to Teir.

Teir whirled and fired, hitting his leafy assailant. But another of the tree creatures Rolf was fighting snatched up a rock and cracked it into the side of his head. Rolf went down as Sarina screamed.

Teir raced over to her. "Use this," he growled, thrusting his shooter into her hand.

"What—?" She didn't continue, because she saw Teir whip out a hidden weapon. Before he could flick the control, a tree creature grabbed him from behind, lifting him off the ground. He flipped himself around in its grasp and knuckled it in the eye. With a moaning shriek, the attacker let go. Landing on his feet, Teir activated his weapon, aiming a fiery blast at the trees hovering over Lord Cam'brii.

Sarina fired the shooter as one cast up a limb to throw a rock at Teir's head, and it toppled over with a hideous sizzling and a puff of foul smoke.

The others moved back, their dark, gaping eyes seeming to grow even blacker.

"Sarina, see if you can rouse Lord Cam'brii," Teir urged. "We've got to get out of here!" He wondered what had happened to their backup. The other guards should have arrived by now.

She scurried over and knelt beside the fallen councilor. His face was pale, and a purplish bruise discolored his temple. "Rolf, wake up!" She shook him desperately. He began to moan and opened his eyes not a moment too soon.

"Captain!" he shouted.

Teir felt a stinging pain in his arm, the same arm that had been wounded before. He pivoted, thrusting a roaring wall of flame at the tree that had pierced his flesh. He jumped back as its bark caught fire and exploded, sending an intense wave of heat in his direction.

"Are you all right?" Sarina asked Rolf. He nodded and slowly rose to his feet. Then she hurried to Teir. "Your arm—let me see it."

His flesh tingled when she touched him, a strange feeling but not unpleasant. Sarina parted the tear in his shirt and gave a sigh of relief. "It's just a scratch." She gently touched the jagged edge of the wound, and her fingertips warmed as she smoothed away the blood. Then she wiped her hand on a nearby leaf and glanced around. The tree creatures were vanishing into the surrounding jungle.

"Let's get out of here before more of them show up," Teir gritted. "Lord Cam'brii needs medical attention."

The councilor was swaying on his feet, and Sarina ran over to support him. With Teir's assistance, they made it out to their speeder. Still there was no sign of his men or of Cam'brii's contingent of guards. Concerned, Teir activated his data link.

"Sorry, sir," his squad leader said. "We're still at the vehicle exchange station. All transport was halted due to a systems malfunction. Communications have been jammed as well. We were unable to get through to you. The computer just came back on-line."

Frowning, Teir gave him a quick rundown of what had happened. "Meet us at the Wellness Center," he ordered. "I'll get to the bottom of this later. Someone must have been in league with the Twyggs, setting up the ambush."

Lord Cam'brii's injury was slight, the medic at the Wellness Center told them. He ran an instrument over Cam'brii's temple, and the councilor's blurred vision and headache cleared at once. Passing a shaky hand across his forehead, Cam'brii sat up on the examining table and turned to Teir.

"Thank you, Captain, for your vigilance."

"Just doing my job," Teir answered.

"What kind of weapon were you using, if I may ask?"

He grinned. "It's a Vilaran flamer. We use them against the jaegger beasts in the Uta Wastes."

"Quite effective," Cam'brii commented. "Who do you think sent the Twyggs?"

"Assuming they were after you, probably the Souks. But I'm not sure you were the target." Sarina and Cam'brii stared at him. "I was waiting back there for you, and all of a sudden a couple of Twyggs jumped me. I got them off and started running in your direction to warn you."

"They knew you were guarding us. They might have been trying to knock you out of commission before attacking us."

"Maybe." Teir wondered what would have happened if the Twyggs had managed to disarm him.

Would they have gone after Cam'brii or Sarina, or was he himself their prey? He had a funny feeling about the whole thing.

"I have to file a report, and I'd prefer to do it in person," he said, running his hand through his hair. Actually, he wanted to check on the transport system snafu. "My people are at their checkpoints outside and so are your men, Councilor. You should both be safe if you return immediately to Spiral Town."

"I think I'll show Sarina around the Wellness Center as long as we're here."

"Are you sure you feel up to it?" Sarina asked him.

"I'm fine." Rolf seemed pleased by her concern.

"Teir, have the medic look at your arm," Sarina urged. "That cut should be cleaned."

Teir nodded curtly as Lord Cam'brii led her out. The medic came over and took a look at him. "Is it here, where your shirt is torn, Captain?" Teir grunted affirmation as he felt the medic's probing fingers. "I'm afraid I don't see anything, sir. Are you sure this is the spot?"

Teir looked for himself. The skin on his arm was perfectly smooth. There wasn't even a trace of a scratch. "By the corona, you're right!" he said, astonished. His eyes narrowed as he recalled the tingling sensation he'd felt at Sarina's touch. The Great Healer—could it be possible?

No, he told himself quickly. He didn't believe in the legend.

Saluting, he bade the medic farewell and left.

Sarina felt oddly drained as she followed Rolf around the Wellness Center. The medic rejoined them, showing her the diagnostic beds which probed a body with a sensor scan, then presented a diagnosis and therapy options. Many diseases had been eradicated, including cancer. It was amazing they couldn't conquer the plague, Sarina thought.

Thinking about Abby, she asked if there was an effective treatment for paralysis victims. She'd seen the wards for patients with traumatic injuries and acute illnesses but had noticed none for chronic disabilities.

"Paralysis?" queried the medic, a fresh-faced young man who looked about twelve years old. He wore an amber colored tunic over black trousers, with the Coalition insignia embroidered over the left breast, and Sarina assumed, having seen other medics dressed in the same garb, that it was the standard issue uniform for medical personnel. Rolf whispered to her that the medic's metabolism was slow but his age was advanced. He was probably fifty-two annums.

"Paralysis is no longer a problem for us," the medic said.

"Really? How so?"

"We have the ability to reconnect severed neurons or generate new ones, given the proper conditions."

"Can you show me?" Sarina asked excitedly. If she were allowed to return to Earth, her friend could use such a gift.

The medic promised to teach her, and they left, soon arriving at Rolf's residence. Once they were in the living area, Sarina broached the subject.

"It's out of the question," Rolf said, his brows drawing together in annoyance. "You may not go back to your home."

"Why? I just want to see everyone once more, and help Abby walk again," she lied. "Then I'll come back and marry you."

"Your duty lies here," he insisted.

"I'm thoroughly sick of that word!" Sarina groaned. "You don't really care for me at all, do you? You ask about my home and family but no matter what I say, your response is always the same. You might as well admit your interest in me is mere pretense. As far as you're concerned, I'm just a pawn in some great galactic game!"

"A very important game." Rolf leaned forward, clasping his hands in front of him. "As Great Healer, you'll be in a position of considerable influence. Think what miracles you'll be able to accomplish in your new role. In the meantime, it is imperative for you to support the First Amendment. You've reviewed our history enough to know the slavery issue is a pivotal point in strengthening Coalition unity. Your advocacy at this time is crucial."

"I'm never going to become the Great Healer, and I don't give a damn about your blasted First Amendment!"

Anguish twisted his features. "We must end the terrorist attacks led by the Souks. Getting the First Amendment passed is critical."

"All you care about is your stupid job," Sarina shouted. "No wonder you agreed to marry me. Probably no one else would have you!"

His face whitened, and Sarina felt a flash of guilt. It didn't last long, however. If she couldn't get home, she was stuck with this man who would never love her.

"My purpose is what drives me," he said quietly. "I cannot help being the way I am."

"What happened to you on Nadira?" she asked. "Surely something traumatic must have occurred to influence you so strongly."

He sprang up from his chair. "That is not your concern!"

"Yes, it is. If I'm to be your wife, you must share everything with me. You said so yourself."

"I can't!" With those words, Rolf stalked into his room and slammed the door.

Troubled, Sarina asked Teir about it the next evening. "The only thing I heard," he said, "is that there was some sort of tragedy in Cam'brii's past. But no one will talk about it—either they don't know, or they won't say. He has loyal friends, and everyone speaks very highly of him."

Rolf had a meeting that night, so Teir had offered to take her out. They were on their way to the Pleasure Palace which Teir had told her was located on the outskirts of Bimordus Central.

Teir wore a loose white shirt open halfway down his hairy chest, a black vest and tight dark pants. His shooter was trapped to his hip. His eyes darted about as Sarina and he strode down the dimly lit footpaths. Teir still didn't know who was behind the Twyggs' attack or whom they'd been after. The transport system had apparently broken down on its own, throwing the central computer off-line, and Teir knew he needed to be even more cautious than usual in case something similar happened again. His men knew their destination and were spaced at intervals along the route, watching from the shadows.

At least Sarina appeared relaxed, he thought gratefully. He wanted this evening to be pleasant for her. He glanced at her, drinking in the lovely picture she made.

The air was cool and crisp, and she was dressed warmly in a long-sleeved black velvet top with a softly pleated silk skirt. Her hair was fastened on top of her head with a jeweled comb, exposing her slender neck that was graced by a diamond and gold necklace. Matching earrings dangled from her ears. She looked elegant, almost regal.

Sarina felt his appreciative glance and it heated her blood. Rolf had left her residence without a single look in her direction. His demeanor toward her all day had been cool. He didn't even seem to care that she preferred Teir's presence to his own.

She looked at the captain from beneath her long lashes, giving him an encouraging smile. She enjoyed his company, and she wanted him to know it.

Teir saw her smile and his heart began to pump faster. Impulsively, he moved closer and took Sarina's hand, careful to keep his other arm free should he need to draw his weapon. Gradually he drew her nearer until his arm was around her. She liked the warm feeling of his body and snuggled closer.

Teir groaned inwardly as he felt her lean into his hard strength. It was difficult enough, knowing she belonged to Cam'brii. Being in physical contact with her was sheer torture. Her wedding was next week— Cam'brii probably wouldn't tolerate him being alone with her after that.

The Pleasure Palace, a white-domed three-story marbelite building, loomed in front of them. Teir guided Sarina through the entrance and watched her face as she stared around in awe. The lobby was immense, with directional signs coded in Jawani, the official common language of the galaxy.

Teir pointed to one sign after the other. "The Showroom books the best acts from all over the galaxy. The Natural Eaterie is a gourmet restaurant with 'real' food prepared to order. The Lounge is a bar with over four hundred varieties of beverages, specialties from all our worlds. The Entertainment Center has games where you become part of the action. And the Creative Corner is the real reason I brought you here. I think you'll be especially interested in what it has to offer."

"Then let's go!" Sarina said. She couldn't wait to have some fun. It was so thoughtful of Teir to suggest this. Clinging to him more tightly, she squeezed his arm to show her appreciation.

Teir took a shuddering breath. She looked like an angel, the soft golden wisps of her hair floating about her face, and her eyes flashing silver sparks. He desperately wanted to embrace her and press his mouth to her parted lips.

Instead, he strode forward to a sweeping staircase and led the way to the second landing. "There are several sections in the Creative Corner," he said, drawing her through a set of wide polished doors that hissed open at their approach. "I'll show you the one I think you'll like best, and then we can explore the others."

They walked through several rooms where other guests were performing strange activities. A myriad of colors and sounds and images blurred in Sarina's mind until they entered a large hall lined with a series of small private chambers, most of them with open doorways. A boxlike contraption was attached to the exterior of each chamber. A few of the spaces were sealed, and she heard laughter and voices from within.

"Go inside one," Teir suggested with a twinkle in his eye.

"Come with me," Sarina urged.

"All right." He accompanied her into one of the chambers and ordered the door to close. Blank walls of white surrounded them, backlit so the room was bright. "Lift your arms, and face the wide wall away from the door," Teir commanded.

Sarina did so, and instantly, bright red light flooded the wall in front of her. "Oh my!"

"Try different movements."

As she waved her arms around, Sarina gradually got the feel for what she was doing. Each movement produced a different color, and with finger motions she could direct the colors into lines. If she moved her whole body, a whole section might be filled in with whatever color was being used. "It's an art form!" she exclaimed, delighted.

"You can print out in any medium you desire. The finished work comes out the replicator on the outside. Just order it done."

She turned to him, her eyes shining with excitement. "This is wonderful, Teir! Thank you so much." Obviously he had noticed her silly cartoon murals on the *Valiant* after all, and had offered her this outlet for her creativity. In a rush of gratitude, she stood on tiptoe and kissed him.

When she went to move away, he growled low in

his throat, put his hands on her arms and pulled her closer. "Not so fast," he whispered, suddenly overwhelmed with need. He'd resisted too long. He couldn't deny his desire for her anymore.

Teir's mouth brushed her hair; she felt his warm breath on her forehead, and then his lips were crushing hers. She felt her knees give way as she yielded to his kiss. He tasted like heated brandy about to ignite! She snuggled even closer. Her arms snaked around his powerful shoulders, and she pressed her breasts against his chest. His muscles were rock hard and so strong. She could feel the bulge against her thighs that told her he was aroused, and it excited her even more. Teir's searing kiss made her want to melt. Rolf never made her feel like this. Neither had Robert, she realized with a shock.

Teir tilted her head back so he could kiss her soft, creamy throat. Her moan of pleasure drove him wild. His hand on her buttocks pulled her closer, as his other hand caressed her breast.

"Oh yes," she whispered, an incredible warmth seeping through her as his finger teased her nipple.

"God, Sarina, you're so beautiful," he murmured, kissing her again. His tongue traced the outline of her lips and then probed inside to sample her sweetness. She was everything he'd thought she'd be and more. His hips grated urgently against hers until he thought he'd explode. "Let's find a place where we can finish this," he rasped, pulling back.

"Wait," Sarina protested weakly, uncertain she wanted to go *that* far.

"What for?" His heated gaze raked over her, taking in her flushed face, her heaving breasts. She was every bit as aroused as he was. "We're both enjoying this, so why stop?"

Sarina was torn with indecision. She was powerfully attracted to Teir, yet she was engaged to two other men. The absurdity of her situation made her want to laugh or cry; she didn't know which. Robert was waiting for her back home. How could she face him again if she slept with another man? And Rolf would be furious if he found out; he was a man of honor. The councilor would expect her to be faithful if nothing else. She simply couldn't allow herself to give in, even though pregnancy wasn't a concern—her birth control patch would see her through the rest of the year.

These thoughts took but a moment to flash through Sarina's mind. "I can't," she said sadly. "It's not right. Lord Cam'brii—"

"Is a chunk of ice. I'm not."

Teir reached out to grasp her, intending to dissolve her resistance with a kiss, but she stepped back out of range.

"I said it's not right!" It annoyed her that he was going against the very principles of duty and honor he espoused. "I'm sure Lord Cam'brii wouldn't take lightly his bride having an affair with her bodyguard."

"To Zor with Cam'brii! All he cares about is politics. You're just a means to an end as far as he's concerned. I'll make you feel more than he ever will!"

Sarina had no doubt of that. Rolf inspired no physical reaction in her at all, while Teir made her weak with desire.

"You're right," she said. "I feel nothing when I'm with Lord Cam'brii. But there's still Robert, my fiance back on Earth."

Teir yearned to take her in his arms, but she was suddenly erecting too many barriers between them. "You miss Robert that much?" he asked in a low tone.

"Of course I miss him," Sarina proclaimed, but even as she spoke, the words sounded false to her own ears. "At least, I did at first," she confessed. "I'm not so sure how I feel now. Oh, Teir, can't you at least help me get out of my marriage to Lord Cam'brii?" she pleaded. "I'm unable to consider anything else with that hanging over my head."

Her wide gray eyes captured his, and Teir felt his resolve weakening. Regardless of how she felt about her fiance back on Earth, he cared enough about Sarina to want to help. Perhaps there was a way to assist her without defying the Coalition.

"All right, I'll see what I can do," he said.

Chapter Nine

Two days later, Teir discussed the situation with Ravi. They were in the Pleasure Palace watching the latest Showroom act, a troupe of plumed Sumarrn dancers.

"I can't do anything that would jeopardize my position in the League," Teir muttered, cupping his glass in his palm. Seducing Sarina was one thing; helping her escape her obligation to the Coalition was another. "And I support Cam'brii's antislavery legislation. Sarina could be crucial to getting it passed if she marries him."

"You mean, if she falls in love with him. Are there any indications that this has come to pass?" Ravi asked, studying his friend.

Teir snorted. "Neither one of them cares for the other."

"Perhaps they need more time."

"Their wedding is less than five days away!"

Ravi pursed his lips. "A delay could prove helpful. Forgive me for changing the subject, but has the

Mistress said anything about my cousin?"

"Afraid not." Teir's eyes remained fixed on the stage where a dozen glitteringly costumed females kicked in unison.

"Could you ask her to make further inquiries, perhaps?" Ravi prodded gently.

Teir turned his attention to his companion. "The situation on Tendraa is grave, my friend. No one is able to gain information."

"But Sarina is the Great Healer. She can do what others cannot."

Teir rubbed his thumb along his hair-roughened jaw. "You've got a point—a very good point." His expression turned thoughtful. "In fact, you may have just given me the solution I need."

"Oh?"

"Sarina is the one person who could get permission to visit Tendraa. Your people, who won't allow any other Coalition representatives to come, would be overjoyed to greet their Savior. And a trip there would necessitate a postponement of her marriage."

"But why would the High Council give their approval?" Ravi asked.

"I'll suggest it as a test. Maybe her healing power has already been activated. How would anyone know? If she visits the plague-scourged planet, it'll be an objective assessment of her ability. And while she's there, she can gather information for the Coalition."

"What about the risk of infection?" Ravi's eyes shone with hope but he was still cautious. "If she hasn't developed her power yet, she could catch the disease."

"She can wear a protective shield. And I'll bet I can get approval to transport her." Teir liked the idea even better because it would give him time alone with Sarina. A ten-day trip in such close quarters could only work in his favor.

He rose from his seat, saluting. "I'll let you know what happens. May the faith be with you, friend." His heart feeling lighter than it had in weeks, he left.

When Teir returned to Cam'brii's home, Sarina was seated in the living area, entertaining Mara, an exobiologist, whom Sarina had met at the Wellness Center during one of her visits. The two women were utilizing Cam'brii's personal entertainment system, watching a holographic Vyxian historical drama.

"Hi, Mara," Teir said, greeting the tall, raven-haired beauty.

"Captain," she said, inclining her head in acknowledgment. "I was just leaving." Rising from her chair, she turned to Sarina. "It's getting late, and I have an early consultation tomorrow. Let us meet again soon."

Sarina flashed her a wide smile. "I'd like that very much." She rose to show her friend out, then returned to Teir.

"Where's Lord Cam'brii?" he asked.

"Upstairs working. Why?"

"Turn that thing off. I've got something to say," he ordered.

Sarina took one look at his serious expression and commanded the computer, "End program." The colorful images abruptly stopped. "Raise lighting." When the room brightened, she turned to him. "What is it?" Teir had been politely formal ever since he'd brought her home from their night out. She couldn't help feeling hurt by his aloofness. Didn't he realize she'd chosen the only option available to her? How ironic that she was the one being honorable, when Teir was always so concerned about his duty! Curious as to what he had to say, she took a seat on the lounger, folded her hands in her lap, and waited.

Teir's glance swept over her lithe form. The loose caftan had settled revealingly on her curves. "I've got a way out for you, or at least a delaying tactic." He described his plan.

Her eyes filled with hope. "Do it," she said at once.

Teir jerked his thumb upward. "How do you think he'll react?"

"Rolf is barely speaking to me. He seems deeply troubled, and I think it has to do with whatever happened to him on Nadira. I think he'll tell me about it when he's ready, but it might be good for us to be separated for a time. Maybe he'll work out whatever it is that's bothering him and be ready to discuss it when I return." Sarina gave Teir a brilliant smile. "And I'd be very grateful for the delay." While she spoke calmly, her heart leapt with joy. If they got approval to go, she'd take every advantage of the opportunity to convince Teir to take her back to Earth! This could be the chance she'd been waiting for.

Wondering how she'd show her gratitude, Teir left to seek an audience with Glotaj. To his surprise, the Regent agreed to his plan at once. The Supreme Leader had the authority to make the decision without consulting his councilors, and he even went so far as to check on the status of Teir's ship himself.

"The *Valiant* is ready," he told Teir.

Teir wondered briefly why everything was going so smoothly, but he didn't question his luck. He headed back to Spiral Town to tell Sarina. And eight hauras later, they were on board his ship at Spacedock waiting for clearance to lift off.

"Too bad the rest of your crew couldn't come," Sarina said. She was seated in the copilot's chair beside him. Only she and Teir had received permission to visit Tendraa, so Ravi and the others had to remain behind.

"We'll manage," he said. He'd have her all to himself for the next five days. A quick visit to Tendraa, then they'd be alone again. Ten days altogether. He wasn't going to take advantage of Sarina since she'd stated her feelings so clearly, but it would give him the opportunity to enjoy her company. His every waking moment was filled with her image, and he couldn't seem to get enough of her. If he'd been offered the bodyguard detail now instead of six weeks ago, he'd snatch at it like a man dying of thirst would grab a carafe of water. She had become all-important to him.

They reached orbit shortly after lift-off, and Teir entered a course for the Tendraan system. An escort of four combat ships accompanied them. Teir consulted with the squadron leader, then turned to Sarina who was perusing the controls. She wore her hair loose, he noticed with approval, his gaze wandering down her sleek form.

"Well, here we are," he said with a broad grin, relaxing for the first time in days. The ship was on automatic pilot and he was free to give Sarina his full attention.

She glanced up at him from under her long lashes. "It was kind of you to do this for me, Teir."

"I said I'd try to help," he replied gruffly. "I don't know what this delay will accomplish, but maybe things will be clearer by the time we return."

"It will certainly give Rolf an opportunity to consider what he's getting into. Whatever happened to him on Nadira has affected him greatly. I don't think he's really considered our situation from a personal angle. Maybe he's realizing now that he's about to give up his freedom and wondering if it's worth it."

"Do you think he'd back out?" Teir asked hopefully.

Sarina shook her head. "He's a man of honor. He'll do his duty. Besides, he believes in the legend."

Teir felt uncomfortable discussing her relationship with Cam'brii. "Shall we retire to the lounge?" he suggested. "I could use a bite to eat."

"What are we going to do for five days?" she said, getting up to accompany him. "Are you always going to be busy with the ship? I can help, you know. I've learned quite a bit."

"I thought you were concentrating on health care."

"Yes, but I covered technical operations before that. The subliminal learning technique was quite efficient."

"Technical operations? Focusing on what?"

"Piloting, navigation."

He frowned, wondering at the extent of her knowledge and why she'd chosen that subject when there were so many others that would be more interesting to her.

"We won't need to work all the time," he said, entering the lounge. "Want a drink?" He suggested a mixed cocktail that he thought she would like. Her posture was tense. She needed to forget about Cam'brii and relax.

Sarina looked askance at the pale pink liquid sizzling in the crystal goblet. "What is it?"

"Go ahead, take a sip. Tell me what you think." He cradled his Arcturian brandy as he sat beside her at the table.

She bravely tried the strange beverage. "It tastes like cherries!"

"And what else?"

She wrinkled her nose. "A straight shot of gin."

"Gin?" he repeated with a puzzled frown.

"A liquor we have on Earth. It doesn't bubble, though."

Teir nodded. "Oroxian Zingers are pretty potent, so be careful how much you drink. The carbonation magnifies the effects of the intoxicant."

"I see you kept my mural," she said, nodding to the colorful picture on the wall.

He shrugged. "It brightens up the place."

"You could have told me that when I painted it. You acted as though you hated me."

"I never hated you," he said quietly. "On the contrary, I found you most desirable from the moment I first saw you."

Her heart pounded. "Don't, Teir. You know what my feelings are."

"Suppose you tell me again." He leaned forward. "How *do* you feel about me, Sarina?" He got a whiff of her perfume. The sensuous fragrance sent his blood boiling.

Looking into his clear azure gaze, Sarina knew she'd be lost if she revealed how she really felt. She wanted him, not Rolf, and not Robert, either, she realized suddenly. When had her affection for him actually dissipated? Had it been when he'd postponed their wedding until her promotion came through? Or had it been the disapproval he'd expressed about the welfare case she'd taken on? Maybe she'd never really loved Robert to begin with. Teir, on the other hand, inspired a tumult of emotions she'd never experienced before.

"Is the question that difficult to answer?" he asked gruffly.

"I was thinking about Robert." She saw the flicker of dismay cross his face and hastened to reassure him. "It's not that I miss him," she said. "I was just thinking that I'm really not in love with him, and wondering why I never realized it before. Maybe there wasn't much substance in our relationship to start with."

He didn't want to discuss Robert, but since Sarina seemed to need to talk, he asked, "What attracted you to him?"

She shrugged, thoughtful. "Well, he's conservative, ambitious, intelligent, very success-oriented. I admired his dedication to his job. And my mother approved," she added with a wry smile.

"Did you make love with him?"

Sarina glanced at him but his expression was impassive. "Of course. It was expected."

"Was it—good?"

She took a moment before answering. "We only made love a few times, and I'd never done it with anyone else. I suppose it was satisfactory."

"That's all? Just satisfactory?"

Sarina frowned. "Maybe I've been missing something."

"I'll say you have!" Teir leaned forward. "Let me show you, Sarina. I can make you feel what neither Robert nor Cam'brii ever will."

"He's a lot like Rolf, you know," she went on as though she hadn't heard him.

"Who is?"

"Robert. They're both totally dedicated to their jobs. Mother always said you have to be ruthless to succeed."

Teir sighed and leaned back, folding his hands behind his head. "What else did Mother say?"

"That I have to ignore the sufferings of those around me and concentrate on achieving my own goals. It was expected I would marry someone like Robert. When I introduced them, I saw instant approval in my mother's eyes."

Her mother must have wielded a lot of power, he thought. "And did you ever do what *you* wanted, purely for yourself?"

"What do you mean?"

"Hasn't it occurred to you that you've been following your mother's expectations all your life? What about your own interests and needs?"

She gazed at him, puzzled. "What about them?"

"You told me at one point that you wanted to be a doctor, but your mother discouraged you. She approved of Robert, so you got engaged. When are you going to follow your own heart's desire, Sarina Bretton?"

Sarina looked into his brilliant blue eyes, touched by how perceptive he was. And how thoughtful. Rolf didn't care enough about her to listen. His whole world revolved around the passage of the First Amendment. And Robert—Robert was part of her mother's legacy, one Sarina decided right then to cast away. He had been her mother's choice, not hers, she realized belatedly.

Feeling a weight lift from her shoulders, she regarded her darkly handsome companion. Teir was strong and courageous, yet he was also sensitive and kind. It was a potent combination. An urge grew within her, an urge to show her appreciation and to find out what she'd been missing all these years.

She tentatively extended her hand. "What if I start listening to my heart right now?" she whispered. "Can you show me to my cabin?"

Was that a spark of promise in her pearl gray eyes? "Of course," he said, rising.

Sarina stood and was surprised when the room swam in front of her. Staggering a little, she said, "Wow! You weren't kidding when you said that drink was potent."

"I'll help you." He came around the table and took her elbow, steering her toward the door.

"Whose cabin do I use?"

"You can have mine."

"That's very generous of you."

The glazed expression on her face brought out Teir's protective instincts. He drew her closer as they entered the corridor so she wouldn't trip over the steel ridging on the deck.

The ship's engines hummed beneath them, the vibration barely palpable, and Sarina's pulse thrummed in unison. Just being alone with Teir was enough to send her sensitivity level spiraling. That he was accompanying her to her sleeping quarters sent waves of heat rippling through her. Her flesh burned where he touched her. She couldn't wait until they reached the cabin.

The door hissed open at their approach. Inside, she whirled to face him. He was so close she could smell his masculine scent. "Teir—"

"Sssh, *larla*, let me give you what you want." He bent his swooped head and kissed her.

Sarina felt dizzy, but she was aware enough to part her lips. Teir instantly plundered her sweetness, as one hand supported the back of her head, and the other encircled her waist. She swayed against him, overwhelmed by her need to be closer. He responded by rubbing his lean and powerful body against hers. His broad chest brushed her nipples with teasing strokes, and she felt a hard bulge prodding her thigh. Knowing he was aroused fired her passion even more.

Stifling a moan, Sarina moved her mouth urgently under his. He tasted like brandy, and the strong flavor only served to inflame her desire. Her hands grasped at his hair. *So this is what I've been missing*, she thought in a haze of passion. But it wasn't enough. She wanted more.

Teir moved her over to the bunk. She didn't protest when he gently lowered her and stretched out beside her. His hot breath seared her neck as he whispered her name and kissed her throat. Sarina's head rolled back as he flicked his tongue across her sensitive skin, sending swirls of delight along her nerves. Then his mouth moved up to capture hers as his hand slipped inside the front fastening of her dress.

Sarina gasped as he found her breast. He began tracing her curves, slowly running his fingers over her breast and then down her cleavage. When his fingers brushed her nipple, Sarina moaned and grasped his back. Each time he stroked her, she could feel the muscular ridges rippling under his shirt. The ache between her thighs intensified into a raging storm of desire.

As though he sensed her need, Teir crouched at the foot of the bunk and slowly pulled off her dress. Underneath, she wore nothing but a pair of lace panties.

Unable to control his hunger for her any longer, he yanked off the remaining barrier and buried his head in her triangle of golden hair. Her musky feminine scent drove him wild. He gazed at her, knowing his eyes must be half crazed with passion. Sarina's mouth curved into a smile of pure feminine power, as she opened herself to him.

She was more beautiful than he could have imagined. Touching her sensitive folds, he was gratified by her moan of pleasure.

As he continued to stroke her, she felt herself spiraling toward mindless ecstasy, and was barely aware when he stretched himself across her, having cast off his clothes. His weight was a pleasure almost too great to bear, especially when he ground his hips against her.

"Take me, Sarina. I can't wait any longer."

She grasped his shaft and with a forceful thrust, he entered her.

"Oh, God," Sarina moaned, wrapping her legs around him, straining to get closer. His breath came ragged and fast as he surged inside her, and she joined him in the ageless rhythm of the universe. She gasped as he thrust harder.

Crying her name, his passion exploded. Feeling his molten heat pour into her, she reached her own sublime ecstasy as shudders of pleasure wracked her body.

At last the spasms subsided. She lay, too exhausted to move.

Teir traced his finger along her breast. A thin sheen of perspiration covered her skin. "I always knew it would be wonderful. We shouldn't have waited so long." His breath was coming under control, but his pulse was still racing. She affected him, even now.

She gazed at him with a lazy half-smile. "You're mine for the whole trip. Now that I know what I've been missing, I don't intend to give you a moment's peace!"

He responded with a kiss, afraid that if he spoke he'd reveal his fears. When this voyage was over, he would lose her. She'd have to be returned to Lord Cam'brii.

*   *   *

The next four days were full of desperate love-making. Sarina, too, realized their time together was precious. She didn't know what the future would hold, but she couldn't deny herself any longer where Teir was concerned. He filled her days and nights with ecstasy. Neither one said any words of commitment. It was understood they'd discuss the situation later, on the way back.

That day got closer when the computer signaled the approach into the Tendraan system and Sarina had to face her destiny once again.

In the city of Ingorr on the planet Tendraa, Mantra drew his cloak tighter around his trembling limbs. He'd recovered from his illness, but now his family faced the danger of starvation. Shaking from hunger and fatigue, he despaired of the prophecy ever coming true.

He was foraging in his father's supply station, hoping to find food the looters had missed. It was the first time he'd been out since his return home, for the law stated that if infected persons did not die, their house must remained closed until four weeks after recovery to make certain everyone inside was well. Zunis had been taken to the burial pit some six weeks ago, but Mantra had slowly healed. Their household had just been certified as free of the pestilence.

Not long after the Examiner left, another member of the family had fallen ill, and by not reporting Malika's sickness and Mantra's leaving the house, they were breaking the law. But his family was desperate for food and supplies, and he had had to come to Father's shop. Their rations were barely enough to feed the four of them. How could anyone survive on tubers and a cruet of wine a day? He also hoped to consult a caretaker if he could find one. The posset-drink that had soothed his distemper might be made available to his mother, and he needed to purchase more herbs to fumigate her chamber.

A horn sounded, and Mantra stiffened. When he heard it again, his shoulders slumped in relief. It was just a raker coming to clean the street. He wondered why they bothered. The stench of sewage permeated the city, and even the cold air couldn't dispel it. But the Baynor had ordered the filth to be swept away daily by the rakers, and along with many of the other laws issued by the city's leader to stop the spread of the contagion, nothing worked.

He stepped deeper into the shadows of the room until the scraping noises receded. The floor timbers creaked, and rats scurried about. Soon we'll be forced to eat those horrid creatures, Mantra thought dismally. The shelves were bare; there was nothing left. Only his father's secret cache remained to be checked.

Withdrawing a key from the folds of his robe, Mantra approached the hidden cupboard at the rear of the shop and swung aside the concealing shelf that had once held aromatic spices. A small wooden door set into the wall was still locked.

His heart thumping excitedly, Mantra fit the key into the hole and twisted it. The door swung open, and he gasped as he took in the stash of supplies. By the faith, now they could survive another month!

Casting a furtive glance over his shoulder, Mantra quickly stuffed the contents of the shelves into the wide sash he'd brought for that purpose. Then he tied it about his waist and drew his robe around him. No one would be the wiser should he meet anyone on the street, he figured. Not that there was much risk of that. The city was all but deserted.

He closed the hiding place and started for the front door.

"You, there! Who goes?" a voice called from outside.

Mantra froze in his tracks, realizing he must be visible through the broken glass of the front window.

Someone must have spotted his movements in the darkened interior.

Terrified of being caught with his hoard, Mantra tightened his robe about his body. Then he stepped outside into the twilight. "It is I, Mantra, son of Naars." Three figures approached slowly down the cobblestone street—two humans and one of his own kind.

Humans? Mantra's eyes widened. Inside their shimmering energy shields, they were strangely garbed, both wearing tight leggings and loose tops. The taller one wore boots. As they came closer, Mantra noticed that the smaller one was a female. Her golden hair was pulled into a tight braid down her back. And the Honorable Baynor himself was accompanying them! The Tendraan was lavishly dressed in a cloak and doublet of amber velvet woven with gold and decorated with ruffles of colbertine, leather shoes to match his white silk hose, and a flowing silver wig. Around his throat was an elaborate lace cravat. The visitors must be important indeed to have lured the Baynor out of the sanctity of his keep, Mantra thought with awe.

"Come forward," the Baynor commanded. "Our guests wish to meet the populace and no one else is about." He pressed a thick cloth to his nose and mouth to prevent contamination.

Mantra stooped as though his back hurt in order to hide the bulge at his midsection. Slowly, he shuffled in their direction.

"Mantra, son of Naars, you have the supreme honor of meeting our wondrous Great Healer. She is the holy one who responded to the sacred light of the Auricle. Show your reverence!" the Baynor ordered.

Mantra gaped as he stared at the female. Her large gray eyes looked back, steady and kind. In them he noticed a special spark, a ray of promise for his people. Truly, she was a princess of the stars!

He fell to the ground, pressing his forehead to the

slime running in the street. "Oh, Great One, how we have prayed for your presence! Save us!"

"Please get up," her sweet voice crooned. "My name is Sarina Bretton. I wish to learn of your problems."

"Don't get too close," her companion warned. He was a dark haired fellow with a stern face and piercing blue eyes. He looked intently at Mantra. "Are you by any chance cousin to Ravi, son of Shay?"

"Aye," Mantra said, rising. "What of him?"

"He has been frantic with worry. When communications terminated, he feared for you and your family." He saw Mantra's wary look. "I'm Captain Teir Reylock of the *Valiant*. Ravi is my first mate."

"Captain Reylock!" Mantra was even more stunned at meeting him than Sarina. "It is an honor, Captain. Ravi is fortunate to serve you. Has he accompanied you?"

"No. Only Sarina and myself were allowed to come."

"I'm so happy to see you are well," Sarina said. "Ravi will be relieved. What about your family?"

"Alas, my father and younger sister succumbed to the Farg. I, too, was afflicted, but was fortunate enough to recover."

"Abide you near here, citizen?" the Baynor interrupted.

"Aye," Mantra replied cautiously. Despite the honor of meeting them, he didn't want his own transgressions discovered.

"The time of airing has passed?"

"It has."

"Then show us your dwelling."

"But—"

"I'd like to see how you live," the Great Healer told him with a smile. "And I'm sure Ravi will be interested in a full report—if you don't mind."

Afraid to refuse, Mantra led them down the twisting paths. "In here," he pointed to one house, "all are dead, and the dwelling stands open. No one dares go inside."

He indicated several other houses as they passed. "A man and his wife and their five children, all are gone in that one. Look across the street—the place is shut up. A watchman guards the door." His voice lowered. "I know the family inside. The son and I shared schooling in our younger days." And so he continued as they moved along, showing the Great Healer the horrors of the Farg.

As they rounded the corner onto his street, Mantra's steps faltered. If the Baynor entered his home, he'd discover that Malika was ill. He'd order the dwelling shut at once, and the occupants fined. It wasn't fair, Mantra thought. He'd survived the plague. He should be allowed his freedom.

At the doorway, he stopped. "It may not be safe for you to enter," he told them. "We've just been cleared of the pestilence as of last eve." Malika had taken sick that morn. She'd complained of a sudden violent pain in her head. Then a quarter of an hour later she'd vomited. Putting her to bed, Kairi had noticed the fatal sign on her mother's thigh. Death had been known to occur within hours of such affliction, and Mantra was frightened that she might already be dead.

The Baynor, who still held a scented cloth to his face, nodded in understanding. "The contagion is fierce, Captain Reylock," he said in a raspy tone. "Mantra may be right. The protective shields have not done much good on other worlds."

Sarina answered, her voice firm. "We accepted the risk in coming here, Your Honor. I want to meet the people, and I can't do that if I remain in your home or in the grand palace of your Liege Lord. Show us inside, Mantra."

Nervously, the Baynor glanced at the faded red warning circle painted on the door. "I'll stand guard out here," he quavered, clutching the cloth to his face.

Taking long shuddering breaths, he stepped back a few paces. "I would suggest you not take too long. The noxious vapors might still be hovering about this wretched house." Fearfully, his eyes darted as though he could actually catch sight of the pestilence.

Mantra glanced at the two humans. The man's eyes flickered indecisively, as though he were deciding if it was safe to enter.

"Let's go," Sarina said impatiently, nudging him.

Mantra pushed open the heavy door. At once, he heard his mother's moaning from upstairs. A wave of relief washed over him. At least she was still alive! Hastily, he ushered the visitors inside and closed the door so the Baynor wouldn't hear.

"What's that noise?" Teir growled, feeling the walls close in on him. This had been a stupid idea. The Baynor was right—they had no assurance that the protective shields would work.

Mantra turned to them. "I pray you will not tell the Baynor about my mother's illness," he whispered. He fell to his knees and folded his hands in supplication. "She has been afflicted with the Farg. Please heal her." Tears ran down his cheeks. "We have lost two in our family already, and I fear Malika may be next. Save her, Great Healer!"

Sarina's eyes moistened at his distress. What a sad world, desolate of life and joy, filled instead with sickness and despair! She prayed with all her soul she'd be able to help him.

"Take me to her," she said softly.

Mantra led her up a flight of stairs, Teir trailing behind. Sarina was aware of the risk, but it was worth it if she could help these people. She desperately wanted to be a healer in their hour of need. Maybe the power *was* within her, needing only a powerful emotion to release it. That she had to fall in love might be a misinterpretation. She wouldn't know unless she tried to heal someone, and this was the best chance she'd ever be likely to get.

Flickering lamplight lit the way up the creaky wooden staircase. The moans increased in volume as they ascended. A strange, foul odor met her nostrils at the landing, and Sarina hesitated. Maybe this hadn't been such a good idea after all. Behind her, Teir coughed. She glanced back at him and saw his glowering expression. She shrugged halfheartedly as though to say, *Sorry, but I have to try.*

When they entered the room, Sarina saw a frail female with scraggly auburn hair writhing on a narrow pallet. Her struggles and groans proclaimed her agony. A lamp burning on the floor cast a sickly illumination upon her anguished face. She rambled incoherently, mumblings that Sarina's implanted translator couldn't begin to interpret.

The air in the chamber was stifling—the protective energy shield acted as a filter for microbes but didn't provide a screen against the atmosphere in any other way. A fire blazed in the fireplace under pans and plates holding burning bulbs. Sulfur sticks smouldered around the room, emitting an odor of rotten eggs mixed with putrid smoke. Sarina raised her hand to her mouth to prevent herself from gagging.

A slender young female rose from the bedside. She'd been pressing a cool cloth to the older one's forehead.

"Kairi, what are you doing here?" Mantra cried. "I said I'd be gone just a half-sun. You should have remained in your chamber!"

"Mother was in distress. I had to do something, brother."

"Where is Sita?"

"In our chamber, as usual." Her words were bitter, and Sarina gathered Sita was another sister. The girl's large emerald eyes rested on her. "Who is this stranger you bring among us, Mantra? An offworlder?"

Mantra strode forward and clutched Kairi's arm. "This is the answer to our prayers, the Great Healer, sister!"

Kairi stared in shock. "It cannot be!"

"Truly, she has come to help us."

The girl fell to her knees and raised her hands. "Thank the heavens! We are saved!"

"Please, get up," Sarina said. "Let me see your mother. How long has she been ill?"

"Since this morn," Mantra said. "She took sick of a sudden." Describing her symptoms, he said, "Now her body shakes as though the groundcrust trembles. Alas, I fear she is lost unless you can heal her. Please tend to her, oh Great One!"

"I'll have to shut off my bioshield."

"Don't, Sarina!" Teir rushed toward her.

She whirled around, and saw his ghostly pale face. "It's the only way. The protective shield might inhibit my power. I have to take the risk."

"We didn't come here for this purpose," Teir reminded her in a low tone.

"I know," Sarina said. Their original goal had been merely to postpone her marriage. But the excuse Teir gave to Glotaj was valid. She needed to be tested for her own peace of mind. "If there is any truth to the legend, we will find out now," she hissed. Anything that could help her avoid the execution decree was worth trying.

Teir stared at her. If he believed at all in the legend, he'd have no qualms. But he'd never given credence to magic or myths—at least, not until the cut on his arm had mysteriously healed after she'd touched it. If she had developed the healing power, it must mean she'd fallen in love with Lord Cam'brii!

Though the thought was abhorrent to him, he said, "All right. But reactivate the shield as soon as you're done."

Nodding curtly, Sarina switched off the shimmering bioshield, then approached the sick woman's bedside.

She put a hand to Malika's neck. Her hide was burning hot. The female's lips were dry and parched, her open eyes glassy. "What treatments are you using?"

"We are purifying the air with sulfur and other detoxifying herbs, Mistress," Kairi said. "And I have put a poultice upon her tumor."

"May I see it?" Sarina knew she would be upset, but she had to know what she was dealing with.

Gently, Kairi pulled back the coverlet and raised her mother's nightgown. A festering black boil covered her inner thigh. "Can you not heal her now?" Kairi asked, covering Malika.

Sarina sat on the bed, closing her eyes and taking the ill woman's hand. Ignoring Malika's tremors, Sarina prayed for her power to materialize. She clutched the woman's hand tighter. Malika still burned, still shook. The minutes ticked by.

Sarina's eyes snapped open. "I'm sorry," she sighed. "It's not working. There's nothing I can do."

"What?" Mantra cried, hovering above her. "You are the Great Healer. You must save her!"

"No." Sarina shook her head. "I have no special power."

"That is untrue! According to the Baynor, you are The One. You answered the light from the Auricle."

Sarina rose and placed her hand on his shoulder. "I am touched by your faith, Mantra, but it is misplaced. I cannot be more than I am. And what I am is an ordinary Earthwoman." A deep pit of sadness yawned within her. "Truly, I wish I could help."

"Let's get out of here," Teir growled. He must have been mistaken about the cut on his arm. Perhaps Sarina had seen bark fragments from the Twygg on his skin, and in the frenzy of battle, she'd assumed he had been wounded and that it was blood. Her healing power didn't exist. Either she still needed more time to fall in love with Cam'brii, or the legend was false. "Activate your bioshield," he told her, panicking. "You have been exposed to the Farg!"

"I need to wash my hands first." Sarina glanced

about the room, looking for a sanitary but not finding one. The lighting was poor at best, and parts of the chamber were cast in shadow. Outside, there was a perpetual cold twilight which Teir had told her upon their arrival existed due to Tendraa's great distance from its sun. What little rays there were couldn't penetrate the soot-covered windows. Flickering lamplight and the crackling fire provided some illumination, but the burning herbs and pungent smoke created a haze inside the room. Nevertheless, Sarina noticed the piles of dirt on the wood-planked floor.

Walking around, she found a tall commode, on top of which was a basin of water. Brown flecks dotted the liquid's surface. A cup, half-filled with cloudy water, rested beside it. Sarina washed her hands in the basin, then searched for a towel. A filthy rag lay on a low chest of drawers. Grimacing, she used it. Conditions might be primitive by her standards, but she knew from the knowledge she had gained from the study center that they'd be considered absolutely prehistoric by some of the more advanced Coalition cultures. Perhaps she could still be helpful after all.

"Come on!" Teir urged. He was going to throw up if he stayed a moment longer. Fighting a known enemy was one thing; standing helpless in a sickroom was another.

"Just a minute," Sarina said, irritated. She approached Kairi and Mantra who had been conferring quietly at their mother's bedside. "I might not have any magic," she told them, "but I do have some suggestions that could help."

They both regarded her with skepticism.

"Ventilation is a number one priority. Can these windows be opened?"

"We dare not!" Mantra said. "If anybody heard our mother cry out, they would report us. We'd be quarantined again!"

Sarina gave him a reproachful look. "Suppose you tell me about this method of dealing with the plague." When Mantra finished his horrifying pronouncements, Sarina promised her silence. "I won't tell the Baynor if you promise to carry out my instructions," she said. It was awful how the healthy were confined with the sick. She could understand the need for quarantine, but other methods of disease prevention might work better without causing so much suffering.

Kairi's hand slipped into her brother's. "Tell us what we must do, Mistress," she whispered. "We shall obey."

"As I said, ventilation is important. It's very smoky in here. Has the chimney been cleaned lately?" At Mantra's shaking of his head, she said, "That's number one. Try to open windows if you can, but avoid drafts and keep your mother warm. Fresh water is next. Where do you get your supply?"

"We have a well out back," Mantra replied, his expression showing her that he was absorbing every word.

Sarina instructed him in the technique of boiling water, stressing that the sick woman must be given frequent sips of cooled liquid. Sanitation measures were next, from housecleaning to personal bathing to handwashing.

"How is the contagion spread?" she asked.

"The very air is corrupted by noxious vapors," Mantra said, giving her a look of surprise.

"Where do the vapors originate?"

"Why, from the soil, of course. The poisonous efflux enters the air and is caught by the viscous humors of the body. This puts the blood into an immediate ferment and agitates the spirit."

"What do you mean by humors of the body?"

Mantra and his sister exchanged a look of amazement. "The humors must remain in equilibrium for a person to be healthy. There are four—yellow bile, black bile, phlegm, and blood. They correspond to the four elements of the universe, which are fire, earth, water, and air. The sickness is brought about by a disruption of the elements. In this case, air."

"So how is catching the disease prevented? No one wears masks or take any precautions against airborne transmission that I can see."

Mantra pointed to the fireplace. "The fire helps to fumigate the chamber. By their nitrous streams, the burning sulfur sticks change the nature of the poisonous efflux should it be received by the body. We carry cloths—" he pulled one from a pocket in his robe "—scented with the attar of flowers to refresh the spirit. Holding the cloth over your nose when you are outside helps to avoid contact with the corrupt air." He glanced at her. "There are many other practices, but nothing seems to work."

"I can believe it," Sarina muttered. No wonder these people were so sick. Their treatments were based on erroneous theories about the causation of disease. Since she wasn't sure what caused the Farg, she could only offer general advice.

"If you follow my instructions, it may help. You've already had the disease," she said to Mantra, "but your sister hasn't. Keep her away from your mother. Wash your hands after every contact with her. And get some fresh air in here! You may not believe it, but stale air like this can harbor germs, not the other way around. See what happens if you follow my suggestions."

Someone stumbled through the doorway and Sarina whirled around. "It is my oldest sister Sita," Mantra said, stiffly introducing them.

The girl leaned against the doorjamb, a sardonic look on her face. Her features resembled Kairi's, but without any of the softness. Lines of strain showed under her heavy makeup.

"The Great Healer, is it?" Sita drawled, adjusting her garment, a canary yellow drape that clung to her ample curves. "Have you cured my mother yet?"

She spoke to Sarina, but her interested glance was directed at Teir.

"I'm afraid not," Sarina replied, "but I've given some suggestions that might help. I'll talk to the Baynor to see that you receive adequate supplies."

Kairi came forward, her hand outstretched in gratitude. Sarina took it and squeezed it in her own.

"Thank you, Mistress," Kairi said. "You came to us without fear. That alone gives us hope."

"Perhaps you can convince the Liege Lord of Tendraa to consider a full partnership in the Coalition," Mantra offered, hope kindling in his breast. The Earthwoman might not have any healing power, but she did have influence. The Coalition doctors might be able to teach his people newer methods for treating the distemper.

"I don't know," Sarina said doubtfully. "We only have permission to meet with your Baynor and view the city." She swallowed a lump in her throat. "I'll see that Ravi gets your news." Unable to think of anything else to say, she switched on her bioshield and prepared to leave.

"Wish my cousin well, Mistress," Mantra said. "Would that I could tell him so myself!"

Thinking of Ravi reminded Sarina of all she faced upon her return to Bimordus Two. As she walked back to the ship beside Teir, a heavy weight of gloom settled over her.

Immediately upon her return to Bimordus Central, she'd be forced to marry Rolf. Less than ten months later would come her execution. The latter event seemed inevitable after her failure with Malika.

She glanced at Teir's firm profile. He had tried to help her, she thought. He'd shown her the depth of his feelings for her, even if he hadn't mentioned any words of love. Neither had she, because her emotions hadn't fully crystallized in her own mind yet. She only knew for certain that she couldn't accept a loveless marriage.

They'd put off discussing their future until the trip home. Well, now it was time. She wondered if Teir would agree to what she was going to ask.

Chapter Ten

"I feel as though microbes are crawling all over my body," Teir muttered when they were seated in the command chairs on the bridge of the *Valiant*. He was monitoring the helm controls as they headed out of orbit at sublight speed. Their bioshields had been removed, but they couldn't bathe until the ship was on automatic pilot. "That was the worst world I've ever visited," he added, shuddering.

Sarina grimaced. "The living conditions on Tendraa are primitive even by Earth's standards. I can't understand why their leaders would allow them to remain that way."

"It was a choice the Tendraans made years ago after the Techno War nearly destroyed the planet. You'd think they would have made some progress since then, however."

"According to what Ravi said, progress is anathema to his people." She brushed her hand through her hair. She'd untwisted her braid, and the waves fell down her back. The strands were thick with grime from the world they'd just left.

"Mantra doesn't think so, and there are probably others like him. Tendraa is rich in minerals, and they have a trade agreement with the Coalition. Where do you suppose all the profits go?" Teir raised his eyebrow. "You saw how the Baynor was dressed."

Sarina gasped. "Do you really believe the leaders are hoarding the riches for themselves and keeping their people in ignorance on purpose?"

Teir shrugged. "I'm highly suspicious, that's all. But it's not our business, and if I have any choice in the matter, I hope never to return there."

"Don't let Ravi hear you say that."

"But he agrees with me! He sees complacency as a problem, and unfortunately it's one that is not confined to his planet. Daimon and his group would have liked to maintain the status quo. The ROF came into being because too many changes were hitting the Coalition at once: expansion, threats from outsiders, the Farg. The ROF is responding the same way the Tendraans did—go back to an earlier era. They propose to dissolve the Coalition and let each species fend for themselves. It's isolationism and regression combined, and you've seen what that philosophy has done on Tendraa."

Sarina gazed out the large viewscreen. Tendraa was receding in the distance. From here, it appeared as a large yellowish globe. Cloud belts intermittently covered the surface. A huge brown spot was evident on the northern hemisphere, but a gaseous haze obscured the lower regions. It didn't offer much beauty, not like Earth. She missed the vast blue oceans and green forests of her home. Even Bimordus Central, the dazzling capital city, was built on a barren planetoid. All plant life there was artificially grown.

"Teir," she said, turning to him with a pleading look, "let's not go back to Bimordus Two. I'm not the answer to the Coalition's problems. You've seen that my power doesn't exist. I'm not the Great Healer, and I'll be executed just because I am an ordinary Earthwoman. Please, take me home!"

"You're forgetting what the legend has foretold," he replied in a gentle tone. "Your power will be activated when you fall in love. You just need more time."

"I'll never fall in love with Rolf!"

"You don't know that for certain."

"Why do you want me to return to him? I thought you cared about me."

"I do, Sarina, but it's not my place to interfere with the legend."

"Even if it means my death? All you have to do is transport me to Earth. I'm sure you can think of a way to elude our escort."

"We've gone over this before. I will not take you back to Earth. The subject is closed." He set his mouth in a firm line.

"Then take me someplace else," Sarina suggested. "It doesn't matter where, as long as the High Council can't find me."

He regarded her with a veiled expression. Despite the soot that smeared her face, she was lovely, with her wide silvery eyes and sweet curved mouth. He yearned to do what she asked, to take her safely away from all threats of any kind. But his obligation to the Coalition was clear. His duty was to deliver her back to the High Council for her marriage to Lord Cam'brii. This delay had accomplished nothing except to cause them both more pain.

Hoping to avoid further argument, he put off giving a direct answer.

"Let's discuss it after we get cleaned up," he hedged. "The ship's computer can take over now."

His fingers flew over the nav pad as he programmed in the course coordinates for Bimordus Two, and he initiated the jump to warp speed. The *Valiant* shot into interstellar space so fast that Teir nearly missed the blip on his radar screen.

"Did you catch that sensor reading on your monitors?" he radioed to the squadron leader escorting them. The four combat ships had assumed position as soon as they'd left orbit.

"Briefly, sir, but I couldn't get a fix on it."

"I got the impression the range was rather broad."

"More than one ship entering the system?" The officer's tone implied that was nothing unusual.

"Many more." Teir frowned. He hadn't received any communiques indicating a large squadron of ships was on its way. He and Sarina might not have been given permission to go to Tendraa if that were the case. Was it possible Defense League Command didn't know?

Out of the corner of his eye, he saw Sarina leave her seat, probably heading for the sanitary. He couldn't wait to wash off the remnants of their visit to Tendraa himself. Hurriedly cutting off communications, he rose and followed her.

The sensor reading was forgotten entirely as soon as he glimpsed Sarina in her dressing gown. He'd gotten cleansed and walked into his cabin to find her standing beside the fabricator. Apparently she was trying to decide what to wear. Her blond hair was still damp, hanging in moist strands down her back.

Clad only in a towel, Teir came up behind her and slipped the silken gown off her shoulders. "Mmm," he murmured, kissing her neck. "I've been waiting all day for this. You taste delicious."

Sarina, who had intended to continue their discussion, was easily swayed from her purpose. She let the gown fall to the floor, and thus commenced four more days of lovemaking. Teir was content to enjoy her without worrying about the future, and he kept Sarina distracted so that she didn't have a chance to bring the subject up.

It wasn't until the last day that Sarina found herself alone on the bridge. Teir had gone below to check a linear actuator on Deck Two. She glanced around, wondering if there were something useful she could do. Her eye wandered to the nav console, and she realized they'd never finished their discussion about destinations. Wondering where Teir had decided to take her, she went over to check the coordinates.

"We're on our way to the Bimordus system!" she cried when Teir returned.

She stood with her hands on her hips, her eyes blazing.

"We are returning to Bimordus Two," he acknowledged quietly. "Our trip was just a brief delay. You knew that."

"But I asked you to consider taking me someplace else. I don't want to marry Rolf!" Her voice was accusatory. She couldn't accept a loveless marriage after what they'd experienced together. Didn't he understand that?

"You might still fall in love with him. If there is any truth to the legend, you have to give the councilor a chance."

It was his fault she was turning away from Cam'brii, Teir realized. Making love to her had satisfied his selfish need but was impeding the prophecy's natural progress. In simpler terms, he was in the way. Did he really want to be the one responsible for the Coalition's downfall? That would be the end result if he heeded her plea.

Wrestling with his conscience, he made a painful decision. It was time for him to step aside, and in so doing, give Sarina back to Lord Cam'brii. Though it grieved him deeply, he decided the easiest way was to pretend he didn't care for her. She hated it whenever she heard the word duty, so he'd use that against her.

"It is your duty as Great Healer to form the alliance," he stated in a flat tone. "I cannot countermand my orders, and those are to protect you and return you safely to the High Council." He stood stiffly, his eyes forward. If he looked at her, his resolve might weaken.

"How can you send me into another man's arms, after all we've shared?" she cried, fear striking her heart at his cold demeanor. "You'll be dooming me to a life with a man I can never love! I thought you felt something for me."

Teir's gut twisted. It made him sick to think of her in the councilor's bed. But he merely shrugged. "I'll still be around when Cam'brii bores you."

"Bastard!" she shrieked. "You don't even care that I'll be killed? They'll condemn me because I'm not the Great Healer!"

He hardened his heart against her fury, knowing that he had to provoke her hatred in order for her to return willingly to Lord Cam'brii. "Your disposition is for the High Council to decide," he told her curtly.

Sarina picked up the nearest object, a metal astrocompass, and threw it at him.

He dodged to the side, cringing when the object hit the console behind him with a loud clang. Sarina snorted in disgust and stormed from the bridge. Letting out a breath of relief, he sank into his seat.

He focused on the ship's controls. The *Valiant* was entering orbit around Bimordus Two when Sarina returned to the bridge holding two crystal goblets of wine. She wore a transparent gown of rose-colored gossamer silk, and her golden hair flowed about her shoulders. "A peace offering," she said, giving him a sweet smile. "I understand your devotion to duty, Teir. I'm sorry if I angered you."

He regarded her with suspicion. "What's this all about, Sarina?"

"I decided our relationship doesn't have to end just because I'm going to wed Rolf. As you said, he'll probably bore me. Shall we drink a toast to our continued—friendship?"

Teir sensed she was up to something, but it was hard to concentrate when he could see her body through the thin material of her gown. Even one day without bedding her was like a lifetime of deprivation. He felt himself responding with an irresistible physical urge.

"All right," he said cautiously, standing and accepting the goblet from her outstretched hand. They clinked glasses and drank.

"Shall we retire to the cabin for one last time?" she suggested in a husky voice. Her long lashes shaded her eyes, and he couldn't read her expression. But her sensuous movements were unmistakable in intent.

Teir wet his lips. "We're entering orbit—"

"You don't have to initiate the landing sequence just yet. Can't it wait for one more haura?" Sarina rubbed up against him, sliding her leg along the outside of his thigh. Her warmth penetrated even through his clothes.

"Why are you doing this?" he rasped. It would only make it more difficult for them to part.

"I want you, Teir." Her eyes glittered amorously. "I'll have you any way I can." She held out her hand.

He leaned over the console, putting the landing on hold, and followed her from the bridge.

Hauras later, Teir was wishing he could push back the chronometer to the scene on the *Valiant* and change his response. He was in the communications room at Defense League Station on Bimordus Central, a furious headache pounding in his skull. But it was nothing compared to his rage.

"Reylock?" Admiral Daras Gog roared over the comm unit. "You there?"

"Yes, sir."

"What in the fires of Alpha Gomaran Two is going on?"

Teir's mouth tightened. "Sarina slipped something into my drink, Admiral. She put me in a shuttle, probably by using the mini-levitator we have on board, and programmed it to land on Bimordus

Two. I woke up when a technician in the shuttle bay broke open the door."

"And the *Valiant*?"

"Stolen, sir. Apparently Sarina tricked our escort as well. She used a digitized facsimile of my voice to order the squadron leader to follow the shuttle down." Or so he had been told after he'd regained consciousness.

What a fool he'd been! His head still reeled from the sleeping potion she'd put into his wine. He'd been right to be suspicious about her abrupt change in behavior. Her seduction scene was merely a ploy to throw him off guard. Now she'd stolen his ship and possibly ruined his career. Entrusted with her safety, he'd failed miserably. Teir wouldn't be surprised if a court-martial was in order from the mess he'd created.

"I'll go after her," he growled. "Requisition me a fast patrol ship, and I'll get right on her tail."

"No," the Admiral answered. "The High Council has called an emergency meeting to decide what they want done. You are to report to the Great Hall for a debriefing immediately after we sign off. They will decide what disciplinary action is needed." His voice lowered. "I'm very disappointed in you, Captain. What would provoke the woman to do such a thing?"

"She's always wanted to go home, Admiral."

"If you knew that, you should have taken extra precautions to secure her return to Bimordus Two. You were extremely negligent in your duty."

Teir's hands curled into fists. "I'll make up for it. I can—"

"You'll do nothing! If the High Council releases you, I've got a different assignment for you and your crew."

"What?" Teir replied, stunned.

"We've had a distress call from the Matiaus system. The series of quakes on Mat Four have escalated. The colonists need a supply of bimanthium krystals.

Our only available source right now is on Lapis, and they're in a hostage situation. You're the only one who can defuse this fiasco and get the krystals to Mat Four on time."

"But Sarina—"

"I'll give you two weeks, Reylock. After that, the tectonic plates on Mat Four will start to separate. We don't have the resources available for a mass evacuation."

"Sir, let me detour to Earth first. I'm sure I can retrieve Sarina and then accomplish this mission." He couldn't believe what he was hearing. Not go after the woman? After what she'd done to him? Blast her to Zor!

Admiral Gog's voice came through clear and strong. "Understand something, Captain. Should you make any attempt to retrieve Sarina Bretton, you'll be thrown out of the force." He paused to let his words sink in. "Now, do I have your cooperation?"

"Yes, sir," Teir croaked. He signed off after promising to get the details of his new assignment later.

With great trepidation, he approached the immense set of double doors at the right wing of the Great Hall. The entrance led to the Council Chamber. Inside, the twelve members of the High Council would be preparing for his inquisition.

Swallowing hard, he entered.

The councilors sat in a circle with Glotaj on an elevated throne at the far end. Teir was directed to stand in the center of the circle, facing the Supreme Leader. Feeling like a criminal, he complied. Out of the corner of his eye he glimpsed Mara, Sarina's friend, standing off to the side.

"Report, Captain Reylock," the Regent commanded. Glotaj's sharp blue eyes pierced his as though they could bore the truth out of him.

Teir told them what had happened, leaving out any hint of a personal relationship between him and

Sarina. He blamed her actions purely on her desire to go home.

Lord Cam'brii spoke first. The councilor's eyes were like two chunks of blue ice. "Are you certain nothing unusual happened on the voyage to provoke her actions, Captain?"

Teir sensed the underlying message, and he felt his face flush. "She was upset by the horrors on Tendraa. Her power didn't materialize, and she feared the execution decree. I suppose she felt her only viable alternative was to flee."

Emu shot up from his seat, his thin Sirisian body elongating as he bent forward. "We must retrieve her! The prophecy may still come to pass!"

Daimon's hard-edged voice grated an answer. "I say leave well enough alone. She's not the Great Healer. Let her stay on Earth."

Teir saw Emu's pink skin redden, as he bobbed his bald head in its ruby turban. "We will never know if she is the Great Healer unless we give her the chance to prove herself. Just because she failed on Tendraa does not mean she is not The One. According to the legend, she must fall in love for her power to activate. She probably needs more time. I say the marriage ceremony should take place as scheduled."

Daimon stood slowly and stroked his beard. "You would still wed her, knowing she has run away?" he asked Lord Cam'brii.

The blond councilor nodded. "Sarina is my responsibility. If she returns, I will fulfill my duty. Do we know for certain she is heading for Earth?"

"Mara," Glotaj called to the tall dark-haired female waiting patiently to be summoned.

Mara's homeplanet was Tyberia where the people possessed extrasensory ability. They were able to sense another's emotions, but Mara's power went beyond that. She could actually separate her spirit from her body and travel along the astral plane to project herself into another's life space. This allowed her to see through the other person's eyes. She rarely used her gift, but since Sarina was her friend, she'd readily agreed to the High Council's request for aid.

Mara stepped into the brightly lit circle. "I am ready." She closed her eyes and tilted her head back. No one spoke. Teir saw she was holding something in her hand—a jeweled comb, one like Sarina had worn. He recalled Sarina telling him that Mara needed to hold an object touched by the person in order to trigger her separation.

Through the comb, Mara homed in on Sarina's psychic vibrations. Her ability let her into Sarina's mind, so that she could watch events as they unfolded from her perspective. Mara couldn't picture what had come before or what would happen thereafter—only the immediate present was visible.

An image came to her. "I see what she sees," Mara intoned. "I am on the bridge of a ship, monitoring the controls. Now I am checking the settings." She rattled off a series of numbers.

"Those are the course coordinates for Earth," Teir said excitedly.

"Good," Glotaj said. "Captain, isn't there an emergency homing beacon located on your vessel?" Teir nodded. "Notify Defense League Command to activate it. When we have confirmed the Great Healer's location, we'll decide what to do next. Mara, is there anything else?"

The Tyberian shook her head. "The viewscreen showed normal star space, Your Excellency."

Glotaj inclined his head. "Thank you for your cooperation. You are dismissed." After she left, the regent turned to Teir. "Captain, you will receive a reprimand on your record. See that you maintain your vigilance in the future. I understand you are needed for another assignment. You may go."

Teir's mouth dropped open. That was it? Just a reprimand? Gods, how lucky could he get! He turned to leave, but then he noticed Glotaj's subtle gesture. The regent wanted to see him in his private chamber.

Teir followed him into a spacious office, then waited while he closed the door. The two men faced each other.

Glotaj's tall, black-robed figure was a formidable one. Teir had always had the utmost respect for this man, and it pained him to have caused that look of stern disapproval on Glotaj's lined face.

"Well, Captain? Would you care to tell me what *really* happened on your ship?"

Teir cleared his throat. "I don't understand, sir. I've given my report."

"Did anything unusual occur between you and Sarina?"

"No, sir," Teir lied.

Glotaj's sharp gaze studied him. "I want the truth, Captain!"

Teir felt as though guilt must be written all over his face. Flushing, he said, "Sarina fled to avoid the execution decree, and I can't blame her. It makes no sense to put an innocent to death."

"You sound as though you don't believe in the legend."

"I'm not really sure how I feel," Teir admitted. "I just don't think Sarina has been treated fairly."

"Explain yourself." Glotaj's expression was stern. Teir wished he knew what the older man was thinking.

"Her viewpoint was never taken into account. She was torn away from her life on Earth and expected to adapt without any concern for her feelings."

"You were the one sent to obtain her. As I recall, you didn't have any qualms about the assignment, other than to consider it beneath your dignity."

He must have been talking to Daras Gog, Teir figured. "I didn't know her then, Your Excellency."

"Ah. And you know her better now?"

Teir moistened his dry lips, sensing a trap. Gods,

they could accuse him of treason if they knew he'd been Sarina's lover! His heart racing, Teir sought a cautious reply. "As her bodyguard, I couldn't help becoming more acquainted with her, sir."

"Indeed." The regent studied him thoughtfully. Before he could respond, a knock sounded at the door. "Enter."

Lord Cam'brii stalked into the room. He glared at Teir, then gave a deferential bow to the older man. "I apologize for the intrusion, sir, but I felt this was something that concerned me."

Glotaj sighed. "Very well. Perhaps it is best if the two of you air your differences. It is clear that hostile feelings are involved."

"Captain Reylock desires my woman!" Cam'brii exclaimed. "I've seen it in the way he looks at her. It is dishonorable to covet another man's bride."

"Oh?" Glotaj turned a questioning glance on Teir. "I thought you said nothing happened during your voyage, Captain."

Teir's thoughts were racing. If he told the truth, his career would be over. And who could tell what punishment Sarina would receive if she ever returned? So he lied.

"I didn't touch her, Councilor. I'm aware of my duty. I would say if anyone is at fault here, it's you."

"How dare you!" Cam'brii's face reddened with anger.

"You've hardly paid her any attention," Teir went on, warming to the subject. "When you do, it's only to talk about the First Amendment and how she can use her position to help you. You've made no effort to gain Sarina's love, and if she doesn't fall in love with you, the prophecy can't be fulfilled."

To Teir's surprise, Cam'brii bowed his head. "You're right, and I'm sorry for it. To be truthful, I never expected her to be so keenly intelligent or so spirited."

"Not to mention beautiful, compassionate, and

willful," Teir couldn't help adding. He glanced at Glotaj. The regent was staring at him, a peculiar look on his face.

"I've showed no regard for her feelings," Cam'brii confessed. "She accused me of treating her as a symbol, and I admit she was correct. I forgot the Great Healer is also a woman." He looked at Teir, and it was obvious he was uncomfortable with what he was going to say next. "If Sarina returns, I'll need your help, Captain."

Teir couldn't have been more astonished if Cam'brii had offered to buy him a new ship. "What do you mean?" he asked warily.

"I must win her love. You seem to understand Sarina better than I. Tell me how to please her."

"Can't you figure that out for yourself? Forgive me, Councilor, but if you're genuinely interested in Sarina, you have to make an effort to get to know her."

Glotaj sighed. "Enough, gentlemen. Please be seated. Rolf, you must tell him. It would explain your difficulties." He had addressed Cam'brii by his first name which only Cam'brii's close friends or family used, but Glotaj had a special relationship with Rolf and favored him as his successor.

Cam'brii's face paled but he nodded. He sank into a chair and waited for Teir to be seated opposite him. Glotaj turned his back to them and stood facing a large crystal casement that overlooked the city.

Cam'brii sighed. "This is not an easy story to relate, Captain. I hope when you hear it, you'll understand my problem. Annums ago, I fell in love with a girl on Nadira. As Gayla was not yet of age, we faced a lengthy betrothal period, but we were too impatient to wait. We planned an elopement. Obtaining a spacecraft, we fled, heading for the Hut star system where we could be joined in peace.

"Our ship was intercepted by Souk pirates." His voice took on a note of anguish. "In the battle that ensued, Gayla was killed. I eluded the attackers and headed back to Nadira in our damaged vessel. I felt obligated to return Gayla's body to her parents. She was an only child, which made it all the more difficult for me to face them. As per our custom, I submitted myself for their punishment."

A long pause followed that Teir didn't dare interrupt. Cam'brii's eyes were glazed with pain as though he were reliving the terrible tragedy in his mind.

"Gayla's parents realized the elopement had been their daughter's wish as much as mine," Lord Cam'brii continued. "They blamed her death on the Souks who had attacked us. Instead of exacting vengeance on me, they made me vow to dedicate my life to stopping the slave trade. I entered the diplomatic corps with the goal of getting legislation passed to eradicate slavery throughout the galaxy. Now do you see why getting the First Amendment approved is so important to me? We have to stop the Souk aggressors!"

Teir could see from the fervor burning in the man's eyes that he was driven by guilt and obsessed with the need for revenge. No wonder his goals were all that mattered to him.

"After I arrived at Bimordus Central," Cam'brii went on, "one crisis after another hit the government. Talk of the legend arose, and then the Auricle began to glow. I qualified as the Raimorrdan born under the sign of the circle. So I agreed to marry Sarina."

His voice hardened. "You have to understand that my life is dedicated to destroying the Souks. The prophecy's fulfillment will help get that accomplished."

Teir leaned forward. "Why didn't you tell Sarina all this? It would have helped her to understand you."

Cam'brii looked away. "I should have done so. In fact, I'd made up my mind that I would tell her when she returned from Tendraa."

"I agree with your purpose," Teir admitted grudgingly. "I, too, would like to see the Souk pirates put out of business. But I would suggest you try to forget about them and the First Amendment when you're with Sarina. Tell her about your past, and find out about hers. Learn to love her, Cam'brii, and she might love you in return."

Even as he said the words, a deep ache rose within him. Thinking of her in Lord Cam'brii's arms pained him beyond belief.

"I shall do my duty," the councilor stated. "Sarina is an admirable woman. I will woo her to the best of my ability. May I count on your support, Captain?"

Teir knew what he meant. "I won't interfere."

Cam'brii wasn't going to leave anything to chance. "Glotaj, you won't be reassigning Captain Reylock as Sarina's bodyguard, will you?"

The regent turned to face them. "No, his duties will keep him elsewhere."

Teir stared at Glotaj. The regent was responsible for his assignment to guard Sarina? How could that be? No wonder Daras Gog had told him to look around Bimordus Two. Now he knew who to blame for his orders—the Supreme Regent himself. Had Glotaj arranged for the *Valiant* to be disabled as well? When he gave Teir permission for the trip to Tendraa, his ship was available again, so it was possible. But why go to such lengths to keep him planetside, and then allow him to take Sarina to Tendraa? It almost appeared as though Glotaj had thrown the two of them together on purpose, but that made no sense at all.

Cam'brii was speaking about Sarina. "What are we going to do? Shall we send someone after her?"

Glotaj replied, "Sarina must make the choice at this point. If she returns, it must be of her own volition. If she truly is the Great Healer, her destiny will guide her." He paused. "I've been meaning to tell you this. One of the Twyggs was caught trying to leave Bimordus Two. After interrogation, we found out that they were working for the Souks. Their orders were to assassinate you, Rolf."

The councilor's brow furrowed. "Who gave the order?"

"All we know is that it wasn't Cerrus Bdan. We're still interrogating the Twygg, however, and we'll find out more information."

Teir explained about the computer snafu that had set them up. "The whole transport system shut down," he said. "That's why our backup didn't arrive at the Rain Forest biome."

"Why did you not tell me this before?" Cam'brii thundered. "Someone here must be working with the Twyggs!"

"Leave it to me," Glotaj said. "The Souks must have an agent highly placed in our government—I've long suspected it. That would explain why Cerrus Bdan intercepted you and Sarina so easily when you first took her from Earth, Captain. It's my guess he was after Sarina, not you. Interfering in the legend could prevent the First Amendment from getting passed and that result would benefit the Souks enormously. When the scheme to capture Sarina ended in failure, one of Bdan's compatriots must have sent the Twyggs to murder Rolf. Killing either one of them would accomplish the same purpose."

"Then Sarina still needs to be guarded," Teir warned. "If the Souks know she's on her way back to Earth, they might send someone after her again."

"Maybe . . . maybe not." Glotaj fell silent, thinking. "If the legend is to unfold naturally, events have to take place as they are destined. I think we'll just leave this for now."

"But—"

"No buts, Reylock. You have a new assignment on Lapis. See to it that you make no unauthorized detours."

"Is it wise to leave Sarina unprotected?" Cam'brii asked, concerned.

Glotaj stared into space as though he were seeing

into the future. "I believe it is the course we must follow, gentlemen. The faith be with you. Good day."

Daimon and Ruzbee were having their own conference about Sarina in the ROF leader's private chamber.

"The Earthwoman is a rallying symbol for the Coalition and can only serve to feed the power-hunger of the Raimorrdans," Daimon said, regarding his companion. Ruzbee's manner was quiet, but cunning lit his tawny eyes. An Arcturian, he was of medium stature with short gray hair. He wore the sand-colored cape of a General Assembly Representative, whereas Daimon was dressed in his maroon robe of office.

"What do you propose to do?" Ruzbee asked.

Daimon looked startled. "What am *I* going to do? Why, nothing! Let Sarina Bretton remain on Earth."

"The High Council may vote to retrieve her."

"I'll vote against taking any action."

"Do you think Reylock will stay out of the way?"

Daimon nodded. "He usually obeys orders. Besides, the captain is scheduled for an important mission on Lapis."

"The hostage crisis?"

"That's right."

Ruzbee's eyebrows shot up. Cerrus Bdan would be happy to hear this intelligence. His payment for the information should be generous indeed. Unfortunately, Ruzbee hadn't known about the captain's mission to Tendraa in time to take out both Reylock and the Earthwoman. The small escort wouldn't have been able to protect them against a sizable Souk force. At least he could give Bdan the locations of both of them now. Then the smuggler could decide what he wanted done.

"Emu could be difficult," Daimon mused.

"I'll keep watch on him."

"If anything new develops, let me know. Otherwise, we'll sit tight."

Ruzbee nodded and left. Grinning, he thought what a fool Daimon was. The councilor figured Ruzbee was in his pocket. Instead, Ruzbee used Daimon as a source of information. The mineral-poor Arcturian worlds were dependent upon the Souks for trade. That the Souks used slave labor didn't bother Ruzbee in the least. His world needed the Souks, and he was glad to sell them information known only to the upper echelons of the Coalition government. Occasionally he took a greater risk, such as hiring the Twyggs. That had been a fiasco. Never mind, something else would be done about Lord Cam'brii. Cerrus Bdan wasn't concerned about him anyway. The councilor was his other employer's nemesis.

Snickering to himself, Ruzbee put on his dark glasses as he neared the rotunda. He loved playing ball on several different courts. It kept life interesting.

Mantra had his own concerns about the so-called Great Healer. Having expected Sarina to perform a miracle and cure his mother, he'd only gotten advice from her.

Malika had died the very same evening of the Great Healer's visit. Even his sister Kairi's words of comfort hadn't been able to dispel his gloom. Now Mantra was head of the family. Would his sisters also be taken by the dead cart? Desperate to ensure their survival, he'd adopted the sanitation measures suggested by Sarina. Already his breathing was easier; the smoky haze had cleared from his house. It was almost a miracle in itself what those few changes had wrought.

Maybe, just maybe, the Great One's advice was the vehicle for her aid. Mantra pondered this and decided it must be so. In that case, he had to spread the word. He was chosen to be her disciple; she had come to him.

Fevered by his faith and enthusiasm, Mantra set out for the Liege Lord of Tendraa.

* * *

"Open communications to the surface," K'darr ordered the communications officer from the bridge of the flagship *Krog*. They'd just entered orbit around the outermost planet of the Tendraan system. The Morgot leader stood scowling at the viewscreen and the ice-encrusted globe spinning below. If this conquest went like all the others, it would take weeks to subdue the inhabitants.

"Wait," K'darr said, changing his mind. He needed to see how much time they had left before the prophesies of the legend came true. Maybe they should go directly on to Tendraa. "Get me Cerrus Bdan on subspace radio."

"Er—the trader is back on Souk," the comm officer said nervously, afraid to be the bearer of bad news.

"*What?*" K'darr thundered. His black robe swished around his booted feet as he stomped over to the console. "Grand Marshal Zen-Bos!" His eyes swept the bridge.

The marshal had been listening to the exchange. "Sir?" he said, scurrying over.

"I thought you had contacted Bdan to obtain the Earthwoman for us. What happened?"

"I don't know. Bdan hasn't notified us."

"Why didn't you tell me there was a problem? It shouldn't be taking him this long." K'darr stroked the clinging aguar plant that hung over his shoulder. The leaves were crimson with a fuzzy texture. "If there's been a miscommunication, Grand Marshal, you'll be the one to pay."

Zen-Bos understood what he meant, and a shudder ran up his spine. The aguar plant grew like a weed. One seedling had sprouted and taken over the whole recreation hall. K'darr loved the jungle-like effect and forbade anyone to remove it. Besides, he used it as a fitting punishment for inefficient crew members. K'darr ordered them locked in the rec room for the night. The victims didn't look pretty when they

came out. The plant secreted a slow-acting diges-
tive enzyme that dissolved one's fur along with
the underlying skin. Trapped inside the room, the
victim quickly became entangled in the voracious
vines. Then the lights were turned off, and the enzyme
went to work in the dark. Zen-Bos had heard the
hideous screams himself when passing by.

"Cerrus Bdan is on-line," the comm officer announced.

"I'll take it in the ready room."

K'darr marched into the private conference room
adjacent to the bridge. Taking a seat at the table,
he flicked the comm unit open on his chair. "Go
ahead."

"Bdan here."

"What happened to our contract, Bdan? You were
supposed to capture the Earthwoman and bring her
to me."

The smuggler coughed. "A delay has occurred,
master."

"A delay? What delay?" K'darr barked.

"We had the woman and then got away she did,
helping Captain R-R-Reylock to escape as well."

"You stupid lyphound! I need to know if the legend
is true. Reylock has the key to knowledge; he knows
the location of the Blood Crystal."

"The mystical stone that can predict the future?"

"Yes, idiot! I will consult the Crystal. If it shows me
this woman is the Great Healer, I will use her power
to my own advantage. Capture both and bring them
to me—*unharmed*, mind you."

Bdan pretended to agree, chuckling as he signed
off. K'darr didn't know that his own plan was already
in motion. He had his own score to settle with Reylock
and Sarina before he'd hand them over to the Morgot
leader, if he handed them over at all.

Chapter Eleven

Sarina breathed a sigh of relief as the *Valiant* reached Earth atmosphere. It had taken her a long time to get there, time enough to consider her situation.

She wondered how Teir felt when he woke up and realized what she'd done. He'd probably want to kill her for stealing his ship, but it served him right. Did the man really think she'd return voluntarily to Bimordus Two to face eventual execution? All those sweet words whispered in her ear—how could she have believed him? If he really cared about her, he would have taken her somewhere else. Apparently she meant nothing more to him than a sex partner. He'd even had the nerve to tell her, "I'll be around when Cam'brii bores you!"

Sarina had thought of the sleeping potion as a last resort. Rolf suffered from occasional nightmares. Without explaining the nature of the dreams when she'd asked about them, he had mentioned taking a sedit beverage to get back to sleep. With her new-found knowledge of pharmacology, Sarina reproduced a supply of the sleep-inducing potion using the fabricator in Teir's cabin. Dissolving the powder in his wine had been easy, and her seduction act had worked.

Now she was finally home. Sarina admired the cleverness of the transport method. It utilized molecular alteration like the fabricators but with a different angle. With the speed of molecular motion subtly changed, one object could coexist in the same space as another and be made to appear in any particular configuration. Teir had made the shuttle look like an elevator behind a wall in her office corridor. She came down by the same method since it was already programmed into the computer. But before leaving the ship, she used the fabricator to produce suitable Earth clothing.

It was a Sunday, and the building was closed. She checked her office, surprised that her things were still in place. Having been missing for so long, she thought her belongings would be gone.

Rummaging in her desk, Sarina found some money and her extra house key in a small purse she kept hidden in a drawer. After calling a cab, she went outside to marvel at being home again. The bright afternoon sunshine warmed her skin. A breeze blew off Biscayne Bay, salty and moist, ruffling the pleated skirt of her patterned shirtwaist dress. It was so good to feel the solid pavement beneath her feet! Planet Earth was a beautiful world, one she vowed never to have to leave again.

Not knowing even if she still had a home, Sarina directed the cab driver there anyway and was surprised to find her favorite crimson potted flowers still blooming on the stoop of her townhouse. Realizing it might be futile, she took the key from her purse and fitted it in the lock, expecting it not to work. Surely someone else would have rented the place by now.

Stunned, Sarina stood there a moment when the key twisted as easily as though the lock had just been greased. Though she was happy that her suppositions about her home were wrong, she was puzzled. Since she had been missing for so long, why hadn't her mother taken her personal items and canceled the lease? This confused her the same way her office had. It was as though she'd never left.

Stepping into the foyer, she peered around cautiously. Her umbrella stand still stood by the front door. And there was the blue umbrella she'd bought at Walt Disney World during a downpour.

Suddenly Sarina tensed. Someone was coming from the kitchen! A feminine voice called out, "Who's there?" And to Sarina's astonishment, around the corner walked an exact duplicate of herself.

"Who are you?" Sarina gasped.

"I wasn't told to expect you," the other Sarina replied, looking surprised. "Are you a replacement?"

Sarina peeked into the living area. Her furnishings, her personal items, were exactly as she'd left them. "What's going on here?" she demanded.

Her duplicate closed the door. "I'm Number 1468, revised series. Which are you?" When Sarina just stared at her, the other said, "You *are* an android, aren't you?"

"No, I'm not!" Sarina cried. "I'm human—the real me! *You're* an android?"

"The real Sarina? Oh my!" The android's gray eyes widened.

She looked incredibly human, Sarina thought, stunned. If it wasn't that she's supposed to be me, I'd never have known. "What—what are you doing here? I assume the Coalition sent you."

"I took your place when Captain Reylock came to get you. He transported me to your residence while he went to your office. My signature name is Kayo." She smiled proudly. "I have the new emotions module."

"I see. So you've been substituting for me?"

Kayo nodded.

"What about Robert?" Sarina asked.

The android raised an eyebrow. "He's quite a man." Her substitute began pacing the living room, and Sarina was angered to note the android wore her best clothes. "When I took over, your relationship seemed rather cool. After trying different types of behavior, I noted that I provoked the most positive response when I was pleasant every time we met. The two of you are very close now."

"Oh, no," Sarina groaned.

"Your mother's plans for the wedding are proceeding," Kayo went on. "She'll be sending the invitations out next week."

"Not if I can help it! What else have you done that I should know about?" Sarina stomped into her bedroom, followed by her double. The room was immaculate, neater than she'd ever kept it.

"I've been maintaining your business appointments. By the way, congratulations. You've been made Associate in the firm. You'll be moving into a new office with your own secretary this week."

"You mean I—you—we passed Simmons's test? What was it?"

Kayo grinned. "Pierce Mitchells took you out to lunch with your boss's approval. He plied you with cocktails to get you drunk, then tried to question you about one of the cases you were handling. The purpose, Simmons told me later, was to see if you'd leak information when you were under duress." She giggled. "Androids are not affected by alcohol. Pierce Mitchells was under the table before I'd even finished my sixth drink."

Sarina couldn't help laughing. "You know, Robert never told me the conclusion of his test case. Since you're so close to him now, did he mention it to you?"

"Yes, we discussed it after I passed mine—or rather, yours. He was tested to see if he would take a bribe."

"Ah, I thought so." Sarina went into the kitchen

and opened the refrigerator door, to find it empty.

"Androids have no need for nourishment," said Kayo, watching her with amusement.

Sarina turned and looked into her own clear gray eyes. "Now that I'm back, you can switch yourself off. Or better still, I'll transport you to Captain Reylock's ship."

"The Captain escorted you home?"

Sarina regarded her a moment in silence. Maybe it wasn't such a good idea to send Kayo to the ship. She might signal the Coalition. "Not exactly," she hedged. "You'd better fill me in on what's been going on."

After an hour-long discussion, Sarina went out for her regular Sunday visit with Abby. She couldn't wait to see her friend. Kayo had been taking her place every week, and for that, Sarina was grateful. The thing that had bothered her most during her absence was how disappointed Abby would be when she didn't show up. Kayo had made sure that didn't happen. Apparently some kind of mind transfer had been effected during the initial transport process in which Sarina's memories were imprinted into Kayo's circuits, so Kayo had known everything that was on her mind. It had been easy for the android to step into her shoes.

Behind the wheel of her electrically powered automobile, Sarina thought what a pleasure it was to drive again. Too bad these vehicles didn't take off into the air like the speeders on Bimordus Two, she mused as the car's computer guided her along the encoded lanes. The traffic was congested with all the Sunday pleasure seekers out on the road.

After parking at the rehab center, Sarina went directly to the paraplegic ward. Abby was sitting in a wheelchair, reading a book. Her long black hair was tied into a ponytail. When she spotted Sarina, her delicate features lit up. "Hi! You're early today."

"I couldn't wait to come." Sarina knelt beside her and lowered her voice. "I've got something for you, but we have to go to your room."

"Okay," Abby said curiously. She pushed a lever and her electrically powered chair began to move.

Inside the room, Sarina closed the door and faced her friend. From her pocket she pulled out the neurojet unit she'd obtained from the Wellness Center on Bimordus Two. Mentally she ran over the procedure: *Examine the spine. Locate the damaged nerves. Repair or regenerate.*

"Lean forward," she ordered.

Abby bent from the waist, a look of puzzlement on her face. "What's that?" she asked when she saw the small device in Sarina's palm.

"Something a friend loaned me," Sarina whispered. "You must promise not to mention a word about this to anyone. It's top secret research, still in the experimental stage, and I'm not authorized to use it. But I guarantee it will work." As she spoke, she glided the device up the middle of Abby's back and immediately picked up the signal that identified the damaged area.

"What will work?" Abby queried. "What on earth are you doing?"

"There!" Sarina pressed the unit against her friend's vertebra. She felt a vibration as the regenerating beam shot forth.

"*Ow!*" Abby experienced a sudden jolt to her spine. "What was that?"

"All done." Smiling in satisfaction, Sarina pocketed the neurojet unit.

"I don't get it."

"It's a form of electrical stimulation," Sarina explained. "It works on certain kinds of nerve damage. Let's hope you show results." She knew Abby would, but she shouldn't appear too confident. "Remember what I said. Don't tell *anyone* about this, okay?"

"Whatever you say," Abby agreed. "You seem different today, Sarina. Is everything all right?"

"Sure." Sarina frowned, wondering how Kayo had

acted with her friend. They visited for another half hour; then Sarina hugged her and left. Tears moistened her eyes as she emerged into the sunlight. There was so much good to do here on Earth! But Sarina had concentrated so hard on learning how to cure Abby's paralysis that she hadn't had time to focus on any of the other medical problems plaguing humankind. Frustration tore at her until she remembered Mantra's family on Tendraa. Perhaps there were still ways to help using the newfound knowledge she'd gained.

She wondered if she'd have enough time to try. Teir could show up at any moment to bring her back. Or Cam'brii himself might come this time. His devotion to duty wouldn't let her elude him so easily. The passage of the First Amendment was too important to him, and he saw the legend's fulfillment as essential to Coalition unity.

Sarina considered going to the authorities and asking for protection. But what could she say? That she'd been abducted by aliens? She might offer proof by showing them Kayo or even taking them up to Teir's ship, but did she want to be responsible for establishing First Contact? That was too heavy a burden for her to accept. And if she had no proof, the police would just relegate her to the nut category, along with Elvis sighters and people who claimed to have out-of-body experiences.

What precautions could Sarina take on her own? She couldn't tell Robert—she didn't want to have anything more to do with him, and the sooner he found that out, the better. Her mother? Her friends? Who would believe her?

Stopping off to buy some food, Sarina went home to eat and to decide what to do. Unable to come to any logical conclusions, she roamed, touching the favorite items she hadn't seen in so long: her books, her treasured mementos, her hologram collection and her favorite clothes; the stuffed giraffe she'd had since she was a little girl; the framed photograph of her parents. She'd told Teir about these things, but she'd never asked him about his home, and she realized he didn't have any personal items on his ship. Wasn't there anything special he wanted to remember? Biting her lip, Sarina told herself that didn't matter now.

Kayo wandered into Sarina's bedroom. "You haven't told me why you're here," she said, fingering Sarina's favorite jade silk robe that lay on the bed. The android's long blond hair hung loose, whereas Sarina wore hers in a tight coil at the back of her head.

Sarina sank down onto the bed. She ached with a weariness that went far beyond fatigue. "I ran away."

Kayo's eyes widened. "You *what?*"

"I did not wish to marry Lord Cam'brii."

Apparently Kayo had been briefed as to Sarina's mission. "But you must fall in love and wed him for the legend to unfold!"

"Then the legend will never unfold because I can't fall in love with him. And in less than a year, I'll be executed if I'm not the Great Healer. The Ascension Statute doesn't allow for any exceptions."

"The law was meant to discourage others from usurping the political power that will rightfully be yours when you are the Great Healer," Kayo said. "You fear you are *not* the Great Healer, but the time may not yet be ripe for the Revelation. Events must fall into place as they are destined. You must return to Bimordus Two."

"No way!" Sarina exclaimed. "I'm never going back!"

"You're not viewing things in a broad enough scope," Kayo persisted. "Your life has more meaning than mere existence here on Earth."

"This world is mine, Kayo. I *like* living here. I don't plan ever to leave again."

"But you are destined for greater things. Your life

can have an impact on the whole galaxy. You must not cower here when you're needed by so many others. Where is your courage, Great Healer?"

"Do you have an off-switch, Kayo?" Sarina muttered. She was damn tired of hearing herself referred to as the Great Healer.

Her abrupt change of subject distracted the android. "Of course. It is located here." She pointed to her side.

"Then turn yourself off!" Sarina snapped.

"You do not have the authority to direct me."

"Oh no?" Sarina leaped up and pushed the button herself. Kayo went limp. Sarina caught the android's falling body and gently stretched her out on the bed.

"God, I was giving myself such a headache!" she sighed.

The viewphone rang just then, and her mother's image appeared on the video screen. Ellen Bretton's blond hair was perfectly coiffed, her makeup perfectly applied, making her look ten years younger than fifty-two. "Sarina, dear, I just wanted to confirm our luncheon engagement for Wednesday."

"What?" Ellen never called her *dear*, and Sarina wasn't in the habit of meeting her for lunch. "Oh sure," she said, recovering quickly, "but I forgot what time you said."

"Twelve o'clock. I'll meet you in the lobby. Is everything all right?"

"Yes, thanks." Her mother hung up before Sarina could ask which lobby she meant. Darn it, this must have been Kayo's arrangement. Glancing at the android lying on her bed, she decided to move her out of sight just in case someone should come to visit unexpectedly. After all, she had no idea what other plans Kayo might have made for her. Grunting heavily, Sarina lugged Kayo over to her closet and shoved her inside.

The next morning, she went to work, apprehensive

about any other changes the android might have effected while she was gone. Shuffling through the papers on her desk, she was interrupted by Robert's call.

"Hey, babe, they got the space cleared for you today. You can start the move."

She stared at his familiar face on the viewphone. "That's nice, Robert," she said, swallowing. God, how could she face him in person? She didn't know what Kayo had said or done in her place. Realizing she had no idea where her new office was located, she cleared her throat. "Uh—is my new secretary available? I could use her help with the move."

"Why don't you call *him* yourself and ask?"

"I'm afraid I misplaced the number."

"Here, I've got it written down." He rattled off the figure, then frowned. "Say, are you all right? You look a little odd."

"I'm fine, thanks. Just a little frazzled about the move."

"Well, don't work too late," he cautioned with a devilish grin. "Remember, we've got plans later."

Sarina's stomach clenched. "Sure," she said brightly. "I'll be ready. What time?"

"Come directly to my place after you're finished here. I'm already chilling your favorite wine, and the steaks are marinating in the refrigerator. It'll be a cozy evening."

"Sounds good. See you later."

Sarina tried to occupy her mind by packing up her things. The young male secretary arrived, and she sent him to her new office with a load of papers. Taking a break, she walked to the window and gazed out at the sun-drenched scene. It wasn't very long ago that she was looking at the sparkling water below and daydreaming about space travel. And then her dreams had become reality when Teir Reylock walked into her life.

What was the captain doing now? Sarina wondered.

Was he on his way to bring her back, or had he forgotten all about her? She would never forget him, no matter how badly he'd treated her. His tall, dashing figure, brilliant blue eyes, and disarming grin were forever implanted in her memory, as were the kisses that made her feel like molten lava. Just thinking of him made her body ache for his touch.

Returning to her desk, Sarina opened a drawer and threw the contents into a carton the secretary had brought. The rest of the day passed quickly as she finished packing, met with Mr. Simmons to be briefed on a new client, and established her presence on the upstairs floor.

By the end of the day, Sarina's apprehension about confronting Robert had grown to new heights. Her palms sweaty, she stood in front of his condo building at six-thirty and pushed the door buzzer. They had decided that she would give up her place when they were married. Although Robert had wanted her to move in with him earlier, she'd refused.

Despite herself, Sarina felt a surge of affection at the sight of him. Wearing a conservative blue knit polo shirt and navy slacks, he represented all that was familiar. She felt comfortable in Robert's presence, and part of her regretted what had to be done.

As soon as he touched her, however, her reservations disappeared. "Hi, honey," he said, giving Sarina a lingering kiss that left her cold. In his eyes was a look that she knew too well, and her heart sank. This was going to be difficult.

"Come on in. Have a seat while I get the fire ready." Robert liked to barbecue steaks outside on the balcony.

"I came here to talk, not to eat, Robert," Sarina said firmly. "There are some things I need to say, and they can't wait." She took a seat on the living room sofa.

As Robert approached, she wondered why she'd never recognized her true feelings about him. Robert appealed to her in a brotherly fashion, that was all.

His touch didn't make her melt like Teir's did, and his kisses didn't turn her blood to fire.

Sarina smoothed her skirt, wishing there were a fabricator in the room so she could order a Moranian Flasher to calm her jangling nerves.

Robert sat down beside her and smiled. "I couldn't wait for you to get here," he said in a low, seductive tone. "To tell the truth, I'm not very hungry either." He edged closer and put a possessive hand on her thigh. "What do you say we head for the bedroom?"

Annoyed, she brushed him off. "Please, not now!"

"What's the matter?" Robert asked, puzzled.

Sarina gathered her courage, wishing she didn't have to hurt his feelings. "I've decided this isn't going to work between us," she said bluntly.

He gave her a look of stunned disbelief. Then his expression cleared. "Of course you've been put off by all the postponements, and I can't say that I blame you. I just thought it best to wait until you were established. Didn't you always say one should forge ahead in life, career-wise?"

"That was before—before—I don't feel that way anymore." Clenching her hands tightly in her lap, Sarina said, "Robert, I'm not in love with you."

He stared at her. "But we're perfectly suited, Sarina! We're in the same profession, and it means a lot having a life partner who understands the vocabulary. We're both ambitious. We like the same kind of music and restaurants and shows. We've even joined the same health club. What more could you want?"

"I want a man who arouses my passion, Robert. I'm fond of you, but I don't feel that way when I'm with you. It's not your fault," she hastened to add. "It's me. I guess I've changed. Some things are more important to me now than they were before, like being in love. Sharing similar interests just isn't enough anymore."

Robert ran a hand through his hair. "I don't get it! The last few weeks you've really come on to me, and now you're suddenly telling me we're finished?"

"I'm sorry," she murmured.

He shook his head in bewilderment. "Is it another guy? Is that it?"

Sarina lowered her head. It might be best to tell him the truth—some of it, anyway. "Yes," she confessed.

"But when did you have time to meet this guy? We've been together every day."

Sarina's mind raced for a plausible response. "It's— uh—someone I used to know who'd moved away, someone I really cared for. He's back in the area now and eager to renew our relationship."

"Didn't you tell him you were engaged?"

"No, I—I didn't. I want to keep on seeing him."

Robert was getting angry now. "What about the wedding, huh? Your mother's sending out the invitations next week!"

"We'll lose the deposits, that's all."

"*That's all?* The whole thing means nothing else to you?"

"I'll always be fond of you, Robert . . ."

His eyes narrowed. "If you walk out on me, Sarina, this is it. I won't take you back if you change your mind."

"I understand." Sarina murmured.

Robert stood up, his mouth tightening. "It's going to be very awkward, being in the same building together. Don't expect me to defend you to Mr. Simmons any-more. You're on your own from now on."

"Can't we at least be friends?" she said hopefully, rising to face him.

"No, Sarina. Once we're through, that's it. And you'd better watch what you say in the office, too. I've worked hard to build up my image."

And I would have made the proper wife to go along with it, Sarina figured. His feelings for her had always been related to his ambitions.

"I guess I'll leave now."

She put out her hand in a friendly gesture, but

Robert brushed past her to the door. Swinging it open, he stood aside, his eyes cold. "Good-bye, Sarina."

Sarina left, relieved to have the scene over with. Now she only had her mother to face.

Wednesday arrived, and so did their date for lunch. Sarina had called to find out where they'd agreed to meet. It was in the lobby of the Sheraton at Brickell Point overlooking Biscayne Bay.

"So, daughter, tell me all about your new position," her mother said when they were seated in the restaurant. "I was thrilled when I heard about your promotion."

Slender and graceful, Ellen was dressed in a tailored linen suit with a diamond pin on the lapel. Her gray eyes were reflections of Sarina's own.

Sarina described a few of her cases, but her lack of enthusiasm was evident to her own ears.

Ellen, however, didn't notice. As they ate, she raved about Sarina's promising future, then focused on the wedding. "The invitations are lovely. I'm getting so excited about the ceremony. Do you have any additions to the guest list, dear?"

It's now or never, Sarina thought. "I've called the wedding off, Mother."

"What?" Ellen gasped.

"I told Robert on Monday. Of course I'll pay you back for the expenses you've incurred and I'll take care of notifying the people involved."

"I don't believe this! What happened?"

Sarina sighed. "I realized that what I felt for Robert wasn't love. It was affection, like a sister might have for a brother, and that's not enough to base a marriage on."

"*Love?* Is that what's bothering you?" Her mother leaned forward and fixed her with a steely gaze. "Love has nothing to do with it. Robert is a sensible young man with excellent prospects. He's perfect for you."

"No, he's perfect for *you*." Sarina carefully folded her napkin on the table, then looked her mother in the eye. "All my life you've told me what to do. Now it's time I made my own decisions. I hate the legal profession, Mother, and I don't want to marry Robert."

Her mother put out a comforting hand. "I understand. It's just a case of prenuptial jitters, dear. But you'd better set things straight with Robert before he finds someone else."

"Mother, *I am not going to marry him.*"

Her tone of voice made Ellen gape. "You are serious, aren't you?"

"Yes, I am," Sarina said.

Ellen shook her head, stunned. "How can you do this to me? I like the man, Sarina. You're making a big mistake if you let him go."

"If you like him so much, *you* marry him!" Sarina snapped.

"I've already got a husband," Ellen snapped back.

"Yes, and he suits you just fine."

Sarina had never liked her stepfather. William was a powerful, wealthy businessman who was generous to his wife but ruthless to his subordinates. He wasn't kind and compassionate like her own father had been. Sarina still missed him terribly. He'd died of a heart attack at the age of forty-six, and Ellen had wasted no time finding a new husband. Always practical, she'd cautioned Sarina against being too sentimental.

"By the way," Ellen said as they got up from the table, "I wanted to tell you about the investment possibilities of Anco Solar. The stock price is undervalued right now, so it's a good buy if you're looking to diversify your portfolio."

"Thanks, but I'm not interested." Sarina contributed her money for the bill.

"I'm more experienced than you are in financial matters, Sarina. Since you won't have Robert to support you, you've got to make the right choices now, while you're still young."

"You're probably right. We'll talk about it another time." Sarina gave her mother an obligatory peck on the cheek and left the restaurant without a backward glance.

Disgusted with her mother's opportunistic attitude, Sarina went home. Teir had been right—she should have broken away from Ellen a long time ago. She would have been a lot happier.

Sarina's life fell back into a predictable, lonely routine. Each morning, her bed phone rang with her programmed wake-up call. A flat panel high-resolution TV screen on the wall lit up with the latest news, weather, and local traffic conditions as she dressed.

On the job, she was given a new identification badge that included a tiny radio transmitter. It allowed her location to be pinpointed for incoming phone calls wherever she was in the building, but Sarina preferred to remain in her office. She and Robert were avoiding one another, and it was awkward answering the questions of her co-workers. Everyone was curious about their breakup. Meanwhile, she went through the motions of completing her work with little interest or initiative. It was something to do while deciding what other options were available to her.

The only thing Sarina truly enjoyed was shopping and visiting with her friends. On her days off, she met a few friends and they strolled through the huge indoor shopping malls, replete with levels of escalators and giant glass walls. She had fun window-shopping, eating in the food courts and buying small trinkets.

In a way, the malls reminded her of Bimordus Central, the shimmering pink and white city under a crystal dome. But Bimordus Central didn't have any shopping centers like these. There was an inter-galactic marketplace in the capital city, but the wares were lavish gift items for visiting dignitaries to bring back home. When Teir had once taken her there, Sarina had mentioned the huge malls on Earth and the diversity of items available. He'd promised to show her the modern emporiums on his homeplanet Vilaran if she ever visited.

A strange emptiness filled her whenever she thought about him. It would be so wonderful if he still regarded her with the same warmth and affection he'd shown before they went to Tendraa. If only he were here! Sarina would have loved to show him around her home. She imagined them having fun together, sailing on Biscayne Bay, visiting Viscaya and Fairchild Gardens and the Zoo. She had to admit that her friends were beginning to bore her. They laughed and gossiped and had no concept of any world beyond their own.

But Sarina's eyes had been opened, and she found it impossible to close them again. Despite the feelings of resentment and betrayal she felt toward Teir, the captain's darkly handsome features remained in the forefront of her mind.

At least she'd been able to help Abby. Her friend called excitedly to tell her she'd felt tingling sensations in her legs. The doctors said it was a miracle she felt anything at all. Sarina told her that was wonderful; maybe the nerve damage wasn't as extensive as had been first believed. A few days later, Abby phoned again. She was able to wiggle her toes.

Sarina was ecstatic, but it only increased her dissatisfaction with her job. Being a corporate lawyer didn't allow her to help people the way she really wanted to. Her performance declined. She considered quitting her job, especially when Mr. Simmons began harassing her. Robert probably had a hand in that, Sarina guessed, but she didn't care. This might be just the push she needed. Her secret desire had always been to be a doctor, and that desire continued to grow within her.

She would go to medical school, Sarina decided at last. She'd learned a lot about medicine on Bimordus Two, but not nearly enough. She wouldn't heal with a magic touch, but with the touch of kindness and compassion instead, and maybe that was more important.

Sarina was sitting at her desk fingering her worry stone when she reached this momentous conclusion. It was a smooth stone passed down through the generations from woman to woman. Her grandmother had given it to her, feeling that Sarina's mother wouldn't appreciate it. "This stone has been in the family forever," her grandmother said. "Stroke it whenever you feel blue. It'll help put you in a better mood."

Sarina liked to flick her finger over the pointed end. The last time she'd done it, a tingling sensation had stung her hand. She'd dropped the stone at once, afraid it contained a mineral that reacted adversely with her skin. The lustrous silvery-grey stone had lain untouched in her desk drawer ever since.

Until now. Sarina needed the calming effect she got from stroking the smooth surface. She grasped it in her palm and ran her fingertips over the rounded edges. As she thought seriously about changing careers, an odd tingling spread throughout her hand, similar to the sensation she'd felt before. But this time, instead of dropping the stone, Sarina opened her palm, and what she saw made her gasp in surprise.

The stone glowed with a pulsating light.

As she stared at it, her heart began thumping wildly. The glowing stone looked just like a miniature version of the ancient Auricle!

My God! Was this how it had happened? Was this the source of the answering light that had led Teir to her?

Sarina placed the stone on top of her desk and watched as the glow slowly faded. The last time she'd held it, she hadn't looked at it, hadn't noticed the pulsating light. The last time, she'd been having similar thoughts about being a doctor. Could it be that the legend was right? Could she be the Great Healer after all?

Sarina was stunned. The implications were mind-boggling. Kayo's words came back to haunt her: *You are meant for greater things. Your life can have an impact on the whole galaxy. You're needed by so many others.*

There was only one way to discover the truth, Sarina realized. She'd have to return to Bimordus Two, marry Lord Cam'brii, and try to fall in love with him. It was the only way to give the legend a chance. Maybe if she supported Rolf's goals, he'd warm toward her, and their relationship would improve. She certainly had a personal stake in proving the legend true now!

Her decision made, she moved with alacrity. Selecting a few personal items from her desk to take with her, she drove home and made her plans. She'd write a letter of resignation and mail it to Hiram Simmons. She'd call Ellen and tell her she was going on an extended vacation, and ask her mother to take care of her apartment. She'd phone her friends, including Abby, to let them know she'd be gone. Leaving again would be painful, but hope filled her heart that she could accomplish greater things by her departure.

Kayo was the only problem she had left. If Sarina was going away, Kayo also had to leave. Sarina decided to bring her along. Reactivating the android, she asked Kayo how to transport up to the ship from her apartment. Was it possible to program the shuttle by remote control?

Kayo, pleased at Sarina's desire to return to the High Council, retrieved the shuttle for her. Shortly after dark, it appeared in her driveway configured as a car. The android helped Sarina pack her favorite clothes, books, and treasured possessions into two suitcases which she then loaded into the shuttle.

Outside, Sarina turned to Kayo. "You're coming with me," she said.

Kayo frowned. "Why? I thought I'd be taking your place again."

Sarina shook her head. "That isn't possible now. I've told everyone I'm going away, and I've broken up with Robert. You're not needed here anymore."

Kayo regarded her thoughtfully. "I suppose you're right, but still—"

"And another thing," Sarina went on. "You haven't been acting properly. You went against your programming by behaving differently than I would have. I think your circuits must be defective. We'd better schedule you for a diagnostic test."

"Hmm. Maybe it's the new emotions module," Kayo said. "It may need servicing. All right, I shall accompany you."

Sarina was glad of the android's company when the two of them were back on board the *Valiant*. Kayo was excited. She'd found her experience on Earth fascinating, but she was eager to get on to new learning situations. She did agree, however, to submit herself for testing before getting reassigned. Apparently the Coalition ran a robotics center on Altara II.

"I am not programmed for ship's operations," said Kayo, gazing with bewilderment around the bridge.

"Fine. You can either keep out of the way or follow my instructions," Sarina said, easing herself into the command chair. She tapped the control panel to initiate the sequence that would take them out of orbit.

It wasn't until Earth was receding in the distance that Sarina realized she was placing herself in danger. Occupied as she'd been with learning basic flight operations, she'd never taken the time to learn how to activate the ship's defenses. No one had bothered her on her return to Earth, probably because they were glad to see her go. But now that she was coming out of hiding, any number of her enemies might be preparing to intercept her.

She glanced at Kayo who was staring out the viewscreen. The android could substitute for her in a pinch, but it wouldn't take hostile boarders long to discover their mistake. An android wouldn't read as a life form on their scanners.

Only one person could help her if she were in trouble, and Sarina had no idea where Captain Teir Reylock was.

Chapter Twelve

Teir's mind registered pain at its first sensory input. At first, he felt a general ache throughout his whole body. Then the discomfort intensified until an agonized throbbing gripped his upper arms and drew him back to consciousness.

As the haze in his mind began to dissipate, he slowly opened his eyes. A cave-like setting met his groggy gaze. He was in a huge cavern, dimly lit by flamelights spaced along damp stone walls. The trickling of water could be heard in the distance, along with the faint hiss of the flames.

Vaguely Teir replayed the final scenes he remembered: the completion of his mission on Lapis; the message from his aunt who had suddenly been taken ill; visiting her at the Wellness Center on Alpha Omega Two only to learn that she hadn't summoned him. And then there was the ambush. Several Horthas, huge bull-like creatures, trapped him in an alley, attacking him with their stun whips. The nerve-jarring pain had brought him to his knees, and his last memory was the sting of a syringe pricking his arm.

Trying to shift his position, Teir groaned. He was strung up by his wrists and could barely move. His arms were bound above his head and secured to an overhead beam. He hung suspended in the air, his feet more than three decimeters above the packed dirt floor. Spasms of pain racked his shoulder muscles, causing Teir to clench his teeth against the agony.

Heavy footsteps approached from the shadows. "Awake, are you, Captain?" gloated the deep voice of Cerrus Bdan. "Welcome to the Souk homeworld."

The slave trader sauntered into his line of vision, jowls wobbling in anticipation. The blue-skinned Souk wore a brightly colored caftan, an incongruity in the gloomy setting.

"Like you my dungeon? Long have I awaited for the pleasure of seeing you here."

"You set me up," Teir accused, awareness flooding him along with a surge of rage. "I'll bet you sent the message about my aunt."

Bdan gave a slight bow of acknowledgment. "Waiting for such an opportunity was I. You've caused me much trouble, Captain R-R-Reylock." His eyes gleamed fiercely. "Now will you pay the price." He balled his hand into a fist and drew it back.

Teir saw the blow coming but could do nothing to avoid it.

"This is for taking the *Omnus*," Bdan snarled, smashing his fist into Teir's jaw. "And for arresting my crew, here is another." He hit him again.

Teir's head snapped back with each assault. Combined with the aftereffects of the drug he'd been given, the blows made his head reel. "Given the chance, I'd do it over again," he croaked.

Bdan growled, his face taking on a purplish hue. "Answer my questions will you, or I'll see that you suffer greatly!"

Teir heard a cough in the background. Scanning the

shadows, he noticed Lieutenant Otis, Bdan's second-in-command, watching from a corner. He wondered if Bdan was going to ask the same things the lieutenant had when he'd interrogated Teir on the *Omnus*.

"I want the location of the Blood Crystal," Bdan barked.

A surge of alarm went through him. Otis hadn't asked that question. Why was Bdan asking it now? Who had told him that Teir was the one who held the answer?

"Give me will you the troop deployments for the Defense League," Bdan continued. Teir felt better. That question he would expect from the pirate leader. "In addition, Captain, ask you do I to r-r-reveal Lord Cam'brii's daily routine."

"Lord Cam'brii?" Teir asked, surprised. "Why?"

"Intimately familiar with his habits are you, and someone I know is interested." Bdan grinned, drool forming on his lower lip. "Let's with the first question start, shall we? Where is the Blood Crystal that can predict the future?"

"You won't learn anything from me." Teir's arm muscles ached unbearably. He attempted to shift his position but the drug he'd been given had sapped his strength. He tried to ignore the throbbing pain that shot through his shoulders and focused instead on his captor.

Bdan approached, hands curled into fists. Teir's stomach muscles clenched as he anticipated another blow, but he looked the Souk in the eye, refusing to be intimidated.

"The Blood Crystal, Captain R-R-Reylock. Where is it?"

"Go to Zor!"

"Defy me, will you?" Bdan's fat body shook with glee. "Enjoy this immensely, shall I." From a pocket in his voluminous caftan, he took out a golden orb. The shiny ball sat in the palm of his hand as he thrust it in front of Teir's face. "Know you what this is?"

"A Korion fireball. How did you get one? They were banned after the War."

"Your laws do not apply here, Captain. Know you how the device works?"

Teir nodded grimly.

"It burns the flesh where it touches." Bdan walked to a sideboard and picked up a heavy glove. Donning it, he activated the fireball in his gloved hand. The orb glowed as Bdan advanced. "Where shall we start, Captain? On your face, by the eye? A nice scar on your temple would it leave. Or on your hairy chest? Or should I have you stripped and use it there?" He pointed at Teir's groin and laughed, an ugly snorting sound.

Teir knew the time for taunting was over. Bdan meant business.

"Talk, R-R-Reylock. Where is the Blood Crystal?" Bdan raised the glowing orb threateningly.

Teir tightened his mouth, saying nothing.

With an angry snarl, Bdan thrust his hand forward, pressing the orb to Teir's chest where it was exposed by his open shirt. Burning heat, intensely painful, tore at the layers of his skin. A sizzling sound rent the air. Teir clenched his teeth to keep from screaming.

The searing pressure stopped, and as Teir inhaled a shaky breath, the smell of his own burning flesh filled his nostrils. Bile rose in his throat. Bdan was only a step away, watching him with a gleeful smile. Teir twisted his body, struggling to get free, but he only succeeded in swaying in place and doubling the agony in his shoulders.

"Talk," commanded Bdan, lifting the orb once again.

Teir spat at him.

"Guards!" Bdan shouted. Two Horthas rushed out of the shadows bordering the room. "Strip him," the slaver ordered.

Teir felt a rise of panic. His eyes fixed on the glowing ball outstretched in Bdan's hand, and he realized there was only one way out. Raising one leg, he kicked at the Korion fireball. His foot connected and the orb landed on the ground with a loud crash.

Bdan looked down at the smashed pieces, then up at Teir, his face mottled with rage. "That was the only one I had, you white-livered son of a belleek!"

"Sorry," Teir said, forcing a grin.

Bdan punched him in the face. "Won't cooperate, will you? Perhaps a Morgot mind probe would unleash your tongue."

"You can try. I've been trained to resist them."

"Then how about this?" Bdan pulled a rod from the folds of his caftan.

"You can use the electrifier, but I still won't talk. You might as well kill me and be done with it."

Bdan growled, "One choice do you leave me. Saving this was I, but it is time." He snapped his fingers to the guards. "Bring in the girl."

The Horthas left. When they returned, the beasts lugged between them a slender female dressed in a slave costume and wearing a restraining collar around her neck. As she was thrust into the light, Teir felt the blood drain from his face. "Sarina!" he gasped.

She widened her eyes at the sight of him. "Teir!" She started to rush forward, but the guards held her back, grasping her by the arms.

"May I present my honored guest, Sarina Bretton," said Bdan, gloating at the look on Teir's face.

He stared at her, horrified. What was she doing here? How long had she been Bdan's prisoner? Why had he heard nothing of her capture? She didn't look as though she'd been harmed, he realized thankfully. She wore a slave outfit but it was the skimpy bra and elaborately gilded girdle of a harem girl, not the coarse cloth of a laborer. At least she hadn't been sent to the mines. Bdan must have been keeping her in reserve just for this occasion.

He looked at the Souk, trying to moisten his lips,

but his tongue was dry. "What do you want with her?" he rasped.

Bdan's eyes narrowed. "Owe you both, I do. But decided not have I what to do with the woman. You can help me make up my mind, R-r-reylock. Tell me what I want to know, and go easier on her, it will."

At last Sarina knew why Bdan hadn't touched her. She'd been imprisoned in his harem for days, having been captured by his pirates soon after she'd left Earth's orbit, without any explanation or demands.

Seeing Teir now made it all clear. Bdan planned to use her in order to force vital information from the captain. Sarina's heart twisted within her. If only she could help him! He hung by his wrists, looking more dead than alive. There was an ugly red blotch on his chest and his face was badly bruised. His eyes were glazed with pain, but Sarina knew that he would never have given in if he hadn't seen her. To save her, he would do whatever the smuggler asked.

"Teir!" she cried. "Don't tell him anything!"

"Be silent!" Bdan thrust out the rod he held and a crackling beam of electricity shot forth, hitting Sarina with a painful impact. The Horthas gripped her in place as she sagged.

Bdan pocketed the device and sneered. "Slaves speak only when given permission. Remember that, *sumi,* or use this to control you, will I."

Sarina's hands flew to her throat. The collar was tightening, choking her. She couldn't breathe. Her eyes widened in panic as she gasped for breath.

Abruptly, Bdan released her from the choke hold with a movement of his hand. "Well, R-r-reylock? Reconsidering, are you?"

Teir saw Sarina's all but imperceptible nod indicating that she was all right. The Horthas were still supporting her, but she could stand on her own. He refused to speak.

"Know you who else wants this woman, Captain?"

Bdan growled. "K'darr, chief of the Morgots. Shall I give her to him?"

Gods, what was he going to do? "I don't care," he lied, certain that Sarina understood.

"Of course, I could keep her here in my harem. Much pleasure would she bring me. Does that bother you?"

"No, why should it? I was just hired as her bodyguard."

"Is that all, Captain? My sources informed me there might be between you more than meets the eye."

"What sources?"

"Like to know, would you? Well, which is it to be—the Morgots, or me? Up to you it is. Talk, and I'll make it easy for her."

Sarina was horrified by the alternatives. Either way, she faced an awful fate. Yet she'd almost rather be given to the dreaded Morgots than be manhandled by the ugly hound. A shudder wracked her body.

"Don't, Teir," Sarina begged. "Don't tell him what he wants to know. Remember your duty. What happens to me doesn't matter!"

Duty. The word stuck in his mind even as Bdan barked an order for his slave foreman Ixan to take her away. Teir watched her break free from the guards and start to run toward him. Ixan intercepted her. Whippet-face stepped from the shadows and activated her collar. Sarina fell to the ground, gasping and choking, her hands clutching at her neck. At a signal from Ixan, the Horthas dragged her away.

"Where is the Blood Crystal?" Bdan repeated, approaching Teir. "The female will suffer if you do not r-r-reply."

"Go to Zor! I'll never talk," Teir grated. "I am sworn to protect the location of the mystic stone."

"Time will I give you to think upon it. Consider the things I can do to her, Captain. Terrible, painful things."

With a flick of his wrist, he ordered Teir to be cut

down. The agony of release was unbearable. Teir collapsed on the ground, clutching his cold, lifeless hands to his stomach.

"Put him in a wasting pit," the slaver ordered another set of guards. "We'll see how well you r-r-resist after confinement, Captain. Enjoy your stay in my dungeon."

The Hortha beasts yanked Teir upright, gripping him by the arms. As they dragged him away like a helpless rag doll, Bdan's snorting laughter echoed in his ears.

The days passed without Teir knowing if it was day or night. Fear and anxiety occupied his waking hours as he wondered what had become of Sarina. Had Bdan hurt her? Or was the trader keeping her untouched as a prize for the Morgots?

Worrying about her ate away at his strength, weakening Teir and leaving him with nothing but despair and guilt. If he'd told her the truth while they were on the *Valiant,* they might not be in this predicament. Sarina had wanted to go back to Earth to see the friends and family she'd left behind, but his refusal had compelled her to take action on her own. If she'd known how much he cared for her, she might have stayed. Together, they might have found an alternative to the execution decree. It was his fault that they had been captured by Cerrus Bdan, so it was up to him to think of a way out.

As though his mental torment wasn't enough, Teir's body was further weakened by lack of food, for he was given no solid nourishment. He shivered in the cold and damp. The pit was lit by a single flamelight, but there wasn't much to see. A corroded chamber pot rested in a corner, contributing to the foul odor already present from previous occupants.

Lying on his lumpy cot, he thought about Cerrus Bdan's demands. By virtue of his position as Chief Troubleshooter for the Defense League, Teir had automatically assumed the responsibility for guarding the Blood Crystal's location. Glotaj and Admiral Daras Gog were the only others who knew its secret hiding place.

Fifteen annums ago, an unmanned alien probe had entered Coalition space from an unexplored region of the galaxy. The cylindrical vessel had no markings to reveal its origins or purpose. Inside, under a protective translucent dome, the Defense League force that investigated found a black crystal rock streaked with veins of red. They reported it to Command and were told to take it to the nearest starbase. Twenty hauras after that first report, all communications with the patrol craft were cut off.

Another Defense League vessel was dispatched to follow up. They found the patrol ship intact, but all her crew were dead. From the destructive scene aboard, it appeared that they had killed each other.

Thinking that the crystal might have affected them in some way, the investigators encased it in a specially shielded container and took it to a laboratory at the nearest starbase. Analysis showed it to be made of a foreign matrix impervious to sensor scans. The scientists handling it began to have strange visions of the future. And then the conflicts began. One scientist tried to steal it, hoping to gain great power by using its knowledge of things to come. Another was murdered over possession of the crystal. Its very presence seemed to drive men mad.

The head of the Defense League notified Glotaj of the discovery and the problems associated with it. Glotaj then discussed the matter with the High Council and they decided the Blood Crystal, so named because of the spilt blood of its discoverers and the red veins in the rock, was a dangerous object that needed to be hidden away where no one would be tempted to use it. It was put into the charge of whichever officer held the title of Chief Troubleshooter since he'd be free to make biannual inspections of the guardian site that housed the crystal.

So why would Cerrus Bdan be after it? Teir wondered. Did he hope to discover the result of the First Amendment vote? Did he plan to learn if the legend of the Great Healer was true before deciding what to do with Sarina?

The High Council had debated using the Blood Crystal to learn the Great Healer's identity once the signs of the prophecy appeared. They'd also considered consulting it to learn the outcome of the problems plaguing the Coalition. But the benefits of its use were minuscule compared to the evil it could unleash and it was deemed too dangerous a risk.

Teir himself had never handled the black crystal rock because he'd been warned that its influence twisted one's mind. In any event, he didn't want to know the future. But he took his responsibility seriously and twice an annum journeyed to the guardian to make sure it was secure. He must protect its location even now.

As time passed he grew even weaker. Parched with thirst, Teir eyed the mildew growing on the walls with a view to licking off the moisture. But then his meager ration of water would be pushed through a small hinged opening at the base of the massive steel door and his desperation would be momentarily forgotten. Gradually he lost track of time and began mumbling to himself. His stomach went from gnawing hunger to where he thought he'd vomit if he ate.

Three times a day, when Teir got the water, someone peeked through a grate at eye level on the door. If he was ever going to attempt an escape, he'd better make it soon.

Mustering what was left of his energy, he formed the bedding into an approximate shape of a man. Then he took up his position beside the door, flattening himself against the wall. He stayed there for what seemed like hauras, his leg muscles cramping, clenching and unclenching his fists to maintain circulation in his arms. Footsteps scraped past, and he thought the guard must have looked in. It would take one or two more times, Teir figured, before the guard decided to examine the unmoving figure on the cot.

Hauras later, it happened.

Footsteps approached, then there was a pause as though someone were peering in. A grunt followed, and a rattle of keys. The steel door swung open. A Hortha guard entered, weapon poised. Teir waited until his shadow had passed, then jumped him, desperation giving him the surge of adrenaline he needed. He took the guard's shooter and locked the door from the outside before the guard could make a sound.

Pocketing the keys, Teir surveyed his surroundings. He faced a spacious cavern, prison cells lining the circular walls. A trestle table and several chairs stood in the center. The room appeared to be unguarded, or maybe the Hortha was the only one assigned. Teir wasn't going to wait to find out. He had to find Sarina. But which way to go?

"Don't move," a harsh voice commanded as something cold poked him in the small of his back.

Teir froze, his heart pounding.

"You wish to find the girl?" Surprised, Teir nodded. "This way."

The pressure eased from his back. Teir whirled around to see a hooded figure shuffling off. He hurried to catch up which was difficult considering his physical state. The surge of adrenaline had helped him overpower the Hortha guard, but as it drained, he felt weak from hunger and lack of exercise.

"Who are you?" he croaked.

"A friend," the figure in front grated. Teir couldn't make out its gender. "A Believer in the legend. Follow me. I will take you to the Great Healer."

"How did you know I was going to get out?" Teir asked suspiciously. He cradled the shooter in his hand, ready to use it if necessary.

"I have been waiting. If you had not made a move, I would have found a way to assist you. Be silent. We approach the armory."

Loud buzzing noises reverberated from an open door, the sound of Horthas' voices. They made their way past, then ascended to surface level via a tunnel. Above ground, the buildings took on a palatial grandeur. The maze inside Bdan's complex was like a labyrinth. Teir would never have been able to find Sarina on his own.

The Believer led him through a series of secret passages until they reached the Souk leader's harem. "The woman rests within this room," the voice told him outside a closed door. "You must wait until daylight when she is alone. Others sleep inside, slaves like herself, and Horthas stand guard. I leave you now. I must not be discovered here."

"Wait!" Teir said. "What about that collar she wears?"

"Aim your shooter at a precise angle and it will break off."

"How do we find our way out of here?"

His guide lowered his voice. "Every sleeping chamber has an entrance to a secret passage on the north wall. The passage will lead you outside."

This fellow must be high up in Bdan's hierarchy to be so familiar with palace secrets, Teir thought. "And then what?" He was so weak he doubted he could even make a run for it.

"The woman arrived in your spaceship, the *Valiant*. It is secured at a spaceport some distance from here. I suggest you hide in the forest until you recover your strength, then devise a plan to board your vessel. My compatriots will look for you to render assistance." From his voluminous garment, the stranger pulled out a hunk of bread. "Eat this. It contains carboplex and will give you energy."

"Thanks," Teir said gruffly, taking the offering. He

eyed the robed stranger curiously. "Who are you? I'd like to repay you someday."

"Free the Great Healer. That will be thanks enough." With a rustle of fabric, the Believer was gone.

Slinking back into the secret passage, Teir left the opening slightly ajar. He leaned against a wall, tucking the shooter into his waistband. Then he started breaking off pieces of the bread, careful not to eat too fast. When he'd finished, he thought about what to do. He didn't know how many were inside the sleeping chamber with Sarina. It was better to wait until she came out. Pulling his weapon, he settled down to wait.

Sarina tossed restlessly on the cushioned lounger. The sleeping chamber held eleven other slaves besides herself, and the lack of privacy plus her anxious state of mind inhibited her ability to sleep. Horthas stood guard at either end, and knowing their watchful eyes were upon her didn't help. She turned on her side and contemplated her situation.

Two additional chambers could be reached through connecting archways; altogether, thirty-six females of varying species were in the harem. Each of them, with the exception of herself, competed for the attention of their master. Ava Bet, Bdan's sole *gima*, threw a jealous rage whenever he spent the night with one of them, but gossip was that Bdan liked to rile her. She was the only one chosen for that exalted position, so her title wasn't really threatened. She just didn't want to share his favors.

The surroundings were plush considering the women's status as slaves. Fabrics in bright multicolors billowed from the ceiling, and pillows in matching hues covered the floor. Bdan liked the setting to be pleasing to his eye when he strolled in to select his bed partner for the night.

Sarina cringed every time she saw him, afraid he'd choose her, but the others were eager to be selected. Privilege and power were afforded those so favored. Sarina, however, was assigned the most menial chores and frequent physical punishments. She had lost count of the times she'd felt the lash of Ixan's stun whip in the past few days. Each time the pain was worse than before. Whippet-face seemed to take particular delight in tormenting her, and because the stun whips did no permanent damage, he could beat her as frequently as his cruelty dictated. The choke collar was used often, too, and a lingering sore throat was the wretched result.

This day had been particularly long and she'd barely been fed. Sarina didn't know how much longer she could go on. She wasn't used to hard physical labor, and the work combined with the punishments were taking their toll. It became an effort even to move. Her only consolation was that Bdan hadn't touched her, at least not yet. She wondered what he was waiting for. Maybe he was planning to sell her to the Morgots after all. That would mean Teir hadn't talked, because Bdan implied he would keep her if the captain cooperated. Had Bdan tortured him? Was he still alive? Fear for him chilled her.

Suddenly the door blew open and the room brightened. Cerrus Bdan sauntered inside, accompanied by his personal Souk bodyguards. "You," he said, pointing in her direction. "Come."

Sarina curled into a ball, hoping he was looking at the Polluxite female in the next bed.

"Sarina!" Bdan barked. "Do you defy me?"

She scrambled to her feet before he could activate her choker. "I obey, master," she mumbled, her head bowed.

The guards surrounded her and she was marched out after Bdan. Her heart thumped wildly, and she didn't dare glance around. She kept her head lowered, her eyes down. Where was he taking her? She felt sick with apprehension.

They wound through numerous corridors and then

entered another suite, apparently Bdan's private quarters because the decorations were even more lavish in this section of the palace. Sarina's heart sank as they entered a sumptuous sleeping chamber dominated by a huge circular bed. Raised on a pedestal in the center of the room, it was surrounded by a moat of water. Reflectors covered the walls and ceiling, and hidden lighting cast a mellow glow. A wide dresser was the only other furnishing.

Oh God, no! Sarina thought, staring at the bed draped in gold.

Bdan turned to his bodyguards. "Leave us," he commanded.

The Souks marched out. Alone, she faced Cerrus Bdan. Drool dribbled down his mouth as he regarded her.

"What do you want with me?" she asked in a defiant tone, lifting her chin.

Bdan absently fingered his crimson caftan. "Wish I to see what you have to offer before I make my decision," he said, his beady eyes slowly trailing down her body. Sarina felt as though he were undressing her, though the skimpy bra and embroidered girdle she wore left little to the imagination.

"Let us get more comfortable," said Bdan. *"Bridge!"*

A narrow path extended across the moat. Grasping Sarina's hand, he pulled her to the edge of the water. "Cross," he commanded.

She had no choice. Trembling, she obeyed. Bdan followed her, then ordered the bridge to retract.

"Sit," he ordered. Pointing to the murky water, he said, "The moat is not very wide but it is deep. Creatures live inside it, tiny flegymns. Devour a human can they within fifteen seconds. Luckily, the flegymns do not like the taste of Souk flesh!" He snorted with amusement, and Sarina cringed. It was clear she could not dive into the water to escape him.

Bdan's expression sobered. "Sample your wares,

shall I. No Great Healer are you. A mere Earth-woman—frail, too." He looked her over appraisingly. "Killed a Vilaran female once, did I. Too thin, like you." He roared with laughter, and Sarina's face whitened. "Tell K'darr, will I, that you were nothing special if you die. Off with your clothes!"

"What?" She swallowed uncertainly.

Bdan grasped her and pulled her against his fat body. "Need I use the choker?"

"No—no, please don't," Sarina whispered. He was so overwhelmingly powerful, and she was defenseless, utterly at his mercy.

Bdan put a paw on her breast and kneaded it. After a moment, he thrust her away. "Hurry. I grow impatient."

He was growing, all right. Sarina saw his organ protruding from the caftan below his ample waistline, and it appeared to be enormous. "I can't," she croaked, feeling like she was going to throw up.

"What say you?" he thundered.

Sarina felt the collar tighten around her throat, constricting her neck so she couldn't breathe. She fell back, helpless, clawing at the restraint. Even as she lay there, gasping and choking, she felt Bdan's paws rip away her garments.

Suddenly, a red beam of light pierced the air.

"Who—?" Bdan didn't finish the sentence. He toppled over into the water and sank out of sight.

"Sarina!"

It was Teir's voice. A surge of joy swelled within her. Rolling over so she could see him, she tried to warn him about the moat, but it was useless. All she could do was gasp and yank at the cursed collar.

"Hold on," he said.

A moment later, he vaulted onto the bed using an extended electrifier rod he'd found on a guard outside the room. Casting it to the ground, he knelt beside her.

"Don't move," he said, twisting her head to the side.

He aimed the shooter carefully and fired. The laser beam severed the collar, releasing Sarina from its choke hold. She gulped in huge breaths of air.

"Are you all right?" His voice was raw, his eyes dark with anxiety.

"Yes," she whispered. "The guards?"

"Stunned." He tucked the shooter into his waistband. "We've got to get out of here before they wake up."

"And Bdan?" She stared at the water. No bubbles arose. There was no sign of him in the murky depths.

"Who cares? Let's go."

"Wait, there's a way across." Mustering all her strength, Sarina shouted, "Bridge!"

The bridge extended and as they hurried across, Sarina got a good look at Teir. He was gaunt, his cheekbones prominent, his eyes darkened hollows. The purplish bruises on his face stood out against the pallor of his skin. His ragged shirt hung loosely on him, and she bit her lip when she saw his chest. The wound there was raw and blistered.

"How have you made it this far?" she asked in astonishment. Her throat still hurt, and her voice was raspy when she spoke.

"I managed. I'll tell you about it later. We've got to get out of here!"

He stared at her naked body, his face expressionless. "You need something to wear."

Teir saw in his mind's eye the obscene bluish body of Cerrus Bdan hovering above her, ripping away her clothes. He'd arrived just in time. With a groan, he reached out and pulled Sarina into his embrace.

Several days growth of beard scraped her cheeks. Sarina, wanting him, needing him, wound her arms around his neck and pressed herself against his chest, unwilling to let him go. He'd come for her! He could have escaped, but he'd come to rescue her instead. She knew he cared for her even more than he would admit, and she yearned to give herself to him in return.

As Teir held her, a strange tingling electrified his nerve endings. The sensation spread through his skin.

"I feel funny," he said, jerking away.

Sarina stared at his chest. "My God!"

Teir looked down. Instead of the ugly, raw sore, he saw a patch of unmarred, hairless skin. "The wound—it's gone," he gasped.

"And your face! The bruises have cleared." Sarina couldn't believe her eyes.

"Sarina, how could this happen? Unless—unless. . . ." He regarded her with awe.

A loud banging on the chamber door roused them to action.

"Quick, we've got to go! Here, put this on." He ripped off his shirt and gave it to her, then put his vest back on.

"There should be a way out by the north wall," he said, racing over to the reflector.

Sarina was still stunned by what had occurred, but the fact that the guards were about to enter brought her back to reality. They had to escape. She only hoped Teir's strength would hold out long enough.

"Is this a crack?" she asked, noting a seam in the reflector.

"You're right!" Teir ran his fingers along the edges until he felt something catch. Pushing on the wall, he was rewarded when a section swung out. "I'll go first." He drew his shooter and proceeded forward.

Sarina swung the section of heavy wall closed behind her. Tunnel after tunnel followed; then suddenly they were outside, at the west end of Bdan's complex. The spread of buildings covered a vast area over a desert-like terrain.

"Now where?" she asked, shading her eyes with her hand. The sunlight was so bright after being confined inside for so many days that it all but blinded her.

"That way," Teir answered, pointing. Tree-clad mountains rose in the near distance. "We'll hide in the forest until we figure out how to get to my ship."

"Look!" Sarina gestured to a pen. "Women are trapped there! That's where I was placed when I first came here. They must be new arrivals, waiting for processing." She knew from hearing the guards discussing the latest arrivals that most of the women were sent to the mines. Only a few became palace servers, and on a rare occasion, Bdan chose one for his harem. "Can't we take them with us?"

"No! They'll only slow us down, and freeing them might set off an alarm. So far no one has sounded an alert." He started forward.

"Hold it, Teir!" He halted, and Sarina stood her ground. "We have the perfect opportunity to set those women free. They're human, like you and me. Some might even be from Vilaran, your homeplanet. How can we leave them? There is room in the cargo hold of the *Valiant* to bring them along with us, and it shouldn't be too hard for you to take out the guards with your shooter."

"And what do we do in the meantime, while we're figuring out how to get to the ship? I'm not in very good shape," Teir pointed out. "I don't know where we're going to get food. You're endangering our escape by worrying about them."

"Teir, *please!*"

Damn the woman, sometimes she took compassion too far! "Look, Sarina, those women are being fed," he said to convince her. "They're alive. If we take them with us, there's no telling what might happen. We could all end up dead."

"I suppose you're right," Sarina conceded. They'd be putting the women at a greater risk by taking them rather than by leaving them. "Maybe we can do something later on to help."

Suddenly loud sirens began howling.

"Come on," Teir yelled, gesturing for her to follow as he began running.

Abandoning all thoughts except their own survival, they dashed for the hills. The dust kicked up by their heels clogged their nostrils. The ground was dry and uneven, but the flatness made running easier. The mountains loomed closer, and spread out at the foot was the beginning of the jungle, a thick tangle of vegetation.

Teir glanced back once or twice but kept going. So far no one pursued them, although the sirens kept wailing. His head was beginning to swim from exertion, and his heart thumped furiously. The heat didn't help, either. They had to make the jungle before he collapsed.

Sarina was keeping up with him, but it was a struggle. Her breathing was uneven, and her pulse raced. Her feet were torn up by tiny pebbles on the rough ground. The sun beat upon her back, and sweat poured down her face. But she forgot her discomfort the moment she heard the whine of engines from behind.

"They're coming after us!" she cried, slowing for a look back. Her breath caught in her throat.

Speeders were zooming in their direction, driven by armed Horthas, and the expressions on the beasts' faces were fierce.

Chapter Thirteen

"Hurry!" Teir cried. The edge of the jungle neared as they stumbled forward. A mist rose like a curtain in front of them from the sudden increase in humidity.

The Horthas loomed menacingly closer. She could hear their angry buzzing noises vibrating in the air.

"Keep moving," Teir urged, grabbing her arm and shoving her forward.

The mist cooled their faces like a fine sprinkle of rain as they reached the border of tall trees. Teir welcomed the thickening fog as they penetrated deeper. It was like a protective cocoon, insulating them from the horrors behind them. Thorns from twisting fodus vines ripped at their limbs and sticky spiderwebs netted them, but Teir didn't want to risk using his shooter to clear a passage—the radiation could be picked up on a scanner.

The heat combined with the humidity was devastating. They were both soaked with sweat. Sarina's chest heaved with the effort of breathing. Then the mist lifted, and sunlight filtered through the branches above them. A rich earthy smell permeated the air. All around them teemed the sounds of the jungle.

Pushing past a giant fern, Sarina stumbled. A numbing fatigue had entered her bones, and her steps faltered.

"I've got to stop and catch my breath," she gasped, leaning against a large green stalk. Her chest ached, and her feet were painfully raw. She didn't think she could go much farther. Something dripped onto her arm and she noticed a brownish fluid seeping from the plant. With a small cry, she jerked away. The vegetation was alien; the sap might be harmful.

"We can't stop," Teir mumbled, his steps slowing to a halt several meters in front of her. His head was spinning, and he felt strangely light-headed. He tried to put one foot in front of the other, but his vision clouded. He tripped over a root and felt himself topple over.

Sarina heard the thud as he hit the soft, moist earth. "Teir, are you all right?" She hobbled forward, her feet throbbing painfully with each step. He wasn't moving! Alarmed, she knelt beside him and felt for a pulse. The beat was rapid and thready. "Wake up!" she cried, shaking him, but he remained as cold and still as stone.

Teir had a marvelous dream. Sarina was enveloped by a strange glowing aura. The aura expanded, radiated, became a blinding white light. It was the light from the sacred Auricle. Stories of the legend reverberated in his mind. An ancient people with special powers—from them would come a descendant—that descendant would be The One. When the signs were right, the Great Healer would be revealed. In the dream, Teir saw Sarina touch his wounded arm. The cut vanished. He saw the burn on his chest disappear when he held her in his arms. Her image shimmered in a halo of bright stars and then blurred. She was calling his name. . . .

Teir's eyes snapped open. Sarina's face hovered above his, his name on her lips.

"Sarina—" He tried to speak, but his mouth was so dry he could only croak.

She cradled his head and raised him, pressing a canteen of water to his mouth. He gulped thirstily.

"He's awake," she said to someone out of his range of vision.

Teir twisted his neck and saw two curious, wrinkled faces peering at him. They were Crigellans, a crossbreed of humans and a lizard-like species. For an instant Teir felt alarm. They reminded him of Lieutenant Otis, Bdan's second-in-command.

"They are friends," Sarina said hastily, seeing the look on his face. "Salla and her mate are Believers."

Teir didn't need any other explanation. The robed figure who had assisted his escape had said that helpers would look after them. Now he saw a youth of about sixteen annums looking on. He was fresh-faced, with a thatch of bright auburn hair and an eager expression.

"How long have I been out?"

"For eighteen hauras," Salla answered. "The two moons of Souk have passed while you were still. Now it is morn, and soon the sol will be high in the sky. We must gather nourishment." The old female narrowed her keen blue eyes. "We've left you some canna fruit. Eat and regain your strength. You are weak as a babe."

"What's the plan?" Teir asked. His limbs felt like gelatin.

"You will remain in the jungle until you are fully recovered. This place is called the Thicket of Bayne. Rising yonder are the Koodrash Mounts, on the other side of which is Ruel's territory. You don't want to go there. Bdan inhabits the Nurash Desert on this side, and he has secured your ship at the spaceport on the other end of his complex, beyond the Sand Pit. You'll need full use of your skills to get there safely."

She glanced at her companion. "Etan and I go now. Devin, the boy, will act as guard."

Teir nodded, deciding further questions could wait. The Crigellans marched off.

"I will watch the clearing," Devin said. "There is a pond on the other side of that stand of trees if you wish to bathe."

"Thanks," Teir mumbled. He didn't have the energy to move, let alone scrub himself.

"Here, eat this," Sarina said softly, kneeling beside him. In her outstretched palm was a bulbous purple fruit.

Grabbing the fruit, Teir bit into it, eating voraciously.

"Not so fast," Sarina warned.

"Water," he rasped, incredibly thirsty again. She passed it to him and he gulped greedily.

The effort of eating sapped his energy and he lay back, resting his head on a makeshift pillow Sarina had fashioned from leaves.

"I'll help you wash," Sarina offered, reminding him that he must smell and look like a piece of vorax's forage.

"No, I can manage. I'll take a dip in the pond," he said, groaning at the effort of rising. It would be worth it to rid himself of the layers of filth he'd accumulated. He staggered off in the direction Salla had indicated.

The pond nestled in a small hollow surrounded by tall tropical trees. *Humma* birds sang in the branches, and colorful butterflies swooped low over the flowering bushes lining the earthen banks. A spicy scent tickled his nostrils but it was a pleasant sensation, like a woman's tantalizing perfume.

Teir quickly stripped off his vest and pants and waded into the crystal clear water until it reached his chest. The temperature felt surprisingly warm. Relaxing, he stretched out on his back, enjoying the weightless sensation as he bobbed gently on the

rippling current. Gradually, the soreness seeped from
his limbs. He closed his eyes and let the warm water
envelop him as he floated on his back.

"You can use this to scrub," Sarina's voice said close
to his ear.

Teir pried his eyes open and stood, feet resting on
the sandy bottom. She was waist deep beside him in
the water, naked. In her hand was a spongy mass. "I
found this by the water's edge. Do you need help?"

He glanced at her full breasts. "Yes, I need help, but
not the kind you have in mind," he said huskily.

"Not now," Sarina retorted, although her pulse was
racing excitedly. "First we wash, and then we talk.
You've a lot to answer for."

"So do you," he said, remembering how she'd
drugged him and stolen his ship.

"You're still weak. Let me do this so you can
conserve your energy." She began scrubbing him
and his resentment drained away, replaced instead
with rising desire. Each sensuous movement affected
his skin like electric shocks. Her touch aroused him
beyond belief, and he couldn't restrain the moan
of pleasure that escaped his lips. Purposely, she
seemed to be avoiding his abdomen and his genitals.
Keeping her eyes demurely downcast, Sarina washed
his arms next.

Commanding him to turn around, she tackled his
back, taking an extraordinarily long time across his
broad shoulders as though she were enjoying herself.
Teir was grinning when she faced him again.

"You can do the rest yourself," she said, holding out
the sponge. She glanced below his waistline, raising
her brows at his tumescence.

"Don't you want to finish me off?" he teased.

"We're supposed to be getting clean, remember?"
Nevertheless, she smiled knowingly.

Teir snatched the sponge from her fingers and
proceeded to scrub his lower half while Sarina
watched. It's been so long, she thought, swallowing

as he washed between his sturdy thighs. His shaft was hard and erect, and he glided the sponge up and down its length in slow motion, as if to excite her deliberately. She moistened her lips with the tip of her tongue. When he stooped to wash his legs, she breathed a sigh of relief, but it wasn't to last for long. As soon as he was done, he faced her.

"Your turn," he said.

That devilish grin was on his face again. "I can wash myself," Sarina said, reaching for the sponge.

Teir grasped her wrist and turned her around. "Let me do your back. It's hard for you to reach."

The sponge touched her skin. At first the pressure was strong, but then it lightened and she felt Teir's fingers running feathery movements across her back. It tickled and tingled at the same time.

"Stop," she murmured, squirming. He sponged her buttocks, and then she felt his touch between her legs. Pleasure flooded her as his fingers lingered there.

"Bend over," he said, applying gentle pressure to her back.

Too weak-kneed to protest, she complied. "Oh God, Teir," she said, as he stroked her. Closing her eyes, she surrendered to his tender ministrations. The intimate caresses continued until she felt herself becoming moist and open, ready for him.

"Now turn around," Teir said gruffly, slowly rotating her body.

Sarina looked down, enjoying the sight of him touching her breasts. The sponge was nowhere in sight. Cleanliness was apparently far from his mind at present, as it was from hers. All she could do was moan and thrust herself forward. His thumbs brushed her nipples; then he pinched them, sending exquisite sensations along her nerves.

"So lovely," he murmured, stooping to kiss her breasts.

"Teir, please!" She couldn't wait for him to finish. The ache between her legs was becoming unbearable.

"Don't rush it. Haven't you missed this as much as I did? Let's take our time and enjoy each other."

He bit her nipple and a sharp ache shot to her groin. As his tongue licked her, she closed her eyes and murmured small sounds of pleasure. When he took her nipple into his mouth and suckled it, she groaned.

"Let's lie down," Teir said in a husky voice. He led her to the water's edge and lowered her to a soft carpet of moss. Sarina's damp blond hair fanned out around her face. Teir crouched above her, breathing heavily. His midnight black hair clung wetly to his forehead. Several days' growth of beard shadowed his face. Those tender blue eyes, that mouth poised above hers were all she'd yearned for, dreamed of, during her time away from him. Talking could wait until later. Right now, this was all that mattered. She reached for him, pulling him down on top of her, relishing the feel of his hair-roughened chest against her soft, aching breasts. Squirming under him, she eagerly sought his lips.

Teir clamped his mouth to hers, urging her legs apart with his strong thighs. With a deep groan, he entered her and began his thrusts, slowly at first, savoring the feel of her. She was part of him, this woman, and he never wanted to let her go again. His passion took over and he forgot everything but the incredible sensations spiraling through him.

Sarina clutched at his back. She wanted to be closer to him, joined with him forever. The future didn't matter as long as they were together. She moved her hips to match his frantic thrusts, all gentleness gone now. They'd been apart too long. Waves of pleasure overwhelmed her until she thought she'd burst. When Teir exploded, sending his hot seed gushing into her, she reached the pinnacle. Spasm after spasm of ecstasy cascaded over her until at last, she was spent. But not sated. She'd been starved for him too long.

They slept for a while, naked on the moist bank of

earth, and when they awoke, both were ready again.
This time, as before, their lovemaking was fast and
furious, leaving them exhausted.

"I'm sorry," Teir said. "I wanted to take it slowly so
you would enjoy it more, but I needed you so much.
Next time, I promise it will be better." He leaned up
on his elbow, playing with her hair as she lay beside
him, smiling.

She traced his cheek with one finger. "I enjoyed it
just fine, thank you. But speaking of the next time,
what about now? I just can't get enough of you!"

A teasing twinkle was in her eye as her hand roved
down to the curly hairs on his chest. She tweaked a
silken hair provocatively.

"You witch!" Teir sprawled on his back. "You've
worn me out. I don't have any energy left to do
anything else."

"Well then, I guess I'll have to wait. After all,
you're supposed to be recovering your strength, not
using it up."

He rolled his head in her direction, raising an
eyebrow. "You're just too much to resist, woman."

Sarina kissed him lightly. "Seriously, I'm supposed
to be taking care of you. And Devin could return at
any moment, come to think of it. We'd better get
dressed."

She got up to wash their clothes. They'd have to
wear them wet, but the heat should dry them fast
enough. She didn't count on Teir's wet shirt clinging
to her breasts in so revealing a manner, however.

"If that young fellow sees you like that, he's likely
to want you for himself," Teir said with a grin as he
put on his sodden pants and vest.

"I doubt it. He's too much in awe of me as the
Great Healer. Speaking of which, I think it's time for
our talk."

Teir made a face. He'd much rather talk of love
than of politics.

As soon as he thought the word, he frowned. *Love?*

Where had that notion come from? He stared at Sarina dazedly. What he felt for her was lust, not love, wasn't it? Then why did you miss her so much? another section of his mind asked. Why did you feel as though a part of you had been torn asunder when she left you? Now that he thought about it, he hadn't so much as looked at another woman since he'd met Sarina. She filled his thoughts to the exclusion of everyone else.

By the stars, this was a novel idea! Never having been in love before, Teir wasn't sure how it was supposed to feel. Perhaps he should explore his emotions about Sarina more deeply.

But Sarina still belonged to Lord Cam'brii, Teir reminded himself, and the legend stated that she had to fall in love and marry him, not necessarily in that order, for her healing ability to be activated. Twice now, she'd made Teir's wounds disappear. The first time, the cut on his arm had been mended after the attack by the Twyggs. Then in Bdan's complex, the wound on his chest had vanished and his bruises had disappeared. Her touch had healed him in both instances. Did that mean she'd fallen in love with Cam'brii after all?

His mood abruptly darkened. "Yes, we need to talk," he said in a gruff tone.

Looking around, he found a moss-covered log to sit on, being careful not to get too near the ant garden on an overhanging branch. Spherical in shape and somewhat smaller than a kick ball, it was made of soil and masses of vegetable fibers chewed by the ants. The garden bristled with small, succulent epiphytic plants that sprouted from the surface in all directions. Teir knew if he got too close the ants would swarm and spray him with a cloud of formic acid.

Devin wasn't in sight, and there was no sign of the Crigellans either. Listening to the sounds around them, Teir contemplated what he was going to say. His ears picked up the buzzing of paper wasps along with bird songs and the whir of brambids. Occasionally the screech of a white-faced kayoka was heard. Its cries seemed to echo the torment in his heart.

Teir's shirt still clinging damply to her body, Sarina leaned against a tree trunk, waiting for Teir to speak first. She wanted to hear his reasons for turning away from her on the *Valiant.* As the silence lengthened, she stared at the ground, wondering why he didn't begin. Maybe he was still angry at her for stealing his ship. He had every right to be furious. Sarina had acted in a deceitful and impulsive manner, and she could have cost him his career. But by the passionate way they'd just made love, Sarina had assumed he'd forgiven her. Was it possible she'd been wrong? Trying to quell her sudden fear, she studied a beetle carrying a morsel of rotting fruit.

At last Teir spoke. "Twice now, you've healed me, Sarina," he said, his voice low. "When I was wounded by the Twyggs, you touched me and my wound disappeared. I didn't mention it to you at the time because I didn't believe in the legend. We both know what happened in Bdan's palace. It can only mean one thing. You've fallen in love with Lord Cam'brii. Was that why you decided to leave Earth and go back to Bimordus Two, because you finally realized how you felt about him?"

"How absurd! I could never love that man," Sarina replied.

"Robert, then? Did seeing your fiance bring back a flood of feelings? Is he the one you're in love with?" It didn't make sense, according to the legend, but one of the reasons she had gone back to Earth had been to see Robert.

"I broke off our engagement."

Teir felt a swell of unaccountable relief. "Well, you must have fallen in love with *somebody* for your healing powers to be activated."

He drew his brows together, thoughtful. The legend

didn't actually state that she had to fall in love with the Raimorrdan she wed, just that her healing aura would result from the power of her love. That could be interpreted in different ways. The High Council chose to believe it meant she would fall in love with Cam'brii, but maybe that wasn't so. *Teir* was the one she'd healed, wasn't he? Didn't that mean something? He was the only one who'd inspired her power thus far.

She was gazing at him apprehensively, so he let an impish expression brighten his features. "If it's not Cam'brii, and it's not Robert, I guess that leaves me," he said jauntily.

Sarina's mouth dropped open. The nerve of him, grinning at her like that. "I should say not! After the way you treated me? It was clear you wanted nothing to do with me."

"That was all pretense, Sarina." His expression grew serious. "I knew you were destined for Lord Cam'brii. I really did care about you, but if I'd told you then, you might have chosen me over Cam'brii and that would not have been acceptable."

She sighed. "I think I understood that deep down, but you still hurt me. Am I forgiven for taking your ship? I hope you didn't get into too much trouble."

He brought her up to date on his activities while they munched on ripe sulu berries from a nearby bush. The bushes grew on Vilaran, so Teir knew the berries were safe to ingest.

"You say your aunt raised you?" Sarina asked, curious about his background. Until now he'd never talked much about himself.

Teir nodded. "Aunt Catharta said my parents died in a reactor accident when I was small. She and Uncle Jebs were my only living relatives. We traveled around a lot, Uncle Jebs' business taking us to different planets, but then we settled in a small hamlet on Vilaran. Having had a taste of travel, I hated being confined to one location. But Uncle Jebs' health was failing, and Catharta thought we should stay close to home."

Sarina read the distress on his face. "You weren't happy, were you?"

"I didn't fit in. All the other kids seemed to have such narrow concerns, while I had a different view of life. I wanted to stretch my imagination, roam the stars, have grand adventures. For some reason, Catharta discouraged my views. She gave me the impression my musings frightened her. She became reclusive after Jebs died, never inviting anyone over, and that made our life even more dismal. Yet for all that, she loved me as though I were her own son."

"It must have been a difficult time for you," Sarina murmured. "What made you join the Defense League?"

"The chance for travel, action, excitement. Aunt Catharta, surprisingly enough, approved. She'd learned by then that I didn't like being confined to any one place."

"I understand." Now that Sarina had had a taste of touring the stars, she, too, wanted to explore further.

"I didn't have any trouble getting into the Academy," Teir went on. "Catharta had a connection with Glotaj, and he vouched for me."

"What connection?"

Teir shrugged. "She never explained. I overheard the conversation they had about my wanting to enter the Defense League. To my knowledge, that was the only time they'd communicated. It was all very secretive, now that I think about it. When I asked Catharta about it, she said to forget I'd ever heard his name."

His eyes darkened. "This could be worth pursuing." He explained his theory about Glotaj trying to bring them together by assigning Teir to retrieve Sarina from Earth and then act as her bodyguard.

"But why would Glotaj want to do that?" Sarina

asked. "It doesn't make sense. The High Council has chosen Lord Cam'brii for me."

"I don't know. If Catharta recovers, I'll ask her. She was in isolation at the Wellness Center when I saw her; it's feared she has the Farg. I had to wear a protective shield to visit with her." He paused, preferring to change the subject away from the painful topic of his aunt's illness. "Did you see everyone on Earth whom you'd missed?"

Sarina nodded, warmed by his interest. Stretching, she walked over to a low stump and sat on it. "I told you about Robert. Mother was very disappointed, but that's her problem. The most exciting thing that happened to me involved my friend Abby." She went on to describe her whole experience.

"So because of the glowing stone, you're returning to the High Council?"

"Yes, I must see if the legend is true. I really do want to be a healer, Teir! There's so much good I can do if I have the power. Abby was just a small example, and with her I used a neurojet unit. Think of what I could do if I didn't need tools." The lustrous stone must still be on Teir's ship where she'd hidden it, Sarina figured.

How far would she go to test the legend's truth? Teir wondered. Would she marry Lord Cam'brii? "You'd asked me once about Cam'brii's background," he said, swatting away a buzzing insect. His skin felt itchy, and perspiration trickled down his back. The rising sun made the jungle steamy hot. "I found out what his secret is. It explains his behavior and his antipathy toward the Souks."

When he'd told the story, Sarina said, "That does explain a lot, Teir, but it doesn't change how I feel about either of you. Lord Cam'brii might try to woo me, but I'm not a pawn to be used in his political games."

"What were you planning to do when you returned to Bimordus Two?"

"I will try to fulfill my destiny."

"So you'll wed the councilor after all."

"If I have to, but only because of the legend, not because of the influence I can have in getting his First Amendment passed. As for loving Cam'brii, I don't believe I ever will."

Teir regarded her intently. "How do you feel about me, then? Is there a rational explanation for why your healing power seems to work only with me?"

She brushed a strand of hair off her face, confused by his question and the jumble of emotions it aroused. "What I feel for you is probably what I should be feeling for Lord Cam'brii."

He went over and knelt by her side. "Say it, Sarina. Tell me how you feel." He desperately wanted to hear the words.

His cobalt eyes probed hers as she struggled to explain how much she wanted to care for him, be with him. She reached out and smoothed the hair off his forehead. He caught her hand and turned it palm up, kissing her soft flesh. She gasped as his tongue darted out, licking the cup of her hand with sensuous circular movements that sent thrills down her spine.

"Teir," she whispered, "you're making me want you again." The ache began deep between her legs, and she realized how little of her thighs were covered by Teir's shirt. Her legs were nearly totally exposed.

"Look," Teir said softly, holding out her hand. "Look at the circle."

The circular birthmark on her palm had a faint glow. "It's as the legend states," Sarina replied in awe, gazing at her hand. She'd learned the details from her studies on Bimordus Two. "The Great Healer bears the sign of the circle. The sign will glow like the ancient Auricle." She looked at him. "The legend must be true!" She pulled her hand away, stunned by this further proof of who she was.

"If that's so, why did it stop glowing just now? Look

at your palm again," he said, gesturing.

The circle had reverted to a flat birthmark. What was it about touching Teir that inspired her powers?

They stared at each other but were startled by shouts coming from behind the thicket.

"Quick! Bdan's men seek you!" Devin crashed through the brush. The youth looked panicked.

"Where's Salla and her mate?"

"They fight them off."

"How many are there? Are they Horthas?" Teir said, bolting to his feet and reaching for his shooter at the same time.

"No, they are Souks, armed with stun whips. But there is one among them who is a champion fighter. Salla's mate has no hope against him. You must flee!"

"I'll not abandon them. Take Sarina to safety."

"No!" Sarina jumped up from her perch.

"It is not wise for you to fight," Devin warned Teir. "You are still weak from your ordeal. You need rest and food."

"I've just had both."

A high-pitched scream sounded and spurred Teir to action. Ignoring Sarina's cry of protest, he set off, crashing through the ground cover. Fallen tree trunks impeded his path and huge matted cobwebs brushed his face. Pressing on, Teir came to the clearing just in time to see Salla being manhandled by a giant Souk. Her mate lay on the ground, deathly still.

"Release her," Teir shouted, aiming his shooter.

Before he could fire, something sharp stung his wrist from behind and his numbed fingers dropped the weapon. Whirling, Teir saw that he'd missed the two rear guards who were poised in low-hanging branches. They were swinging their stun whips in his direction again. He easily sidestepped them, but by now the giant had dropped the helpless Salla and was lumbering toward him.

Teir scowled, facing the approaching dogface. So

it was to be hand-to-hand combat, was it? He gave a quick glance backward, but Devin and Sarina were nowhere in sight. Either they were hiding, or the boy was already leading her to safety. Somehow he knew, though, that Sarina wouldn't leave him. He hoped she wouldn't cry out if he were hurt.

He faced the Souk champion and mustered his strength.

Chapter Fourteen

The Souk's build was stocky, with muscles bulging on his arms, broad chest, and sturdy legs. Teir searched for an obvious weakness but couldn't find any. Being shorter than the Souk meant he might be more agile, but that wasn't a great advantage under the circumstances. In his weakened state, a few punches could easily bring him down.

Swallowing hard, Teir assumed a fighting stance and readied himself by bouncing back and forth on the balls of his feet. The Souk neared, and Teir noticed with distaste the drop of spittle on the champion's lower lip. The dogface was actually drooling in anticipation of the forthcoming battle. Behind him he heard scuffling noises, as though the guards were getting into position should their champion fail.

The Souk suddenly lunged, his right knee bent forward, his fist swinging. Teir feinted to the left but was centimeters too slow and the blow caught him on the ribs. Grunting, he kicked out, catching the Souk sideways on his legs. The Souk cursed and whirled around, jabbing at Teir with a stiff hand to the neck.

The blow hit him on his collarbone, forcing Teir to his knees, wincing from the pain. The Souk advanced again. Teir bent his head and butted the champion in the stomach, but it was like banging against a stone wall. The Souk chuckled and grasped Teir under the arms. Lifting him, he encircled his chest and began squeezing.

Teir felt the air being crushed from his lungs and a wave of hopelessness washed over him. They were all going to be captured—he, and the two Crigellans. He only prayed that Sarina was safely away. A strange buzzing sounded in his ears as his vision began to dim. *Not again*, he thought vaguely, just as he lost consciousness.

Sarina watched from her vantage point behind a clump of trees, a safe distance from the two guards Devin had pointed out. She had thought Teir was doing well when he kicked the giant, but now the champion had brought him to his knees. Her heart skipped a beat at the expression of pain contorting his face.

"We must help him!" she hissed to Devin.

The youth glared at her. "You think we would have a chance against two Souks armed with stun whips and their champion fighter? You must go away from here. Come, I will lead you."

He started to rise, but Sarina's hand halted him. "Wait, the giant's got him. Oh my God, he's crushing him!"

She watched in horror as the Souk fighter lifted Teir and squeezed his ribcage. Teir's jaw dropped, and then suddenly he went limp and hung lifeless in the giant's embrace.

"He's killed him! Devin, I've got to go to him."

"He's just unconscious. See, his chest moves. He is breathing."

The Souk laid Teir out on the ground next to Etan, Salla's mate. The guards hovered over all three of them, stun whips crackling as they swung them menacingly close to the old woman. Salla's face showed no fear. Her expression was sublimely calm as she crouched beside her mate.

"I can't leave him," Sarina said, standing.

"Don't be foolish. You can do nothing."

The red-haired boy stood up, and Sarina noticed he was taller than she.

Ignoring his warning, she started forward.

"I'm sorry," Devin said, "it is my duty to take you to safety."

Sarina felt a sharp painful blow to the side of her head. Crying out, she lost her balance. The last thing she saw as she fell was darkness.

Teir pried his eyes open to view an unwelcome sight. He was back in Bdan's gloomy dungeon, strung up by his wrists in the same manner as before. Only this time, Salla and Etan were beside him in the cavernous hall. A smoky scent permeated the air, clogging his nostrils and making his painful intakes of breath even more uncomfortable. That giant must have cracked some of his ribs, Teir thought. Shadows played in the corners of the room, so he couldn't see who else was there, but buzzing noises indicated Hortha guards were present. He peered around, wondering who had ordered their recapture. It must have been Otis, the second-in-command. The lieutenant hadn't been harsh during his interrogation of Teir on board the *Omnus*. Perhaps they could strike a bargain wherein he would regain his freedom. Hope surged in his breast, only to be dashed the next moment.

A figure stepped out of the shadows and approached. Flamelights flickered along the damp stone walls, providing meager illumination. It took Teir a moment to identify the individual.

"You!" he said, stunned.

"Welcome back, Captain," Bdan crooned.

"Where did you come from? I thought you were—" Teir had a vision of Bdan vanishing from sight in the moat surrounding his sumptuous bed.

"Thought you I was dead, Captain? The flegymns in my moat do not feed upon Souk flesh, and an escape hatchway have I underneath. I simply vanished below and reappeared in another section of my complex. A tiresome journey it was, however. Another reason for us to even the score, grrrr?" the smuggler growled. "Finding it irritating, am I, to have to keep hunting you. Simpler would it have been had Loopa succeeded in luring you in the first place."

"So you were backing him!" Teir exclaimed triumphantly. "Was he responsible for sabotaging my ship as well?"

"Of course." Bdan laughed, an ugly raucous sound. "Unfortunately, Defense League Command reassigned you before you could accept his offer." He grew serious. "Disappointed, am I, to see the Earthwoman is not with you. Where is she?"

"Sarina is long gone," Teir lied.

"Gone where?"

Teir tried to moisten his mouth but his tongue was dry, so instead of answering, he shrugged.

Bdan whipped an electrifier out of his robe and hit Teir. Set on low, the current would cause a painful shock but not damage his captive's nervous system. "Not waiting around for answers am I this time, Captain. Sarina did not have time to get offplanet, and monitoring all flights have I been. Where is she?"

Teir's body twitched in pain. "Go to Zor," he spat at Bdan, uncaring of the consequences.

The Souk struck him again, adjusting the power level one notch higher. "Talk will you, Captain R-R-Reylock. Or maybe your friends would rather speak than watch your suffering." He turned his attention to the other captives. "Lieutenant!"

Otis scampered from the shadows. "Master?"

"Know you these two? Crigellans are they, like yourself."

Otis's lizard face was impassive as he regarded the pair. "No, sir. I've never seen them before."

"Good, then mind not will you when they are executed." Otis's mouth pinched but he said nothing. "Found any trace of the Earthling, have you?" Bdan asked.

"Not yet. My men are working on it. There is something I want to show you that is of interest, however."

Otis drew Bdan off to the side and Teir glanced at his companions. Etan was awake, but appeared woozy. Salla was strung up between the two males. She was watching Teir, her expression inscrutable even though she must have been in pain from the uncomfortable position.

"I'm sorry," Teir told her miserably. "If I had been stronger, I might have been able to defeat the Souk champion. Now you're here because of me."

"Do not apologize for your weakened condition. You should have listened to Devin and left while you had the chance."

"I don't desert friends. I'm just sorry you're involved." He looked away, avoiding her gaze. "It seems I've met nothing but failure lately. Even on Lapis, our mission succeeded but lives were lost. And now it seems we're doomed. I don't understand what's been happening. Before Sarina came along, my crew and I had no problems. All of our assignments were successful. Now, things just keep going wrong." He hung his head in defeat, his body throbbing in a hundred places. His arms felt like they were pulling out of their sockets. "I hope Sarina was able to get away," he mumbled.

"Do not sound so hopeless, Captain." Salla's ageless eyes regarded him wisely. "Sarina is safe, but you must complete a quest before you see her again."

"What do you mean?" His tone was glum. They

were in a no-win situation as far as he could tell. If Sarina had escaped, he didn't see how he would ever see her again. Bdan undoubtedly would put him to a painful death so he couldn't cause any more trouble. The prospect didn't thrill him.

"The legend has yet to be fulfilled, and you are the key to its attainment," Salla said encouragingly. "The Blood Crystal can reveal what must be done." She paused, wincing in discomfort.

Her aged limbs must be tearing apart, Teir thought, anguished that he had caused her pain. Beside her, Etan writhed, but his wrists were securely bound above his head like theirs. Teir wriggled his fingers but could feel nothing. His hands were numb.

Salla took a deep breath. "Listen carefully. My energy seeps away, but there is more I must tell you. It is you, Captain Reylock, who is destined to marry the Great Healer."

"What do you say?" Teir asked, dumbfounded.

"Consult the Blood Crystal," Salla said mysteriously.

"How is it that you're so knowledgeable?" His eyes narrowed. Maybe this was some trick of Bdan's to get him to reveal the location of the magical rock.

Salla nodded to her chest. "The amulet around my neck, do you see it? It is a glowstone, Captain. We are of the people—you, I, and the Earthwoman. There are others like us—"

"R-R-Reylock!" Bdan roared, marching over to them. "What means this?" In his palm he thrust out a data link. On the display were the entry codes for the *Valiant*.

Teir looked him in the eye. "It's not mine. You emptied my pockets when you captured me the first time."

"Is Sarina on her way to your ship?"

"I told you she's long gone. Where did you get that?"

"Found at your hiding place in the Thicket of Bayne

was it, according to Lieutenant Otis. Who does it belong to, then? These two?" He turned his furious face to the Crigellans.

"It is not ours," Salla replied quietly. "We would not have advised the Captain to return to his ship. It is too heavily guarded."

"Whose is it?" Bdan bellowed. "Where is the girl? Talk, or start terminating you one by one, will I." He shot up the power level on his electrifier as though he meant it.

"Wait," Teir said, seeing him take aim at Etan. "You still want the location of the Blood Crystal?"

If he could divert Bdan's attention from Sarina, she'd be one step ahead. And Salla had advised him to consult the crystal. How better to serve both goals than to take Bdan there and elude him? For the first time, hope surged in his breast that he might escape.

Bdan stuck his ugly face in front of Teir's. "Decided to cooperate, have you, Captain?"

Teir assumed a defeated expression, which wasn't hard to do. "I'll take you to the Blood Crystal, but only if you let my friends go free."

"Give me the location!" Bdan snarled, raising the electrifier.

"No! I have to go with you. The guardian will only open to me. We can take the *Valiant*. She's fast, and the coordinates are already in the computer."

Bdan held a whispered conference with Otis. "There's no reason to take him," the smuggler said to his second-in-command. "Trying to trick us is he. Analyze the files we can ourselves to get the information."

"He's probably got it encoded so you'd never break in," Otis responded, his brow wrinkled. "And you don't know anything about this guardian. You could take along his friends to ensure his cooperation."

"Good idea," Bdan growled. He turned back to Teir. "Very well, agree to your proposal do I. However, your friends will be released only after I have possession of the Blood Crystal."

Teir feared this might be so, but he'd deal with that complication later. "We go in the *Valiant*, then?" This was a crucial part of his plan.

"So be it." Bdan barked an order to the Hortha guards, and the three were cut down.

Giving them no time even to rub the circulation back into their numb hands, Bdan commanded them to march. Soon all three captives, Bdan and Otis, and a contingent of mixed Hortha and Souk guards were on their way through a series of tunnels.

Eventually they emerged into the blazing desert sun. The *Valiant* was secured in a huge hangar complex a short walk away. It brought Teir a measure of comfort to see the sleek lines of his ship. Running his hand over the metallic surface, he almost purred his pleasure. She'd help him in his escape, this great galactic bird of his. He only had to get to the controls.

Bdan wasn't about to let him get off so easily, however. He made Teir and the two Crigellans sit in the lounge while he and Otis piloted the ship. The three prisoners sat around the conference table, a silent group, ringed by guards. The viewing ports were closed, apparently under Bdan's orders. Teir could tell when they were underway by the vibrations.

At last Bdan entered the lounge. "Well, Captain? Need some information do I."

"Ah yes. Our destination?"

"Indeed."

"I'll have to use the ship's computer. There's a terminal over there." He nodded to a corner of the room that held a small console.

"Tell me will you and I'll enter the data."

"That won't work," Teir explained patiently. "The system will only respond to me. This particular entry is voice activated. Security, you understand."

"I see." The Souk appeared to consider. "All right,"

he agreed with obvious reluctance, "but watching you shall I be. No tricks, R-R-Reylock."

Bdan lumbered over to the console after him to observe over his shoulder. Teir was careful to keep his expression bland, but as his fingers flew over the control pad, his heart soared joyously. He was coding in the sequence that would repel unwanted intruders from his ship. This wasn't the right time to activate it, though, not with Bdan watching him so carefully. He'd have to wait for a better opportunity. As an added precaution, he ordered the computer to record Bdan's voice in case he needed to fake the smuggler's gruff tones in the future.

That left one more thing to do. If they were going to take the shuttle down to Taurus, Teir would need a remote unit to gain control of the vessel from his getaway point. That way, once he eluded Bdan and his guards, he could summon the shuttle and leave the others stranded.

"What are you doing?" Bdan snapped suspiciously.

"Just opening the path for voice command," Teir replied, finishing on the keypad with a flourish. "Computer, locate coordinates for code name Onyx, authorization Reylock, Gamma Alpha Two."

Coordinates ready, responded the computer in a sultry female voice.

"Lay in a course," Teir ordered.

Course locked in.

"Activate."

Course set for location code name Onyx.

Teir let out a long breath. "Voice activation off." He turned to Bdan. "Done," he said.

"Where are we heading, Captain?" The slaver hovered over him, his rolls of bluish flesh quivering. The ship rocked slightly, and he put a paw on the wall to steady himself. The skirt of his voluminous purple and gold caftan swayed.

If Teir had been flying, there would have been no sensation of movement at all. He knew how to fine-tune the controls, but Otis wasn't as familiar with the ship's operations. He could use that in his favor, Teir determined. "We're going to Taurus," he answered.

"Taurus is in the Quantum sector. Weeks will it take us to get there!" Bdan exclaimed angrily.

"Not if you go at warp eight. It should take us ten days at the most. I assume you checked the fuel capacitators?"

"Fully charged are the krystals."

"Then we'll have no problem. Tell Otis to increase power."

"Why did you not tell me this sooner?" Bdan thundered, face distorted in anger.

Teir grinned. "I'm in no hurry."

"Try my patience, do you, R-R-Reylock. Know I the location now. Expendable are you."

"No, I'm not. You still need me for the guardian, remember?"

"Grrrrr," the Souk growled. He passed on the order to Otis to increase speed, then apparently decided his stomach took precedence over further activities. He stalked over to the fabricator and conjured himself a snack. Joining the Crigellans at the table, he ranged his bulk across two chairs and sat down.

"May I have permission to use the sanitary?" Teir asked mildly.

Bdan studied him through narrowed eyes. "No harm can you do from there, I suppose," he said, slurping up a bowlful of live Rigelan slugs. "Geemus will accompany you to make certain you behave." He nodded to one of the Souks standing guard.

Teir washed and shaved, then entered his state-room. There, under the close supervision of his vigilant guard, he changed into a fresh blue shirt and navy pants with a black leather vest. When the ship rocked again, causing the Souk to momentarily glance away, Teir's hand shot underneath the slight overhang of his desk and grasped the small rectangular object fixed in place. Bending over with a pretended cough, he slipped the remote unit into his inner vest pocket. Suppressing a grin, he combed his hair, then went back into the lounge.

He offered Salla and Etan some refreshments, then sat down himself with a bowl of nourishing stew and a drink of his favorite Arcturian brandy. He was going to need all his strength for the ordeal to come.

Bdan, who had gone to the bridge to consult with Otis, sauntered back into the lounge. He bombarded Teir with questions about the ship and insisted on a tour. Teir rattled off a series of technical instructions that would confuse even Datron as he led the fat Souk about. The hidden compartments and security arrangements remained secret as he pointed out only the obvious.

The next days passed with agonizing slowness. Bdan took over Teir's cabin, and Lieutenant Otis occupied Ravi's. That left the remaining two cabins with double bunks for Teir and the Crigellans. Geemus, the guard, was assigned to share with Teir. Bdan wasn't taking any chances of leaving him alone.

Teir was careful to keep his remote unit on his person at all times. He changed his shirt and pants each day, but kept the same vest. Geemus never saw fit to frisk him, and Teir made sure the guard's suspicions weren't aroused.

Confined for the most part of the journey to the lounge, he spent time in conversation with Salla and Etan.

"I hope Sarina is well," he told them, mentioning her name for what must have been the hundredth time.

"Did I not tell you that what is meant to be will come to pass?" said Salla patiently. She and her mate were playing a game of Boks using a backlit board and colored tiles on the dining table.

"Yes, but I can't help worrying about her. Are you sure she got off Souk? Where is she now? Is she trying to find me?" Questions, endless questions, plagued him. If only he knew for certain she was all right. If only he could speak to her, hear her voice. He sighed, not realizing how his concerns were etched upon his face.

"She'll be all right," Salla reassured him, patting his hand. "In fact, I sense she will soon be with friends, and in particular, one who cares about her."

Teir's head jerked up. A friend who cared about her? Who could that be, unless it was Lord Cam'brii? Was Sarina returning to him after all? A terrible fear took hold of him, fear that he might lose her to the councilor. By the corona, he couldn't let that happen!

His escape took on a new urgency, and he began counting the hauras until they reached Taurus.

On the planet Tendraa, Mantra faced his own challenge. He'd been granted an audience with the Liege Lord. The whole future of his disease-ravaged planet might depend upon what happened during this interview, so he had to think carefully about what to say.

The journey from Ingorr had been long and arduous. He'd joined a caravan leaving from the posting station at Cameron, and passing through the icy Kougar Chills. Weeks later, Mantra had reached the capital city of Lazore on the coast of the Bazmayan Sea. At least it was warmer here. His breath merely steamed instead of freezing in his nostrils.

Cold and tired, he'd put up at a local inn to wash and rest. Then he'd presented himself at the palace gate, armed with a letter from the Baynor of Ingorr and endorsements from other town leaders he'd met along the way. Word traveled fast. Those cities that had implemented the measures suggested by the Great Healer were already showing declines in the incidence of disease, and thereafter Mantra's advice had been sought all along his route. Mantra had no trouble getting an appointment with the leader of Tendraa.

He stood nervously in an anteroom, unable to appreciate the elaborate gilded wallpaper, carved cornices, or plush velvet drapes that met his eyes. Part of him wondered where the credits had come from to decorate the palace with so many ornate furnishings. Mostly, he kept himself busy by rehearsing his speech.

All rational thoughts flew from his mind when he was ushered into the grand presence of the Liege Lord Cyng Navin. The Receiving Chamber flashed brilliantly with gold. It was so bright that he had to squint as a pageboy led him forward toward a raised dais. The Liege Lord seemed almost dwarfed by the immensity of the throne he occupied. Mantra bowed deeply, and it wasn't until he heard the command to rise that he was able to study his leader at length. He noted the Liege Lord's sharp brown eyes, the shock of coal black hair and his tall rangy physique.

Cyng Navin regarded him just as intently. Mantra knew that Navin hadn't become the leader of Tendraa by virtue of his birth alone. He had been born into the ruling dynasty, but it was his charisma that had propelled him to dominate planetary politics. He'd risen through the ranks and was proclaimed Liege Lord at a younger age than any of his predecessors.

"The faith be with you, citizen," said Cyng Navin, making the sign of the circle with his hand as though giving a blessing. "What brings you to us?"

Mantra cleared his throat. "I have seen the light, your worship. The Great Healer herself came to me."

"Aye, I have heard of your good deeds. You have been spreading the word even as you come. What is it that the Great One revealed to you?"

"She gave us the means to help ourselves, Liege

Lord." He rattled off the sanitation measures Sarina had suggested, then told of his own implementation and the positive results. "Neither of my sisters have fallen ill. We breathe easier, and our hide has thinned to its former softness. I say we must make a mandate throughout the land. The Great Healer has spoken; we must heed her word."

Mantra dropped to his knees and clasped his hands together. "You have never seen such sweetness and compassion, Your Worship. The woman called Sarina is like a miracle come alive. Truly, she is a representative of the Ancient Ones as prophesied in the legend. The sacred light shines in her eyes. I myself saw this wondrous sight. If we do not follow her decrees, I fear our people may perish!"

Tears came unbidden to his eyes. "I lost both my parents to the Farg, and my younger sister Zunis. I pray we do not see a resurgence of the horrifying visitation. Kairi is very dear to me—another sister, sire. I could not bear it to lose her, too. Everyone must do as the Great Healer says in order for us all to be protected!"

"Why does the Great Healer not cure the sick?" asked Navin, his brow wrinkled in thought. The bejeweled crown on his head bobbed when he spoke.

Mantra slowly rose to his feet. "That puzzled me at first, sire. But then I saw that it was a test of faith for us to heal ourselves." Straightening his shoulders, he let his gaze fall pointedly to a side-table holding a crystal goblet of wine and a gleaming silver-cast dish of fruit. "Surely we have the resources to make widespread change," he said meaningfully.

"Change is what caused the downfall of our people in the past," Navin said in a stern tone.

"That is because we were not prepared, and the changes came too fast. These are small measures I am proposing."

"Ummm." The Liege Lord rubbed his cheek, wondering what it would feel like to have soft hide again. The smoky haze that permeated the cities wreaked havoc on one's outer body layer, and although Navin's hide was smoother than the average fifty-two-annum-old, it still felt rough to his touch. And because of the Farg, he'd been practically isolated in his palace. It would be so good to stroll the streets again and shake people's hands as he had in the early days of his reign.

"We'll give it a trial," he agreed, "first in Lazore. If I see positive results, I shall issue a decree. In the meantime, Citizen Mantra, I have a mandate for you."

"Yes, your worship?" Mantra asked, feeling a great sense of accomplishment. His main purpose had been achieved. The word of the Great Healer had been accepted.

"I have been thinking about this long and hard, and I feel the time has come. We need a representative to go to the Coalition central government so we can keep abreast of news regarding the Great Healer. She might have more of these pronouncements such as the ones she has given you. Since you were chosen initially, I now appoint you to be our ambassador."

Mantra's mouth dropped open. Ambassador to the Coalition! How could this be? It was a dream come true! "Are you thinking of applying for full membership?" he asked cautiously.

"No! We do not want interference in our policies, just information."

"But—"

"You will follow my directives, citizen, will you not?"

"Of course, sire," Mantra mumbled, bowing.

"I have another piece of news you must take with you." The Liege Lord pushed himself up from the throne and began pacing the dais. "You may not be aware of this, but some advanced machinery was preserved from the Techno War. Our palace houses a large communications room. Most of the equipment is not used, but we have been monitoring the long-range sensors. They have picked up a large alien force orbiting the outer planet of our system. It appears their intent is hostile."

"Morgots!" Mantra exclaimed, terror striking his heart.

Navin looked him in the eye. "We know they will come here. Tendraa is rich in flavium. They can use the mineral to produce weapons of immense destructive magnitude."

"But mining of flavium is forbidden for that very reason."

"You think the Morgots follow rules?" Navin laughed. "It is why they enter this sector. Our planet has the largest flavium source in the galaxy. The Morgots wish to possess it."

"We must ask the Coalition for help," Mantra pleaded.

"No, you must ask the Great Healer for her assistance. I do not want the political bungrats on Bimordus Two getting their claws into our culture. That is what led to the Techno War the last time we sought partnership in the Coalition."

Mantra saw the Liege Lord would not budge in his opinions. "Very well, I shall approach Sarina. When do you wish me to depart?"

"Immediately. My daughter, Tami, will assist you with the preparations." His gaze swept over Mantra. "You'll need to see Popus, keeper of the wardrobe. As our representative, you must be suitably attired."

He tapped a hidden gong by the throne and a door at the rear of the chamber slid open. In walked the most beautiful girl Mantra had ever seen. Her age could be no more than eighteen annums, he figured. She was of medium height, slightly shorter than he, with a slender figure draped in a glittery jade-colored cloth. The drape complemented her luminous green eyes and provided the perfect backdrop for her long russet hair. Gazing at her delicate facial features, Mantra thought he'd never seen a complexion so lovely. The creamy beige of her hide was smooth and unflawed. High cheekbones and a slightly upturned nose went perfectly with her pouting mouth. He wondered insanely what it would be like to kiss her, then abruptly cast the thought aside. He was here on business, not pleasure.

"Citizen Mantra, may I present my daughter Tami," said Cyng Navin.

Mantra bowed deeply. "My lady, it is an honor." He was glad he'd taken the time to wash and change into his best robe, but he couldn't even come close to her brilliance. It was a good thing the Liege Lord would have him properly outfitted for his journey.

"Your transport has already been arranged," Navin continued. "Everything you need will be aboard. I will expect your first report within seven days after your arrival on Bimordus Two."

Dismissed, Mantra understood he was to leave with Tami. He followed her out the rear door and through a series of corridors into a salon.

"Please be seated," she said in a musical voice. Every movement she made was dainty and graceful, he noted wistfully.

Popus, the keeper of the wardrobe, shuffled in to take his measurements. When he was finished, the portly gentleman stroked his beard. "You maintain your weight well, citizen. I have many excellent garments that will suit you." Turning to Tami, he asked, "Shall I have them sent directly to the spacecraft, Your Highness?"

"Please," Tami said, "and make haste."

She ordered refreshments. When the small cakes and wine were delivered, she smiled at Mantra. "You have a brief time before the transport is scheduled for departure. Do you have your own belongings that you wish to have brought to the ship?"

"Aye." Mantra gave her the name of the inn.

Tami gave instructions to a servant to retrieve Mantra's baggage. "Now, Mantra, tell me about this mission you undertake."

Mantra knew her mother was away visiting relatives, so Tami was taking her place as hostess. Still, it felt strange to speak so freely to a young lady in such an unaccustomed manner. They were alone, the servants having withdrawn and Popus having hurried off to complete his task.

"I go to seek the council of the Great Healer," he said. Noting the interest on her face, he proceeded to tell her of his own experience with Sarina. His face glowed as he spoke of the Earthwoman's compassion.

"I have prayed for the Great Healer to save us," Tami responded. "I am sorry she was unable to help your parents and sister."

Her look of caring took Mantra by surprise. "What is important now is that we were graced with her presence. The legend is coming true. Peace is in the future. But achieving it might still be difficult." He sighed. "Alas, I fear the Great Healer may not be able to help our people overcome the dire threat that now appears. The Morgots are on their way to strip the resources of our planet and enslave our people. Your father refuses to beseech the Coalition for aid."

"Surely the Morgots would not come hither while the pestilence overwhelms our land!"

"That is exactly the sort of situation they thrive upon. For some reason, the Morgots are immune to the visitation. According to my cousin Ravi, they've been conquering planets stricken by the plague."

Tami's face paled. "What are we to do?"

Mantra wanted to take her lovely hand in his and comfort her. "Help your father see that we cannot fight this alone. We must have the assistance of the Defense League. He wants me to ask the Great Healer for aid. I shall do so, but I fear her powers will not be enough. Tami, for the sake of our people, talk to your father about this."

She nodded emphatically. "I shall follow your advice, Citizen Mantra." She smiled, and her face radiated such beauty that he didn't want to leave. "And now I believe it is time for your departure." She stood, and Mantra followed suit.

The words escaped his lips before he could stop them. "Mistress, may I have the honor of calling upon you when I return?"

"Aye, sir, that would please me," Tami said, raising delicately arched eyebrows. "I find your mission exciting. Long have I thought that more should be done for our people. There are many inequities on Tendraa. Things have been static for far too long. The time has come for a change."

Mantra couldn't help himself. He stepped over and took her hand. "It warms my heart that you feel as I do about these things. Perhaps we can talk more of this."

Tami blushed and lowered her eyes. "I shall be monitoring the communications room for your news."

"Then I shall be certain to report often." He held her hand a moment more, then released it.

"Attend me now, and I'll show you the way to your vessel. Lightspeed on your journey, citizen."

"The faith be with you, lady."

A short while later, Mantra was seated in the cockpit of a space transport with only a two-member crew for company. As he readied himself for his initiation into space travel, his heart thumped with excitement. Wonder of wonders! He was going where his cousin Ravi had gone before him.

He strapped on his safety harness and stared out the viewscreen. His life was about to change, and he hoped to be the one to usher in a new era of enlightenment on his planet. The Great Healer had chosen him to serve her and implement her pronouncements.

Somehow, he'd deal with the Morgot threat as well. His faith would guide him along the right course.

In his pouch he held a parchment from the Liege Lord. It was a letter of introduction, authorizing him to represent the people of Tendraa. He'd have to present himself to the General Assembly for ratification of his appointment. Once that was done, he'd seek an audience with the Great Healer. And if his cousin Ravi was on Bimordus Two, they'd enjoy a warm reunion.

Hope filled his heart for a brighter future, and it glowed with faith and love almost as brightly as the light from the ancient Auricle.

Chapter Fifteen

Total darkness met her eyes. Sarina blinked once, then several times more. She was lying flat on her back and could see nothing despite the fact that her eyes were wide open. Forcing herself to remain calm, she waited for her vision to adjust to the dark. A throbbing headache told her she was quite alive. Indeed, the last thing she remembered was Devin warning her that his duty was to bring her to safety. Then he'd apparently cracked her on the head to ensure her compliance.

So where was she? Why did she hear no sounds? The surface she was lying on was cold and hard. Raising a hand, Sarina gasped when her palm met an obstruction. Running her fingers along its outline, she was alarmed to discover that the surface seemed to enclose her. She tried to roll to her side but found the space was too tight. Panic began to flutter in her breast.

Oh, God! She couldn't see and she couldn't hear! She was encased in something that totally surrounded her. A coffin came to mind. Had Devin knocked her cold and left her for dead? Or had he placed her in this box, knowing she was alive? Maybe he was a spy for the Souks after all.

She began banging her fist on the hard surface. Hollow clangs of metal rang in her ears. How was it possible that she could breathe? She listened more intently and then heard a faint hissing noise. So there was air in here, or at least an opening somewhere.

"Help!" she screamed, banging more fiercely. After a few more cries, she was gasping for breath. She stopped, realizing it might be wise to conserve what little air there was. If she couldn't calm the rapid pounding of her heart or stop hyperventilating, she'd probably pass out from sheer terror. Her body went cold and began to tremble.

"Teir," she whispered, craving the comfort of his presence. "Where are you?"

A vision of the Souk champion hovering over the captain's prostrate body came to mind, and she knew he was a prisoner, too. Tears squeezed from her eyes at the memory of his helplessness. Was this to be their fate, then? They'd die apart, never to see each other again? Good God, it was too much to bear.

Her sobbing blocked out the squeaking sounds, but when she heard them, she began screaming and banging on the metallic surface with renewed desperation.

A hatchway opened above her, and bright light streamed in. Sarina shut her eyes against it.

"Hush," said a voice. "You must remain quiet."

Sarina cracked her eyes open just a slit. The eraser-pink face of a Sirisian male peered at her. "Who are you? Where am I?"

"You're on board a cargo vessel bound for Bimordus Two. You were smuggled aboard from Souk several days ago."

"Several days ago!" It seemed like she'd just seen Teir and the others. "What about my friends?"

"Devin remained behind. He fights for freedom with other Believers on Souk. Of the rest in your party, I know not. No one else on this vessel knows you are here. I gave you a drug to keep you quiet for most of the journey, but we arrive at Bimordus Two within the haura so it was necessary for you to awaken. You must remain inside the container until we land and off-load the cargo. The other crew members are sympathetic to the Souks."

"I'll die if I stay in here any longer!" Sarina protested. She started to sit up, but he pushed her down brusquely.

"Do as you're told, or I'll inject you again and put you back to sleep. You endanger us both by making noise. Your ordeal is nearly at an end. Please try to be calm. Careful—I close the hatch now."

"Wait!" Sarina thrust out a hand, but he waved her back and sealed the lid. Blackness overtook her once more. If I just lie still, I'll be all right, she told herself. Think about the legend. Believe in it, and everything will turn out happily. Believe. . . .

Time must have passed, because suddenly her area was flooded with light. Squinting, Sarina allowed the Sirisian to help her out of the container and into a standing position. Her knees buckled, and she swayed against him.

"Easy, Mistress," he said, stretching out his long body to accommodate her. "You are free now. Give yourself a moment to adjust."

"I can't see!" she said, shutting her eyelids. "The brightness hurts my eyes. What is this place?"

"We have arrived at the Spaceport on Bimordus Two. The cargo is being unloaded now. You have to go before you are noticed. I regret that I cannot accompany you myself, but my absence would be noted."

She rubbed her eyes, then pried them open again. This time, the light didn't hurt as much. She looked at her rescuer. He wore a pale yellow turban on his bald head and a tan tunic. "Thank you for helping me. Your name is . . . ?"

"It does not matter. I am honored to help the Great Healer. You have much work to do. The universe is torn by strife, and disease is rampant. You are the star we have prayed for to bring us out of darkness."

"Well, I don't see how I'm going to accomplish anything alone. I needed you to get me out of that coffin just now." If Teir were at her side, she could do so much more, Sarina thought sadly. She *had* to find out what had happened to him.

"Here is a cloak for you to wear," the Sirisian said, handing her a dark brown cape. "You'll be able to blend into the crowd if you are not so—er—unusual in appearance."

Glancing down, Sarina flushed with embarrassment. Teir's shirt was ripped in several places. Her long legs were exposed, and her feet were bare. Of course, she couldn't walk around in public like this! Gratefully, she wrapped the garment around herself and drew the hood over her blond hair.

"Come, I'll show you the way out." The Sirisian took her arm and led her through another storeroom to an exit. "The faith be with you, Mistress. I shall pray for your success."

"Thank you again for your assistance." He bowed and left her standing in the open doorway, alone.

Sarina looked out at a bustling scene of activity: spaceships taxiing to and from hangars, cargo off-loading, uniformed officers shouting instructions. From the position of the sun overhead and the coolness, she figured it was early morning. Maybe Rolf would still be in his quarters.

She knew of nowhere else to go. If he rejected her, she'd seek sanctuary from Glotaj.

Afraid of being spotted by the crew of the cargo vessel, Sarina slunk through the shadows until she came to a people-mover terminal. There she boarded a tram, trying to remain as inconspicuous as possible.

She found a seat and scanned the directory display for the correct stop.

In fifteen minutes she was facing the entrance to Spiral Town. Rolf must be home, she thought, recognizing the guard detail patrolling the building's perimeter. The sergeant in charge marched over, greeting her with surprise. Sarina asked him not to notify the councilor of her arrival.

As the sergeant let her into the building, Sarina wondered how Rolf would react when he saw her. Given the way she'd deserted him, he'd probably be furious. He might even order her to leave. Trembling with apprehension, she climbed the spiral staircase to his level.

As for what she'd say, Sarina had made up her mind that she would go through with the marriage if that was what it took for the prophecy to come true. Initially, she'd wanted to become the Great Healer to cure people like her friend Abby. Now, she hoped to use the political clout of her exalted position to help Teir. Any sacrifices she had to make along the way were worth it if she could free him from the Souks. She'd do anything, even if it meant sleeping with the councilor.

Resolutely, Sarina approached Rolf's door and placed her eye in the retinal scanning device, wondering if it was still programmed for her parameters. She needn't have worried. After a brief flash when the scanner read her eye, the portal slid open soundlessly.

Rolf was exercising on the living room carpet, wearing a pair of shorts and nothing more. Seeing her in the doorway, he jumped up, his jaw dropping in astonishment. "Sarina!" In two long strides he was beside her. His eyes raked her up and down. "By the stars, where have you been? What's happened? How did you get here?"

Sarina averted her gaze from his muscular chest. "It's a long story. May I come in?"

"Of course!"

He stood aside while she passed him and seated herself on the double lounger at the opposite end of the room. He ordered the door shut, grabbed a towel and wiped himself dry, then turned to face her.

"You've been hurt," he said, a look of concern replacing his stunned expression.

"No, I'm all right. I'm just glad to be here."

"Let me get you a drink. You look as if you've been through a terrible ordeal." He brought her a cool beverage, then hovered protectively in front of her.

"You must have lots of questions," Sarina began, moistening her lips.

"I've been worried sick about you."

"Perhaps I should start at the beginning." She gave a long sigh, partly out of relief. At least he wasn't angry with her. "I left because I was afraid of the execution decree, and I was also anxious to see my friends and family back home. I took advantage of the opportunity to flee."

"You made a fool out of Reylock."

"Teir deserved it. Anyway, let me tell you what happened when I went to Earth."

"What do you mean, he deserved it?" Rolf said, picking up on her words. "What did Reylock do to you?" For weeks, he'd been wondering what had happened to her. For weeks, he'd been doubting the legend's validity while striving to refute the accusations of Daimon and his followers. Now Sarina suddenly reappeared, and Teir's name was the first on her lips.

"Dammit, I knew something happened on that ship!" he said, unable to suppress a surge of jealousy. "Did Reylock try to seduce you? Is that why you ran away, because you feared being dishonored?"

"No, you've got it all wrong! He said he wanted nothing to do with me. Teir explained later that he—"

"Later? The captain was ordered not to pursue you! Where is he?"

"He's a prisoner somewhere on Souk—I hope."

"You hope?"

"Either that, or he's dead."

"What in Zor are you talking about?"

"Sit down and I'll tell you."

"Very well." He perched himself on the edge of a chair. "Go on. I'm listening."

Sarina's eyes roamed over his nearly naked form. Rolf's muscles gleamed—he must have spent more time than she'd thought working out in the physiolab each day. He certainly maintained a virile physique. With his great height, curly blond hair, and piercing blue eyes, he was undeniably attractive. But for all his appeal, she felt no desire for this man. No matter how hard she tried, Teir was still foremost in her thoughts.

Taking a deep breath, Sarina described her sojourn on Earth, her experiences with Abby and the stone, her capture by the Souks, and the reunion with Teir in Bdan's dungeon. She was about to tell him about healing Teir, but then thought better of it because it would justify Rolf's suspicions that something significant had passed between the two of them. She'd have to inform someone else, perhaps Glotaj. According to Teir, the regent seemed interested in their relationship, and she needed to talk to him anyway.

Rolf frowned, as though what he was going to say next was difficult. "Before you left for Tendraa, I was unable to relate to you on a personal level. I didn't realize how difficult this situation was going to be. I'll admit I didn't treat you with the proper respect. Now that you've returned, I'd like to make amends. We'll spend time together and get to know one another more intimately. If you will have me, I still wish to wed you."

"Yes," Sarina said, trying to put some enthusiasm into her voice, "the marriage ceremony can be rescheduled. Speak to Glotaj and arrange the date."

Rolf smiled. "We must celebrate!" He rose and walked over to her. Holding out his hands, he pulled her to her feet. "With you by my side, we can accomplish anything. I know the legend will come true!"

Sarina closed her ears. She wanted to be at Teir's side, not the councilor's. Why couldn't she have stayed with him on Souk? At least then she would have known what had happened to him. This way, she suffered the agony of not knowing. When she saw Glotaj, she intended to ask the regent to investigate, but for now, Sarina didn't feel up to going out again. There would be questions asked, and she was content to let Rolf, who had left to see the regent and the High Council, handle them for her. All she wanted was to rest and bathe.

Rolf returned by the dinner haura, elated with his news. "The High Council rejoices at your return. They seek an audience with you tomorrow morning so they can hear your news firsthand. Our wedding date has been set for seven days hence. Glotaj will officiate at the ceremony, which will take place in the Assembly Chamber—it's the only place on Bimordus Two that can hold so many guests! A reception is planned in the large conservatory located in the Nutrition Pod." His eyes twinkled happily as he regarded her.

"Will your parents be attending the ceremony?" Sarina asked, wondering what her future in-laws were like. Meeting them was not a prospect she anticipated with any joy.

His mood change was abrupt. "I don't think they will come."

Sarina noticed his downcast expression. "Teir told me about the tragedy in your past. Surely they don't still hold that against you?" His silence gave her the answer. "But you are second son to the Imperator. You told me yourself you would assume the title of Prince after we wed."

"My position in the family does not change, only

my father's attitude. According to our law, he does not have the authority to disinherit me. It is enough that he has never spoken to me since my disgrace."

"And your mother?"

"She has never defied him. I have sent word to my elder brother, but the journey would take too long for him to get here in time."

"I'm sorry."

"Don't be. I shall have my vengeance when the Souks are defeated. I live for that day!"

Troubled, Sarina occupied herself by creating Rolf's favorite dish on the fabricator. She served it to him at the dining table, then got a plate of pastagillo noodles with vegetables for herself and joined him. Summoning an appetite was difficult. She felt guilty being in such plush surroundings when Teir was still imprisoned on Souk. And Rolf's words had indicated that revenge was still his driving motivation. He may still be intent on using me to achieve his goals, Sarina realized. But then she was using him, too.

"I hope our marriage works," she told him. "I want the legend to come true."

"Even if it doesn't, Glotaj has requested a repeal of the execution decree," Rolf told her between bites. "The vote is scheduled to go before the General Assembly next month; then the High Council must ratify the statute."

"Do you think it will pass?" Sarina asked eagerly.

"I hope so, but there are still those to whom your presence is a threat, and they may vote against the measure."

"You mean Daimon and his followers in the Return to Origins Faction?"

Rolf nodded glumly. "The ROF has been gaining power in your absence. I have ordered a new detail of guards to escort you about town. You must maintain caution in your movements."

* * *

The next day, Sarina made her report to the High Council. Emu was ecstatic when she related the account of the stone.

"It glowed while you were thinking about being a healer!" the Sirisian counselor exclaimed. "You see, it is a sign that you are indeed The One!"

"You have this wondrous object with you?" Glotaj asked, his demeanor solemn.

She stood in the center of the semicircle, facing him. "No, I hid it on Teir's ship when the Souks captured me. It might still be on the *Valiant*. Can't you send someone after Captain Reylock? He could fly the ship to the nearest Defense League outpost if you'd free him. I'm sure he knows a way to get on board and elude the Souks' defenses. That was part of our escape plan."

Glotaj shook his head. "You don't even know if the captain is still alive."

Emu spoke up. "Pardon me, Your Excellency, we could consult Mara. She gave us direction when Sarina went away."

"Please, ask her to help us!" Sarina cried, recalling her friend's special ability to see through the eyes of another.

"The captain's disposition is the concern of Defense League Command," said Glotaj coldly. "I'll notify Admiral Daras Gog. This falls under his jurisdiction. We have more important matters to pursue. Council is dismissed."

But when the meeting was over and the regent turned to leave, he cocked an eyebrow at Sarina, indicating that he wanted to see her outside.

She told Rolf to wait for her in the antechamber while she entered Glotaj's private office.

"Please be seated," said the regent. He closed the door and turned to her with a smile. "I didn't mean to be so brusque, but there are things we must discuss that are not for everyone's ears. I want you to know that I *am* concerned for Captain Reylock's welfare."

Hope swelled in her heart. "Then you will send someone after him?"

He held up a hand. "We don't have enough information. I would suggest you consult Mara on your own. Your Tyberian friend may agree to use her power to aid you. She helped us when you stole Reylock's ship. From her, we learned you were on your way to Earth. But do this quietly. If you get anything definite to go on, let me know and I'll pass the word to Admiral Gog."

"Why can't you consult her?"

Glotaj's eyes darkened, and he began pacing, his hands folded behind his back. His black robe swished at his heels.

"Remember the attack on Lord Cam'brii by the Twyggs? We learned they were sent by the Souks." He told her about the central computer snafu that had brought the whole transportation system to a halt and prevented their backup guards from reaching them. "We suspect the Souks have an agent here who is a highly placed government official. The agent would have been responsible for hiring the Twyggs and sabotaging the computer network."

"So you don't want this spy to know you're interested in Teir's situation?"

"Oh, the spy knows I'm interested, but not that I'm doing anything about it. When Reylock disappeared after visiting his aunt on Alpha Omega Two, Admiral Gog put a tracer on him. Unfortunately, we had no clue as to his whereabouts until you told us. You had commandeered his ship, and eventually the homing beacon on the *Valiant* was pinpointed to Souk. But how or why the ship ended up there when you were supposedly on Earth, we couldn't guess. The signal terminated, so we assumed the Souks deactivated the device.

"We've heard rumors of an underground movement on Souk but they weren't confirmed until now. We still don't know how to contact these people. Occasionally captives have escaped, but there's never been an organized pipeline. I think the assistance you got was because of who you are."

Sarina paled. "I hope I haven't hurt Teir's chances of escape by mentioning Devin and the others in front of your councilors. Do you suspect the spy to be one of them?"

Glotaj's brow furrowed. "I do not wish to make guesses at this point. I have some suspicions but haven't been able to fix them on anyone in particular. However, you do understand why I wanted to pursue this topic in private?"

"Of course," Sarina said. "I'm sorry. I didn't realize—"

The regent waved a hand. "If the resistance leaders on Souk want to establish contact, they'll have to make the first move. The only thing I can do at this point is pass information on to Admiral Gog."

"I see." Sarina folded her hands in her lap. "Tell me, Your Excellency, why did you have Teir assigned to retrieve me from Earth and then to act as my bodyguard? You also allowed us to go to Tendraa together. Was there some reason why you wanted us to be together?"

The regent regarded her impassively. "Captain Reylock is a top officer in the Defense League. I simply thought he would be the best person for those jobs."

"Why did you aid his admission into Defense League Academy? Teir told me you knew his aunt."

Was that a flicker of alarm she saw in his eye? "That is not your concern," Glotaj said.

"Everything about Teir is my concern. What are you trying to hide, Your Excellency?"

"I am merely attempting to protect Captain Reylock. Do not inquire further into his background. It could be dangerous for him."

"Why?"

"I can tell you no more."

"I healed him," Sarina blurted. "Twice, I made his wounds disappear."

"What?"

When she described the occurrences, Glotaj rubbed a hand over a face suddenly lined with concern.

"So, it comes to pass," he murmured in a barely audible tone.

For a long moment he didn't say another word. His expression showed a shifting of emotions, as though he was trying to make a weighty decision.

At last the regent looked at her, a cold mask hiding his thoughts. "Speak of this to no one, and proceed along your present course. Let me know what you learn from Mara."

"What about the wedding, Glotaj? It's scheduled for six days from now."

"Destiny will show you the proper path, child."

"Let's hope you're right," Sarina said dryly. Rising, she wondered if protocol demanded that she bow or curtsy. Deciding to do neither, she left.

Rolf was pacing the antechamber when she appeared. Silently, he led her outside. Sarina paused on the hilltop, gazing at the brilliance of the city below and feeling a flash of comfort. Was this place becoming her home? *No*, her mind answered. Your home is wherever Teir is. Her heart cried out for him, wishing he were there beside her.

Rolf turned to her. "What did Glotaj want?"

"He just needed a few more details about the Souks, so I went over my story again," she lied. She wasn't about to tell him they had spoken about Teir.

"I think you should put all that out of your mind and try to relax. Let's go to the Pleasure Palace. I'm free for the next couple of hauras."

Sarina had no desire to waste time at the city's arts and entertainment complex, but she didn't want to offend Rolf. There would be time enough to see Mara afterward. "All right," she agreed.

Requisitioning a speeder, they zoomed to the massive structure and parked in an adjacent terminal. "What would you like to do?" Rolf asked, obviously eager to please her.

"I don't know," Sarina said dispiritedly, remembering the last time she had been there. Teir had made her so happy by appreciating her love for art. Thinking of him suffering on Souk, she didn't feel like having fun.

Noting her unenthusiastic response, Rolf suggested they have a cold drink in the lounge and talk. He asked her about her family and friends on Earth and what she had accomplished while she was home.

Sarina found herself responding, telling him about her life there and the people she'd known. Somehow, the subject drifted to Robert.

"You didn't regret leaving him this time?" Rolf asked, studying her.

"No, I realized he didn't attract me at all. He's too rigid in his views. All that matters to him is his job and the image he presents."

"His dedication sounds admirable."

"I suppose it would, to you," she said. When she saw the pained look on Rolf's face, she hastened to add, "I'm sorry. I didn't mean—"

"Yes, you did. My role is extremely important to me. But so are you, Sarina. I promise to give you the attention you deserve."

Seated beside her, he leaned over to kiss her. Sarina felt the warm pressure of his lips and suppressed an urge to pull away. She had to fall in love with him if she wanted the legend to come true, and that meant enduring his physical advances. The councilor wasn't displeasing. He just didn't arouse her passion the way the captain did.

As soon as Rolf left for a meeting with the High Council, Sarina paged her friend Mara and asked if they could meet. She chose a public eaterie, so the guards following her would think she was just

enjoying herself with a friend. She didn't know if
they reported her movements to Rolf or not, but
the fact that they surrounded her wherever she
went inhibited her freedom. She was grateful for
their presence, though. Too many different political
factions opposed her and Rolf, and Teir was no longer
available to act as bodyguard.

She spotted the tall, raven-haired beauty approaching the eaterie. Striding over, Sarina gave Mara a
quick hug. They exchanged excited greetings and then
went inside where Sarina selected a corner table so
they could watch the entrance. She'd learned a few
things from Teir, she thought wryly.

After ordering a light snack, Mara fixed her knowing gaze on Sarina. "So you return to Bimordus Two,
my friend."

"Yes. I think the legend might be coming true after
all." She filled Mara in on events.

"I helped locate you after you escaped from Captain
Reylock's custody, you know."

"Yes, Glotaj told me."

"I sensed you were not happy."

"No. I was angry with Teir." Realizing what she'd
let slip, Sarina hastened to cover up. "I mean, the
captain wouldn't help me go back to Earth."

"He was only doing his duty."

"Yes, I know." She compressed her lips, reliving
the memory of her suffering over his callousness.
Then the purpose of his behavior came to mind.
He'd been sacrificing his own happiness to push her
back to Rolf. How ironic that she'd returned to Rolf
of her own accord! Now it was she who was making
sacrifices for Teir. "Mara, I could use your help."

"Oh?" The Tyberian took a sip of her wagmint
tea.

"I want you to tell me where Teir is."

Mara put her teacup down and leaned back, a frown
on her face. "This must be serious."

"Yes, it is. Please, Mara! I've asked Glotaj for help

in locating Teir, but the government has no contacts on Souk. I don't know of any other way to get news. I just want to know that he's all right." She didn't mention Glotaj's interest in the matter, or the regent's suggestion that she pursue this avenue on her own. "I know you require an item of his, something he's touched. I have his shirt, but I wasn't able to go home on the way here to get it. Could we meet later, maybe at your place?" She'd put the shirt through a cleansing, unable to discard the one thing of Teir's she possessed.

"Fine. How about coming by at twenty hauras?"

Sarina agreed and they parted. Outside, she hopped on the people-mover, chuckling at the curses of her guards as they scrambled to get on after her. She headed for Spiral Town, wanting nothing more than a bath and a long nap. She wanted time to pass quickly until she saw Mara again, but Rolf was waiting for her.

"I'm sorry I had that meeting," he said, following Sarina into her sleeping chamber. "I would have liked to have spent the rest of the afternoon with you. Where did you go?"

Sarina took her data link from her dress pocket and placed it on a countertop. Standing before the reflector, she began untwisting her long braid.

"I met Mara for a snack."

"How is she?"

"Fine." She began brushing her hair. Rolf placed his hands on her shoulders from behind and she stopped, the brush poised in her hand.

"Why do you resist me?" he said softly, breathing into her ear.

"Pardon?"

"You know what I mean. Every time I touch you, you cringe."

"I—I don't mean to."

He caressed her upper arms. "Reylock isn't coming between us, is he?"

"How could he? He isn't even here."

"He's in your thoughts, though. I will not tolerate disloyalty, Sarina."

Pivoting, she faced him. "You have my allegiance, and I'll support your goals. Isn't that enough?"

"No, it's not. I may have felt that way before, but things have changed. I'm a man, Sarina. You're going to be my bride. I need your full attention."

"You have my attention. Just remember that affection can't be forced."

"But you're making it difficult for me. I want the legend to come true, and so do you. If I'm willing to work toward that end, you should do your part."

"You're right," she said, lowering her head.

Rolf tilted her chin and kissed her. Sarina endured his caresses as his hands roamed her body. She tried not to think about Teir, but she couldn't help herself. Every spare moment, she was wondering what had happened to him. As Rolf's mouth moved over hers, she wept inside. It wasn't his embraces she wanted!

After dinner, Sarina dashed out for Mara's. Luckily, Rolf was busy with a conference call upstairs so he didn't argue when she said she was going to visit her friend. Under a bulky maroon sweater, she wore Teir's shirt tucked into her long black skirt. Hopefully the guards that accompanied her wouldn't notice anything unusual.

Mara was waiting for her. "Did you bring it?" she asked, showing Sarina into the small apartment she shared with Hedy, a medic from the Wellness Center. Sarina greeted her roommate, and then the two of them went upstairs to Mara's loft-style study.

"I wore his shirt under my sweater," Sarina replied with a grin, pulling the outer garment over her head. She unbuttoned the shirt and took it off, replacing the sweater.

Mara took the shirt from her. "Do you want to begin right away?"

"If you don't mind. Rolf might get upset if I'm gone too long."

"He is very attractive, Sarina. There are many females who would like to be in your position."

"I know. I wish I could feel differently toward him."

"The captain still holds your affection?"

Sarina grinned weakly. "More than that."

"What about your wedding?"

"The arrangements have been made." Her gown had arrived, and the gossamer silk material was beautiful. She'd felt guilty trying it on, however. This marriage to Rolf wasn't right. *Destiny will move you along the proper path*, Glotaj had told her. It seemed to be moving her inexorably toward the wedding ceremony. Unless something miraculous occurred, Sarina supposed she'd have to go through with it.

"But if you don't want to wed Lord Cam'brii—" Mara said, confusion in her dark eyes.

"I want the prophecy to come true, Mara. I'll do whatever is necessary to fulfill its terms."

"You're supposed to fall in love with him."

"The legend states that I must marry a Raimorrdan who is highly placed and was born under the sign of the circle. The power of my love will activate my healing aura. Those are the exact words, Mara. They don't say I have to fall in love with the Raimorrdan I wed, do they?"

"Well, no, but—"

"I never thought about it before, but maybe the meaning is different than how the High Council interpreted it. Maybe it isn't Rolf I'm supposed to love. Maybe it's—"

"Teir?" Mara supplied.

"I healed him, Mara," Sarina whispered. "Twice, I made his wounds vanish."

"How could that happen unless you're in love with him?"

Sarina stared at her friend. "Why have I never

realized it before? No wonder I don't feel anything toward Lord Cam'brii. I *do* love Teir! I think about him constantly. I can't wait until we're together again. Oh, I hope he's all right!"

"But what of the legend that states you're supposed to marry a Raimorrdan?" Mara asked, her eyes warmly sympathetic.

"I don't know. Glotaj seems to think everything will work out the way it's supposed to." Suddenly her gaze narrowed suspiciously. Just what had the regent meant when he said it was dangerous to inquire into Teir's background? She'd have to find out. In fact, it suddenly became imperative that she learn more about Teir's heritage. Was it possible. . . . No, surely Glotaj wouldn't let her marry the wrong man!

"Let's begin," she said eagerly. "Tell me about Teir."

Mara clutched the shirt tight against her chest. Closing her eyes, she let her mind wander. Emanations from the garment reached her psyche and stretched out into the farthest corner of her mind. Her consciousness responded, rising and floating away, out of the confines of space, across the reaches of the stars. . . .

"Mara!"

Sarina's choking cry broke her trance, and Mara's eyes snapped open. "What is it?" Mara said, alarmed by the pallor of her friend's face.

"I don't feel well. I think I'm going to—" Sarina dashed across the room to the sanitary and vomited into the receptacle. Moaning, she sank to her knees.

"You are ill!" Mara exclaimed, following her.

"My head hurts," Sarina croaked, holding her hands to her temples. Her vision swam dizzily, and her body felt as if it were burning up. Feeling her stomach begin to heave again, she propped herself upright and leaned over the receptacle.

"Hedy, come upstairs!" Mara shouted to her roommate.

"What's the matter?" the medic asked, rushing up the flight of steps.

"I don't know. She got sick all of a sudden."

The two women stared at Sarina. Her face was a ghastly hue.

"Wait, I'll get my mediscan."

A moment later, Hedy returned, holding a triangular object. Running it over Sarina's body, Hedy couldn't stifle the gasp of horror that escaped her lips when she read the diagnosis.

"Lord Cam'brii must be notified immediately!" the brunette said in a voice laden with disbelief.

"What is it?" Mara cried.

Hedy looked at her with a grim expression. "If these readouts are correct," she said, "our Great Healer has contracted the Farg!"

"Oh, no!" Mara paled as the implications sunk in. Sarina had the dreaded plague, and they'd all been exposed.

Chapter Sixteen

Mantra heard of Sarina's illness the moment he set foot on Bimordus Two. The whole settlement was talking about it. Fears ran rampant that the disease would spread, even though she'd been quarantined in the Wellness Center. Murmurs of doubt had arisen about her as the Great Healer, for if she possessed the power, why hadn't she healed herself? The High Council was in a turmoil, and Mantra had to wait to be presented as the new Ambassador from Tendraa.

At last he gained an audience and received approval for his appointment. The High Council was greatly pleased that the Liege Lord of Tendraa had assented to sending a representative, and Mantra was authorized to sit in the General Assembly. Mantra beamed with pride when he received his sand-colored cape of office. Because of Tendraa's status as an associate member, however, he was not permitted to vote.

Glotaj was shocked when Mantra informed them about the Morgots. "Why have we received no intelligence to this effect?" he demanded of his councilors.

"Lord Cam'brii, contact Admiral Gog and find out what's going on. The Morgots must not be permitted to take Tendraa. If they get hold of the flavium resources, the Coalition is doomed."

"Pardon, Your Excellency," Mantra said. "My Liege Lord expressly forbid me from asking the Defense League for assistance. He requested I consult the Great Healer for her advice in this matter."

Glotaj waved a hand in the air. "The Great Healer is not available. You can tell your leader that the entire Coalition is threatened by the Morgot presence. Upon my authority, a force will be assembled to oppose them. You've done well, Ambassador. If we are successful in repelling the invaders, you can take credit for saving your world."

Admiral Gog was astounded by the news when Rolf contacted him via the comm unit at Defense League Station. "Have the Morgots been able to expand the molecular alteration technology to cloak their vessels? We haven't been able to convert anything of that size. I don't understand how the fleet got past our sensors otherwise. Be assured, Lord Cam'brii, I'll get on this at once," he barked.

"Any news of Captain Reylock?" Rolf asked. If he could bring Sarina a positive report, it might help her recovery. He was terribly concerned about her prognosis.

"Not so far. Our intelligence in that region is limited. We sure could use his help, though. Reylock's our best strategist."

Rolf had to agree. The captain was a formidable opponent in the art of war. His unorthodox tactics and brilliant maneuvers had made him the youngest captain in the League. "Keep me posted," he told the Admiral. "Cam'brii out."

Mantra was just leaving Defense League Station after inquiring about his cousin Ravi. The duty officer had informed him that Teir's crew members were due to return later that day. Surprised to see Lord Cam'brii striding by, Mantra hastened to his side.

"My lord, may I accompany you to see the Great Healer?" he asked, falling into step beside the tall, blond man. With his regal carriage and noble profile, Lord Cam'brii made an impressive figure. Mantra felt awed by his presence.

"I'd be honored by your company," Rolf said graciously. "I understand you met Sarina on Tendraa?"

The two exited into the bright afternoon sunshine and turned onto a busy walkway.

Mantra related all that had occurred during her visit, including the effects of the sanitation measures she'd suggested. "It is truly a miracle what those few changes have wrought. The Liege Lord has agreed to mandate the orders throughout the land. I come to seek her advice."

"I fear she can give you none. She is gravely ill."

Having already had the pestilence, Mantra didn't need to don the protective energy suit like Lord Cam'brii. He could walk right into her cubicle and sit at her bedside.

When they arrived at the Wellness Center, they headed for Sarina's cubicle. When Mantra entered it, he was shocked by her appearance. Sarina was weak and thin, and her livid complexion and red, burning eyes told him that she was indeed smitten by the plague.

A flicker of surprise lit her eyes when she saw him. "Mantra," Sarina whispered through cracked lips.

"I have been made Ambassador to Tendraa, Mistress," he told her gently, touching her forehead. Alas, she was burning up! "I am to seek your counsel."

Sarina laughed weakly. "I fear your faith in the Great Healer is misplaced. I will not survive this affliction." Her face twisted in agony, giving credence to her words.

"Nay, do not speak thus! If you indulge in gloomy thoughts, you will surely bring about a fatal result.

I shall aid you." He spoke to her for a few more minutes, then sought the medic, a lean young woman with short black hair, in charge of her care. "What is being done for her?" he asked, as though his knowledge could help in this sterile setting of modern medicine. This world was full of wonders, and he couldn't wait to explore, but his duty was first and foremost to the Great Healer.

"We can only treat the symptoms," the medic said. "When her temperature rises, she slips into a delirium and mumbles incoherently. We give her medicines to lower the fever and assuage the pain."

"The blisters must be drawn," Mantra said. "May I assist you?" Taking charge, he told the medic what he required.

The medic, giving him a strange look, obeyed. She knew the Ambassador had survived the Farg, so perhaps his knowledge would be helpful.

When Mantra returned to her room, Sarina had fallen into a state of insensibility. She was rambling on about Captain Reylock and someone she termed the fat dogface. Even in her unconscious state, her countenance proclaimed the agony she endured.

Ripping away her covers, Mantra examined her body. He found one plague-spot on the inside of her thigh and another ugly boil under her arm. Hastily drawing the blanket up so she wouldn't be chilled, he waited for the medic to arrive with the spirit of sulfur for the posset-drink he'd ordered, and the mallows, lily-roots, figs, linseed, and palmara oil to make poultices for her sores.

Sarina opened her eyes and fixed her gaze upon him. It was clear she did not know who he was, because she heaved a deep sigh and began talking to him as though he were Captain Reylock. Mantra wondered at their relationship. Was the Great Healer not betrothed to Lord Cam'brii? Had not their wedding been postponed because of her illness? He shook his head, puzzled.

The medic entered and silently handed him the requested items. "I had to create the alexipharmics you requested on the fabricator," she said. "Half these things are unheard of here, but the programming extends to Tendraa so you are lucky."

The medic's speech was incomprehensible to Mantra. What was a fabricator? It did not matter; he had what he needed. Laying out the items on a table, he said, "I need some means to heat the poultices."

The medic pointed to an alcove inset in a wall. "You can use the fabricator in this room. Just place whatever you want in there and order it to raise the temperature."

Fascinated, Mantra asked for a demonstration. Truly, this was a miracle! You could create anything out of thin air! Pushing aside his curiosity, he focused his mind on the purpose at hand.

After applying the warm poultices to Sarina's tumors, he roused her long enough to get her to take the posset-drink. Then he gave her a dose of mithridate mixed with Venice treacle. Placing a cool cloth on her forehead, Mantra sat back and waited. Not everyone responded to this treatment, as evidenced by the death rate on Tendraa. But Sarina was fortunate in that her illness had been caught in its earliest stages.

Within the haura, moisture broke out on Sarina's skin, a good sign. She writhed on the narrow bed, ranting and raving, as the sweat poured from her. At last she calmed and sank into a tranquil slumber. Mantra felt her forehead. Her skin felt cool. Rejoicing, he called the medic in to wash and change her. Offering a prayer to the Almighty, Mantra refreshed the poultices, reapplied them, and drew the covers over her.

When Sarina awoke, she was so weak she could barely lift her head. But her breathing came easier, and the terrible throbbing pains from her sores were gone. Ravenously hungry, she demanded nourishment which Mantra provided. He got a kick out of using the fabricator, and while Sarina was sipping a strengthening brew, he ordered a meal of Stuntorian stew and a carafe of ale for himself. He'd been so engrossed in caring for his patient that he hadn't thought to take nourishment earlier.

A commotion at the door made him look up, and when he saw who was there, a wide grin broke out on his face.

"Ravi!" he cried, stepping outside to greet his cousin.

The two embraced, and then Ravi introduced him to the rest of Teir's crew who'd come to inquire after Sarina. They remained in the anteroom, safely outside the confines of the quarantine area.

After a while, the others left, leaving Ravi and Mantra alone.

"How does your family?" Ravi asked. "I was sorrowed to hear of the passing of your parents and your sister Zunis."

Mantra gazed at him. "Alas, I would have thought no worse disaster could befall us, but now the Morgots are attacking the outermost planet of our system."

Ravi's jaw dropped in surprise. "The Morgots!"

"Glotaj has ordered the League to muster a defense."

"Aye, I'll bet he doesn't want the Morgots to get the flavium resources on Tendraa! I'll have to see that we're assigned a ship," he said excitedly. "The forthcoming battle will be a decisive one. Is that why you came, to request aid?"

"In truth, I was sent to consult the Great Healer."

"The Liege Lord still refuses to participate fully in the Coalition?" At his cousin's nod, Ravi said, "He is a foolish old man."

"Not so foolish," Mantra replied, remembering the riches in the palace. "Just stubborn and prideful. I have set his daughter Tami to work on him to try to change his mind. In any event, it does not matter. A force will be sent regardless."

He sighed heavily. "I did not wish to leave Kairi and Sita alone. I hope they will fare well. The Baynor has supplies delivered to them daily, thanks to Sarina, but they still must remain shut in the house."

"What did Sarina do on Tendraa that so impressed you?"

Mantra told him, and then their talk turned to the Great Healer's current condition.

"She's been grievously ill. In the height of her distemper, she kept crying out for Captain Reylock," Mantra mentioned.

"The captain is missing," Ravi said solemnly. "They were on Souk together. Apparently she fears he is either captured or dead."

"Why does she take so much interest in him?"

Ravi lowered his voice. "They have a tendre for one another. It was quite evident even when she was first aboard the *Valiant*."

"But she is betrothed to Lord Cam'brii. The wedding was postponed due to her illness."

"Hush, here comes her bridegroom now."

The two men watched as Lord Cam'brii approached, his stride long and purposeful.

"What is this news I hear? Sarina is recovering?" Profound relief shone in his eyes. "I shall be eternally grateful to you, Ambassador." Donning a protective energy suit, he hastened into Sarina's cubicle.

Her eyes fluttered open when she heard sounds of footsteps approaching. "Rolf," she said, her voice weak and low.

"Are you feeling better?" he asked, concerned at how pale she still appeared. Her hair clung in moist tendrils at the sides of her face and spread about her pillow like a halo.

"The pain is gone, but I feel terribly weak."

"Rest easy. Everyone is asking about you. You must get well."

"Has anyone else become ill? Mara, Hedy, or yourself?" They'd been most directly exposed.

"No, and our researchers are puzzled. It was thought the pestilence was highly contagious. Yet no one else on Bimordus Two has succumbed. It is assumed you were infected when you were on Tendraa, and the incubation period was lengthy. It is possible that those of us who were exposed will become ill suddenly like yourself, but I for one hope that will not be true!" By the Gods, he hoped hers was an isolated case on Bimordus Two.

"I hope Teir isn't ill!" she exclaimed, thinking he'd been on Tendraa with her.

Always her thoughts are for the captain. Rolf grimaced. "You were both wearing the suits, weren't you?" If it didn't work for them, it might not work for him, either. Even though he'd already been exposed, he was hoping the contagion wasn't infectious until symptoms broke out. In that case, the suit should protect him if it worked.

"I shut mine off," Sarina confessed. "I wanted to test my healing power, and I thought the energy barrier might be obstructive. Teir kept his on the whole time. I hope he's all right!"

"You can't ask him, can you?" Rolf said, then instantly regretted his choice of words when he saw her stricken look. "Sorry, Sarina. I can't help it. We're supposed to be married soon, and all through your delirium, you kept raving about Reylock."

"I did?" she asked in a small voice.

He nodded grimly. "Nevertheless, our wedding *will* be rescheduled. Eat, and regain your strength."

Mantra shuffled in soon after Lord Cam'brii left. "What grieves you, Mistress?" he asked, seeing her melancholy expression.

"I wish I knew what happened to Teir." She studied him a moment. "Mantra, would you do me a favor?

Would you send for Mara, please? You can have her paged."

Later Mara visited her. "Captain Reylock is alive," she told Sarina right away.

"How do you know?" Sarina gasped, a flood of joy surging through her.

Lowering her eyelids, Mara confessed, "I used my power while you were sick, hoping I would have good news for you when you recovered. I didn't bother to *see* much, however. I'll do it again now that you're awake, and maybe it will give you a clue as to his location."

She returned that night with Teir's shirt hidden under her work clothes. Waiting until they were alone, Mara drew the white fabric to her chest. Closing her eyes, she swayed back and forth until the vision came to her. With awful clarity, she looked directly through Teir's eyes. "I see what he sees," she intoned. "There is fire—a raging wall of fire. The heat blasts my face."

"You can feel it?" Sarina croaked. Her throat was dry with apprehension.

Mara nodded imperceptibly. "I am moving back, changing direction. Bubbling and hissing noises reach my ears. There are others behind me. I feel apprehensive about their presence. Oops, I nearly stepped in a pool of boiling liquid! See how it spits hot mud into the air."

"Where is this place?" Sarina asked, wondering if Teir were in his own version of Hell.

Mara shook her head, her eyes squeezed shut. "A lizard man is watching me. He wears a strange uniform and doesn't look friendly."

"Lieutenant Otis!" She shouldn't be surprised. The Crigellan was Bdan's second-in-command. He must have taken over when the slaver drowned in his moat.

"And there's another . . . a Souk with the face of an ugly bloodhound." Mara described his features.

"Not Cerrus Bdan? I thought he was dead!" Shocked, Sarina asked, "What is he doing?"

"He is pointing at me and shouting. Now he flicks his wrist. Aargh, my throat constricts. Something is choking me!" Mara snapped out of the trance, abruptly opening her eyes.

"A slave collar," Sarina whispered. "He lives but is restrained. Oh, Mara, what shall I do?"

"At least he is alive," Mara reminded her.

"Yes, but as Bdan's slave! Oh, I cannot bear it. I must help him!" Tears threatened, but Sarina pushed them back. Weakness wouldn't help either one of them. "Has Teir's crew returned?"

"They've been back for some time and have quite annoyed the medics over you. I believe the Polluxite, Lieutenant Wren, sits in the anteroom with Mantra."

"Send him in! And Mara, thanks," she finished lamely.

Mara winked and left.

A moment later, Wren hastened into her room. "Sarina, you look much better," the navigator said.

"Teir is alive." She got straight to the point. "He needs our help. Cerrus Bdan still has him."

"How do you know this?" Wren queried, scrunching his layered eyebrows.

"Mara used her special power. Can you go on a rescue mission?"

"To Souk?"

Sarina regarded him solemnly. "Actually, I'm not certain of his location."

Wren rolled his eyes. "Then how do you expect us to go?"

"The place is full of fire and bubbling pools of mud."

"It sounds like Zor."

"No, it was outside, not a fiery underworld."

"I'll ask the others, but unless you have more specific information, I'm afraid it's not enough to go on. We've requested to join the fight against the

Morgots in the Tendraan system."

"The Morgots are threatening Mantra's planet?" The Tendraan hadn't told her, but then, he was considerate enough not to worry her with additional problems when she was so weak. "When will you know if you've been reassigned?"

"Within the next few days. I wish we had the *Valiant* . . . and her captain."

"Me, too."

After Wren left and Mantra entered the cubicle, Sarina expressed her frustration to him.

"Mistress, you can do little else to aid Captain Reylock, but you can do much to help others," he told her, kneeling at her bedside. "Your words of wisdom have already wrought great changes on my planet. You are much needed here!"

Emu came in and told her of the dissension within the government, dissension fueled by her indisposition. "You must show the populace you are well," said the Sirisian, stretching his rubbery face for emphasis. "It is time for you to assume your position."

"I have no special powers," she told him bleakly. "Wouldn't I have healed myself if I did? The legend is a farce." Healing Teir must have been a fluke. Either that, or her healing power worked on wounds but not on diseases.

"Do not be so quick to cast away your faith! It could be that your recovery is attributable to some innate quality within yourself. Many others have died on Tendraa using the same methods of treatment," Emu added. "And what of the long incubation period you experienced? Usually it is a matter of days, or even hauras. It could be that the special quality within yourself was fighting the sickness all this time. No one else on Bimordus Two has fallen ill.

"Another thing: Think about the method of transmission. If you were contagious, others would be sick by now, assuming there is a short incubation period. Some other factor must be involved in catching the disease. You have much work to do, Mistress."

"His words make sense," Mantra told Sarina. "Use the resources available to you, *Mira*. Find out why your case was different. It could be because you are the Great Healer."

"But you survived, Mantra. You did the same things for me that helped you."

"Aye, but I got sick directly after exposure."

"Emu may be right," Sarina agreed. "I'll discuss it with Glotaj."

She sought a private audience with the regent a few days later, immediately after her discharge from the Wellness Center. Glotaj appeared to be unimpressed by her theories.

"Your blood and tissue samples were sent to the Timosian Research Station where our greatest scientists have gathered to study the Farg," he said. "I don't believe they found anything unusual."

"You can't explain how I healed Teir, either," Sarina pointed out, "but it did happen. I think my reaction to the disease deserves further analysis."

"If you ask me, your healing power could use investigation, although it's always possible you might contribute something of importance to our body of knowledge about the Farg with a fresh approach." He studied her, thoughtful. "I suppose you'll have to go to Timos yourself."

"I'd be glad for the opportunity to do something useful," Sarina said quietly, but she was secretly elated by Glotaj's suggestion.

"Rolf isn't going to be happy about another postponement, but I think this is more important. I'll give you two weeks, no more." The regent paused. "It appears that the repeal of the execution decree is not going to pass," he warned her solemnly. "Daimon's supporters have grown. Immediately upon your return, the wedding must take place."

"Agreed." Sarina thought a moment, wondering

how best to broach the subject that really concerned her. A flash of inspiration gave her the opening she needed. "What about Teir? Since I healed him, shouldn't he be part of this research?"

Glotaj gave an exasperated sigh. "He can't participate if he's not here."

"I might have a clue as to his whereabouts. I did consult Mara as you suggested."

"And?"

His expression was wary, and she spoke quickly, describing the session.

"By the moons of Agus Six, that place sounds like Taurus!" Glotaj's face paled. "If the captain is there with Cerrus Bdan, it can mean only one thing. Bdan is forcing him to retrieve the Blood Crystal. I must notify Admiral Gog at once."

"Why? What's wrong?" Sarina cried, alarmed by the panic on the regent's normally placid countenance.

"The Blood Crystal can predict the future, but its use is influenced by the forces of evil. If the wrong people get hold of it, the results would be catastrophic. Reylock must be intercepted."

Chapter Seventeen

The *Valiant* reached orbit around Taurus eleven days and fourteen hauras after leaving Souk. A seething, hot volcanic planet, Taurus's terrain was known to be inhospitable and harsh.

In preparation for the shuttle departure, Teir was allowed on the bridge. Looking at the viewscreen for the first time on the voyage, he noticed an escort of two Souk patrol craft. They'd put a slight damper on his escape plan, but he should be able to manage, Teir figured, dismissing them for now.

"We'll need special gear," he told Bdan, listing his requirements for the arduous journey ahead. The Souk stood beside him, gazing out at the cloud-covered globe below. Otis, sitting in the pilot's seat, had put the ship into standard orbit and was awaiting further instructions.

"The landing site is on a flat bed of rock some distance from the guardian," Teir told them. "The climb will be treacherous. I suggest you leave my friends on board the *Valiant*. They'll only slow us down."

"Very well. Lieutenant Otis, join us will you for the landing party. Vivak will stay on board. Flight training has he, and he can watch the elders as well. Geemus and Wyeth go with us. Help carry the equipment can the two Hortha guards."

Teir quickly totaled up the number in the landing party: three Souks, two Horthas, and one Crigellan, besides himself. It shouldn't be too difficult to elude them. He knew the secrets of the mountain. They didn't.

Vivak, a tall, lanky Souk, took over the controls while the landing party made preparations. Once outfitted, they headed for the shuttle bay. Since the climate on the planet was hot and the atmosphere was tolerable, extra clothing wasn't needed. Bdan, however, changed into a tunic and baggy pantaloons to be practical. Still, Teir wondered how he'd get his bulk over the peaks and crevices below. Aside from Bdan, Teir was the only one not wearing a tool belt. Bdan wouldn't allow him to carry any equipment.

In the shuttle bay, Bdan grasped him by the shoulder and whirled him around. "R-r-remember, Captain, my prisoner are you. You make any attempt to escape, and I'll use an electrifier to punish you." He took the rod out of his tunic pocket to show Teir.

Teir gritted his teeth. "You're holding my friends captive on the ship. I won't step out of line." Of course, if his plan worked, they'd all be free as *humma* birds soon enough. But in the meantime, he had Bdan's unpredictable rages to contend with. He'd seen the heavy links of inertia manacles sticking out of the Souk's pantaloons pocket. If Teir acted up, no doubt those handcuffs would be slapped on his wrists in no time. It wouldn't matter how difficult they'd make his progress. The slaver would enjoy his suffering.

Compressing his lips, Teir opened the hatch to the shuttle and took over the helm. Bdan lowered himself with a grunt into the copilot's seat. Otis and the others filed in, taking seats in the rows behind them. After they'd fastened their safety restraints, the shuttle door hissed closed and locked. Teir began the departure checklist. Pressurized air whooshed on, and the countdown sequence began automatically. The shuttle bay door slid open, revealing the black starry backdrop of space. With a neck-jerking thrust, they were out, soaring into the airless vacuum. Teir changed the heading, and the shuttle nosed downward. They dropped at top speed toward the planet's surface.

Teir made a smooth landing and powered down. Removing his harness, he stood and led the way to the hatch.

"Hold, Captain!" Cerrus Bdan said. From yet another pocket, he took a thick circular band.

"A slave collar!" Teir exclaimed. "No, you wouldn't dare."

"On the contrary, Captain, gives me great pleasure does this."

With a nod from Bdan, the two Horthas gripped his arms. Teir struggled futilely as Bdan snapped the collar around his neck.

"Damn you!" he protested, enraged.

Bdan gloated gleefully. "Extra insurance is this. Trust you not, do I. You try any tricks, and—" He flicked his wrist and Teir felt the collar tighten.

"You've made your point," Teir croaked when the pressure was released.

Swallowing his anger, he opened the hatchway. A flight of steps automatically unfolded down to the ground. The stink of sulfur wafted upward, and Teir wrinkled his nose. Determinedly, he started down the steps. At the bottom, he waited for Bdan, Otis, the two Souks and the two Hortha guards to catch up. Luckily, Bdan wasn't leaving anyone behind to guard the shuttle. That would have made his own plan more difficult. As it was, it wouldn't be easy to get away.

The trek ahead of them appeared fraught with perils. Mountains rolled and peaked in a terrain made gray and bleak by countless volcanic eruptions. Heavy rains had loosened the tons of ash dumped on the slopes, causing cement-like slurries of mud to rush down streambeds in torrents called lahars. As a result, the landscape was barren, all vegetation having long since been obliterated.

Even as they stood, an eruption occurred in the distance. Plumes of superheated gas and ash spewed from the mountaintop, blackening the sky and shaking the ground with violent tremors. Lightning flashed overhead, strange streaks of blues, greens, and reds, while all around them rose pillars of steam, escaping from ground vents and crevices. Hissing, bubbling noises issued from pools of mud, heated by the fiery magma underneath.

Bdan coughed. "Arrgh, this planet is cursed. Full of fire is the air."

"We'd better move," Teir said. The whole region was unstable, including the mountain they had to climb. He didn't want to get caught in a pyroclastic flow.

Feeling less confident than before, Teir indicated the direction they were to follow. As protector of the Blood Crystal, he'd been to Taurus many times before, but only once to this particular location. Twice an annum, he had made a solitary journey to check the seismic instruments placed near the guardian. If all was stable, he left until the next time.

During his last visit he had seen signs of imminent eruption on the mountain housing the guardian, so Teir had changed its site. Although his primary assignment was to ensure the safety of the guardian's location, he also had to make certain no one else ever discovered it. The planet's desolate terrain had discouraged visitors, which made the last part easy— until now.

He took the lead, Bdan following, then Otis and the four guards. They crossed a stream, scrambled over a bed of boulders, and passed through a narrow canyon lined by sheer towers of rock. Then they entered a relatively straight pass over bumpy terrain made eerie by towering lava tree molds.

"This is easy," he lied, carefully choosing his steps. The gray rocks sprinkled with black dots were easily visible when you knew what to look for, and Teir had placed the rocks himself in precisely this order for just such an occasion. He counted the seconds, waiting for the scream of someone behind.

A crash sounded, then an unearthly howl. Whirling around, Teir feigned ignorance. "What was that?" The two Horthas were missing, he was pleased to note.

A large hole yawned in the ground. "They fell through!" Otis exclaimed, looking stunned. The others came over for a look.

"It's a lava tube," Teir explained, striding over and peering down into the black pit. "They must have broken through a thin spot. Watch where you're walking."

Bdan flicked his wrist and Teir's throat constricted. "Trick us, will you? You lose any more of my men, and I'll manacle you." When Teir's face started turning red and his breaths were choking gasps, Bdan released him.

"Damn you, I can't lead this group effectively if you question everything I do," Teir gritted, rubbing his neck.

"Lead on," the Souk slaver commanded, ignoring his protest.

Teir didn't have time to argue. He'd noticed the gray ball growing just below the nearest peak. Watching it blossom into a billowing pyroclastic cloud of hot gas, pumice and ash, he warned the others, "We'd better hurry. That doesn't look good." Another tremor shook the ground and he glanced around for a better route. "This way," Teir cried, leading the group through a pass toward the other side of the mountain. Looking behind, he saw the rolling cloud of superheated ash race down the slope.

It took the better part of three hauras for them

to reach the base of the mountain they needed to climb. By this time, earthquakes were coming fast and strong and the yellowish sky had turned an ominous shade of slate. Ash fell like powdery beige snow. Teir insisted on having the slave collar removed before he went any farther.

"It's too dangerous from here on," he told Bdan, shouting to be heard over the claps of thunder. To their right, a fountain of flame burst out of a crack in the earth's crust. To the left was a steep incline, the path they were to follow.

"All right," Bdan grumbled, "but my electrifier will I not hesitate to use if you cause trouble. Understand?" He choked Teir one more time, enjoying the sight of the captain brought to his knees, clutching at his neck and gasping for air. Abruptly, he released Teir's restraint and pocketed it.

Bdan was in a foul mood. He'd been sweating profusely during the past half haura of exertion. His bluish skin had paled to a sickly color, and his eyes kept darting about. No doubt he wished to finish this excursion as quickly as possible. Teir, hating the slaver more than ever, resolved to push him off the nearest peak at the earliest opportunity. But he was so busy watching his footing that he didn't get the chance.

Resuming the pace, Teir led them carefully through a section of boiling hot pools where heated mud spattered and spewed into the air. Then he began the ascent. Glancing back, he noted that the two Souk guards took up the rear. They were going to be a nuisance, he thought grimly. His plan was to reach the guardian, also known as the Cave of Crystal, then escape through the secret passage to the other side of the mountain and the sea below. Once on the beach, he could summon the shuttle using the small remote unit in his inner vest pocket. But he had to get free of the others long enough to do all this.

A huge blast rocked the air as part of the erupting

mountain blew apart. Red-hot lava cascaded down the nearby slope, exploding when it hit the sea on the other side of the volcanic range. Against a sky now black with ash, the effect was a pyrotechnic show worthy of a miniature supernova.

Rocks began to fall, frothy lava that was blown aloft and cooled into clumps of sharp-edged pumice. "Take shelter!" Teir yelled as glassy shards began piercing his skin. He sidestepped to a ledge under an overhang, and they huddled there, waiting for the cataclysm to calm.

After a brief consultation, they donned breathing gear and night goggles. The darkness equaled that of a sealed room, and Bdan's eyes when he looked at Teir were as large as saucers. "Are you leading us astray, R-R-Reylock? As desolate as Zor is this place! I like it not." His jowls quivered as he spoke.

"We'll get there," Teir assured him, "unless a lahar doesn't get us first. They can roar down the slope without warning." Even as he shouted to be heard, a stream of basaltic lava flowed by like a river of syrup. Cooling, it hardened into black glassy swirls. "Don't step there," he warned the others. "It's still boiling hot."

They'd gone a few hundred meters ahead when Teir stopped and turned to Lieutenant Otis. "I need the surveyor's theodolite," he said to the Crigellan. The officer looked ill. His face, what Teir could see of it through his breathing apparatus, appeared light green and his brow was moist.

"What are you doing?" Bdan croaked as Teir set up the piece of equipment.

Teir focused the instrument on a palm-sized reflector he knew to be spaced higher up on the mountain. Locking in on target, he activated a small laser beam that leaped to the reflector and back. "I'm measuring the distance. It's 4680 meters. That varies less than a few centimeters from my earlier measurements, meaning there's no dangerous swelling of the cone.

We can proceed." He folded up the device and gave it back to Otis.

After midnight, a light rain began to fall. Teir was genuinely afraid they might be caught by a lahar. He urged them on as pillars of steam rose all around them. Finally, the clouds of ash dispersed enough for a faint light from Taurus's two moons to brighten the climb. They reached the summit just as dawn broke on the horizon in a brilliant red display.

"We have to descend into the crater," Teir said, pointing to the steaming, sulfurous caldera below.

"You joke!" Otis said.

They packed away their breathing apparatus and night goggles and stared into the seething crater.

Teir inserted a thermometer into a crack that showed red just centimeters below. It was hot, but not volcanically feverish. He glanced down at the lava dome, smoldering like an ominous fuse. "You see that opening?" he said, pointing to a dark mouth gaping at the opposite rim. "It leads to our destination, the Cave of Crystal."

Bdan's fat body shook with fatigue. "We rest here, Captain. Go no farther can I r-r-right now."

"I could go down with Otis and bring the Blood Crystal back up to you. He'll make sure I stay in line," Teir suggested mildly.

"Go nowhere will you without me," growled Bdan. "Trust you not, do I." He glared at Teir. "Soon shall we see if you have earned your rewards."

"What rewards?" Teir asked sarcastically as he sank onto the ground's hard surface to gain a much needed rest. His clothes were covered with a coating of ash, and his skin was encrusted with grime. He wiped his mouth with the back of his hand and then looked with disgust at the black dust that came off.

"Your friends will go free when we get back to Souk. Told you I keep my word, didn't I?" the slaver said, giving him a sly smile. He too plopped on the ground, panting.

"And what happens to me?"

Bdan grinned wickedly. "Have plans for you, do I."

Teir saw the direction of his glance. "They don't include pushing me into that pit of molten lava, do they?" he asked dryly.

Bdan grunted his laughter. "R-r-read my thoughts, do you? No, Captain, a better idea have I."

Teir didn't ask what it was. He didn't intend to be around long enough to find out. "I don't think we should spend too much time here. A strong quake could rock us right into the caldron. There's only one safe way to descend."

After they'd taken nourishment, they began the final trek. The distance appeared to be short, but it took them a good part of the morning to reach the opposite rim. It was midday when they approached the opening to the cave.

"Use we flame torches or goggles?" Bdan asked, hesitating in front of the pitch-black hole.

"Flame torches. They'll give us wider vision."

Taking the sticks from Otis and igniting them, they trailed single-file into the yawning gap. The passage dipped and they had to crouch, hobbling along half-bent until they rounded a corner and reached a larger opening. Here the path split in two directions.

"Which way?" Bdan panted behind him.

"We'll take the path to the right," Teir said, leading them over a flat slab of rock and into another tight passage.

They continued to wind through a maze of tunnels, steam hissing from vents in the rock face surrounding them. The temperature was hot despite the elevation, and sweat streaked Teir's face.

For a moment he thought he'd lost the two Souk guards bringing up the rear. He was rushing along as fast as he could despite the obstacles, and when he glanced back at one point, only Bdan and Otis were to be seen.

"Captain!" Bdan called as he tried to squeeze his bulk through a particularly narrow passage. "Go too fast, do you!"

"I can't help it if you're not in shape," Teir said, grinning. He was hoping the two Souks were lost for good.

The smuggler grunted and pushed himself through the tight opening. "Halt!" he commanded, waiting for Otis to catch up to them. "Leading us in circles are you. I told you what the punishment would be for disobedience." He whipped out his electrifier.

Teir held up his hands. "Easy, Cerrus. The path to the guardian is complicated. We must take the exact route."

"Take me to the chamber that houses the Blood Crystal!"

"That's what I'm doing. We're almost there."

"Liar!"

Bdan blasted him. The shock threw Teir against the wall. He banged his head against an outcropping of rock and slid to the ground, dazed. His nerve endings burned with pain.

"You do that again, and I won't take you anywhere," he gritted.

"Get up!" Bdan shouted.

Just then, the two guards staggered into view, one of them dragging the other.

"Sorry, master," grunted Wyeth as they joined the others. "Wanted to turn back did Geemus. Convinced him did I to follow orders."

"Turn tail, would you?" Bdan bellowed to his henchman. "Stand aside," he ordered Wyeth.

Flicking a switch on his electrifier, he aimed it at the quaking Geemus. As the Souk screamed, Bdan pushed the trigger. A crackling light shot out, and Geemus vaporized instantly.

He turned to Teir who was watching, frozen on the ground where he'd fallen. "Take us now, R-R-Reylock, or it's all over for you, too."

Teir put a look of defeat on his face. Heaving himself upright, he sighed, "Very well. This way." But inwardly, he grinned. The odds were now three to one. The rest should be easy, unless Bdan decided to shackle him with those manacles dangling from his pantaloons. He'd better seem very cooperative.

At the end of a twisting passage, he stopped.

"Now what?" growled Bdan, coming up behind him. They faced what appeared to be a dead end.

"This is the entrance to the guardian," Teir said, fitting his hands into two grooves carved into the rock face. A grinding noise followed, and the whole section of rock slid open in front of them.

Bdan gasped as a sparkling chamber was revealed.

"This is the Cave of Crystal," Teir said, striding inside.

Dazzling stalactites and stalagmites of gleaming black crystal shone in the lights from their flame torches. Water dripped down the walls, adding to the dazzle, and silvery-white boloxite columns graced the cavern. The effect was surreal in the artificial light.

Bdan indicated that Otis and Wyeth were to guard the entrance, more so that Teir couldn't run out on them than from fear of anyone following. Teir almost laughed. They didn't know the secret of the guardian. With one push of a hidden control, he could move the entire Cave of Crystal to another preset location, using phase emission technology. The guardian simply vanished from one spot and showed up in another. That was how he had been able to keep the Blood Crystal safe from the cataclysms of nature. One hint that the mountain was about to erupt, and Teir changed the site. Since Bdan and his cohorts were present, he'd use his private escape route, the one that would take him down to the sea. Now all he had to do was get near the chute.

"The Blood Crystal, where it is?" Bdan asked, aiming the electrifier at him.

"This way." Teir stalked across a river of cold

flowstone and pointed to a raised pedestal in the center of the room.

"I see nothing!" Bdan exclaimed, joining him. "Is this some trickery?"

Teir glowered at him. "A word of warning, Cerrus. It is said that whoever uses the Blood Crystal is touched with evil."

Bdan laughed uproariously. "I'm already evil, Captain! Get it for me."

Glancing at the electrifier still pointed in his direction, Teir clenched his jaw. He'd hoped he wouldn't have to go this far, but there was no way around it. He couldn't make his move to get away just yet.

He set his palm on the flat surface of the pedestal. The blank whiteness was lit by a momentary glow. Standing back, Teir watched as an opening gaped and the gleaming black crystal slid upward into view. It was cone-shaped and streaked with veins of red that glowed in the light from their flame torches like rivers of blood.

Bdan lumbered closer and snatched it up. "Test it, will I." But as he held the glassy stone in his palm, nothing happened.

"What is this?" he growled, turning to Teir. "Why does it not show me the future?"

"Maybe it doesn't work with people who already have darkness in their souls."

Suspicion dawned in the Souk's beady eyes. "A decoy must this be. Where is the r-r-real crystal?"

Teir regarded him calmly. "You're holding it, Cerrus. You asked me to take you to the Blood Crystal and I did. You didn't tell me to get it to work for you."

"Then do it!"

"I don't know how. I've never touched it myself."

"Arrgh!" Bdan howled with rage. "You lie! Kill you, shall I!"

As his finger moved on the electrifier, Teir threw himself into a flying somersault, snatching the crystal

out of Bdan's hand before hitting the floor. He rolled
toward the far wall as a jagged streak of electricity
singed the air by his ear. Slapping at a raised knob
on the ground, Teir drew into a crouch just as an
ominous rumbling began. Bdan snarled and fired
again, and Teir dodged to the side just in time. He
charged for the section of wall etched with a barely
discernible white circle. The last thing he saw before
the wall crumbled and swallowed him up was the
astonished look on Bdan's face.

Feet first, Teir slid downward in total darkness.
He was racing along inside a giant slide carved
into the mountain's interior, straight down to the
sea. Grasping the Blood Crystal firmly in his hands,
he closed his eyes so he couldn't see the terrifying
blackness below.

He landed abruptly. One moment he was hurtling
through darkness, and the next he came to a bone-
jarring halt on a bed of powdery volcanic sand.
Opening his eyes, Teir saw it was still daylight
outside, though a gray haze obscured the sea. He
rubbed his face. His jaw was rough with stubble, and
his eyes were gritty from dust. Blinking, he glanced
at the object in his lap.

The Blood Crystal was cold and lifeless, albeit oddly
beautiful. Was it true what Bdan had said, that this
was a decoy? Had he too been tricked? Was this
just a piece of ordinary volcanic rock? Holding the
black crystalline shape in his hands, he pondered its
sleekness. Surely such cool, perfectly even sides were
unusual.

He remembered the worry stone Sarina had mentioned, although hers was silvery-gray and rounded,
with a pointed end. Thinking of her brought him pain.
Where was she? Was she safe? Salla had said Devin
was taking care of her. Had the youth managed to
get her off Souk? The first chance he got, he'd have
to check on her whereabouts.

By the stars, he missed her! Staring out at the

bleak expanse of black sand beach, he felt an ache of loneliness so deep he wanted to cry out. He grasped the crystal tighter, clutching it against his chest as though it could conjure up an image of her, showing him where she was.

And as his very soul yearned for her, the red streaks on the stone began to glow. The glow spread, expanded, until it encompassed the entire black crystal. With it came a tingling sensation in his hands.

Stunned, Teir stared at the Blood Crystal. The haze around it shifted and shimmered. Through the growing brightness, he saw Sarina's image linked to his in an aura of light.

What did this mean? His heart thudding in his chest, Teir wondered if the Blood Crystal was predicting the future. Were they to be reunited after all?

As he watched, Sarina's aura separated from his. Another image, this one a miniature version, glowed in her belly. The brightness overall expanded, radiated, and their auras were joined once again in a halo of light.

Gods, Teir thought, could this be true?

He dropped the stone as though it were fire. Instantly, the vision extinguished, and the Blood Crystal lay lifeless in the sand.

Teir whipped out the remote unit from his vest pocket and activated the sequence that would summon the shuttle. In less than ten minutes, it landed on the flat expanse of beach stretching before him. Grabbing the Blood Crystal, he raced into the waiting vehicle.

His mission was clear. Salla had spoken of a quest, and now he knew what it was. He had to discover his birthright. She'd said it was he, not Lord Cam'brii, who was destined to marry the Great Healer. The Blood Crystal had just shown this to be true. The proof was in his heritage. He had to visit his aunt on Alpha Omega Two to find out what she knew.

By now, Bdan and his cohorts would have dashed

out of the guardian. The Cave of Crystal would have vanished before their eyes, having been sent to its next preset location. Bdan would discover the shuttle was gone, but he wouldn't be stranded for long. One of the two combat vessels orbiting around Taurus would rescue him. Teir had no time to lose to put the rest of his escape plan into action.

Placing the stone carefully on the seat beside him, he pushed the throttle forward and lifted off. Once he took control of the *Valiant*, he'd blast those two Souk vessels out of the sky. He wouldn't let them rescue Bdan. Let the Souk leader be trapped on the planet's volatile surface! His jaw clenched as he imagined the pleasure he would get from destroying his enemy. The idea of annihilating Bdan thrilled him. His palms grew sweaty with anticipation and he licked his lips with eagerness. And then his gaze fell upon the black crystal on the seat beside him. The red streaks were again glowing like burning embers.

By the stars, the thing was affecting him! It was working its evil into his mind!

Abruptly changing course, Teir headed back toward the planet's surface and touched down near the Cave of Crystal's new location. Carefully, he delivered the stone to its receptacle. It had shown him the future, but it had touched him with darkness. The stories about it were true. The Blood Crystal needed to be kept hidden until more could be learned of its origins.

Deciding he would need to reevaluate the hiding place later, Teir resumed his flight. The air inside the shuttle seemed lighter, and he aimed its nose toward the *Valiant*.

Days ago, when he'd first set course for Taurus, Teir had surreptitiously keyed in a sequence on the computer that would allow him access to command functions on the ship. Now, seated in the shuttle, he sent the signal to open a channel to the *Valiant*'s command center. He requested that the computer use his digitized recording of Bdan's voice to order the Souk on board to initiate docking procedures.

When his console lit, informing him that this order had been carried out, Teir activated another preset sequence. This one would release a round of Nokout gas on the bridge. The Souk would be unconscious when Teir went aboard. Teir would drop him off along with the Crigellans at the nearest Coalition outpost. Then he'd head for Alpha Omega Two to visit his aunt—assuming she hadn't succumbed to the Farg. That possibility threw him for a moment, but he decided to deal with any obstacles as they occurred. And always, foremost in his mind was the need to check on Sarina.

He was on his way to seek his future, and she was a vital part of it.

Teir's crew was on board the vessel assigned to take Sarina to the Research Station on Timos. Satisfied that Admiral Gog was pursuing Teir on Taurus, she'd agreed to leave as long as she was kept posted as to his progress. When she requested Teir's crew be allowed to accompany her to Timos, Admiral Gog had agreed. They'd been assigned to the *Hornet*. The sleek cruiser was on her way to join the force assembling against the Morgots, but Sarina could be dropped off along the way.

"Ravi," Sarina said a couple of days into their journey, "did Teir ever talk much about his childhood?" She was remembering her conversation with Glotaj when the regent warned her not to inquire into Teir's background. Now she found it imperative to learn as much about him as she could. Somehow she felt it was relevant to her future.

"Nay, Mistress. The captain wasn't one to dwell upon the past."

"I'd like to learn more about him. What was the date of his birth?"

"I believe it was stardate 2140, or in Earth chronology, the year 1978."

"That would make him twenty-nine annums, the same age as Lord Cam'brii."

"Correct. He holds the unique achievement of being the youngest in the Defense League to reach the rank of captain."

"What more do you know about him?"

"He lived with his aunt and uncle. When he was young, they traveled around. Later, they settled in a small village on Vilaran and that's where the rest of his youth was spent. I gathered his relatives were of a reclusive nature."

"That village—what was its name?" Sarina asked eagerly.

"I'm sorry, *Mira*, I do not possess that knowledge."

"I think I'll study up on Vilaran history."

Finding an available computer terminal in the mess hall, she seated herself, then drew up the files from the Cultural Data Bank.

Using Earth chronology as a reference, Sarina learned that the last hereditary Preim of Vilaran was born in 1918. A descendant of the House of Raimorrda and sovereign leader of the Retti dynasty, he ascended to the throne and ruled as a cruel despot until a bloody revolution in 1978 overthrew the empire and established a worldwide republic. Thus ended the Retti dynasty. The Preim and his entire family were murdered by revolutionaries. The youngest victim, a great-nephew, was but a babe when his life was forfeited, but the people of the land did not regret their actions. They lusted for the blood of the Rettites who'd forced the population into a life of poverty and toil. Even now, so many annums later with an elected government in power, hostile feelings still ran high against the aristocracy.

Teir had been born the year of the revolution and raised after the Republic came into power, Sarina figured. But that wasn't relevant to his current situation, was it? There must be something else Glotaj was hiding. Had Teir committed a crime in the past, something that could come back to haunt him? Was that why he'd run off to join the Defense League?

Wren interrupted her. She knew he was excited, because his wings had unfolded and were flapping at his back. "You have a message coming in from Command! Follow me to the Ready Room. You can take it in there. Maybe they've located the captain!"

Her pulse racing excitedly, Sarina followed him into the compact conference room. She waited until he left, then sat at the long table and established a commlink. Admiral Daras Gog's face projected onto the wall. "I got a ship to Taurus," he said in his gruff tone. "There wasn't any sign of the Captain or anyone else on the planet's surface."

"How is that possible?" Her voice rang with disappointment.

"They did pick up a particle beam emissions trail. Each vessel has her own signature exhaust, so to speak, and this one was specific for the *Valiant*. We know she was there, and it appears a couple of Souk vessels were in the vicinity as well. Unfortunately, the trail of the *Valiant* vanished so she can't be traced."

"Could they have gone back to Souk?"

"It is my belief the captain escaped and covered his trail so he wouldn't be followed."

"You mean he took control of the *Valiant*?"

"Aye."

"So where is he now?"

"Your guess is as good as mine. If he's on the loose, he'd better report in. Tell him that if you hear from him before I do."

"Of course." She frowned. "Would there be some reason why he wouldn't want his whereabouts to be known?"

"He could fear it would put Bdan on his trail again, but it's highly unusual for Reylock not to check in.

I've put all outposts on the alert. If anyone spots the *Valiant*, they're to call in immediately."

Out the observation ports, Sarina saw the Timosian star system rapidly approaching. Signing off, she went to get ready for departure.

"At least the captain got away from the Souks," Wren told her. He'd been distressed when Sarina told him Teir still hadn't been located. "The *Valiant* will show up. Give him time. He must have his reasons for not communicating with you."

"Yes, I would imagine so," Sarina said vaguely, but she felt hurt that he hadn't contacted her right away. Didn't Teir know how concerned she was about his safety?

"You'll be going down to Timos in a shuttle," Wren was saying. "Someone will be sent to bring you back to Bimordus Two. We're heading directly to Tendraa from here."

"Good luck," Sarina said, feeling sad when she said good-bye to Teir's crew. They'd become her friends, and she worried about them being in battle. "Contact me when you can," she pleaded.

The chief scientist at the Timosian Research Station, Wagroob, was less than friendly. Courteous but cool, he conducted Sarina on a brief tour and asked what she hoped to accomplish by her visit.

"We're too busy to offer instruction," he admonished her, apparently unimpressed by her status.

"I didn't come to learn. I came to help," she said, irritated that they obviously considered her visit a burden. "Glotaj seemed to think you might want to run more tests on me since I recovered from the Farg. Apparently the long incubation period I experienced was most unusual."

"Indeed." He eyed her with renewed interest. "I suppose there can't be any harm in testing you further. We might learn something new. Come this way to the laboratory, please."

Sarina fell in step beside him as he proceeded down a long corridor. "After we're done in there, I'll assign you a workstation," Wagroob said. "Do you have any background in microbiology?"

"Just what I've learned on Bimordus Two." She'd spent hauras in the study center using the subliminal learning device, reviewing data on the Farg.

"Sometimes I think we're too close to the material we're examining," Wagroob said, "and it might be the one clue we're missing that would piece together the whole mystery of the Farg. You'll see what I mean if you review our findings. Someone like you with little background in science might actually be of more help than you realize. We need a fresh viewpoint, someone who can see the bigger picture, so to speak. If you need help interpreting the data, the computer can assist you."

Sarina was at her newly assigned work station the next day when another call came through from Admiral Gog.

"We've just got word from an outpost in Sector Zero-Niner that the *Valiant* off-loaded two Crigellans and a Souk."

"Where is that?" Sarina asked, her heart thumping excitedly. News at last!

"Not far from Taurus. The Crigellans are not being very communicative, and the Souk claims to have been tricked by Reylock. Unfortunately, the ship left orbit before security could get an explanation from her pilot."

"And now?"

"She could be anywhere."

Frustrated, Sarina terminated the link. Dammit, why didn't Teir contact her? He was somewhere in the galaxy in the *Valiant* for purposes that eluded her, and he hadn't inquired after her at all? What was wrong? Didn't he care anymore?

She turned back to her work, worried and upset.

*   *   *

Teir had managed to elude the two Souk combat vessels that were orbiting Taurus, fooling them with Bdan's voice as he'd tricked Vivak on the bridge of the *Valiant*. Afraid they might discover his ruse before he got out of sensor range, he'd used evasive maneuvers and maintained radio silence to cover his escape. He dropped the Crigellans and Vivak off at the nearest Coalition outpost, and then headed for Alpha Omega Two to interview his aunt.

Inquiring about Sarina was still uppermost in his mind, but he'd listened in on subspace frequencies and heard her name mentioned. Satisfied that she'd made it to safety, he was concentrating on his current mission. He needed something solid to go on regarding his heritage before contacting her personally.

Aunt Catharta was suffering from an infection of the lungs, not the Farg, Teir discovered when he stalked into her room. He noticed at once that she looked considerably more frail than the last time he'd seen her. Her finely chiseled features were shrunken and pale.

When she saw him, a smile curved her mouth. "Teir! Back so soon?" Her voice warbled weakly.

"How are you, Aunt Catharta?" He stooped to kiss her wrinkled cheek.

"Much better, now that you're here." She saw his look of concern. "Seriously, the medics say I made it through the worst of this seizure. I just have to get over a lingering infection." Taking a wheezing breath, she added, "I'm not sure that I can."

"Nonsense! You've a strong constitution," Teir reassured her, patting her hand as he seated himself at her bedside. The Farg having been ruled out, he didn't need to wear a protective energy suit. "I've come for a reason. Tell me about my parents."

Catharta avoided his eyes. "There isn't much to tell."

"You said they died in a reactor accident. How old was I?"

She withdrew her hand from his clasp. "You were just a babe. But we've been through this before. Why now?"

"It's important." He fixed his gaze on her, waiting.

"Very well. You were eight weeks old."

"Where was I living?"

"In the city of Minna, where you were born."

"Who informed you of the accident? Were you and Uncle Jebs also in Minna at the time?"

"Aye, we were." She stared at a spot on the ceiling.

"And you were my mother's only living relative, is that right? So you were given custody of me?" When she nodded, he went on. "I was an only child, of course." He saw something flicker in her eyes and panicked. *"Wasn't I?"*

Catharta directed her gaze at him. "Is there a reason for these questions, Teir?

"Yes. I've found my mate but I can't join with her until I learn my heritage."

"I don't understand."

"It's the Great Healer, Aunt." He told her how he'd met Sarina and how their relationship had progressed.

Catharta's eyes widened. "You're the one! I can't believe it! Yes, yes, I can. Listen—you must journey to Minna. The proof of your birth is there." Her shoulders sagged, and her expression saddened. "It is time for you to learn the truth, Teir. I'm not really your aunt."

"What?"

"Jebs and I were living in Minna. We'd just had our first child, a male. The babe wasn't two months old before he died in his cradle, the cause being unknown. It was a time of terror and strife in the land. 2140 was the annum of the revolution." Catharta's hands picked at the covers, and her mouth quivered.

"My sister, knowing how we grieved for our lost child, made us an offer that same afternoon. If we would entrust her with our son's body, she would give us a living child in exchange. We were to ask no questions but to raise him as our own. No one else knew of our tragedy."

"Where would your sister get another babe to substitute for yours?"

"She worked at the Manor, a maid to the preimess. Such a lovely young girl! Rite had recently given birth to her second son. But let me back up a bit and fill you in on Vilaran history. The Preim, a cruel despot, lived in the capital city of Theal. He and the Preima had one son. His brother, Gregor, lived in Minna with his wife Ana. They had two daughters. Rite was the youngest. She married and had two sons."

"So Rite's two sons were the Preim's great-nephews?"

Catharta nodded, her gaze distant. "Because of the Preim's cruelties, feelings against the aristocracy were running high. It didn't matter that some were innocent, like Rite and her family. All were branded traitors by the people. When the revolutionary fervor swept the land, mobs of angered citizens charged the citadels. My sister warned Rite, but the girl was too innocent to believe the people would rise against her when she had done nothing to harm them. But then word came that the palace at Theal had been stormed. The Preim and his family had been slaughtered along with all their servants. A horde was gathering in Minna that very day."

Catharta took a long, shaky breath before she continued. "That was the same day my beloved babe passed on. My sister, when she came to share our grief, had an idea. She rushed back to the Manor and spoke to Rite. At last Rite was ready to listen. Servants were fleeing the Manor in terror, and Rite, desperate to save her infant son, agreed to the switch. It was done right before the mob broke through the gates." Catharta closed her eyes at the pain of the memory. "The preimess was unable to save herself or her elder son."

"So they were all murdered?" Teir still wasn't clear how this related to him.

"Aye. When the revolutionaries charged into the nursery, they found a dead infant in its cradle. It was assumed the babe died of natural causes, although some wondered about the brown hair color. My sister urged Jebs and me to flee. Our babe now had dark hair, hair as black as midnight, and some of our neighbors might notice the difference. It was you, Teir. You were that babe."

"But you claimed to be my aunt, not my mother!"

"We traveled far from Minna, and I thought it would be easier to explain the difference in our looks. No one else would be the wiser in our new location."

"What about your sister? Did she make it out of Minna?"

"Jannis is there still. You must find her. She has the proof of your birth. It has been a burden to her all these annums. Even the most distant relatives to the Preim were executed. To this day, an edict remains condemning the royal family to a death sentence. Memories last a long time."

"But the other members of his family weren't evil!"

"It doesn't matter, Teir. You walk on dangerous ground if you return to Vilaran to seek proof of your heritage. You must do this in secret."

He nodded solemnly. "Where will I find your sister?"

"Jannis has a small abode in the bremen section of town—her last name is Reylock, by the way. I put out that you were her child but that she was unable to raise you on her own."

Recalling that it was Glotaj who had helped him be accepted into the Academy, Teir asked, "Tell me, Aunt

Catharta, where does Glotaj fit into this?" He still called her aunt despite knowing the truth. She had raised him and loved him, and he'd always consider her to be his adopted aunt and love her.

Sighing, Catharta let her head fall back onto the pillow. "Your great-uncle the Preim was a descendant of the House of Raimorrda. Because Glotaj was also a Raimorrdan, I sought his aid on several occasions. He alone knew who you really were. For your own safety, he kept silent. There are still those on Vilaran who would see you dead."

"But why? I'm no threat to anybody."

"You are the only surviving member of the Retti dynasty. As such, you could be restored to power as the new Preim if the royalists predominated."

Retti . . . Rite . . . *Teir*. Jumble the letters around and that was where his name had come from. But it was ridiculous to believe that someone would want to kill him over an age-old revolution.

Something his aunt had said suddenly registered. He was a descendant of the House of Raimorrda! "Did the aftereffects of the supernova reach Vilaran?" Teir asked excitedly. Perhaps the same reasoning that applied to Lord Cam'brii could be applied to him regarding the sign of the circle. As a Raimorrdan, he might qualify under the legend as mate to Sarina!

But Catharta shook her head. "The only cataclysm on Vilaran that annum was the one caused by the people's blood lust. It still exists; you must be cautious if you go there."

"I'll be discreet in my inquiries. I have no desire to get embroiled in Vilaran politics," Teir assured her.

Catharta sat up and grasped his hand. "I love you as I would my own son, Teir."

"I love you, too." He squeezed her hand, then leaned over and kissed her. His eyes were moist as he got up to leave. He promised to contact her after his sojourn to Vilaran, but her health was fragile. This might be the last time they said good-bye.

As Teir made his way back to the spaceport, the implications of what he'd learned rang in his head. He was a Raimorrdan! As the only living member of the Vilaran royal family, he could consider himself to be highly placed. That left being born under the sign of the circle as the remaining requirement he had to meet to get the High Council's approval to wed Sarina. He couldn't claim the same atmospheric disturbances that had led to Lord Cam'brii's birth being interpreted that way, so what of his? He'd just have to find out on Vilaran, Teir supposed.

It was imperative that he contact Sarina, but he wasn't sure where to find her. Contacting Defense League Command as soon as the *Valiant* left orbit, he was at once patched into Admiral Daras Gog's office.

"Captain?" boomed the Admiral's voice over the ship's comm unit. "Where in Zor are you?"

"I can't tell you, sir. I need to contact Sarina. Did she make it to Bimordus Two?"

"Aye. Her marriage to Lord Cam'brii was about to take place when she fell sick with the Farg."

"What?"

"Don't worry, she recovered," the admiral said in a dry tone. Then a note of worry crept into his voice. "You haven't caught it, have you?"

"No, I'm fine. Where is she now?" He had to speak to her, make sure she was all right. By the stars, her marriage hadn't already taken place, had it? He held his breath, waiting for Gog's answer.

"I'll give you her current location if you give me yours," the admiral offered.

"Dammit, *where is she?*"

Gog gave a heavy sigh. "This isn't general knowledge, Reylock, but she's at the Timosian Research Station. She'll be returning to Bimordus Two for her wedding in a few more days. When are you planning to report in for duty? Maybe I can get you assigned to transport her."

"There's something else I have to do before I surface. I'll be in touch, Admiral."

"Reylock, wait! You blasted renegade. You don't have leave to take time off. I order you to report in for a debriefing—"

Teir severed the link, cutting off communications. He didn't want the admiral or anyone else to know where he was heading.

Leaning back in his seat, he thought about Sarina. She had suffered the plague! What a horror! If only he could have been with her, cared for her. Storms of the sun, she'd nearly married Cam'brii. Their wedding had been delayed only because of her sickness. Now she was due to return to Bimordus Two and the marriage would go forth. He must prevent it!

Leaning over his console, he put in a call to the Research Station on Timos.

Chapter Eighteen

"I request permission to retrieve Sarina," Lord Cam'brii said. He stood facing Glotaj and the semicircle of councilors in the Council Chamber. A special session had been called because Sarina was requesting an extension of her visit to Timos. "You said she would return in two weeks, and our marriage ceremony was rescheduled accordingly. You can't change the arrangements now!" he protested to the regent.

Daimon and his supporters in the Return to Origins Faction were becoming more powerful in Sarina's absence. Soon they'd have enough signatures on their petition to move up the vote calling for a dissolution of the Coalition. If that ever passed, all Cam'brii's efforts against the Souks would have been in vain.

"I agree with Lord Cam'brii," Emu said, stretching his long neck. "Another delay is unacceptable. In my opinion, the Great Healer should not have been granted permission to leave in the first place. What has she accomplished at Timos?"

"Nothing!" Daimon's tone was harsh. "The woman is a useless Earthling. I've told you before, she has no power. You're all deluding yourselves if you believe she can rid you of the problems facing the Coalition. Sarina hasn't made any contributions to our knowledge of the Farg. She dabbles in experiments beyond her ken!"

"And how are you so well-informed?" Emu sneered. "Are you in communication with your friend Wagroob who heads the station? I understand you're one of the largest contributors to his private fund, Daimon."

"That has no relevance here. Look, we've held far too many special sessions on account of this supposed Great Healer. She fell sick and couldn't even heal herself. You're all nothing but fanatics, waiting for a Savior who doesn't exist. I'll show you the true way! If we go back to our original boundaries, we'll have a decent chance to fight off the Morgot invaders. We won't need to rely on anyone but ourselves."

"You're wrong!" Cam'brii said. "Even as you speak, a Defense League force engages the Morgot fleet in battle. We must remain united."

Tension filled the air as thick as fog. Glotaj motioned for Lord Cam'brii to be seated; then he spoke. "We are here primarily to make a decision regarding Sarina's request. Is she, or is she not, granted additional leave?" He kept his expression impassive so his own opinion wouldn't influence the vote.

Seven to five voted against her remaining on Timos. Cam'brii voted against, and so did Emu. Daimon cast his vote in favor of letting her stay, not because he felt she would accomplish anything on Timos, but because her return meant her marriage and he didn't want that to take place. It would only increase her status and give added power to the Raimorrdans.

Daimon was solemn and thoughtful as he left the Council Chamber. In his private office, he summoned Ruzbee for a meeting. The short-statured Arcturian didn't take long in arriving. He'd been prowling the halls, trying to get news of the Great Healer. The Assembly representatives weren't aware of Sarina's location, only that she had left on a mission of import.

"We've got to do something," Daimon said, pacing his office with his maroon-colored robe swishing at his feet. Stroking his beard, he faced the Arcturian. "Already the Earthwoman manipulates our central government. It is wrong, Ruzbee, wrong!"

"Where is she?"

"She works at the Timosian Research Station trying to find a cure for the Farg. She's just asked for an extension of her stay. It's been denied, and Cam'brii is being sent to retrieve her. He leaves within the haura. The wedding will take place immediately upon their return."

"So what bothers you?" Ruzbee asked warily, wondering what Daimon was getting at or if he just wanted to complain.

"She is a thorn in our side!" Daimon exclaimed. "As Lord Cam'brii's bride, she will be perceived as supporting his goals. In that case, we may not get the votes we need for self-determination." His eyes narrowed. "We must ensure that she does not marry the Raimorrdan!"

"What would you do?"

The councilor's eyes grew crafty. "Lord Cam'brii is on his way to Timos. If he never arrives there, the matter would be resolved."

"You mean . . ." Ruzbee pretended to look shocked.

"It's for the good of the people! Our government has lost control. The Morgots and the Farg run rampant across the galaxy. We must save ourselves!" Daimon's voice lowered. "The Coalition leadership is strongly in favor of the Raimorrdans, and if this marriage takes place, they'll remain in control. Power must be restored to the people."

He drew a long breath and fixed Ruzbee with a

glare. "Do you understand what I'm saying?"

Ruzbee nodded. "Might it not be better to wait until Cam'brii picks up Sarina? If they were intercepted on the way home, both would be removed as a threat."

"Good idea, but how? Too bad that Twygg assassin is dead. He might have given us some useful information."

"Someone poisoned the poor fellow with mushgum, probably to silence him." Ruzbee gave a sly grin. "I might know someone else who could make the necessary arrangements . . . for a price."

"Do it," said Daimon.

"As you wish."

Clicking his heels together in a salute, Ruzbee scurried from the room. His cunning would pay well this time. His Souk master would give him a generous bonus for the information about Cam'brii. Ruel was just waiting for another opportunity to get at the man, and this setup was perfect. In addition, Ruzbee would pocket part of Daimon's payment to Ruel. Acting as liaison, he was entitled to a cut. And he'd make sure the trail led from Daimon to the Souks in such a way that the councilor would take the fall if their plan failed.

Cerrus Bdan was looking forward to his next encounter with Captain Reylock. Bdan had just returned to his compound on Souk. He, Otis, and Wyeth had been rescued by one of the escort vessels orbiting Taurus, but only after a long and fearsome wait on the fiery surface. He didn't have anything to show for his journey, and that rankled. Bdan hated the captain more than ever.

"Waiting for you is a Morgot emissary, master," said one of his lieutenants anxiously.

A spark of fear ignited in his breast. K'darr would be furious that he hadn't obtained the Blood Crystal. He'd have to tell the emissary that Reylock had led them to a decoy. Hopefully, the truth would be enough of a defense. K'darr did not treat failures kindly.

The emissary didn't look very pleased when Bdan greeted him in the Reception Hall. Otis and Wyeth had come along, and Bdan could sense their apprehension. The Morgot was huge, towering over all of them. His opaque eyes, as he glared at Bdan, were as cold as the black crystal had been.

"Where is the Blood Crystal, Souk? I must take it to my leader."

Bdan gave a look of confidence he didn't feel. "Have it not, do I."

"What! Why not?"

"Tricked us did Captain R-R-Reylock. He led us to a decoy."

"Where is he now?"

"Got away did he, but we'll track him." Bdan had tried to pick up the *Valiant* on his long-range sensors, but the captain's trail had been cold by the time he'd left Taurus. Those fools in the escort vessels had been tricked by the son of a belleek. Now Reylock could be anywhere.

"What about the Great Healer?" barked the emissary, contempt in his tone. "Do you have her for me to bring to K'darr?"

The blue color drained from the slaver's face. He was beginning to wonder if the emissary was empowered to pass judgment on his own. "Had her, did we, but she escaped. I'll find her, too." At his nod, his guards moved in closer.

"K'darr will be most upset by your failure. His Eminence would have waited to confront you himself, but he is engaged in battle in the Tendraan system, a battle he would have foreseen if you had been able to obtain the Blood Crystal for him earlier." The Morgot's dark brown fur ruffled with ire. "Our fleet's supply route has been cut off. K'darr may be forced to order a retreat. He will blame you, Cerrus Bdan, for not fulfilling your contract."

"Send troops will I to assist," Bdan said quickly, his jowls quivering nervously. "Make good my word, will I."

The emissary shook his head, unaware of the encroaching Souks. Bdan's bodyguards were encircling him, anticipating a hostile move. Unnoticed by them all, Otis slinked toward a side entrance.

"The price for failure is death, Cerrus Bdan." He reached a paw inside his armored doublet. Instantly, the Souks drew their shooters. "You may kill me, but we shall die together." He pulled out a round orb and held it up. "This detonator is set to explode in—" he checked the reading "—two point five seconds. The time for apologies is over, Souk."

Bdan's mouth gaped. The Morgot was on a suicide mission! They were all going to be. . . .

Otis stumbled through the archway into the next chamber just as a blinding white light exploded behind him. He didn't need to look to know that his master and those surrounding him had been vaporized. He had work to do.

Otis was a Believer. He'd been the one who'd released the magnetic lock to Reylock's prison cell on the *Omnus* when Sarina was trying to free him, and he'd been the robed figure who had assisted the captain in the palace. He was a Crigellan, and like Salla and Etan, he worked toward making the prophecy come true. His position was dangerous but it had served him well. He'd get a new master now, but he still could be useful, feeding information to the resistance movement on Souk. One day, he dreamed of liberating those of his people who were enslaved here. But for now, Otis had to appear to be part of the Souk hierarchy, even if it meant going against his basic principles.

Devin would be his contact now that Salla and Etan had left. He hoped Reylock had been able to free his fellow Crigellans from the Souks. He'd try to find out, but communications of any kind with off-worlders were still too unreliable. The underground movement needed to establish a regular connection with the Coalition for purposes of information exchange and support. It was something he would work on in the coming months.

Otis wiped the smile from his face and put on a grim demeanor suitable to the terrible news he was about to deliver to Bdan's troops. A brighter day was dawning now that Cerrus Bdan was gone, but there was still much work to do.

Seated at the computer console in her private cubicle at the Research Station, Sarina was reviewing her data. She hadn't yet been informed of the High Council's decision regarding her request for an extension of her visit to Timos, but she hoped she would be allowed to stay. At last, she felt as though she was making progress. She'd used an online tutorial to boost her knowledge of scientific methodology and then had begun to sift through the multitude of data gathered on the Farg.

Unable to form any outstanding conclusions, she'd tried a different approach by overlaying the planets affected by the Farg with the ones conquered by the Morgots. Conveniently enough, they were all rich in natural resources, almost as though the disease had been selected for purposes beneficial to the warlike Morgots.

The origin of the disease still remained unknown. Since planets of every size and geophysical configuration were visited by the pestilence, it was difficult to isolate the factors involved in disease transmission. This was one area that had the scientists stymied, and Sarina, despite her findings regarding the Morgots, couldn't piece the two together.

The observation had been made that planets closer to their suns were less virulently attacked than those farther away. This led to the theory that heat might work in enervating the Farg. Yet when heat treatments were used, they had no effect on the victims. The only treatments currently available were palliative, not curative.

Superstitions remained in force, and nearly every culture affected claimed that a comet had preceded the dreadful pestilence. Yet astronomical observations could not confirm these reports.

The data were confusing and too fragmented for any sense to be made of them. It was like pieces of a puzzle that needed one clue for them all to fit together, yet none of the greatest brains in the galaxy could figure it out. Sarina frowned. There had to be something significant here.

Take those comets, for example. She wouldn't have thought people to be so superstitious in this age of interstellar communication. Yet every one of the planets claimed a malevolent force was at work.

Perhaps it was, Sarina mused, studying the graph on her screen. But if those comets didn't show up on astronomical charts, then where did they come from? Could one be traced? It was said cosmic dust from a comet's tail seeded the atmosphere of the planet affected. What if the tail contained something other than ice and dust particles?

Her eyes lit with excitement and she summoned Wagroob. "It seems strange that a comet supposedly appears over each planet right before the plague strikes. Has any evidence of this actually been found?"

Wagroob looked at her askance. "No one can predict where the Farg will strike next, so how can we send a probe to take measurements?"

"The Morgots are in the Tendraan system now. Where would it benefit them to go next?" she asked, pointing out her overlay.

"Why, Vilaran, I suppose. That system is the closest, and if your theory about natural resources are correct, Vilaran has deposits of piragen ore that would be useful for spacecraft construction."

"Send a probe there, Wagroob, and have it wait for a comet. I'll bet one will show up before the Morgots leave the Tendraan system." With luck, the Defense League would push them back and they'd never make it to Vilaran, but many other planets could be helped by the knowledge that might be gained if she was right.

"I'll see that it's done, Mistress." For the first time, respect shone in the scientist's eyes. Her comm unit buzzed and he squared his shoulders. "I'll let you know what happens."

He stalked from the room just as Sarina flicked the switch to receive the call. Her cubicle had only an audio link so she couldn't view the speaker.

"Hello?"

"Sarina!" It was Teir's voice.

"My God, is that really you? Where are you?" Her heart pounded wildly.

"Never mind. Are you all right?" His voice was gruff with worry.

"I'm fine, but I miss you. I need to see you! What's been happening?"

"I escaped from the Souks. I've learned a lot, Sarina. You and I are meant to be together. You must stay there on Timos until I can get you."

"But where are you now? What are you doing?"

He hesitated. "I'm going to the planet of my birth. It's my belief that I'm the Raimorrdan who is destined to wed you, but I have to get proof to show the High Council."

"Let me come with you!"

"No, it could be dangerous. Wait there for me. I love you!" The audio link went dead.

"Teir, no!" Silence met her ears. Sarina stared at the console, stunned. What had he said? *He loved her.* Dear God, she loved him, too. Why hadn't he given her the chance to tell him so?

Then the rest of his words sunk in. He was the Raimorrdan destined to wed her. How could that be?

According to the legend, she was supposed to marry a Raimorrdan who was highly placed and born under the sign of the circle. Rolf was the only one who met those criteria.

Or was he?

She remembered Glotaj's warning not to inquire into Teir's background. Now Teir was journeying to Vilaran to get proof of his birth—proof that he was a Raimorrdan, too? But he'd still have to meet the rest of the criteria if indeed he was the one meant by the legend. It certainly made sense for him to be the chosen one. She loved him, and she had healed him.

Sarina rubbed her temples. The answers must be on Vilaran. But what if she was right and that planet was the next target for a comet? Would Teir be infected with the Farg? She had to warn him!

The thought of his being in jeopardy again brought tears to her eyes. But why had he mentioned that going to Vilaran could be dangerous? Did he already know about the comet, or was there some other reason he wasn't sharing with her? How could she wait to see him, knowing he might be her true destiny? Her soul cried out for him, needed him. She yearned to feel his touch, to hold him in her arms. *Oh God, Teir, I want you so badly!*

Her sojourn to Timos had been partly to investigate the Farg but also to avoid her marriage to Rolf. She'd known in her heart all along she couldn't wed the councilor. Now Sarina wondered how she'd be able to tell him.

She wouldn't have long to find out.

Wagroob stalked into her cubicle after the dinner haura. "I've just received a message that Lord Cam'brii is on his way to bring you back to Bimordus Two. He says you are to be ready to leave at once. His estimated time of arrival is twenty-one hundred hauras."

Sarina stared at him. So her request for an

extension had been denied. Rolf was coming for her in person to bring her back for the wedding. She hadn't expected to have to face him so soon. Oh God, how was she going to tell him the marriage was off?

"Thank you," she whispered, waiting until Wagroob left before covering her face with her hands.

The two geckos watched Cam'brii's small transport ship begin the descent into Timos's atmosphere.

"We'll wait until he picks up the Earthwoman; then we'll follow them at a safe distance," Orr, the one in charge, said. He rubbed his steel, dented in several places, reminders of unpleasant past encounters. "When they're out of sensor range from Timos, we'll open fire."

"Yes," Pah confirmed.

He wasn't a big talker. Sitting in the copilot's seat of their small fighter vessel, he was monitoring the planet's surface as Orr watched Pah's antennae quiver.

"I hope we don't have to wait long. I'm anxious to get home and replenish my nectar," Orr said, his own antennae trembling with anticipation.

"I had a long drink the last time, after we freed the *Omnus* for Cerrus Bdan."

Pah turned his huge, round eyes to Orr, who admired the sleek, unmarred surface of Pah's red-shelled body.

"His brother Ruel pays better. I think we should stick with him," Orr answered.

"We'll see how prompt he is after this job."

That should be easy work, Orr thought to himself. Cam'brii obviously didn't suspect anyone was following him, and Orr had been careful to keep out of his sensor range. Now all they had to do was wait.

Sarina heard booted footsteps coming down the hall and knew at once it was Rolf. Nervously, she stood and straightened her metallic blue jumpsuit, then patted her hair into place. She'd braided a section off her face and the rest hung down her back. A blue ribbon was entwined through the braid.

"Sarina, you look lovely!" the councilor exclaimed, striding into her open cubicle. He beamed at her with approval. In two long steps, he was standing in front of her and pressing his mouth to hers.

Sarina stepped back. "No, Rolf. We have to talk. Computer, close portal." The door hissed shut behind them. "Please, take a seat."

Puzzled, he complied. "What's this all about, Sarina? I thought you'd be happy that I came for you."

She sat on the edge of the lounger and folded her hands in her lap. "I'm not going to Bimordus Two," she said quietly.

"What?" His face showed astonishment.

"I want you to take me to Vilaran."

"Vilaran? Why Vilaran?" His eyes narrowed. "Wait a minute. Isn't that where—"

"Teir was born. Yes, that's why I must go there. Rolf, I have a lot to tell you. It's time you learned the truth." And she proceeded to relate all of her relationship with Teir.

Rolf's emotions ranged from anger to dismay to resignation. He'd always thought there was something between the two of them, and he'd been right. He would never win Sarina's love now. For a moment, he felt a flash of anger and jealousy directed toward Reylock, as well as wounded pride, but then an odd sense of relief overwhelmed him. Perhaps this was the way things were meant to be. He'd never really loved Sarina, and if he didn't marry her, he could remain faithful to Gayla's memory.

"So Reylock is saying he's the one destined to marry the Great Healer?" Rolf was still concerned about the legend and its significance for his political goals.

"Teir claims he's a Raimorrdan. He's going to

Vilaran to get proof. I said I wanted to go, but he told me it was too dangerous."

"Dangerous? Why?"

"He wouldn't say. Listen, Rolf, I came up with a theory about the Farg. All the infected planets were visited by a comet before the pestilence took hold, but none of these comets were recorded on astronomical charts. I think they may somehow be responsible for spreading the plague, and that they're linked to the Morgots. Each one of the planets involved is rich in natural resources and would benefit the Morgots after a conquest.

"Wagroob and I figured out that the next likely target is Vilaran. I don't know if this is what Teir meant or if there's some other reason. Glotaj might know. He told me it was dangerous to inquire into Teir's background. He could have been referring to something that happened on Vilaran in Teir's past."

Agreeing with her, Rolf put in a subspace call for the regent, using his personal data link as a scrambler.

"Ah, the legend comes full circle," said Glotaj's clear voice over the comm unit. "So be it. It is time for you to learn the truth. Reylock is a descendant of the former Preim of Vilaran. The entire royal family was wiped out in a revolution in 2140, the annum of his birth. Teir was exchanged for a dead infant so that the revolutionaries thought the royal babe had died. Instead, Teir went to live with an adopted aunt. His identity was never revealed to him because of the danger involved. It would be an instant death sentence for his heritage to become known."

"A death sentence!" Sarina cried, listening over Rolf's shoulder. "My God, we have to warn him!"

"He probably knows this already. That's why he told you it would be dangerous," Rolf said. "Go on," he told Glotaj.

"Teir can only be going to Vilaran for one reason. He's realized that his destiny is to marry Sarina!"

"But how is that possible? I'm the one who meets all the criteria!"

"So does Reylock. I've never been sure which of you was the right one, but it seemed more sensible to choose you for the bridegroom, Rolf. With your position and regal bearing, I thought it would be easier for the Great Healer to fall in love with you. Reylock is more rough-edged, and I felt he might not appeal to her as readily. Besides, he was unaware of his heritage. Just in case I was wrong, however, I threw Reylock and Sarina together so they'd have a chance to get to know one another. In the end, it would be Sarina's choice." He paused. "Teir still has to come up with proof, however, before the High Council will give their approval. I cannot do that for him."

"What is the proof?" Sarina inquired eagerly.

"That is not for me to say. You are not to go to Vilaran," Glotaj warned. "Return at once to Bimordus Two."

"I have another reason for wanting to go there," Sarina said in partial truth. "As I told Rolf, Wagroob and I have a theory about the Farg. If we're right, Vilaran will be the next planet struck by the pestilence. A comet will appear, as it has all the other times. Wagroob has sent a probe to take readings. If I'm on Vilaran, I can make on-site observations." She explained her findings regarding the Farg.

"It's too dangerous. Return here at once."

"We'll keep you informed," Rolf said, terminating the link. Slowly, he turned to Sarina. "I think we should go to Vilaran. Your theories about the Farg are valid and should be investigated firsthand. More importantly, Reylock may need our help. I want the legend to come true as much as you do."

"Then let's go!" Sarina cried.

Orr sat up excitedly in his seat. "Here they come!" A small vessel was just leaving the spaceport on Timos.

Adjusting the controls, Orr moved his ship until they were just out of visual range.

"He could pick you up on his sensors," Pah warned, his antennae bristling.

"So what? We could be part of the spaceport traffic for all he knows. Let's make sure of their heading before we take pursuit. Cam'brii will probably take the same route back to Bimordus Two as he used in getting here, but we don't know that for certain."

A few minutes later, Orr shouted, "They've broken orbit! Let's go after them." He increased speed, warming up the laser cannon at the same time.

"Wait, their ship is turning. What the—"

"They've changed direction!" Orr exclaimed, punching in the new coordinates on the nav unit.

"This is not the heading for Bimordus Two. Maybe we should see what they're up to."

Orr shook his head. "Let's just get the job done."

Pushing the control level forward, Orr narrowed the distance between the two ships. Then he threw his head back and trilled a battle cry, a harsh shriek that echoed throughout the cockpit.

Unidentified ship approaching, Rolf's onboard computer warned.

"Shields up," the councilor ordered, scanning the sensor readings. "It has the outline of a gecko vessel," he told Sarina who was seated in the copilot's chair beside him.

She squinted at the monitor. The crab-like shape of the vessel was unfamiliar to her. "Could they be passing by?" she asked.

"I doubt it. Their weapons systems are armed. Hold tight, I'm going full about."

He grasped the control column and maneuvered the ship into a tight turn. Sarina felt the pressure of her safety harness as she was thrust forward in her seat.

"They're firing!" she gasped as a white flash erupted from the gunports of the other vessel. A dull thud rocked the ship as a hit was taken.

"Damage?" Rolf requested.

His expression was calm, Sarina was glad to note, as her own pulse raced with fear.

No damage. Shields are holding, the computer replied.

"Look out, here comes another!" Rolf threw the ship into a stomach-wrenching drop.

"What kind of defenses do we have, other than the shields?" Sarina asked when she was able to speak again—that last maneuver had knocked the breath out of her.

"We're loaded," Rolf said. "I wouldn't have come for you without an escort otherwise. This ship is small but she's well outfitted. Try to raise them on the comm unit. I'd like to know why they're targeting us."

Sarina tried but received no answer. Another flash of laser fire lanced out, pounding their ship. "They're gaining on us!"

"I'm readying the torpedoes. We're not going to fool around." His fingers danced over the controls. "Okay, we're locked on target. Fire away!"

The gecko ship dove quickly and the torpedo hit a piece of space debris instead, exploding with a fiery display.

Rolf cursed. Sweat beaded his brow as he saw how well the gecko vessel was keeping on their tail despite his best maneuvers. It reminded him of another time, another place, when he was also in a small ship being attacked. Only then, it was Gayla with him, and the Souks were the aggressors. A red haze obscured his vision, and he heard Gayla's voice calling to him amid the fury of battle. *"Rolf . . . !" Gayla needed him. She'd been hurt.*

"Rolf, pay attention!" Sarina said sharply, drawing him out of his trance. "They're firing again—"

Another blast hit them, this time penetrating the shields. An alarm sounded. The hull had been breached, and an automatic shutdown sequence for the second level compartment went into effect.

"We've got to go to lightspeed," Rolf said. "I have to drop shields."

"They'll blast us!"

"We can't get away from them otherwise." Reylock would have known how to do it, he thought. Although Rolf was a skilled pilot, the captain was better at getting out of sticky situations. "I'm going into a dive. While we're coming out of it, I'll drop the shields. Can you initiate warp speed when I tell you?"

"Of course."

"All right, let's do it."

The tactic worked. Rolf went into a sharp dive, then when they were zooming out of it, he dropped the shields. Sarina pushed the lever for lightspeed and the space in front of the viewscreen blurred into starlines.

"We've done it!" she exclaimed, immensely relieved that the unexpected conflict was over.

Rolf glanced at her after checking their heading. "I wonder how they got onto us."

She raised an eyebrow. "What do you mean?"

"Not too many people knew where you'd gone, and only the High Council members were aware of my journey here. Add two and two together, and what do you get?"

Sarina shook her head. "I don't know. What?"

"A leak in the High Council. It's well-known that geckos do the dirty work for the Souks. Someone must have revealed our location to them."

"So you think the Souks were behind this attack?"

He nodded grimly. "Probably. I'll check it out later, but I think this must be another attempt to impede the passage of the First Amendment. The sooner we get you and Reylock together, the better. The legend must unfold. I just hope he isn't running into trouble on Vilaran."

Gazing into Rolf's solemn blue eyes, Sarina swallowed. She had the awful feeling that trouble was an understatement for whatever situation Teir faced on his homeplanet.

Chapter Nineteen

As one of the six founding members of the Coalition, Vilaran was a major scientific and cultural center in the northwest quadrant of the galaxy. Theal, the capital city, had undergone a transformation since the revolution, twenty-nine annums ago. Once mainly a feudal fortress, now it was a thriving modern metropolis with tall skyscrapers, people-movers, and intergalactic marketplaces.

Teir flew into the spaceport and then caught a commuter flight to Minna. He didn't think there was any real danger in the *Valiant* being well-known. Those who knew him as Teir Reylock wouldn't question his background. The reason given for his visit was simple: he wished to see his 'mother,' Jannis Reylock.

The only problem was, he had no idea how to find her. Catharta had said her sister lived in the bremen section of town. That didn't tell him much, so he walked into the comm center at the flight terminal and requested a local directory. There was no listing for a Reylock anywhere in Minna.

Teir grimaced. He should have known it wouldn't be so easy. Jannis's position as maid to the preimess might have put her in danger in the early days of the republic. She was probably used to covering her tracks. Either she no longer lived here, or she kept a low profile by not being listed in the directory.

He headed outdoors to continue his search on foot. The bremen section of town was an attractive area of tree-lined streets and individual residences painted in colorful pastels. Teir felt an inner glow of warm satisfaction to be home. The breeze felt fresh on his face, and heat from the bright sol shining overhead warmed his skin. A fragrant scent floated in the air, perfume from white keela blossoms. Under other circumstances, he'd have liked to linger and enjoy the sights, but not now.

The city's main marketplace was in a central location, so Teir went there first. Farmers from outlying organic cooperatives sold their produce in the glass-domed, climate-controlled hall. Many people preferred to prepare their own nourishment instead of using fabricators, or else they wanted a break from the high-tech pace of life, so fresh fruits and vegetables were always in demand.

Teir strolled the wide path between stalls, admiring the mixture of modern and ancient techniques at work. Samples of the wares for sale were attractively displayed at each stall, but the items were actually obtained only when someone ordered them. Conveyors whisked the goods from warehouses to the point of delivery. This way, the natural produce was kept in ideal temperature storage until needed.

Colorfully dressed vendors loudly hawked their goods to the morning crowd. Teir glanced around, his gaze settling on an old woman wearing a scarf over her head like a refugee from Lutto. She might be able to use a few extra credits.

Sauntering over to her fruit stall, Teir pretended to admire a purple pommus. Round and shiny, it appeared to have a firm texture and smooth skin. "How much?" he asked, pointing.

"Five credits," said the old woman.

"I'll give you fifty if you have the information I need," he offered. "I'm looking for someone named Jannis Reylock."

"Don't know her." The vendor's face closed.

"I'll double the price. One hundred credits." When the woman shook her head, Teir hissed, "One thousand!"

The vendor leaned closer, bending over her stall. "You might ask Old Man Naggers. He's been around town longer than I have."

"Where can I find him?"

"Seek your answers where the water flows upward before it falls down."

"Huh?" He waited for a fuller explanation but it didn't come. Great, Teir thought as he strode away after giving the woman fifty credits for her trouble. Now what?

Getting hungry looking at all the food, he bought a salt bread and munched on it while deciding what to do next. His first task would be to find a body of water.

It was midafternoon by the time Teir discovered the steps. He'd been to several lakes and ponds, but none of them flowed upward, and no one answered to the name of Naggers. He was about to give up when he reached the Centorium, the seat of the provincial government. It was across a wide square from the palatial Museum of History. In front of the long rectangular Centorium building was a fountain which consisted of a plume of rainbow-colored water cascading onto a series of steps. The water on the steps flowed upward, into a pool surrounding the plume.

Teir glanced around but saw no one who bore the slightest resemblance to anyone called Old Man Naggers.

"Can I help you?" a curt voice behind him said.

Teir whirled, facing a uniformed sentry. "I was just admiring the fountain. I'm a visitor here."

"Is that so?" The sentry gave him a keen look of appraisal. "You might consider visiting the museum across the square."

"Thank you, I'll try that later," Teir said, moving on. The flag flying atop the Centorium meant the provost was in residence, and apparently loiterers in front of the government building were not encouraged.

Vilaran was divided into provinces, each one ruled by a provost appointed by the central Parliamentary government which was itself elected every eight years by the populace. The provosts had full authority to administer the laws within their realm. Each province, in turn, was divided into districts headed by a justice. Teir hadn't known that Minna was the seat of the province, but the significance of it wasn't lost on him. That museum across the street might at one time have been the Manor where he was born.

Teir wandered off toward a row of shops on a side street, looking for a place where he could query the local inhabitants, and soon found a saloon nestled between a data card supply shop and a jeweler's.

Chimes sounded when he pushed open the door. The atmosphere inside was stale, reeking of liquor. He made his way past a loud group of locals and took a seat at the bar. "Do you accept universal credits?" he asked the bartender.

"Aye, that we do. New to these parts, are you? What'll it be?"

The bartender's long gray hair fell forward, shielding his face, but Teir glimpsed sharp brown eyes in a wrinkled visage.

"A cosh of your local, please." He handed over a data card for his banking credits to be debited. "I'm looking for a man named Naggers."

The bartender paused in filling Teir's carafe, but swiftly carried on until froth spilled over the brim.

With a soft *plunk*, he put the carafe in front of Teir and handed back his data card. "What's the nature of your business?" he asked gruffly.

"I was told Naggers could help me locate a lost relative."

Teir pocketed the card, noting that twenty extra credits had been charged. He took a long swig of the bitter brew, then nearly choked when the bartender said, "I'm Naggers."

"You are? I need to find Jannis Reylock," he blurted out.

"Who?" Naggers grabbed a rag and casually polished a brass fitting.

"Jannis Reylock. I'm Teir Reylock, her son," he lied.

The man's eyebrows shot up and he gave Teir a sharp glance. "Never knew Jannis had no son."

"So you *do* know her!" Teir exclaimed, leaning forward.

Naggers nodded slowly, his dark eyes sweeping the room to see if anyone were watching them. Groups of men were sitting around clusters of tables, drinking and talking. The loud chatter in the room would preclude their being overheard, and no one else sat near the bar.

"You saw my name when you charged my data card," Teir said quietly. "You know I tell the truth. I tried to locate Jannis at the comm center, but there are no Reylocks listed in this city." When Naggers didn't respond, Teir said in as sincere a tone as he could muster, "I was sent to live with my aunt when I was just a babe. Please, I'll be happy to reimburse you for your trouble if you help me locate my mother."

Naggers glared at him. "It's not credits I want, young'un. I'll tell you what. I'll let Jannis know you're here. If she wants to see you, then we'll take it from there."

Teir looked at the man's set mouth and nodded. "When will I know?"

"Come back tonight at nineteen hundred hauras."

Teir finished his brew and left. He had no intention of hanging around for several more hauras. Checking the back of the saloon for alternate exits, he found an opening onto a narrow alley and situated himself behind a public connector pole and waited. If he was right, Naggers should be coming out soon.

Sure enough, about fifteen minutes later, the old man hobbled out the rear door of the saloon. He'd drawn a cloak around his shoulders, but his scraggly gray hair was unmistakable. Teir followed him at a discreet distance. The man was good, as though he was used to evading shadows, but Teir was even better.

Naggers ended up taking a people-mover to a sparsely occupied section of town on the outskirts of the bremen section. There were no pretty rows of houses and well-tended lawns here. This area was desolate, almost rural. Teir followed Naggers on foot some distance, leaving the paved roadway and walking across a meadow until he came to a small farm near a forest. A cottage stood amidst vegetable fields which were laid out neatly in the back. A formal garden graced the front lawn. On either side were groves of tall trees, dark and mysterious even in the late afternoon light.

Teir slunk into the shadows behind a tree and watched as Naggers announced his presence to an electronic door sentry. The door opened and the old man disappeared into the cottage.

Less than ten minutes later he emerged and hastened away. Teir didn't bother to follow him, being more interested in the occupant of the cottage. This could be where Jannis was hiding out.

When Naggers was out of sight, Teir approached the front door. "I'm a friend of Catharta's," he told the electronic sentry.

The door swung open. Facing him was a plumper version of his aunt, with blue eyes and silvery hair pulled back into a bun. She wore a comfortable work dress in a colorful print pattern.

"Who are you?" she asked, her tone curt. Her keen eyes looked him over with obvious interest.

"I'm Teir Reylock, *mother*."

Her mouth gaped open. "You can't be! He's . . . he's . . ." Speechless, she stared at him.

Teir held out his data link for her to persuse his identification. "Catharta sent me here. May I come in?"

He glanced around. The surrounding trees seemed to be encroaching on the tiny house. An eerie feeling pricked the hairs on the back of his neck, and he swallowed apprehensively. Surely Naggers hadn't had time to set him up. The old man had come directly here from the saloon. Still, it was with a feeling of foreboding that he went inside at Jannis's invitation.

"Why are you here?" she asked, closing the door and facing him.

Teir had expected her to be friendlier. "I've come to inquire about my background," he said. "Catharta told me what she knew."

"Why?"

"I need proof of my birth."

"You don't want it. It's dangerous for you here. It's dangerous for *me* for you to be here!"

"What possible danger can there be now?" He glanced around the comfortably furnished living area, wondering if she were going to ask him to have a seat.

"There are those who miss the old aristocracy," Jannis said in a low voice. "They would put you on the throne in an instant if they had the chance. By right of birth, you would be Preim."

"I don't want to be Preim," Teir said impatiently. "I'm happy with my position in the Defense League. Besides, the blasted government is a republic now. Why should they care?"

"The death sentence remains in effect. Any royals found are still under orders to be executed."

"But that's absurd!" By the stars, it reminded him of Sarina's situation with the High Council. How incredible that someone would want him dead now because of what had happened twenty-nine annums ago!

"Nevertheless, it remains a threat," Jannis said. "You must leave at once."

"After you give me the proof I seek."

Jannis put her hands on her hips. She was small like Catharta but very determined in her expression. "Why do you need it?"

"Can we sit down?"

At her nod, Teir took a seat in the living area. After Jannis sat in a lounger opposite him, he began his story, telling her about Sarina, the legend, and where they both fit in.

"I've heard about the Great Healer!" she exclaimed, excited. "Yes, yes, it could be true! You *do* meet the criteria, but I never thought—"

She rose, rushing over to embrace him, and Teir stood and endured a crushing hug.

"I loved the preimess as I would my own daughter," Jannis said, sniffling. "Ah, what a tragedy! But thank the stars you are well and strong!" She regarded him fondly. "I wish we had time to get to know one another better, but you must not linger. Come—the items you seek are buried in the back. I have not looked at them since the day I took you from my dear lady the preimess, and gave you to my sister Catharta."

He followed her outdoors, into a field in the back where rows of leafy greens grew.

"I sell my vegetables to one of the vendors in the market," Jannis explained, picking up a small trowel along the way. "It gives me an income, and I prefer the quiet life. They killed all the other servants, you know. I was lucky to have escaped. I feared they'd come after me, so I stayed in hiding for many annums. Even now,

I often get the feeling I'm being watched."

The air was getting cooler as the sol began its descent. Teir glanced apprehensively at the surrounding forest as he and Jannis walked down a dirt lane between rows of vegetables. She asked him about his work and he told her about his ship, his crew, and some of their missions. He stopped talking when his boots sank into a puddle of mud and he had to yank them out with a huge sucking noise.

"It rained recently, so it's quite wet out here," Jannis said. "Don't worry. It's drier up ahead, and your valuables are well protected. In truth, I shall be glad to be rid of them." They came to a break in the row of plants. "Here is the spot." Handing him the trowel, she stepped aside.

Teir crouched down where she'd indicated and began digging. His heart thumped excitedly. What was this proof he so desperately needed? He'd soon find out. The tool struck a solid object, and he cleared away the dirt to find a small leather chest.

"Lift it out. Don't worry, you can't damage anything." Jannis watched while he raised the chest from the hole. "Put it down there. I'll open it and you can remove the contents; then we'll rebury the chest. I don't want it in my house."

Teir placed it in front of her, then watched while she scooped up her skirts and crouched beside him. An old keypad-style lock was in place, but obliviously Jannis knew the code. When the faint click sounded, she gave a grunt of satisfaction and stood up.

"Open it, Teir."

Gingerly he lifted the lid. Inside, in a waterproof pouch, were three objects. One was a heavy gold chain with a medallion. Another was a signet ring, also made of gold. And the third was a smooth silvery-gray stone with a lustrous finish and a pointed end.

"I understand the stone belonged to your maternal grandmother," Jannis said. "I have no idea of its importance, but the preimess insisted I keep it for you. The medallion and the ring display the crest of the Retti dynasty."

Teir put the rock in his pocket and examined the other pieces. "What does this crest represent?" It was circular with spokes around the circumference.

"It is the sol. Originally, the preim's authority was believed to come from divine right. The ancient peoples worshiped the sol, and they believed the preims were their god in human form. The preims used the sol as a symbol of their authority." She paused. "The position of preim has always been hereditary, and you are the last of the line."

"I'm not interested in being any blasted preim. I just want to marry Sarina." Teir took the medallion and hung it around his neck, hiding it under his white shirt. The ring he put in his inner vest pocket.

"Don't let anyone see them," Jannis warned as he put the chest back in the ground and refilled the hole.

Together, they started back toward the cottage. Teir hadn't noticed how far out in the fields they'd gone. Now as they headed back through the narrow dirt lanes, he heard an ominous rumble in the air.

"What's that noise?" he said, feeling uneasy.

Jannis glanced at him vacantly. She hadn't been paying attention, having been lost in memories of the past. Now as she heard it, she gasped. "Speeders!" They looked back, and both saw the black dots on the horizon at the same time. The dots were rapidly growing larger.

"Who are they?" Teir asked, increasing his pace.

"Sentries. They must have found out about you. Hurry!"

"They may not be coming here."

But as Teir ran, he glanced over his shoulder and saw that the speeders were definitely headed in their direction. There must be a dozen of them and they're riding two-seaters, he thought with alarm. Blast! If he had landed with a shuttle, he could have used his remote unit to escape. But since his ship was at the spaceport, he was trapped.

"How could anyone know about me? Do you think Naggers told them?"

"Naggers wouldn't betray me. They must have been keeping watch using long-range sensors. I've always felt I was under surveillance." Jannis huffed and puffed and finally came to a standstill.

"Come on!" Teir yelled, stopping and turning. The speeders were nearly upon them.

She sighed. "It's no use. I'm sorry, Teir."

He drew his shooter as the speeders landed, surrounding them only meters from the cottage. Uniformed sentries, weapons aimed, jumped out and encircled them.

"Lower your shooter," an officer commanded, stepping forward.

"I'm Captain Teir Reylock of the Coalition Defense League. You've no right to detain me!"

"Drop your weapon!" the officer snapped.

Realizing he was hopelessly outnumbered, Teir gave a grunt of disgust and threw his shooter to the ground.

A couple of other speeders landed, troopers accompanying two civilians. Teir knew at once they were men of authority.

"I am Provost of this province," said the portly gentleman with graying hair. He pointed to the tall man beside him. "This is the Justice of Minna. What is your business here, Captain?"

"I came to see my mother," Teir said defiantly.

The provost nodded to a sentry, and the soldier stalked over. "Arms up," the sentry ordered.

"Go to Zor!"

The clicks of triggers readying met his ears. Hastily, Teir complied. The sentry frisked him, emptying his pockets and relieving him of his hidden blade and Nokout gas grenade. Teir was ordered to remain standing, hands on his head, while the two civilians examined his belongings.

"Data link, a set of data cards, one rock—and what is this?" The provost picked up his ring. "A signet ring with the royal crest! How very interesting, Captain."

Straightening, the provost strode to where Teir stood motionless. He ripped open Teir's shirt and gave an exclamation of triumph. "A medallion with the emblem of the Preim! So, you've come back to claim your inheritance, have you?"

"Don't be ridiculous," Teir said, flushing. "Those are souvenirs, that's all. I'm just visiting Vilaran. Let me go back to my ship, and I'll leave at once."

"Come now," crooned the justice, a malevolent looking fellow who was as thin as a rail. "You might as well be truthful with us. We know who you are."

"Of course you do. I just told you," Teir said, lowering his arms. "I'm Captain Teir Reylock—"

"*Silence!* We always knew the infants had been switched. The dead babe had dark brown hair, not black like yours. We've been keeping watch on the preimess's maid for annums, waiting for you to return. Now the sentence can be carried out at last."

"What's that?" Teir croaked, although he knew the answer.

"Death!" the justice intoned with an evil grin. "Move the woman out of the way," he ordered his troops. "She'll be next," he told Teir. "All traitors to the Republic are executed. Never again will the taint of imperialism contaminate our culture. Prepare yourself, Captain. You're about to meet your ancestors."

"You can't do this!" Teir shouted as the sentries dragged Jannis away. The old woman didn't even whimper. Her expression of terror had changed to one of sad resignation. "I'm an officer in the Defense League. Glotaj, the Supreme Regent, will be enraged if you harm me."

"Glotaj has no authority here. This is a local

matter," the provost instructed. He stood on the sidelines, content to let the justice do the dirty work.

"Ready!" the justice said.

The sentries took aim.

"No!" Teir screamed, throwing himself at the nearest trooper. The man's rifle butt caught him on the temple and he crashed to the ground. Bleeding, he lay there, despairing of his life and his lost future. In another instant, it would all end.

Sensing that something catastrophic was about to occur, Sarina had urged Rolf to go at warp speed to Vilaran. They'd arrived at the spaceport and checked through the dockmaster's manifest to find the *Valiant* listed.

Rolf had asserted his authority as a member of the High Council to gain entry to the vessel. Using the ship's scanners which were programmed for Teir's molecular pattern, they were able to locate him on the outskirts of Minna. It was Sarina who suggested using the shuttle to reach him.

"It's faster than surface transportation and is equipped with defense systems. We don't know what kind of situation we'll be facing." She couldn't help feeling an overwhelming sense of doom.

Rolf agreed. He had a bad feeling, too. Reylock should never have come here alone. If anything happened to him, it would interfere with the legend's fulfillment.

"What's going on?" Sarina asked anxiously as they approached Teir's position. Dozen of figures were milling around on the ground and she couldn't make out which one was his.

"We'll find out soon enough," Rolf said grimly. His mouth set, he brought the shuttle down for a landing. Sarina was out of her seat in an instant, dashing for the hatchway. She hit the release and the hatch popped, the steps unfolding to the ground. Behind her, she heard Rolf call out a warning.

She ran outside. Dear God, Teir was lying on the ground, his head bleeding, and soldiers were aiming weapons at him! He caught sight of her, and she saw a flash of joy in his eyes just as a mean-looking official shouted, "Fire!"

Sarina screamed as the weapons discharged. Teir's body jerked and then he was still.

"Teir! Oh God, no!" She crashed through the barrier of troops and knelt beside him. The lasers had torn through his layers of skin, leaving jagged scorch marks where they'd burned through to his insides. She scooped him up in her arms, cradling his broken body. His skin was ashen, his breath rattling in his throat. Sarina hugged him to her, sobbing his name. *Don't die, Teir. I love you so. Please don't die now that we're together again!* Tears ran down her cheeks. She couldn't lose him, not now.

As she held him in her arms, sobbing and conscious of nothing but her love for him, a strange sensation tingled along her nerves. At first it felt as though a charge of electricity were building inside her body. All Sarina's sensory fibers vibrated with an intensity she'd never felt before. The feeling shifted, settling in her hands. Her right palm grew warm, then fiery hot. Sarina looked down. The circle birthmark on her palm was glowing. Without knowing exactly what she was doing or why, Sarina turned her palm toward Teir. A beam of light shot out from the glowing circle. It radiated over Teir's body, enclosing him together with her in a pulsating energy field.

Closing her eyes, Sarina let her aura bathe them both in the light of love. And then something incredible happened. All of a sudden, she was a separate entity, hovering in the air. She could see her body down on the ground with Teir. His aura was being pulled into hers, and they merged, one consciousness, one being.

And then they separated to rejoin their bodies, and the bright light faded.

Teir's eyelids fluttered open. A slow smile curved his mouth as he looked up at her, his head in her lap. "Sarina," he whispered, awed by what he'd just experienced.

"I know," she said. "I love you."

"I love you, too." Aware that his body was healed, he drew her down and kissed her with all his pent up passion, hungering for her taste, her touch. He never wanted to let her go.

Sarina's response was just as powerful. Not caring who was watching, she entwined herself in his embrace. His powerful arms enveloped her, and she closed her eyes, reveling in his touch. His tongue boldly probed inside her mouth and she met it with her own greedy thrusts. This wasn't enough. She wanted more of him.

They became aware of Cam'brii talking, explaining the legend and their part in it to the astonished soldiers and their superiors.

"Forgive us, we had no idea who you were!" the provost said, throwing himself on the ground in front of them. Teir and Sarina sprang apart, embarrassed.

"Yes, yes!" the justice said, his pallid complexion even more colorless than usual. "We didn't know you were the Raimorrdan of the legend."

While Teir stood to accept their apologies, Sarina rose and faced Rolf. He gave her a deep bow. When he straightened, his gaze was full of wonder. "You truly are the Great Healer. You have shown this day what you can do. I will do everything in my power to assist you and your chosen one."

"I owe you my thanks," Teir said gruffly, turning to him. He held out his hand to the councilor.

Rolf took it, and the two shared a firm handshake. "Did you get the proof you need for the High Council? Although after I tell them what happened here, they shouldn't require it."

Teir retrieved his possessions. Holding out the signet ring and the medallion and pocketing the rest, he said, "Here is the proof that I am highly placed. But I have yet to find where I have been born under the sign of the circle."

"I can help you," said Jannis, who appeared still dazed by the miracle that had occurred. "You were born in the preimess's chamber at the Manor, now the Museum of History. The answer you seek is there."

They set off immediately for the former palace. Teir and the old woman went with Rolf and Sarina in the shuttle. They landed on the wide lawn bordering the town square, followed by the sentries on their speeders who had now been assigned to act as their armed escort.

The museum was closed for the day, but the justice knew the combination to open the door. Commanding the lights to rise, he led them inside. "The preimess had her chamber on the second floor," he explained, leading the way up a wide curving staircase. Sarina gazed around in wonder. The palace was ornately decorated. It was amazing the contents had been so well preserved.

The beauty of the preimess's chamber took her breath away. Obviously restoration work had been done here, because the silken coverlet on the fanciful carved bed appeared in prime condition, as did the matching rose-colored drapes. But what caught her attention the most was the emblem on the wall above the preimess's bed.

"This is where Teir was born?" she asked Jannis whom Teir had introduced her to.

"Aye," Jannis said, staring at the same symbol that transfixed Sarina.

Teir frowned. "I don't get it," he said, glancing around.

"Don't you see?" Sarina said, pointing to the emblem. "*That* is a circle!"

Teir gazed in the direction she indicated. "That's

the crest of the Retti dynasty. It symbolizes the sol. See the rays coming out of the—" Then it dawned on him what he was about to say. *Out of the circle.* Of course! The evidence was right before his eyes. No strange astronomical event had heralded his birth. He'd been born under the sign that had served his family for eons. "Storms of the sun, I think that's it!" he exclaimed, turning to Sarina. Joy shone in his eyes. "Do you know what this means?"

"Now we can be wed, my love. Nothing will stand in our way!"

Turning to Jannis, Teir said, "Will you come to Bimordus Two to be my witness, since you were present at my birth?"

"I don't think it's necessary for her to travel all that distance," said Lord Cam'brii. "If you record a mini-holovid with your data link, that will serve the same purpose. And you have the ring and medallion." Teir now wore both, no longer afraid to display his heritage. No one would dare challenge him after what their leaders had witnessed.

"Then there's no need to remain on Vilaran," Teir said. "What of your transport?"

"We ran into some geckos on the way who weren't too friendly. My ship is in need of repairs. I suggest we all return to Bimordus Two on the *Valiant.*"

Agreeing, Teir addressed Jannis. "I owe you a debt of gratitude. You saved my life when I was a child, and you kept my secret safe all these years. What can I do to repay you?"

Jannis smiled, her eyes crinkling with happiness. "Seeing you alive and well is payment enough. I just want to return home."

"I'm sure that can be arranged." He spoke to the justice, then returned. "A sentry will take you on a speeder whenever you're ready to go." Touching her shoulder, Teir said gruffly, "Remember, if you ever need anything, call on me."

He walked outside with Sarina and Cam'brii.

"It certainly is dark," the councilor remarked, glancing overhead. "Is sol setting always so abrupt here?"

"Not that I recall," Teir said, peering at the blackened sky. A strong breeze ruffled his hair, and an eerie whistling noise hummed in his ears.

"The sky looks weird," Sarina said with a shiver. She clung to Teir, her arm in his.

"Look!" Cam'brii cried. They all glanced in the direction he indicated, and their jaws dropped in horror. A bright dot was evident far above in the darkened sky. It grew larger, closer, and then became a glowing ball streaking across the heavens. Behind it trailed a putrid yellow stream of dust.

"The comet!" Sarina exclaimed.

"So your theory was correct," Rolf said to her. "Do you think Wagroob had time to launch his probe?"

"I hope so. Let's get to the *Valiant* and ask him."

They filed into the shuttle and hurriedly lifted off. Sarina explained her theories about the Farg to Teir on their way to the spaceport. Not much later, they'd secured themselves inside his ship and were preparing to depart.

"I've got the Research Station on subspace radio," Teir said to Sarina on the bridge. Cam'brii sat beside him in the copilot's seat, and Sarina had moved to Wren's nav console off to the side.

They put Wagroob on the viewscreen and Sarina saw his excited expression. "You're on Vilaran? How in Zor did you get there? Never mind—did you see it? The telemetry readings were incredible."

"Yes," she replied. "It streaked overhead like a ball of fire."

"And it had a dust tail, right?"

"Right. You could almost see the yellow particles falling from it like a light rain."

"That was no comet. It's an artificial satellite. And those dust particles were full of altered molecules."

"What?" Rolf and Teir said in unison.

"We haven't been able to isolate the disease organism before because it's not an exact organic phenomenon," Wagroob explained. "Someone used molecular-alteration technology to change the infecting organism in such a way that it couldn't be detected using normal scientific methodology. We picked it up by running a scan analysis of the cosmic dust. The infectious particles in the dust fall to the planet's surface, entering the water supply, and there you have it! An entire world is contaminated."

"My God!" Sarina exclaimed. "But who—?"

"The Morgots, my dear. You said yourself they benefited most from these conquests because each planet infected with the plague is rich in natural resources. It all makes sense. The Morgots have been manufacturing these disease-laden satellites and disguising them as comets. They send them over the planet they want to take over, and the satellite itself self-destructs after the planet's atmosphere has been seeded. It's a brilliant concept. Comets have always been regarded as harbingers of evil, and these modern days are no exception. The Morgots have been playing on our superstitions."

Teir spoke up. "Now that you know how it's being done, Wagroob, can you stop the Morgots from releasing any more of these deadly satellites?"

"I hear the battle in the Tendraan system went in our favor. The Morgots were forced to retreat. They must have launched this satellite before the tide of battle turned against them. I don't think we'll need to worry about another comet coming our way for quite some time."

His voice deepened. "Sarina, if you truly are the Great Healer, you need to think about the people of Vilaran. They have all been exposed to the plague, and so have your friends. Do something about it." With those words, Wagroob signed off.

Teir and Rolf both turned in their seats to stare at

her. "Me?" she said, feeling put on the spot. "What can I do?"

Teir got up and walked over to her. "You healed me with your love. Do you think it's strong enough to heal a world?"

Chapter Twenty

Teir powered down the ship so Sarina could go outside and try to help the people of Vilaran. When they emerged from the *Valiant*, they stood in front of the entrance to the huge spaceport. It was still busy despite the late hour. Travelers bustled to and fro, intent on their business. Bright flamelights lit the walking paths, and speeders zoomed down wide paved streets. The warm night air was perfumed with the scent of keela blossoms.

"Now what?" Sarina asked.

"Well, do your thing," Teir said.

"Right here? What if nothing happens?"

Teir's tender blue eyes were full of faith and love. "You can do it," he told her. "Try raising your palm, the one with the birthmark."

Rolf stood off to the side and watched. He saw Sarina lift her hand in the air and close her eyes to concentrate. Reylock was a lucky man to have won her love, he thought. Longing for Gayla hit him deep and hard. Sarina hadn't been meant to take her place.

Yet as he saw how happy Teir and Sarina were, he yearned to share that kind of closeness again.

Opening her eyes, Sarina glanced at Teir. "Well? Did I do anything?"

"The circle didn't even glow," Teir said, disappointed.

Slowly, she lowered her arm. "I just can't do it. I don't know how to control my healing power. It works with you, but that's all."

Rolf stalked over to them. "You're forgetting something. The legend states you have to wed your Raimorrdan. You and Teir have been joined in spirit, but not in name. Your healing power may have been activated by your love so that it works for Teir, but in order for you to aid others, you and he must be wed. Otherwise, the terms of the legend are not complete."

"But that means we'll have to return to Bimordus Two to get the High Council's permission," Teir objected. "It might take weeks. My people will die before we return."

Lord Cam'brii appeared thoughtful. "May I make a suggestion, Captain? We could request a conference call to resolve the matter. If the High Council gives their approval, you can be married here."

Sarina laughed. "Do you really think Glotaj would agree to that after all the fuss about my marriage?"

"I will see to it." The councilor requisitioned a speeder and they departed for the government center. Once there, he asked a sentry to rouse the President under his authority as a Coalition official.

The President had apparently heard of their earlier adventure. A mature woman dressed in conservative business attire, she came hurrying down the steps of the great Parliament building to greet them herself. "What can I do for you?" she asked.

Rolf instructed her, and so it was that they found themselves seated in a deliberation room inside Parliament. A call was patched through the comm center to Glotaj, and the recent events were described to him.

"Congratulations!" the regent exclaimed, his image being projected onto a wall. "Captain Reylock, I hope you understand my reasons for keeping your secret all these annums?"

Teir grimaced. "Considering the reception I got here, yes I do, sir."

"My best wishes to you both. Rolf, I hope you're not too disappointed?"

Lord Rolf Cam'brii gave a wry smile as both Sarina and Teir looked at him. They sat together holding hands across the table. "Sarina is a remarkable woman, and the captain is a lucky man to have her," he said without any hint of resentment. "Now what about getting the High Council's approval? We have to go forward with this matter so I can get back to Bimordus Two. I have a lot of unfinished business to attend to."

He had the problem of the geckos to deal with. Someone in high government circles had betrayed him to the Souks. Rolf hoped that when the First Amendment passed, as he was certain it would, the assassination attempts would stop. The Souks would no longer be after Sarina, but they might still target him until the vote was cast. He had to learn who their mole was to stop the leak of information.

"I'll summon the councilors to tell them your news," Glotaj was saying. "Remain there, and I'll get back to you."

They terminated communications. While waiting, Teir suggested they get something to eat from the fabricator. They had just finished their meal when Glotaj's call came through. This time when his image appeared on the wall, he was not alone. He sat in the Council Chamber with the other eleven members. It didn't take long to convince them to approve the wedding on Vilaran. Daimon objected, but he would have protested anyway in order to delay a marriage that would mean trouble for his cause.

Rolf promised to holovid the wedding so it could be seen live on Bimordus Two, and then Teir and Sarina received the blessings of the High Council before signing off.

The President of Vilaran was ecstatic. "The Great Healer is going to be married here! The legend is coming true on our own soil. How thrilling!" But then her fervor cooled. "I have already received reports of people falling ill. I pray that you will be able to help us fight this pestilence. The arrangements for your marriage will take place at once."

Rolf accompanied her from the room to assist in the preparations. The President had to gather her parliament and retrieve Jannis, who Sarina and Teir requested be present. The local justice would officiate. The holovid equipment had to be set up and the Grand Hall decorated. There was much to be done, and very little time in which to do it.

Left alone, Teir and Sarina looked at each other.

"Are you sure this is what you want?" Teir asked, thinking about Cam'brii's aristocratic bearing. Teir had come from a royal bloodline, but he hadn't been raised that way. "I mean, my lifestyle might not be conducive to your position," he told her uncertainly. "You might be expected to reside on Bimordus Two."

Sarina regarded him tenderly. How sweet that he still needed reassurance. "If my power expands after we wed, I'll have a lot of traveling to do," she said quietly. "Many different people will require my services. Besides, I want to see the whole galaxy! You don't think your crew would mind if I joined you on the *Valiant*, do you?"

Teir laughed, a rich throaty sound. "They'll be thrilled to have you aboard. Oh, my sweet, I love you so." He pulled her into his arms and lowered his head. Sarina reveled in the pressure of his lips, the masculine taste of him. She opened her mouth, letting his tongue plunder hers, meeting it with her own. Running her fingers through his hair, she thought about how much she loved him. She couldn't wait until they were alone to do this—and more—every day.

"Pardon," Cam'brii's voice said.

They broke apart, their faces flushed, both turning toward him questioningly. Beside him stood a young woman, obviously embarrassed to have come upon them in each other's embrace.

"This is Zeem. She'll help you get ready for the wedding ceremony, Sarina. I'll assist you, Captain," he told Teir.

"I appreciate all the help you're giving us, Lord Cam'brii," Teir said in a gruff tone.

"Please, call me Rolf." And the two men left.

Sarina looked after them, smiling. She was fond of Rolf and hoped the two men would become friends. Following Zeem, she entered a confusing maze of corridors. They ended up in a suite of rooms which was available for visiting dignitaries.

"I'm going to get dressed for the wedding while you use the sanitary," Zeem told her. "Do you wish nourishment first?"

"No, thanks. We ate earlier." She should be tired, Sarina thought, glancing at the soft bed in the sleeping chamber, but she was much too excited. She went into the sanitary to wash and remove her clothing.

Zeem was already dressed in a jade green gown when Sarina came out. The yellow yoke of office around her neck signified that Zeem was a high official in the Vilaran government. Her shiny black hair was twisted atop her head under a tall green headdress replete with tiny bells that jingled when she walked.

"What am I to wear?" Sarina asked. She hadn't even thought about a wedding gown.

Smiling, Zeem went over to the fabricator. A few

minutes later she had produced a complete ensemble, down to the hosiery and satin shoes.

"It's beautiful!" Sarina exclaimed when Zeem had laid the wedding dress out on the bed.

"Go ahead, put it on."

Zeem held the gown up so Sarina could step into it. The fit was perfect. Zeem then closed the back with some kind of invisible fastener and handed Sarina a gold mesh belt to cinch her waist. The silken folds of the gown flowed to the ground as Sarina walked over to a reflector to gaze at her image. The gown's billowy sleeves were lined with gold lamé in rich contrast to the ivory color of the dress. A golden chain outlined the bodice, glistening with an inlaid crystal pendant. Completing the effect was an ivory lace veil that Zeem draped over Sarina's head and shoulders.

"There's more?" Sarina asked when Zeem went over to the fabricator again.

Zeem returned holding a glittering object. "This crystal tiara will hold your veil in place." She set the tiara atop Sarina's head as a chronometer chimed the haura. "Just in time! The ceremony is about to begin."

Equipment had been set up to beam the wedding across the entire planet using laser satellites so everyone could see it on their holovid units. In addition, a relay would project the images to Bimordus Two so the congress could watch in absentia. Billions of eyes would be focused on them, Sarina thought nervously, and then those same billions would be watching to see if her healing power materialized.

A hush fell over the assemblage as she appeared at the entrance to the Grand Hall. A long aisle stretched before her, and she could see Teir at the opposite end. Rolf, Jannis, the President of Vilaran, and a robed justice waited on a raised dais. A sea of faces stared at Sarina as she walked with a confident stride, grateful for the quiet music in the background. Her face broke into a radiant smile as she got closer to Teir. He was wearing a white military dress uniform with gold braid, and he looked magnificent.

Teir's eyes widened as Sarina approached. Truly, she looked like a goddess! Her thick golden hair cascaded over her shoulders and down her back under the lace veil, and her lovely features seemed carved from the finest porcelain. Gliding down the aisle, she moved with the grace of a dancer. His proud blue eyes met her loving gray ones.

Teir strode forward to meet her. Bowing at the waist, he grasped Sarina's hand and kissed it. Then he led her up the steps to the dais.

After Rolf and Jannis took up positions on either side of them, the justice began the ritual, finalizing it when Teir placed his signet ring on Sarina's finger and kissed her.

Congratulations were shouted from far and near. Beaming with joy, the newlyweds held hands and rushed outdoors. Responding to the cheering crowds, they raised their clasped hands to the sky.

And from their joined hands shot out a glowing ray of light. It expanded, enveloping them in a pulsating energy field. The crowd gasped and fell into a stunned silence as the glow spread upward and out until it became a blinding radiance that surrounded the globe.

Sarina and Teir felt their bodies tingle with electricity. Once again, their auras joined and melded into one. They reveled in the feeling of being united. But there was work to be done, so they reluctantly stepped apart. Their separation broke the circle of light and the radiance extinguished.

At Sarina's urging, the main water supplies on the planet were tested and found clean; no harmful plague organisms were to be found. The miracle had happened. Sarina and Teir had cleansed Vilaran and all her people of the Farg.

* * *

On the way back to Bimordus Two, Sarina and Teir stopped off at Alpha Omega Two to heal Aunt Catharta. They brought Jannis along to stay with her sister during her convalescence, a welcome surprise.

From there, they journeyed to Tendraa to practice their newfound power, and linked up with Teir's crew who were patrolling the area after the Morgot defeat. The crew were reassigned to the *Valiant*, and they all returned to Bimordus Two.

At last Sarina and Teir were able to meet with Glotaj and the High Council. Rolf had gone on ahead, taking his own transport back to the Coalition capital. He'd learned that Daimon had transferred credits via a middleman to the Souks right before the gecko attack. Since an economic embargo was in effect against the Souks, the transaction was illegal. Daimon confessed he'd set up the ambush for Cam'brii, hoping to prevent his marriage from taking place. Forced to resign in disgrace, the ROF leader admitted the legend was true, but it only reaffirmed his belief that the Raimorrdans were too powerful.

The Liege Lord of Tendraa sent a message to the Coalition that he wished full partnership. After the defeat of the Morgots and the visit by the Great Healer who had eradicated the Farg from his planet, he wished to proceed into the modern age. His petition was accepted and Tendraa entered into full diplomatic relations. Now a voting member, Mantra was offered the vacant position left by Daimon on the High Council. He eagerly accepted.

Several important votes took place. The execution decree, although no longer applicable, was declared invalid and struck from the legislative books. The ROF's proposal to dissolve the Coalition was voted on and defeated. And the First Amendment passed, much to Rolf's enduring delight.

The councilor wasn't totally satisfied, however. There were rumors that someone on Souk still had a price on his head, and these rumors were confirmed by another assassination attempt. It was thwarted by an alert troop of guards. Now that the First Amendment was no longer an issue, Rolf wondered why he was still a target. Teir had told him about Bdan's demand to learn his personal routine. Who had made the request and why? Obviously the Souks still had a mole in the government who was reporting on his movements. It was a problem that remained to be solved. Daimon apparently wasn't the only one leaking information.

Souk pirate attacks on civilian vessels continued to take their toll of lives and captives. With his obligation to Gayla's parents always in mind, Rolf determined to stop the Souks once and for all. When a communication arrived from the resistance leaders on Souk requesting assistance from the Coalition, he volunteered to go to the planet and establish contact.

While on Souk, Rolf also intended to find out who was behind the assassination attempts and why someone wanted him dead. He had a chance to discover the identity of the mole as well. Intelligence reported that the *pashas* were congregating at a special conference and the paid informant would be present. It was a chance to accomplish all his goals at once and he leapt at it with alacrity.

As Rolf strolled toward the rotunda in the Great Hall with his fellow councilors, Glotaj, Sarina, and Teir, he gazed fondly at the legendary duo. Along with the regent, they were the only ones aware of his impending secret mission to go undercover to Souk. Once he left Bimordus Two, it would be a long time before he'd see them again.

"We have much to be thankful for," Glotaj said as they approached the Auricle. All of them wore dark glasses except for Sarina and Teir. "The Morgots have returned to their homeworld, and the Farg is finally being eradicated. Two major threats to the Coalition have been removed. We owe you a debt of gratitude, Sarina." Glotaj smiled at her.

"Wagroob figured out why the Farg is sensitive to my power," she replied, eager to explain. "The disease organism is sensitive to radiant energy. Planets closer to their stars are less virulently affected—not because of the heat or visible light from the suns, as was first suspected, but because of the invisible radiation, the same kind of electromagnetic energy that my healing aura provides. He thinks that is why my incubation period was so long. My body was trying to fight off the disease, but my aura wasn't strong enough yet to be successful."

Methods of treatment had already been devised that were effective against the Farg. Hundreds of worlds were being irradiated with a form of energy that was harmless to the inhabitants but deadly to the disease organism. Sarina had learned, to her dismay, that her healing powers were limited in effectiveness to those illnesses or injuries responsive to the invisible radiation. Unfortunately, she couldn't cure every ailment that would ever exist.

At least she was able to use her healing aura alone, as it seemed to be strengthening with use. Uniting with Teir was like a booster. At first, she'd needed him to initiate her power. Now, it was no longer necessary for her to touch him physically. Their spiritual link was enough.

Calls for her services were frequent. The *Valiant* was assigned to transport her wherever she was needed. So far, Sarina had found her role highly gratifying. Teir was happy because he was still able to perform as chief troubleshooter for the Defense League. There were always areas of conflict or natural disasters that called for outside assistance, so they both had their work cut out for them.

Halting in front of the Auricle, Glotaj said, "This is where it all started. The Auricle glowed, and it led us to you, Sarina."

"Look, it's similar in shape to my worry stone. That's what I wanted to show you." She'd retrieved the lustrous silvery-gray stone from its hiding place on Teir's ship and had requested they all gather here. Now as she held it up, Teir drew out his own stone, the one left him by his maternal grandmother. Both his stone and Sarina's were like the stone amulet worn by Salla, the Crigellan female on Souk. Teir had told Sarina about Salla, wondering what the stones signified, and she'd replied that they'd find the answer here.

Clutching their respective stones, Sarina and Teir held hands. To nobody's surprise, the Auricle's glow increased and a circle of light shot out from the monument. From within the blinding brightness, a holographic image of a woman's face materialized.

"My name is Malryn," she told them, waves of pure white hair framing her youthful face. "Welcome, Sarina. For eons your coming has been foretold. I sent this herald to summon you and later to tell you this story.

"I come from a planet called Shimera. We were an advanced race of humans who sought to understand the complexities of the mind. We were able to expand our knowledge of brain function and improve our ability to control thoughts. And then, among a group of highly sensitive individuals such as myself, a new phenomenon emerged. We became able to manipulate our aura, the electromagnetic field that surrounds the body. We could even transfer the energy from our aura into another being. We began to call ourselves Auranians.

"Our difference frightened others who were skeptical about our power. The phenomenon was not completely understood, and even though we used it only for good, such as to heal the sick, there were those who feared the power could be turned to evil. An atmosphere of fear and doubt prevailed, and a terrible persecution forced us to flee the planet. Terrified for our lives, we scattered among the stars. Search parties were sent out to scour the solar systems and eliminate us, such was the fear of the power of the Aura, a fear that it could reach all the way back to Shimera itself to punish the aggressors. But we wished only to be left in peace, so we hid among alien populations, interbreeding and diluting the bloodline until we faded from memory.

"Through a mistake in navigation, Sarina, your ancestors reached the planet Earth. The small group settled in Salem, Massachusetts. When one female revealed her power by healing a sick child, she was accused of witchcraft and burned at the stake. The female was survived by a daughter. As a result of her mother's death, the girl believed the power to be a curse. She suppressed her own innate ability and warned her children against expressing altruistic emotions for fear they would trigger the power. As the gene passed down through the generations, so did her warning. For eons, the power lay dormant— until your birth. You were destined to awaken the collective consciousness, to rouse the other Auranians into declaring their heritage. Thus will begin a new age of love and peace."

Sarina broke in. "But how did you know this?"

"It was foreseen by the Blood Crystal."

Teir gasped. "You had the Blood Crystal? Is that where it originated?"

"No," Malryn said, turning her somber gaze on him. "It comes from a place you cannot imagine. But it had arrived on our planet and we consulted it. It showed us what was to come, and it also predicted the destruction of the planet. But that was to happen later, after its evil spread throughout the land and we Auranians were already gone."

"So it survived the destruction of your world?"

"The Blood Crystal is not of this sphere of life, so it endured. What happened to it then and how you came upon it is beyond my scope of knowledge."

She turned to Sarina. "Since my power was particularly strong, I was selected to send you this missive. Knowing our world would someday be annihilated, we each took with us a token that would remind us of our heritage and act as a means of identification. Those are the glowstones you and your mate hold. Into this larger repository that you call the Auricle, I embedded my message and sent it hurtling into space, knowing it would someday reach you. Now that my responsibility is fulfilled, I go to rest."

"Wait!" Sarina cried, but the image of the woman's face had already dissolved. A long moment of silence ensued while the listeners were rapt in concentration; then Sarina turned to Teir. "I'm an Auranian," she whispered with new understanding.

Teir looked at her. "I must be one, too. That's what Salla meant. She said, *We are of the people.* There must be many others as well."

"We'll have to find them," Sarina stated.

Teir recalled the vision he'd seen on the planet Taurus. The warm light in Sarina's belly represented their child, a child who would be the offspring of two Auranians, the first such to be publicly acknowledged in centuries.

"Malryn had said you would awaken the collective consciousness," he told her. "I think once other Auranians see that it is safe to reveal themselves, they'll make open declarations of their ancestry, too. We won't have to worry about finding them. They'll find us."

He paused, gazing at her with adoration. "Through our child, the power of a lost people will be restored."

"Our child?" Sarina asked, wondering at the knowing light in his eyes. "What do you mean?"

"You'll find out soon enough, my love." He lowered his head and kissed her.

Epilogue

Mantra went home. Dressed in his ambassadorial robes of office, he strolled down his street, greeting those neighbors who'd survived the terrible Farg. How joyful it was to hear their laughter. How satisfying to see the doors opened wide to accept the fresh, clean air. The last vestiges of the plague were gone, and the people were no longer living in a cloud of fear. The threat from the Morgots was past. Peace and harmony prevailed, just as it had in the beginning, and so it would be in the end. Life revolved in a circle, Mantra concluded, a circle of light. His work was to keep that circle revolving.

The journey had just begun.

Nancy Cane would love to hear from her readers. Please write to her at: P.O. Box 17756, Plantation, Florida 33318. A self-addressed stamped envelope would be appreciated for a personal reply.